Angel On My Shoulder

Julie Poole

To Heather
With angel blessings
and best wishes

Julie Poole

x

Angel On My Shoulder by Julie Poole

Acknowledgements:

Acknowledgements are made to the following, whose work I have mentioned in this novel:
I'm Free: Pete Townshend: The Who: From the album Tommy (1969)

Love is all around us: Reg Presley: The Troggs (1967) covered by Wet, Wet, Wet (1994)

Sarah: Phil Lynott, Gary Moore: Thin Lizzy: From the album 'Black Rose: A Rock Legend'. (1979)

She's the One: K Wallinger: from the album 'Egyptology' (1997). Covered by Robbie Williams in the album 'I've been expecting You' (1998)

She: Charles Aznavour and Herbert Kretzmer (1974).

It's a Wonderful Life: Frances Goodrich, Albert Hackett, and Frank Capra: Liberty Films. (1946)

Forest Gump: Winston Groom (novel)
Eric Roth (screenplay): Paramount Pictures (1994)

Harry Potter books – JK Rowling: Bloomsbury (2001-2011)

Special Thanks:

I would like to thank the following people for their help with the development and production of this book:

Titan Inc. – for helping me to finally publish my book and see it come to life. You have made my dreams come true! Thank you.

Sandie Rogers – your resilient, patient friendship has lifted me, held me and inspired me always.

Heather Ross - for ploughing through each and every chapter as I wrote them, always waiting for the next instalment with baited breath. Your encouragement and excitement kept me going and helped me to believe in this book even more than I already did.

Christopher Poole – for your unending patience as you read through every line, every paragraph, and every chapter, despite it being written for women! Your constructive criticism and ideas have been invaluable and have without a doubt, improved it, developed it, and enhanced it on every level.

ST – thank you for being the inspiration for several of my characters.

MH – thank you for supporting, advising, cajoling, and accepting my obsession '*Angel On My Shoulder*', as I developed, pampered, preened, pushed and pulled her into life.

And... to all the men, friends, and experiences that I have known, enjoyed, hated, loved and lost over the years; each and every one of you have contributed in some part to the characters, the story and the magic. Those experiences have at times given me inspiration, constipation, desperation, complication, and frustration, and I wouldn't be who I am without each and every one of you crossing my path at some point in my life. Good, bad, indifferent, my most fabulous dream or my worst nightmare, you have all played a part and I wouldn't change a thing!

To my mother, thank you.

To my children, Tom, Chris, and Charlotte; thank you for loving me despite my chaos, my individuality, and my weird and different way of seeing the world, life, and love. I love you all dearly and am so grateful for you being in my heart and part of my life.

And finally, of course….. to the Angels; I thank you.

Julie Poole

Cover design by Rebecca Poole from Dreams2Media
Book design by Titan InKorp LTD
Editing by Titan InKorp LTD

Printed in the United States of America and United
Kingdom
www.titanpublishinghouse.com
Titan InKorp LTD © is registered by the UK ISBN agency
on the international ISBN Agency's Publisher Database
ISBN - 978-1-78520-026-7

Dedication

I dedicate this book to all of the
Sarah's of this world.
Don't ever give up... look up...
For the Angels are there, watching over you!

Prologue

Clarabelle sat on Cloud 322 with her brother, musing the problem.

'I just don't know what to do with her, Clarence,' she sighed. 'Three days and nights she's been crying now and nothing I can do or say is snapping her out of it, nothing at all. I just don't know where to turn to next!'

Clarence patted his sister's wing reassuringly. Her feathers were flat, he noticed, flattened by her worry over her ward.

'It'll be all right, Clarabelle, dear, really, it will. Don't give up; don't lose the faith; she'll get there in the end, promise.'

'I'm going to get sacked if I don't sort this soon, I'm sure,' she worried on. 'Demoted! I'll end up down in transport with Fred and Frank if this goes on! Twenty years and no progress, no progress at all. What *will* they think of me 'upstairs'?'

'Don't panic, my dear. She's about as low as she can get now, rock bottom I'd say, which means there's only one way to go… and that's up.'

'It's not just that, Clarence, it's my Ruby Review next week! I just can't go in there and say to the bosses 'no progress' again; I just can't! Two a year for twenty years and each one's been the same… 'Anything to report Clarabelle?' they ask, and me saying, 'No, sir, no progress,' Her head hung in shame at the thought of it, hoping and praying she wouldn't have to say those dreaded words, yet again!

1

'Well, my dear sister, you did ask for a challenge when you took this one on, didn't you, eh?' He smiled as he looked at her reassuringly, gently. He'd done his best to support her, to be a mentor to her over the years, being that much more experienced than her, but he wasn't sure he'd been much good at all really.

'Challenge, yes! Impossible, no!' she was saying now, a quiet desperation in her voice. 'I need a miracle, a miracle I tell you.' She looked longingly at him, hoping that her big brother would be able to come up with a solution, a plan, anything. They looked down at the cloud in unison as they pondered, noticing its lumps and bumps. Don't make them like they used to, they decided.

Peeking over the side of the cloud, they looked down onto the sleepy, small town far below them where Sarah lived, somehow hoping the town would give them the answer if they looked at it for long enough. It gave no reply. Redfields was a big village: a pretty high street with a few shops, a chapel and an old pub, the cricket ground and pavilion, the small school, the duck pond in the centre with its willow trees, set amid open parkland; the whole thing wrapped up and parcelled by fields of rolling countryside. The larger town of Redville lay eight miles east; the main road between the two, busy at this time of day, rush hour. They watched with interest, distracted for a moment as the people and traffic rushed here and there, intent on getting to work and school; their attention fully focused on their

2

busy lives, completely oblivious to this interaction taking place high above them on Cloud 322.

Peering down at the town, their minds on the problem at hand, they both jumped with a start as a dark figure flew past them at speed, descending towards 'downstairs', a long-cloaked shadow of blackness trailing behind.

'Hi, Frank,' Clarabelle shouted after the figure, waving.

'That wasn't Frank; that was Fred!' corrected Clarence, thinking how they really should slow down. *Giving everyone a start like that, most unnerving!* he thought

'Was it? Oh, I thought it was Frank!' declared Clarabelle, 'Though all these Grim Reapers look the same, don't you think?'

'Mmmm,' agreed Clarence, watching the reaper. They did go fast, and being so dark and shadowy it *was* difficult to tell them apart, although when they did slow down long enough to stop for a chat, you always knew which was which. He turned his attention back to his sister; *she looked so lost, bless her!*

'So what are you going to do about your Sarah then, my dear?' he asked. Clarabelle shrugged in a defeated manner, sighing deeply as she raised her eyebrows and her shoulders at the same time. *This is most unlike her*, thought Clarence. *Very worrying indeed!*

'More support, guidance and help?' he suggested kindly.

She shrugged again, lost as to finding the solution to the problem that was 'her Sarah'. She

3

shook her head. 'I don't know, Clarence, I just don't know,' she said sadly.

Clarence didn't know either. There must be a solution; he just had to find it! He thought about his suggestion of more support, dismissing it quickly. It wouldn't work. *Hadn't worked so far, had it? Not in twenty years!*

'Mind you, you've tried that, repeatedly… doesn't work,' he added, scratching his head. There must be a solution, there simply must! Suddenly, a new idea came to him.

'Or—' he hesitated, thinking it through slowly. 'How about, maybe, if a few more things go *wrong!* We're always trying to make it *better,* but what if we made it *worse* instead? I think it's time for a new strategy Clarabelle! If she gets to the point where she gives up – and she's close now – she'll *have* to turn to you, *have* to let you help her. We *need* her to let you help her to get you through this review. Yes, I think if a few more things to go wrong. That should do it!'

Clarence beamed, positively beamed! This would work, he was sure of it. They'd tried everything else. Yes, this would work; it simply had too! He grinned at Clarabelle. 'She'll get there, eventually, your Sarah, promise! Just keep plugging away, she can't resist your help forever.'

'Yes, that *may* work. Make it *worse* for her, not better!' Clarabelle felt a hint of hope and gently began to smile. 'Most of them 'downstairs' turn to us lot when the chips are *really* down, don't they? Maybe a few more chips, then?' *But what could they possibly create to go wrong for Sarah that would encourage her to let them help at last!* She wondered. Her feathers began

4

to lift as she saw a possible solution to the problem that was 'her Sarah'. *It was simply a matter of finding something more to go wrong, rather than trying to put things right!* 'Nothing to lose, nothing to lose!' she chirped, and radiated a beam that shone all around her, illuminating her faded halo back to its natural brilliance.

'Hi, Fred,' they both called, as the dark angel flew past them again, this time on his way back 'upstairs' with his newly-collected soul, closely followed by a beautiful white angel trailing behind him.

'Hi, both,' shouted Fred as he flew past them, breaking the speed limit again! 'Come on, Ursula,' he shouted, looking behind him at the trailing angel, 'we haven't got all day you know, have to get this one 'upstairs'.' Ursula flew faster, trying her best to catch them up, but these Grim Reapers, blimey, they just flew so blinking fast!

Clarabelle and Clarence watched as the three shadowy figures continued on their journey: the two angels and the retrieved soul, on their way to 'upstairs' for their review.

'I don't know how I'll feel when he comes for me and Sarah, you know,' Clarabelle admitted to her brother, 'but that's a long way off yet. Still have years to go before he comes for her. I think we're down to fifty-two years, three months, fifteen minutes and thirty-five seconds before it's her turn. I just hope it isn't going to take me most of that time to make her happy, although the way we're going I'll be lucky to get her there in time for Fred, or is it Frank, at all!'

5

'Now there's a thought! Clarabelle dear, I have it! I have the idea! The solution! Have to clear it with 'upstairs' first of course. We'll need Fred's help too, if he can slow down long enough! And what's his name, thingy, the one in charge of the tunnel?'

'Who? Oh, you mean Huber, the manager of the tunnel of light where the souls are collected from? Oh goodness, Clarence, I'm not ready to hand my Sarah over to Fred yet; she's got years left in her still! I know we want something to go wrong, but I'm not letting my Sarah be killed off!'

'No, no, my dear! I wasn't thinking of handing Sarah over to the Reapers, not at all, but we said we need a miracle, yes? Someone could *nearly* die! Right in front of her, of course, scare her a little. Then you could do a bit of life saving, a *little* miracle? Show her your power; that should get her attention, maybe even a little respect? She'll start listening to you then. You never know, she may even surrender completely and let you do your job… for once!'

Clarabelle thought about it for a moment then beamed happily. She turned to Clarence thoughtfully.

'It seems like a good plan Clar, but who's around her that we could 'miracle' on? We can't go causing illness; that's not allowed. And it would have to be someone already destined for a problem, and be someone close to her that she cares about or it wouldn't have a big enough impact.'

'You leave it with me, my dear. I'll see what we can sort, but it's going to have to be quick if we're going to get you through this Ruby Review without you being sacked. Next week is it? Well then, today, I think, yes, today, we shall arrange a little miracle for

6

today.' Clarence scratched his head again as he thought it through. 'May have to bring something forward, I'll need clearance for that. Give me a few hours; I'll need to talk to Fred. He does get excited when we have some near-death experiences as you know. I'll need to make sure he doesn't get carried away and cart them off completely, just need him to keep them in the tunnel for a little while, giving you a chance to do your thing.'

'Absolutely! And you make sure he gives them back, whoever it is that you choose!' Clarabelle said firmly.

She knew what Fred was like and Frank was even worse! Always disappointed when they had to give a soul back, both of them sulked for days! But she wasn't having any proper death around her Sarah, oh no, not on her watch! A *pretend* one would be all right, just as long as it was in everyone's best interests of course.

Clarabelle's wings were full again, Clarence noticed. Full of hope and happiness, thank goodness! Her halo was glowing all around her as her faith restored. It would be all right! He'd help her get Sarah where she needed to be. They just needed to pull a few favours, or she really would be in trouble with the bosses. Clarence knew they'd been making allowances 'upstairs' for Clarabelle's continued failure. Sarah was, after all, her first ward, and she hadn't long qualified as a fully-fledged Guardian Angel when she took her on all those years ago, bless her! She couldn't be expected to get everything right and, to be fair, Sarah was a pigging nightmare, *so*

7

resistant to help, just like a lot of them down there!
Just didn't know what was good for her. Poor
Clarabelle!

'Go on then, Clarabelle dear, off you go. Back
to it,' Clarence instructed. 'I'll meet you a bit later
today once everything's in place.' And he flew off to
make his plans.

Clarabelle felt so much better. She beamed
with delight as she watched her brother disappear. 'It
will be alright; we'll sort it!' she chirped to herself.
'And a miracle! I do love a miracle or two, just makes
the day. Smashing!'

Chapter 1

Sarah stared pensively through the bedroom window watching the early morning sun light up the nearby hills, her chin resting on her hands, propped up by her elbows on the windowsill. Tears glistened in her sad turquoise-blue eyes; her long chestnut hair, normally so shiny, hung limp around her oval face, coming out in sympathy with her. The pain was beginning to pass now after three days and nights. She had gone from her bed to the window and back again over those three days, barely leaving the room. She hadn't eaten, her head spun, and her stomach was retching just at the thought of food; her pain so all-consuming had reached into the very depths of her. There had been some respite for sleep now and then, but on waking it was present yet again and somehow took her over, drawing her back into its dark embrace. She'd sworn in those three days that she'd actually heard her heart crack as it broke, smashing into a million pieces of sharp spiky metal, which stabbed into her chest and stomach relentlessly. Sometimes the agony had been so great that she thought she might actually die! She hadn't, of course, but she knew that the worst of it would pass in time, and it seemed that that time might have actually arrived!

The cause of all this agony and grief? A man of course! Yet another 'he's-the-one' relationship had ended in held-back tears in her favourite restaurant

Gino's, a lovely little bistro on the outskirts of the larger nearby town, Redville. Quiet and dimly lit, it had charm, character and a wonderful chef and Sarah did like her food. What a night! The bastard hadn't even let her finish her steak before he announced, so matter of factly, that this just wasn't working out, they wanted different things so he wanted to call it a day. His words had cut through her heart as easily as her knife had cut through the perfectly cooked, tender steak she had just started enjoying. Then he expected her to finish her meal! Of course she hadn't been able to eat a thing after that and she loved steak. The pig even wanted to stay friends! As if, for God's sake! Don't men know anything?

She hadn't seen it coming, not at all. The night before the last supper they had even made love and how beautiful it had been. He had held her in his arms, gazing lovingly into her eyes, stroking her hair adoringly, and holding her like he would never let her go; loving her with every inch of his soul, tender, loving, soft, and gentle, with real care and depth. Yeah, right! Depth of a bloody puddle it turned out to be, because there he was the very next night telling her it was all over. She knew why, of course: she had wanted more. Why was that just so scary, nay, terrifying for most men? To want more than to just be a girlfriend, to actually want a relationship to develop into something deep and meaningful? She had so carefully chosen to ignore the signs which had been present from the beginning, and continued to be present all the way through to its inevitable conclusion; she was so blinded by her love for him

10

that it wasn't exactly rose-coloured glasses she had
been wearing, more like blackout blinds!

When he'd told her so calmly and coldly that
it was over she had stood up straight, mustering all
the strength, dignity, and will that she had, stretching
her 5' 4" frame to its full height for effect, and
flounced out of Gino's so fast that her feet had hardly
touched the ground. It must have been fast, she
recalled, because she hadn't even felt the pain from
those bloody lethal five-inch heel shoes she was
wearing, shoes that absolutely crippled her at the best
of times and that was when walking gingerly, picking
out her steps carefully so as to avoid those menacing
little gravely bits that make you feel like you've just
stepped on hot coals. She certainly wasn't going to let
him see her cry, so she'd had no choice really. The
steak had had to be sacrificed. What a waste! And the
dress! A whole week's wages on that new blue size
ten number, which so enhanced her eyes apparently,
(so the lady in the shop had said) and which almost
made her look like she had a cleavage, with its low
neckline. Not that Sarah had any kind of decent
natural cleavage, but with a little help from the
'essential accessories' she had looked her best and she
knew it. 'Essential accessories' were nothing to do
with belts, bracelets, and bangles, of course. They
were the 'essential' bits that Sarah couldn't live
without. The *really essential* stuff! Stuff to go *under*
said new dress: a fabulous deep-plunge 'pull 'em up -
push 'em in, seriously-padded gel bra', which she'd
discovered in the depths of Redville's main
department store's lingerie department. And thank
God for 'essential accessory' number two, the special

11

knickers, the absolutely 'can't-live-without' essential knickers, which flattened the ever-increasing WWB beautifully. 'WWB' was, of course, the 'wibbly wobbly bits' that her body now seemed to sport: her tummy, ever increasingly saggy and droopy with each year that passed, no longer tight and firm like it used to be ten years before. And the bum! Where had that pert bottom gone that she had been so proud of in her youth?

She wasn't exactly fat, she knew that, but her body had seemed to change shape alarmingly in the last ten years, getting looser, flabbier and wider, especially around the hips; the previous flat tummy of her youth long gone. Her mates all told her she was paranoid, of course, that she had a lovely figure and to stop moaning, but Sarah didn't think so, no, not at all! The knickers had smoothed it off a bit and pull it in a bit, and helped her fragile confidence somewhat and, admittedly, she reluctantly knew, she was probably more of a size eleven now, or even, God forbid, *a twelve*, but she refused, absolutely *refused* to buy anything unless it was a size ten, no matter how tight and uncomfortable it was. It had all gone horribly wrong. The knickers had helped, but clearly not helped enough.

'Oh God!' she cried out loudly at the window, staring at nothing in particular. 'What is the point? What is the bloody point?'

'Precisely, Child!' piped up Clarabelle, just at that moment when Sarah did so not want to hear from her, just back from her meeting with her brother Clarence, and full of beans. 'Precisely!'

12

'Oh, Clarabelle, just leave it! Can't I have a rant in peace just now and again?' cried Sarah, in the full flood of her disappointment and misery.

'Now, child, you know that's only the ...'

But Clarabelle didn't have time to finish what would have been her so eloquent reasoning, given half the chance, before Sarah spat her disgust in a 'humph' and stomped out of the bedroom into her en-suite bathroom, slamming the door in Clarabelle's beautiful and concerned face.

'Can't I have any bloody peace?' she ranted to herself. 'Couldn't she just leave me alone for two minutes? Always so damned positive about everything!' All Sarah wanted was a whole five minutes of feeling sorry for herself. She'd earned it; she deserved it. Life was shit sometimes and didn't she know it right now! *Jesus, the rest of the world seemed to be constantly pissed off and she wasn't even allowed a five-minute moan!*

Sarah stared at herself in the bathroom mirror, looking with horror at her puffy tear-stained eyes, her hollow cheeks and her sallow grey skin. *Three days grieving was enough, more than enough and it had to stop and stop right now,* she thought grimly. She pulled herself up with the tiny bit of strength she had left inside her and held her head high. Staring at her reflection she said to the image in the mirror in the firmest voice she could muster, 'Listen here, my girl. He was a pig. He didn't deserve you. You are worth more. Now pull yourself together, get in that shower, and sort your sorry arse out right now!'

'I couldn't agree more,' piped up Clarabelle, 'he was indeed a pig, as you say,' although she did

13

feel it was a tad unfair to pigs to be compared with Rob. Such kind creatures!

'Yeah, yeah, vacate please,' Sarah ordered, holding the door open to a concerned Clarabelle. She needed to be on her own to try to pull herself together. 'Go!' she ordered again. Clarabelle went, knowing not to argue with Sarah when she was like this.

She's turning a corner, which is good, Clarabelle thought to herself happily. *At least she was out of bed and contemplating a shower. This was progress, tiny progress, but still progress. Smashing!*

Sarah climbed wearily into the shower cubicle and stood under the water, letting it wash over her head for a full five minutes before turning her face towards the powerful jets of warm and soothing water. She imagined it washing away all the hurt as she scrubbed her tear-stained face till it was raw (at least it brought back some colour!) She massaged shampoo into her limp and sad hair till it squeaked louder than Jessica Rabbit (who was Jessica rabbit anyway?), and she scrubbed her body with the thing that is meant to exfoliate but is actually a sadomasochist's tool of choice. She even shaved her legs and underarms. By the time she got out of the shower she was feeling stronger, brighter and ready to face the world again, just!

Her bedroom was at the top of the old three-story house, occupying the entire floor with windows on three sides; it was light, airy and spacious. The windows were open, allowing the fresh scents of the

countryside to permeate the room, scents that lifted
Sarah's spirits even more. The front views scanned
the small town of Redfields a quarter of a mile away;
the side view spanned across the valley with its trees
and sloping green hillside, while the rear view
reached far across open farmland. This room was
Sarah's sanctuary. She loved this house with a
passion. Built some two hundred years before, its old
stone walls had faded gently with time. Its large
original wooden window frames, long since rotten,
had been replaced sensitively with modern white
double-glazed units since Sarah had taken over its
ownership five years before. It was an impressive
detached house, sat at the end of a small lane on the
fringes of the town that she had spent most of her life
near or in; it wasn't an overly large dwelling, but the
extra floor at the top of the house made all the
difference. It also boasted a large garden, bordered by
a tall hedge that separated her from the adjoining
fields and which swept gently from the front gate
around the sides and across the back, protecting her
cottage garden with its trees, plants, herbs and
flowers within its warm embrace.

As she walked down the stairs in her fluffy,
comforting dressing gown, her hair still wet, wrapped
in her softest towel, she took in the beautiful hallway
with its high Victorian ceilings, the ornamental
coving, and the beautifully carved wooden spindles
on each stair as she always did. The early morning
spring sun shone through the stained glass door,
filling the hall with different coloured lights, creating
a rainbow effect on the wooden floor, its warmth

15

releasing the fragrance of wax and polish into the hall. The whole place shone with vibrancy, colour, and beauty. Sarah felt her spirits lift once more as she passed by her living room, its door wide open inviting her to admire its beauty. The large marble fireplace with its black wrought-iron hearth filled with coals and logs stood majestically, commanding the attention of the room and all who entered. She absently looked out through its wide French doors, ignoring the heavy drapes which adorned the windows with their lush satin and gold vibrancy, looking beyond them into the cottage garden, which faced the rear of the house. Seeing the beauty, the colour, and the vitality she felt a peace descend that had been missing for days.

In the neat and tidy kitchen overlooking the side garden with its large, sweeping willow tree, Sarah made herself a cup of tea piling three sugars — for shock — into the large mug. (Yes ok, the shock was three days ago, but she needed a sugar rush!) She took it into the garden, passing the herbs in the pots, which framed the winding red-bricked path, touching them distractedly as she walked by, releasing fragrances of basil and mint into the air all around her. Sitting down on her favourite swing seat, enjoying the early morning sun, Sarah didn't notice the spring chill, she just saw the beauty around her and felt the peace. Slowly she turned her face towards her left shoulder and smiled.

'Sorry,' she said, 'I do get in a state sometimes, don't I?'

Clarabelle simply smiled a sweet, non-assuming smile. A smile that was filled with the ages of wisdom and light that comes naturally to an angel.

Sarah didn't know how long Clarabelle had been with her; it seemed like forever. She knew that Clarabelle's job was to keep her happy and Clarabelle always wanted Sarah to be happy, seeing it as her great mission to cheer her up, get her to look on the bright side, and generally stop her feeling miserable. That was great, lovely most of the time, but sometimes, just now and again, it was really annoying! *Well, quite a lot of the time actually*, thought Sarah.

Clarabelle was Sarah's Guardian Angel and she took her job very seriously. She had introduced herself to Sarah some twenty years previously when Sarah was just seventeen, a time before she knew or understood any of the 'weird' stuff that she had since become accustomed to. She had simply appeared one sunny morning when Sarah had been sitting at her dressing table, examining, with horror, the latest zit on her chin in the mirror when she had looked up and saw what she thought at first was a fairy sitting on her shoulder. It was as clear as day and Sarah had frozen in shock, looking at it and thinking *what the bloody hell is a fairy doing sitting on my shoulder?*

'A Fairy!' laughed the thing in amusement and indignation, 'A Fairy? No Child, I am an *Angel!* Your Guardian Angel! And I *can* hear your thoughts you know!' she grinned. 'My name is Clarabelle,' and then the thing had twirled around, taking a sweeping

17

bow and waving her arm in the air, all very theatrical and everything! She had made this introduction with momentous gravity, glowing and floating around Sarah just like something out of Cinder-bloody-rella! Sarah had nearly had a coronary, then she'd nearly had a stroke, and then she thought perhaps she was hallucinating. With the possibility in mind that she might be stoned as opposed to be going completely potty, she had felt a little better.

'I must have had too much booze at the party last night,' she declared. *Frieda! It would be her fault! She was always trying something new to spice up her parties; she'd probably put something in the punch.* She was always experimenting with something or other, was Frieda: new flavours, images, looks, hair colours, and Sarah wouldn't put it past her to have tried something more adventurous and more dangerous. However, the Angel had assured her that she was neither hallucinating nor was she going potty and as the months and years had gone on, she'd gotten used to Clarabelle sitting there, interfering as usual. Whenever Sarah was lost, low, confused, or otherwise out of sorts, Clarabelle was there with her pearls of wisdom, positive outlook, and understanding, whether it was welcome or not!

Clarabelle appeared to Sarah to be about six inches tall. She was dressed in a long white gown and even had 'The Full-Monty-Wing-Thing' going on (right down to the floor with feathers and everything!). She had a golden light all around her, just like a halo - like the angels described in the fairy tale books of her childhood. Her hair was golden too,

18

curling just past her neck and onto her shoulders in soft waves and her eyes were the clearest and brightest blue she had ever seen. She looked about thirty, Sarah reckoned, but Clarabelle had said that she was ageless and she was, of course, utterly beautiful.

'Clarabelle! What kind of name is that?' Sarah had laughed to the miniature fairy thing. 'Sounds like Clarence, the crazy angel out of that film that always makes me cry. What was it called, the one with the guy with the voice, what was his name? Ah yes, James Stewart. *It's a Wonderful Life*, yes, that was it. You know the one where a bell rings every time an angel gets its wings?'

Well, apparently, (so she was informed on the day of the introductions) Clarabelle was Clarence's sister! For God's sake! How you could be related to an angel in a bloody Hollywood film she hadn't quite understood even to this day, but Clarabelle had assured her that most of the ideas for the good films were put in the writers' heads by angels or other important bods 'upstairs'. (That's 'upstairs' where the angels live, so Clarabelle had said. She doesn't call it Heaven, Sarah recalled, she just calls it, 'upstairs'.) Clarence had, so he had told his sister, inspired the writers of that particular masterpiece and had made sure his name was in there somewhere. Well, you can't have those Hollywood writers claiming all the credit for ideas given by 'upstairs', can you? Even Angels like a bit of credit, you know.

They were close, Clarence and Clarabelle, and had been for eons Clarabelle had said. Worked together and everything apparently, though Sarah didn't

19

really understand that bit and as she hated to look stupid, had never really pushed the point. At the time, when she'd first appeared to Sarah back then, Clarabelle hadn't long qualified up through the ranks of 'Guardian Angel-ship' and Sarah was her first ward. Clarence, her brother, (the one from the film!) was her mentor, apparently and according to Clarence, Sarah was a challenging ward. Nice! Ward! What kind of word was that anyway? Project, mission, protégé, anything was a better description than 'ward', surely? Well, I mean, what is a ward to anyone other than an angel? It's a long, boring room with cheap, nasty curtains, where you felt like shit and where everyone told you what to do. Come to think of it, maybe she was a ward after all!

'So, my dear, what are we going to do with you, then?' Clarabelle smiled at her with her 'concerned' face on. 'I did offer to help, but you wouldn't let me. In twenty years, you've never allowed me to help you and life could have been *so* much easier for you if you had, my dear.'

'Yeah, yeah, I know,' sighed Sarah, 'but if I'd asked you if he was 'The One', you'd have told me that he wasn't, and then I wouldn't have gone out with him.' Sarah hesitated briefly, thinking. *Hmmm, and then I wouldn't have spent the last six months being led up the garden path and back down again, would I?*

'Maybe next time you'll let me help?' suggested Clarabelle quietly, kindly, a request that she had made often over the last twenty years, but which hadn't yet got past first base.

'I'll think about it,' replied Sarah reluctantly, moving over to sit under her favourite apple tree.

20

She breathed in the scent of the apple blossom, which surrounded her, trying to regain some peace. She had planted the seeds of this tree with her gran when she was just four years old, counting the pips out of the remains of the apple core, which she had just eaten, and placing them carefully, one by one, into the ground. She'd nursed the fledgling plant over its first year, watching with amazement as the first shoots sprouted, watering and feeding it and watching it grow as tall as her throughout her childhood years. In time, eventually, it became taller than her, growing into an adult tree and blossoming beautifully the way that Sarah hoped that she herself would, one day. She was still waiting, but her tree had given her blossoms in the spring, apples in the autumn, shade in the summer and peace all year round. It would always be her favourite. She loved this time of year in early spring when the ground was so fresh with new life and new hope, the next generation of seeds and buds being born right there under her feet. *Amazing*, she thought, not for the first time. *The miracle of nature is so amazing.*

Her thoughts drifted back to Friday night and Rob. It had been a huge shock, him dumping her at Gino's like that. She had thought they were fine, more than fine actually. He'd led her to believe that they had a future, that this was going somewhere. Sarah thought about that again now. There had never been any *actual* evidence of his love, words, words, plenty of words, but no real evidence. Plenty of sex, mind you, oh yes, plenty of that!

21

Why did I believe him? she wondered now. They'd had fun, of course, loads of it: nights in, nights out, even a week's holiday in the Canaries. That had been magical. *God, was that only ten days before? It was probably the holiday that had made him run.* She'd seen it as a practice run for when he moved in; he had obviously had a reality check at the thought of having to act on some of his empty promises and legged it.

'Another player,' she said sadly, 'and I was played beautifully, magnificently and thoroughly. Tosspot!'

'Tosspot indeed,' agreed Clarabelle, patting Sarah's shoulder sympathetically, wondering quite what a frying pan had to do with Rob, though she did *love* pancakes! She didn't understand half the insults that had been thrown about in the last few days, but she was doing her best.

Ben would be pleased, though. Her brother had never liked Rob, clearly seeing through him in a way that Sarah herself had never managed to do. 'Smarmy' he had said once and that was it. He hadn't said another word on the subject of Rob. 'No comment' was all he ever said whenever she had brought up Rob.

Sarah and Ben adored each other and were very close. They were chalk and cheese in everything except looks. Ben's life was everything that Sarah's wasn't: successful, fulfilled, happy, and sorted, while Sarah's was a mess of never-ending change and chaos. She had never settled into anything and envied her brother's life of stability. She didn't begrudge him any of it; she loved him, but she did envy him. How did he manage to do it? What made his life so successful and hers such a disaster?

'No comment,' piped up Clarabelle with a wry knowing smile.

'You sound like Ben. I bet he wouldn't say "no comment" this time,' said Sarah in reply.

'I bet he wouldn't either,' agreed Clarabelle, 'but don't let it get to you, my dear. He loves you and worries for you.'

'Yes, I know he does and he never gets it wrong, does he, my perfect brother! Happily married for five years. Gina's just so lovely and so perfect for him, not to mention a beautiful baby son, fabulous home, and a successful career. Perfect judgement every time,' said Sarah in frustration, feeling her own judgement so sadly lacking.

Wonderful Ben! Five years her junior, she'd idolised him since his birth when she had been just the right age to pretend that he was a doll. She had dressed him up in her favourite dolly outfits, driving him around the house in her doll's pram despite his loud yells of protestation, especially about the frilly pink bonnets she'd insisted he wore. Thirty-two years old now, he was six feet tall and really very handsome, not dissimilar to Sarah in looks with his turquoise-blue eyes and chestnut hair. He was also loyal, charming, funny, gorgeous, sorted and right! But then he always seemed to get everything right; first time, every time. Not only had he found his perfect partner, his soul mate, his lifeline, but Ben's first job had been right for him too, straight from school into the bank. He'd worked his way up the corporate ladder and was doing well. He'd been there fourteen years now, she realised. Sarah didn't know what it was to be still in the same job for fourteen weeks! *Well, maybe fourteen weeks, but not longer than a year, that's for sure,* she admitted to herself. More than that, Ben was really content with his lot! Sarah, on the other hand, had never felt content with anything, ever, neither a relationship, nor a job. There'd been many of both — well, she was quite attractive so there was no shortage of offers from men, and she wasn't stupid so had always been able to find work. It was *keeping* either or both for any length of time that had been the problem, a problem that had been on going now for twenty years, which, as far as Sarah was concerned was just a wee bit too long. At thirty-seven and a half, life seemed to be going nowhere fast!

The only stability she'd had within her life was her home. Her gran had left it to her when she died five years earlier, leaving Ben some money instead. The cash she left for Ben had been almost the same amount that Sarah's father had left for her when he had died eleven years previously. Her gran had always worried about Sarah and as her son had left her grandson his house, she wanted to leave her granddaughter hers, feeling that this was only fair. Sarah had always loved this old house, spent loads of time here when she was growing up (always happy to escape mother), and she was absolutely thrilled when her gran told her that it was to be hers when she was gone. Not that she wanted to lose her gran, but that was inevitable. She was eighty-eight after all and anyway, Sarah had taken death with a pinch of salt since Clarabelle's arrival.

24

As her thoughts flitted to memories past, Clarabelle's voice brought her back to reality with a bump.

'Do you think, maybe child, you might let me help you a bit? I can make life so much easier for you if you'd only let me try?'

'Hmm, yes, maybe,' considered Sarah reluctantly, 'but you know how I like to make my own decisions; you know how independent I am. I can't go running to you like I'm five years old, that's pathetic! Sometimes I get it wrong,' she hesitated, 'ok, most of the time I get it wrong.' She stopped for a moment, contemplating her poor judgement of Rob. *She really was crap, wasn't she! Didn't have a bloody clue! Maybe she would do better if she let Clarabelle help?*

'I tell you what, let me have a think about it. That's the best I can do, ok?'

'Oh yes, dear, that's fine, just fine. And don't you worry, my dear, I will only help when you ask me to. You know the rules we lot have to work to; we can't help you unless you ask. One day you may want my help, until then I'll stand by your side quietly and not interfere.'

'Yeah, right! That'll be the day!' muttered Sarah under her breath, but she was smiling. *Clarabelle not interfering? Yeah sure, like that's gonna happen.*

'Oh, you'd be surprised, my Child. Now, dear, stop beating yourself up about Rob and your judgement of him; it isn't good for you, you know; it damages the soul, not to mention the aura and well, the negative energy you emit, my dear, it's like waves, big waves of sadness, makes my feathers all

25

dark too. Look!' she said, brushing away a speck of grey from one of her pristine white feathers with a sigh.

'Yeah, yeah, I know. You've told me a thousand times.' Sarah impatiently raised her eyes because of the lecture, as she saw it, from Clarabelle.

Clarabelle smiled. 'What you must do now, child, is focus on today. Let the past go, put it behind you, move on, dust yourself off and brush yourself down. Now, go and do something with yourself, child, you look a frightful mess, then go to work. And hold your head up, Sarah! You have nothing to be ashamed of. The day they make mistakes a sin is the day I quit and I don't intend to quit, ever! Trundle off now, dear, off to it.' With those words of wisdom ringing in her ears, Sarah sped off to her bedroom to prepare for a day of being single, again!

As she walked back into the house and up to her room she realised that she was coming slowly back to her normal state of mind. She knew that she wasn't out of the woods yet with the 'getting over Rob' thing, but she also knew that she was through the worst of it. *Maybe I'll concentrate on sorting out a proper job, put my energy into that instead of some tosspot,* she thought with a smile. *Yes, I'm going to sort out the rest of my life first and bollocks to the male species. Maybe I'll even let Clarabelle interfere!* With that thought, Sarah smiled the smile of acceptance, reflecting on the pain she had been through for the last few days, thankfully now passing with time and with Clarabelle's help, whether she realised it or not.

26

'A five minutes' moan would have helped though, if I'd been allowed!' she grumbled and began to dry her hair ready for work.

Clarabelle rushed 'upstairs' to tell Clarence the news. She was finally beginning to see a chink in Sarah's armour; she was finally getting through. This was huge progress! Huge!

'This is definitely the time to strike, strike while the iron's hot!' she squealed in delight. 'We absolutely, definitely need that miracle. Yes, must be today! It must be today, while the chink is still visible.'

Clarabelle was delighted. For the first time in twenty years she was actually making progress. 'I wonder who we're doing the miracle on?' she mused to herself all excitedly. 'Can't wait, can't wait!'

Chapter 2

Sarah stood in front of Mackenzie's store trying really hard to feel cheerful and more or less succeeding; she took a deep breath, unlocked the door and marched in.

'Morning, Mr. Mackenzie,' she called into the darkness of the closed shop, the tinkle of the old bell above the door still ringing in her ears as she relocked the door behind her. 'How are you today?'

The old shop stood warm and welcoming, as it had for the last one hundred and twenty years. Standing at the end of Redfields High Street, the store had been converted from three Victorian cottages late in the last century by its then owner 'Old Man Mackenzie'. Seeing fit to add to Redfields bakery, clothes store and food store, the new all-purpose General Store 'Mackenzie's' had been an instant success. In time, and a generation later, the old external buildings at the rear were also converted along with the derelict land. Once the original outhouse, shed and privy, all three had been rebuilt to form a small office, toilet and tiny kitchen area. They adjoined the main building; the shop's long counter dividing the area between the staff and the customers. The derelict land at the back, originally the gardens of the three cottages, was now the car park for the store.

Sarah walked into the semi-darkness of the shop. The low ceilings, adorned with many rows of electric strip lights, which oversaw each of the small,

narrow aisles, were not switched on yet. The shadows
bounced off the mirrors and glassware by the door as
they vied for position with the early morning sun
peeking through the small windows. Musty with the
smell of time, old wood, and love, the shop stood, as
it always had, oozing character from every crevice, its
shelves piled high with every conceivable item that
the local townsfolk might need. The general store
tried to be all things to all people, although its goods
were not fresh or perishable: from cushions to
candles, from screws to paint, Mackenzie's tried to
meet each and every need in its appreciation of the
continued loyalty of its local customers.

Mr. Mackenzie appeared suddenly, popping
his head up from behind the ancient wood and glass
serving counter, giving Sarah a start. At only 5'3" he
wasn't much bigger than the counter and looked a bit
like an elf, standing as he did with his hands on his
hips, his wide cheerful grin and his sticky-out ears.
All he needed was the pointed hat and he'd complete
the picture perfectly. His suit, beautifully pressed,
and shoes, polished to within an inch of their life,
matched the neatness of his starched white shirt and
completed the overall image. You could not fail to
notice the ex-army 'smartness' that Mr Mackenzie
wore with pride, despite his small size and advancing
years. At eighty years old he should have retired ages
ago, but this shop was his life and Mr. Mac intended
to leave his shop carried out in a box. He'd never
done anything else (apart from his national service
stint); he'd worked here since he was a nipper with
his dad; then dad had died and he'd taken over and

that was that. The third generation in his family's store, he saw himself as the keeper of it, the protector. *What was it with some people and stability?* Sarah seemed to be surrounded by people who had found their calling. *You never know, maybe some of it may rub off on her; well, she'd been here ages now - nearly eight months!* Mr. Mackenzie smiled broadly at her.

'Fine, thank you, Sarah. Did you have a nice time with your young man the other night? Big dinner, wasn't it … at Gino's, did you say?' he enquired politely. He was a nice old boy and wasn't to know that Sarah had had neither a nice time, nor had she had a big dinner. She smiled and nodded, moving towards the pricing gun on the counter; she picked up the price list in an attempt to avoid the question. She began to get on with labelling the stock as Mr. Mackenzie busied himself opening up the store for the day. It gave her time to think, what to say, how to reply.

'Just tell him the truth, dear. The truth will always serve you,' piped up Clarabelle from her left shoulder.

'I suppose so,' she grunted. Having accepted it herself — almost — it was quite another thing to admit it to other people, especially her boss. Admit that she'd been dumped. *Dumped! Lovely word! Does wonders for the ego, does that! Erm … Mr. Mackenzie, having been shagged senseless for months, at his every convenience and in every position, my tosspot boyfriend has got bored with me and dumped me without decent explanation or warning and over my favourite steak, and in my best dress. What do you think of that then, eh?*

30

No, perhaps not! The old boy's eyes would pop out of his head; he'd have an asthma attack and probably drop dead on the spot (he didn't look too good today, actually), then not only would she look like a sad sap, she'd be a murderer to boot. Perhaps go with Clarabelle's idea then? Sarah took a deep breath.

'It wasn't a very good night, actually, Mr. Mackenzie,' Sarah paused — *go on, say it once, it'll get easier every time after it's been said once* — 'we broke up; we're not together anymore.'

There, she'd done it. It was out and the world now knew that she was a dumped, rejected saddo. Great! Well, they would by the end of the day. This was a small town and gossip was gossip. It would travel on the mighty gossip highway and be old news by tomorrow. She'd just have to ride out the storm of 'oohs' and 'aahs', and 'what happened?' from every Tom, Dick, and Harriet, not forgetting Harriet's cat! She sighed.

'Oh, Sarah, I am sorry to 'ear that,' said Mr Mackenzie in genuine surprise. 'Well, it's 'is loss if you ask me. Fine girl, you are. Any man 'ud be proud to 'ave you as 'is missus. The boy's a fool and no mistakin'!' With that and a bemused shake of his head, Mr. Mackenzie disappeared into his office at the back of the old store to make his rounds with the news. Sarah heard the telephone click and cringed. Here we go, hot subject for the rest of the day. Mackenzie's would never be busier than in the next few hours as everyone with a life even sadder than Sarah's came into the shop to gawp at the girl who'd gotten dumped *again*. Damn it!

31

'Now stop being paranoid, Sarah,' Clarabelle piped. 'You know he's not like that, and no one's going to come in just to gawp at you. He's actually on the phone to his May to invite you to theirs for tea to cheer you up. He's checking with May that it's ok with her before he invites you. Really, you do let your imagination run riot sometimes, my girl.'

Here we go again with the interfering, thought Sarah, but in her heart she knew Clarabelle was right. Mr. Mackenzie wasn't like that and anyone he did tell he would tell out of concern, probably to save her having to do it herself. Sarah immediately felt guilty for her unkind thoughts towards the elderly man, a man whom she had grown very fond of, even come to love. As he returned from his office he was smiling as he walked towards her, carrying a cup of tea that he'd made especially for her; she blushed with embarrassment. He'd even put a couple of biscuits with it that he must have taken from 'May's special tin'. God bless him! She knew exactly what he was going to say, Clarabelle was never wrong and sure enough, he smilingly said,

'May and me was wonderin' if you'd like to come for yer tea with us tonight, Sarah? Nice bit o' cake for afters an' all. Be better than going 'ome to that empty 'ouse of yours, won' it, eh? Let us look afta yer, eh, watcha say, luvie?'' He smiled a twinkly crooked smile from his aged and kindly face and Sarah beamed back at him.

'Bless you,' she said, 'you're my answered prayer, Mr Mackenzie. That'd be lovely, thank you.' She genuinely meant it and was pleased to be invited. She hadn't been looking forward to going home that

night; she'd only be stewing on Rob again and
probably get down or mad or both.

Since she'd been working there the last eight
months, Mr. and Mrs. Mackenzie had almost become
surrogate grandparents to her. She cringed again at
her unkind thoughts earlier. Clarabelle was right,
they'd never gossip about her, not intentionally
anyway and never maliciously; they were good folk.
Staunch Christians, old school with their hearts most
definitely in the right place and they put up with a
fair bit from her, bless. Between her friends Frieda
and Angela popping in on a regular basis for a chat
and of course Clarabelle going on all the time, it's a
wonder she ever got any work done at all.

Mrs. Mac didn't come in very often these
days, not with her legs as wobbly as they were, but
Mr. Mac was here every day, seven in the morning
until six at night and had been for most of those
seventy-odd years. He'd caught her talking to
Clarabelle on more than one occasion since she'd
been there and she'd never had the heart to tell him
the truth. Whenever he'd asked who she'd been
talking to, Sarah had always replied, 'Just talking to
myself, Mr. Mackenzie. You don't get any backchat
that way.' Just imagine his face if she'd told him the
truth! *Oh, just chatting to my Guardian Angel, Clarabelle.*
She lives on my shoulder mainly, but at other times she
just pops up wherever. May I introduce you? He'd have
her locked up for being nuts or possibly for
blasphemy or something equally biblical. She knew
that a lot of church folk accepted the concept of
Angels, but she also knew that for them to accept that

we *all* have a Guardian Angel and some of us could actually *see* them and *talk* to them, well, that was just too much for most folk. Fair enough, really, it did sound potty, even to her.

The day passed quickly and it didn't seem long before Sarah was waving goodbye to Mr. Mackenzie as he locked up the store. She had brightened up as the day had gone on, throwing herself into her work, keeping her mind off Rob as best she could, and her spirits had improved vastly.

'See you in a minute, then,' Sarah called out as she left the store, cycling off down the road towards her house. She only lived ten minutes away from the shop and usually walked or cycled to work, but the Mackenzie's lived three miles out of town and Sarah wanted to go back home for her little car. She planned to follow Mr. Mackenzie back to his house in her own car so that she could drive herself home afterwards. He'd offered to run her home later, but she'd refused. He really didn't look too well today and she'd already decided that she wouldn't stay too long, so that he could get some rest. A bit of company would do her good, she knew, even for a couple of hours. If she spent the evening alone she'd probably start crying again and there'd been enough tears over the last few days.

'So,' she said to herself, 'no more tears, no more men, let's just stay single, eh, till we've worked out how to do it right.' *Right? Blimey, she couldn't have got it more wrong! Ten out of ten for effort, and zero out of ten where men were concerned.*

34

'Let's just get from zero to two on the "having a bloody clue" score sheet before we get involved with anyone else!' She smiled wryly to herself. Decision made, Sarah felt good, empowered and hopeful. It was a change, a different way and a way that Clarabelle would definitely agree with.

'God, I'm appeasing Clarabelle at last,' laughed a surprised Sarah as she cycled along the lane quickly.

While this new thinking might have surprised Sarah, Clarabelle, sitting on her shoulder as usual, fell off with the shock! Picking herself up quick smart from the muddy lane, noticing that she'd only just missed a rather menacing puddle, not to mention an alarmingly close cow pat, Clarabelle scooped up her muddied and rather ruffled feathers, flicked away a stray clump of sticky mud from her chin and flew after Sarah as fast as she could manage, catching her up just in time to jump in the car with her.

'What happened to you?' grinned Sarah, seeing the state of the normally beautifully composed and spotlessly clean Clarabelle, who was now cleaning and preening her feathers and trying to focus on what was to come. Clarabelle smiled quietly. She just hoped the boys were ready. She *certainly* was!

Heading back over to the store, Sarah was glad she'd decided to take the car. Her little banger was old and battered but was hugely reliable. The old mini was scratched and dented; its paintwork long since faded, but she loved it. *There!* she suddenly realised, *she did have something that she'd hung onto; she'd had that car forever!*

35

'Yes, well. Ok, only because I can't afford to replace it, I know. Now don't you start piping up!' she chipped in to Clarabelle before she had a chance to say anything. Clarabelle just raised an eyebrow, a muddy eyebrow at that, trying to look innocent, but her eyes said a different story. Sarah could have used her inheritance to get a decent one, she knew, but she'd always had a feeling that it was for something important. She didn't have a clue what though!

Sarah drove back to the old store with some urgency so that she didn't have to keep Mr. Mackenzie waiting any longer than necessary. May had said six o'clock for tea and May was more accurate than Big Ben. As she pulled up outside the back of the store at five forty, expecting to see her boss sitting in the little red van, Sarah was surprised to find it was still in its parking place and he was nowhere to be seen. The lights were off in the L-shaped extension, she noticed, meaning he wasn't in the office. *Maybe the kitchen?* Sarah was unable to see the rear door of the store from the car park, hidden from view as it was by the office.

'I wonder where he is?' she said with some concern.

Clarabelle grinned. She had just managed to pluck the last bit of dried mud from her feathers. *Smashing! Great timing. Off we go!* She put on her most important, most commanding voice possible and could almost hear an invisible director call 'action' as she piped up,

'He is ill, my dear, go to him quickly!' It was an instant and urgent reply and Sarah ran from her car without hesitation, her heart pounding, her blood racing in her ears.

If Clarabelle says go quick then this is bad, she thought to herself, fear engulfing her as she ran. *Please don't let him die,* she called out in her mind. *Let him be ok, please God.* But as she ran around the corner towards the rear entrance of the store, Sarah could see him lying near the old green door he'd been trying to lock when his heart attack had come with such force. He wasn't ok; he was far from ok! The coronary had literally knocked him off his feet and at eighty years old, his feet weren't that stable these days.

'Help!' screamed Sarah as loudly as she could. 'Help! Get an ambulance, somebody.'

The back street had been deserted, but her screams for help held such an urgency that several people arrived at once from nearby buildings. Jim was first to get there, running out from the closed bakery next-door to see what was going on. He took in the situation immediately and ran back inside to call an ambulance while Sarah propped up Mr. Mackenzie's head with her jacket. Laying him on his back, she could see immediately that it wasn't good. He was grey, cold and, with a start, Sarah realised he wasn't breathing. His thin frail frame looked even frailer now that he was lying on the floor, and he was so still. His thin white hair was dirty from the pavement; his jacket that was always so beautifully washed and pressed lay crumpled and creased beneath him. He looked so old and so withered and…so…dead!

'Oh my God! No!' shouted Sarah. 'No, no, no!'

She immediately began mouth-to-mouth on him, not really knowing what she was doing other than what she'd seen on telly, but at the same time knowing that she had to do something. As she pumped, somehow, somewhere, a part of her knew that it wasn't going to be enough. His heart had stopped, there was no pulse and more, there was stillness in him that she had seen before a long time ago, years ago; a stillness just like when her dad died. She froze for a moment and then burst back into action. On automatic pilot, Sarah stayed focused on the job in hand. With a will of iron, Sarah muttered between clenched teeth and between each breath of air that she blew into his cold and still mouth,

'No, you're not going yet,' she said it over and over at him as she pumped his chest harder and harder,

'You're not going yet. It's not your time, come back!'

But the old man lay still and cold, with a heart that lay eerily silent. Looking to her left shoulder she suddenly and desperately screamed,

'Help me, Clarabelle! Help me to get him back.' Before she'd even finished saying the words, Sarah felt the heat rise and a force so powerful it made her tremble all over begin to travel down from her shoulders into both her arms. A light as blue as the brightest topaz poured out through her hands and into the chest of Mr. Mackenzie like a laser beam. She was tingling everywhere as if an electric current was pulsing through her whole body. Sarah was motionless, frozen as she watched and felt the heat and light of Clarabelle's energy through her hands and then with a jump, Sarah felt the still and silent heart under her hands beat suddenly back into life. Seconds later, sirens were wailing and blue lights flashed as the Ambulance screamed around the corner to a jolting halt beside her. Sarah got up shakily and stood back to let the paramedics do their thing.

'His heart stopped for about five minutes,' she said to them, not knowing how she knew that. She looked at the men in confusion, blurting out,

'You need to know that. I don't know why you need to know that, but you need to know that.'

'Alright, Miss,' one of them said. 'What's his name?'

'Mr. Mackenzie.... Edgar.' She stood watching helplessly as they put an oxygen mask over his pale face and a drip into his frail arm; they lifted him gently then onto the waiting stretcher, wheeling it quickly towards the open doors of the ambulance.

'Would you like to go with him, Miss?' the paramedic asked.

'No, no, thank you.' Sarah shook her head. 'I'll go and get his wife. May needs to know. I'll meet you there.' Sarah's voice seemed to be coming out of her mouth in little gasps, as if she couldn't string a sentence together anymore. For the second time in a few minutes, she went into automatic pilot, focusing on the next job. Fetch May, look after her, make sure she was okay, and be there for her.

Clarabelle stood back delighted with herself.

'Good job, boys!' she said happily as she turned to Clarence and Fred. 'Just enough to give her a scare, but not too much aye?' The three angels laughed, joined by a fourth grinning happily from the side lines.

'I've been wondering for an age how I was going to get him to retire and let go of this blinking shop,' admitted Edgar's angel. 'This was a good plan. Thanks, guys.'

'Must go, chaps, still more to do. See you later, byeeeee.' shouted Clarabelle as she flew after a panicking Sarah.

Sarah ran to her car as the paramedics loaded the stretcher into the ambulance. With the oxygen mask over his face he was pale and still unconscious, but the greyness had gone, thank God. Sarah just knew he was going to be alright. She didn't yet know how she knew, she'd figure that one out later, but she knew he'd be fine. Now she had to concentrate on May. Poor May! She wasn't so well herself. Her tiny little body looked so frail at the best of times, but she was a wily old bird. Sarah knew she had a will of iron and a grit stronger than Chisholm. 4'9'', size two feet (Sarah knew that because she'd bought her new slippers for Christmas last year,) May had a frame the same size as a nine year old. She wore children's shoes and clothes. Tiny or not, May had beaten many adversities in her life, she'd handled many disasters through her years and Sarah just knew that she'd cope with this.

She drove quickly through the quiet country roads to the Mackenzie's house getting there within minutes. Passing fields and hedgerows, the smells of the countryside all around her, none were noticed in her haste to get to May. Jumping out of the car, she ran to the door of the old rambling farmhouse, opening it without ringing the bell.

'May? May? It's Sarah, where are you?' she called as she ran into the old and worn house.

'Kitchen, dear,' came the reply. As Sarah walked quickly into the kitchen May smiled at her and then looked behind her. Seeing no one there, she looked back at Sarah in confusion.

'May, now come and sit down for a minute,' Sarah gently said, leading a confused and bewildered May to the nearest chair at the large pine table. 'Now May dear, I don't want you to panic, but Edgar may have had a heart attack.' *Edgar?* She'd never called him that before and it seemed strange on her lips, but she knew it was the right thing to do, to make it more personal, softer on May, less of a shock.

'He's on his way to the hospital, May. I was with the ambulance. When you're ready we'll get your coat darlin' and I'll take you to him.'

May sat frozen to the spot, the colour draining out of her face with each word that Sarah spoke. Her white curly hair seemed to get five shades whiter, as did her face. Her legs began to shake under the table, seeming to reverberate all around her body until her teeth were chattering.

Shit! thought Sarah. *She's going into shock.*

She pulled a glass quickly out of the cupboard and pouring the nearest thing she could find into it, Sarah placed it between May's shaking fingers,

'Drink this, May, it will help,' she said calmly. It was brandy. *Oh, thank God,* she thought.

41

'You're welcome!' came the reply from her shoulder as Clarabelle glowed and beamed at her, having located the brandy some time before in readiness. 'Blanket I think too Sarah?'

'Yes, yes, blanket.' Sarah nodded in her daze. Leaving the trembling old lady for a second slowly sipping the warming brandy, she ran up the old wooden staircase looking for something suitable to wrap around May's shaking shoulders and found a shawl laid out on a blanket box that sat at the foot of what was clearly May and Edgar's bed. Sarah took in the old antique furniture, the chintz curtains and suddenly felt an invader into what was so clearly private and personal space. Grabbing the shawl she ran quickly down the stairs back to the kitchen and placed the warm crochet softness around May's shoulders, holding the wrapped and packed May tight until her shaking started to calm down. She noticed that the glass was empty and guessed correctly that May had, after the initial few sips, more or less downed it in one. After a few minutes the old lady pulled out of Sarah's hold, stood up and without speaking, nodded mutely towards the door. Sarah guided her gently from the kitchen, along the hall and towards her waiting car, managing to get May's still trembling body into it, they sped off as fast as her little car could go to Redville hospital. She didn't know how many speed limits she broke on that journey. Later, she could not recall the drive whatsoever, wondering if they just were beamed in by The Enterprise and Scotty!

****

42

May and Edgar had been together for sixty three years, since they were seventeen years old and were totally dependent on each other. May was in a frightful state at the thought of losing him and shook all the way to the hospital. Frightful state or not, as Sarah drove up to the front doors of the accident and emergency unit, May's grit must have kicked in and she leapt out of the car as it screeched to a halt, practically summersaulted herself through the doors in her haste to get to 'her Edgar', leaving a stunned Sarah to go and park the car.

She didn't later recall parking the car, or if she'd put any money in the meter, or of going through the A&E doors herself. All she could remember was looking at her hands as the memory now of what had happened in the last half an hour hit her like a sledgehammer. She began to cry. Slow, long, gulping sobs escaped from her mouth as she sat on the hard chair in the sterile, white room. Sarah realised that she was in the family waiting area, but couldn't remember how she'd got there. May was nowhere to be seen. Her gulping, hiccupping sobs gently subsided as she sat up from her hunched stance and took in her surroundings. The room was stark, lifeless, and soul-less. There were a few magazines on the side table, long since out of date. A lone picture of a solitary flower hung on the wall, too small to be effective or interesting, a brief gesture to make the room more appealing to families as they waited. Sarah noticed the smell of antiseptic, bleach,

43

misery, and worry all rolled into one, with a smattering of hope on the side.

What the hell was going on? What had happened back there? Chaotic thoughts raced around her head, bumping into each other and making no sense at all! *God, she'd been so afraid, and yet so calm. She'd known he was dead but she'd got him back somehow. What was it she'd been ranting? 'It's not your time?' How did she know that?*

'Ok, Clarabelle, what just happened there?' she asked quietly.

'Simple, my dear. It wasn't his time, not really, although it could have been if he'd chosen to, but he didn't have to go right then. You asked for my help and I gave it. Simple!'

'You mean you really did bring him back? I just witnessed a miracle?' Sarah asked in utter astonishment.

'Not just witnessed, dear, you were part of it. Never underestimate the power of positive thinking and of not giving up. You didn't want him to go. I was there and able to help, so I did. We always help when we're asked you know, just not always in the way you may think. Sometimes we help by helping them to go, sometimes we help by helping them to stay. He stayed! He'll be alright now, although some changes will have to happen, you know that don't you?' asked Clarabelle kindly

'Yes, yes, of course. I mean, he shouldn't be working so hard at his age should he? He's eighty!' said Sarah, trying to understand what Clarabelle had just said, but it just wasn't sinking in. What she was becoming aware of though, was Clarabelle's light. It

44

was so bright, much more so than usual. She was positively glowing and she seemed delighted with herself.

'So, you put what exactly into him, to get his heart going again?' enquired Sarah in a dazed stupor.

'What we always use, dear; love, light, energy, stuff like that. And I am delighted! It's always a delight to be able to help when we are asked you know. I just wish it could be more often.'

'But it felt like an electric shock to me. And what the hell was that blue light? It was coming out of me, out of my hands!' Sarah was close to hysterical. She felt totally bewildered now, her mind couldn't understand, couldn't comprehend. Clarabelle smiled, stretched and then began to beam a glow all around her. It sank into Sarah's shoulder and a gentle warm heat slowly and gently soaked right through her. Sarah immediately calmed down and relaxed, right from her head to her toes. *Amazing! Who needs aromatherapy when she'd got Clarabelle, and she was so much cheaper!*

With that, the door opened and May walked in, smiling with relief, accompanied by a doctor, who looked to Sarah to be about twelve. He was stood in front of her wearing a white coat, so he must be a doctor. (Mind trying to comprehend child dressed as doctor who must actually be doctor – *does not compute – abort, abort* – Sarah's mind was definitely flipping!) *Abort, abort? First I'm beamed in by Scotty and now I'm turning into a Dalek,* she thought, looking around for Doctor Who and the Tardis! The child/doctor approached, his fair hair flopping over his forehead into his eyes; he was covered in freckles and spots.

45

Yep, you're not going mad, he has major acne! God, someone should get him a doctor, there are tablets for that these days you know, Sarah thought in astonishment, the irony not escaping her. He was about as tall as May, which made him a goblin, or an elf, or a spotty teenager!

'I prefer the goblin idea myself,' said Clarabelle mischievously.

Jesus, it must be the light – she's making a funny, thought Sarah in shock.

Then the Goblin piped up, 'He's through the worst of it now but he needs to rest. We'll keep him in for a few days and run more tests, just to be sure that there won't be any more attacks. I understand that he collapsed at work?' The doctor's voice sounded about as old as he looked; high pitched, as if it hadn't broken quite yet. Just her luck! In a hospital surrounded by dishy doctors, she gets the man-child-goblin – typical! Although there was a time and place, and Sarah had to admit that this was neither, not really, but then…. *perhaps he had a nice colleague?*

'Sarah!' Clarabelle's voice rang in her ear and the inappropriateness of her thoughts reverberated through her like a sharp slap.

Sarah nodded mutely to the child/man. Jesus, she must be getting old.

'I thought it was policemen who were supposed to look younger as you got older,' she whispered to Clarabelle. To think that this sprat was in charge of people's lives was even scarier than the 'blue light electric thing' that had happened earlier.

'God, I need a valium or a youth transplant, or something,' Sarah muttered and realised that the

46

goblin/child was still speaking/squeaking at her and
May.

'He won't be working for a while and my
advice to him would be to retire completely,' the
goblin/doctor/child said, and then he walked, (or
did he skip - Sarah wasn't sure,) briskly out of the
room. May was nodding to herself, clearly agreeing
with the retirement idea.

Well, he would be too old to you, Sarah thought.
Anyone over fifteen's probably too old to you!

Sarah didn't know if he was off to a meeting,
to save a life, or to go to the playground and spin on a
roundabout, but she didn't care. It was official – Mr.
Mackenzie was going to be all right.

May gabbled on all the way back in the car ten
to a dozen and Sarah let her. She knew it was nerves,
the relief and despite the late hour, after she'd taken
May into the house and plied her with sweet tea,
Sarah rang May's nephew to come around to look
after her. Then with a huge hug Sarah left them to it,
it was family time now. As she was leaving, May
apologised to her about the shop, but said of course,
they wouldn't be opening up tomorrow, and added
almost without thinking, that if she had anything to
do with it, they wouldn't be opening up again at all,
ever!

So, thought Sarah, *my boyfriend's gone and now
my jobs probably gone, all in twenty four hours, but hay
ho, at least Mr. Mac's alright and that's all that matters.*
And in the scheme of things, it kind of put it all into
perspective for Sarah and she smiled happily to
herself as she drove home. She felt exhausted as she

climbed into her bed a few minutes later, the processing of it all could wait until tomorrow. She didn't have anything better to do now, did she, except for sorting out where she went from here and there was plenty of time for that! *Maybe time to let Clarabelle help,* she heard herself vaguely thinking, and after getting over the shock of that thought, Sarah fell into a deep sleep.

****

The morning broke with blazing sun, birds singing and a beautiful hue falling across the valley. Sarah woke with it and felt strangely alive, optimistic and energised. She had absolutely no idea why. She'd just lost both her man and probably her job, and all in a few days. Still, there were other jobs and there were certainly other men. (That she did know, there always were!) But she didn't want to go there, not at all, not now and the way she felt right at that moment, not ever! The job was important though, hugely important, and she wondered what would happen to the shop and her along with it. Trying not to worry, she showered and dressed quickly, going straight to the hospital to see Mr. Mackenzie. As she walked down the stark and sterile corridor of the hospital ward with the uninspiring bunch of flowers she'd grabbed in the foyer shop on her way in, she was delighted to see him sat up in bed, being pampered and preened by May along with most of the staff, and Sarah noted with amusement, he was loving every minute of it.

48

They talked through what had happened as
Mr. Mackenzie, (call me Edgar,) gushed and thanked
her repeatedly for saving his life and saving May, and
saving the shop and saving the world and Sarah
waited for the universe to be thrown in as well. He
wasn't going to be going back to work and that was
official. The shop was to be sold and Mr. Mac was
retiring with his May, (I've neglected her for far too
long,) and retiring to Brisbane, Australia to be with
his long lost son and grandchildren, (who'd have
thought it!). And Mr. Mac, (call me Edgar,) had then
assured Sarah that she would always be his surrogate
grand-daughter and that he would never forget her
etc. etc., and then, Mr. Mac, AKA Edgar, passed out
with a smile of sheer bliss on his morphine-stoned
face!

Chapter 3

The shop was to be sold. May was on a mission to action it all whilst Edgar was still in the land of morphine and still in the mood to retire. Her Chisolm grit had kicked in and May was on fire. An estate agent was already on his way and the board was going up within the hour. The accountants had been ordered to prepare the accounts ready for sale and there was no going back. It was over. Job number three hundred and fifty, (or was it twenty two? – she always did have a tendency for exaggeration) was over and Sarah was heading to Redville's job centre, again, to see Jane. They were on first name terms now, well, she was in there so often they were almost like family. *Here we go again,* thought Sarah, and kissing them both goodbye, she left the pair to it in their relief and happiness to be alive and to be together, and disappeared off to see Jane.

****

The apparently 'unemployable' Sarah sat under her favourite tree a few hours later with her feet tucked beneath her and contemplated. Jane had nothing at the job centre that she hadn't already tried. It was a small area and whilst she was liked, she also had a reputation of getting bored easily and not staying. Employers wouldn't touch her, not in Redfields nor in Redville and the thought of unemployment filled her with dread.

50

'Don't panic now, child,' said Clarabelle.
'There are other options you know!'

'Yeh? Like what?' worried Sarah quietly,
trying to stay calm and keep her increasing panic at
bay.

'Is that an invitation to interfere?' enquired
Clarabelle with an excited grin, 'For if it is, I have a
suggestion, and it's a good one!'

Sarah sat quietly and thought about it. *What
would be the harm? To let her guide me like she's been
wanting to for so long? I did say yesterday that maybe it
was time to hand over the reins and start doing it
differently.* Sarah wasn't sure. She'd always done it on
her own, and true, she'd always messed up, but that
was a small detail. *What if she didn't like Clarabelle's'
suggestion? What if she didn't want to do it? What if she
started taking over, running her life for her?*

'Well then, child, you don't do it!' said
Clarabelle interrupting her thoughts again. 'You
listen to the suggestions, you choose if you like the
options and then you act. I simply suggest that maybe
there are other options that you haven't considered,
other choices you haven't thought about.'

'Well….' Sarah hesitated. She took a deep
breath then spoke slowly and deliberately…. 'Well,
okay then, go for it. What do I have to say? Clarabelle,
please help me or something like that?' The words
stuck in Sarah's throat like little gravelly bits of glass
as she said them. She felt sick and scared as if she was
giving away power, showing her vulnerability, letting
someone else make decisions for her and she didn't
like it; she didn't like it one little bit! But she also
knew, without a shadow of a doubt, that it was safe.

51

This was Clarabelle for God's sake, not Genghis Bloody Khan! Clarabelle loved her; she wouldn't see her go wrong. *Yes, well, mother loves me, but she'd see me go wrong and she'd revel in my failings,* she thought, *but again, that was mother and this was Clarabelle!* And she knew for the first time in her life that she was ready, ready to hand over the reins of her life, (a bit,) and she could always say no, couldn't she?

'Well, that's good enough for me,' squealed Clarabelle in delight, wondering quite what had taken her so long to get Sarah to this point of surrender.

'And no, you don't actually have to say anything. Your intention of wanting help and of being willing to be helped is actually all I need, but if you want to actually *say* the words 'Please help me,' I'm more than happy to hear them. After all, Sarah, I've waited a long time for them and you really could do with the practice child!' she laughed.

And with that Clarabelle began to talk. She outlined her plans for Sarah's future employment as she sat bemused and bewildered at this new development of allowing outside help for the first time in her life. As she listened, her excitement grew at Clarabelle's ideas and plans for her. They sat and debated and talked until the wee small hours, watching the spring night draw in together under the apple tree. An excited and not a little unafraid Sarah, not to mention a frozen solid Sarah, (it's alright for angels, they don't feel the cold – probably the feathers!) went to bed ready to begin her life anew. A life of being guided, directed, and helped along a successful path. A path, according to Clarabelle which would lead to Sarah's ultimate happiness. Everything Clarabelle had said had made sense and every obstacle Sarah had put in the way Clarabelle had expertly sidestepped. Tomorrow she would go and see Ben and she would start to practice this new phrase in her new faze, 'Hey, Bro, I need some help.'

****

'And so that's what I want to do, Ben. I need you to help me with the paperwork side 'cos you know what I'm like with all that banking stuff. And the house will be the collateral, so that's got to be sorted too, and accounts at suppliers and stuff and Dad's money will be the deposit and it's all gonna be fine.' Sarah gabbled on with her plans as Ben listened avidly to her, trying to keep up, as attentively and alert as one could be when discussing major business and bank loans at this unearthly time of the morning.

She had driven to the nearby larger town of Redville and banged on the front door of his large Victorian terraced home at just after 7am, launching herself at him with a gusto of 'we need to talk' as she rushed around his kitchen making tea, banging cups around in her haste. It was now 7:30am and Sarah was nursing a cold cup of tea that hadn't had a sip taken out of, because Sarah hadn't paused for breath long enough for her lips to reach its edge!

'And we need to go and see Mr. and Mrs. Mackenzie together and get the shop off the market and get this all agreed and we need to do it today, ok?' Sarah raised her voice in order to get Ben to agree and agree he did. His head nodded

53

thoughtfully as he muttered quietly to himself. He always did that when he was thinking.

'Well, you have worked in shops for years. You practically run Mackenzie's anyway don't you? You *should* know enough to be able to make it work, in terms of suppliers, customers, profit and loss, pricing etc. and it is an established business with an already established clientele, so the risk is minimal to both you and to the bank.' Ben was trying his best to put his business head on, trying to stay focused and keep up. 'The collateral is there of course, in the house. The main issue is the cost of the purchase. Of course, you still have Dad's money, you can use that as the deposit and you borrow against the house, but it's a matter of how much you'll need to borrow and whether the business will sustain the borrowing, Sarah. There may be a better way though,' Ben paused as he thought through the options from a business point of view. 'You could buy the whole building, then sell the top floor and recover the costs through that. There's a flat above the shop, isn't there?' Ben enquired thinking on his feet now, as he moved towards the kettle and another much needed coffee. He'd been up half the night with baby Joe and his head was still fuzzy with sleep. Gina was still out cold, practically comatosed, same with Joe, he deciding that his sleep pattern at twenty months suited him far better to be in the land of nod early morning rather than in the night when he was *meant* to be asleep. Ben reckoned he did it on purpose, just to cause havoc, little minx!

'And no, we are not going to see the Mackenzie's right now, Sarah,' said Ben as he stepped

54

on a discarded squeaky toy rabbit hidden against the kitchen cupboard, making him jump in his half asleep distracted state. 'It's 7.30 in the morning! And anyway isn't Mr. Mac still in hospital?' he asked. Sarah nodded, she'd forgotten about that.

'And I need to go to work, Sis. Sorry, but I can't just rock up late without notice. We need to give it more thought first.' He paused, absent-mindedly moving a toy rattle away from the kettle, watching his sister's face fall at his remark and added quickly, 'I can meet you at lunchtime though, any good? We should have all the options we need explored by then. That will give them time to at least get themselves dressed before we turn up on May's door or at his hospital bedside.' He smiled at her encouragingly. 'I think it's a brilliant idea, Sis. You go and talk to Mrs. Mac first, aye, see what she thinks, then maybe go with her to the hospital to discuss it with Mr. Mac, alright?' he grinned. Sarah nodded with relief as Ben added, 'And of course I'll help you! What's the point of having a banker for a brother if he can't help his favourite sister now and then, but I bet if I'd said it was a crap idea you'd have changed the 'B' to a 'W' wouldn't you?' and he pushed her playfully as he watched the kettle, willing it to boil faster in his desperate need for more caffeine.

'Let me grab another coffee and a shower while you get some more details together. Annual turnover, profit and loss account, value of the shop. Go online and see what the agents got it up for, most of the info we need should be on there and I'll see you in a mo.' Ben disappeared off, clutching the coffee he'd just made into the abyss that was his upstairs.

'Told you it'd be fine, didn't I?' squealed Clarabelle in delight. 'Told you he'd help!'

'Yes, yes, you told me. It actually wasn't too bad, asking him, you know.... for help. Was quite easy, actually, easier than I thought and he does so know his stuff. If Ben says it's do-able, it's do-able! And Ben said it was a great idea. Hell!'

'Heaven actually, child, heaven! And are you going to go with the idea of the new stock, the new lines, I suggested? I can help you find the right suppliers you know?' Clarabelle smiled serenely, delighted with herself and her new found advice-line. She knew that this would be the making of Sarah. It would give her the sense of permanency that she needed, of stability and of commitment. There was no way that she would get bored with this because it would be hers. She'd never allow it to fail with her beloved house being the security for it; she wouldn't risk losing that! She could also change the business, develop it and grow it, along with her confidence and belief in herself. Sarah's self-worth was just rubbish! It was why she kept finding herself with men who treated her so badly. How many times had she told her that when she cared about herself properly, she would find a man who would care about her properly? But deaf ears as usual, only now... now there was a shift. It had taken five years longer than anticipated to get there, but they were finally getting there.

Yes! Thought Clarabelle. *We're on our way at last! Now all I have to do is make up for the lost time. Never too late, never too late,* she bustled, *but a lot to do!* And with that, she nipped upstairs to have a word

with her own brother and tell him the good news.
She'd need his help, she decided, and may even need
to call in some of the others.

****

Sitting on Cloud 322, Clarabelle was beaming,
positively beaming!

'So there we are, Clarence! She's finally asked,
so it's all systems go because we have an awful lot of
making up to do here now to get her square. This
was the hardest part, getting her to surrender, but
we've cracked this one now. I estimate she will be
where she needs to be within herself in
approximately six months but we're a few years
behind schedule. Do you think it's too late for the
other things? Do you think we're in time?' she
questioned. 'We all know they have the right to
choose their own path and time, but time waits for no
man or woman, and I just don't know if it's too late
for her to connect with Simon now, or those two souls
waiting to come in for them.' Clarabelle sat heavily
down on the cloud with a bump. It was a bit rough
this one, she noticed. *Just don't make them like they used
to!* She thought as she patted her behind. Thinking
about Simon then, she asked her brother, 'Where is he
within his own life now, Clarence? Do you think we
can keep him hanging on another six months before
he gets fed up and goes and finds someone else?' she
fretted.

'Now don't be silly, Clar,' laughed her angelic
brother. 'If he does it wouldn't work, would it? The
girl wouldn't be the right one! Mind you, there's

57

loads down there like that aren't there. Yes, maybe you're right. I'll have a word my end and we'll square it all between us.' He patted her shoulder reassuringly. Nodding to himself, he continued, 'You know just like I do that those two were meant to be together, all planned even before they set foot down there this time. It's set, ordained, fate, destiny, it's organised and arranged and it will be so!' he declared, scratching his chin and musing the problem. 'I'll ask the boss if I can have a word with Nathaniel, Simon's angel, see if we can't get our heads together. I know he's had a rough ride keeping Simon stuck where he is these past five years or more. That boy is so ready to settle down now it's beyond belief! Nathaniel won't be able to keep him where he is for much longer that's for sure, but somehow we've got to think of a way to drag it out a bit longer. We just can't risk allowing them to get together yet, not until they're both ready, they'll stuff it up! You say she isn't ready yet, definitely? Another six months?' he asked.

'No, she's nowhere near ready yet,' Clarabelle said, shaking her head sadly. 'Her confidence and her self-worth are just rubbish, almost non-existent! We've got to get those up before we can bring in Simon and we've got to get her belief in herself up too, and on top of that we need to sort out her assertiveness. What she puts up with is just unbelievable, especially from that mother of hers!'

'He won't go for a weakling!' declared Clarence. 'He's a strong man and he needs a strong woman. If you say you think six months to get her where she needs to be then we'll just have to hold him off for that long. I don't think Nathaniel's going to like it though, but leave it with me. You sort the job side, I'll sort the love life side.' Clarence hugged his sister, smiled reassuringly and went back to work.

'Six months!' declared Clarabelle to herself, trying not to worry. 'I have six months to make up five years?' Ever positive, never giving up, Clarabelle just knew she could do it!

Chapter 4

Sarah sat holding her head with one hand and with the other, clutched her stomach, which appeared to have a will of its own this morning. Head drooped and hanging, she gazed in the mirror opposite her bed at her puffy face, reddened with the alcohol from the night before, eyes blood shot and half closed, she groaned.

'Why do we do it? Oh, why, why, why?'

'We, child?' Clarabelle asked with a wry smile. 'I think you'll find that 'we' don't do any such thing! 'You' do this poisoning to your poor body, not 'we'! And where has it got you, mmm?'

'Yeah, yeah, yeah!' Sarah groaned. 'Don't start, Clarabelle! I am so not in the mood for one of your 'told you so' lectures this morning. My head's dropping off, my eyes hurt, my stomach's been ripped out and put back in the wrong way, and my mouth tastes like a donkey's bum. I will never, ever, ever drink again!' Sarah threw herself back onto the pillow, pulling the covers back over her aching head in protest at the reflection in the mirror forcing her to witness the results and realities of alcohol abuse, and willing abuse at that! She shrivelled up, curling her lamenting, poisoned body into the foetal position in defence to the world.

The night had been wonderful though, she thought as she lay in her pit/death-bed. 'I'm dying, I am truly definitely dying!' she wailed.

60

'Was it worth it?' Clarabelle asked, raising a disapproving eyebrow.

'Totally, definitely, absolutely!' Sarah grinned the grin of the naughty and the wicked with a smile that said, 'Yes, it was bloody worth it!' The smile reached into every part of her malfunctioning water craved, dehydrated body with a gentle little glow. They had celebrated into the wee small hours and then some, staggering home singing 'show me the way to go home' in appalling disharmony, at top volume all the way up the high street, down her lane and into her house. Shit, she'd have some grovelling to do today! How many neighbours had she woken from their peaceful, restful sleep? How many dogs had barked their owners awake in their panic at the horrendous noise that drowned their sensitive ears, noise that drunken humans called 'song'?

Ben had come up trumps. Over the last two weeks the sale of the shop had been agreed, the forms completed and the loan approved, so it had been decided to go out and celebrate Sarah's newly found destiny – joining the ranks of the world's shop-keepers. Her friends Frieda and Angie had been there for the celebrations of course, and they could knock them back like teenagers; only none of them could hold it like teenagers anymore. The under twenties who never seemed to get hangovers and could get up and get on with their lives the next day without dying the death that the over twenties die; and the even more appallingly particularly vicious death that the over thirties die! It seemed to Sarah that life was very unfair sometimes as she felt the full force of her hangover as her head spun again. *I'm turning into her from the exorcist!* she thought then, wondering if her head really, actually was going to spin a full 180 degrees, spin back, and then fall off!

Thinking back to the night before, she grinned. Ben had been the sensible one of course, but that was only because of baby Joe who would probably be up screaming half the night and for whom he needed to be in at least a semi-state of capability. Ben was nothing if not sensible, sharing the celebrations with the girls with just one glass of champagne and then he was onto soft drinks. Gina had been a different matter, bless! Babysitter sorted, her rare night out and the ability to let go had done wonders for the baby-bored-housewife. She had got totally wrecked on three glasses of bubbly, giggling stupidly at absolutely anything! Ben had left with a smile as he'd manoeuvred Gina out of the door, saying to Sarah over his shoulder as he guided, half carried his happy and very drunk wife towards the exit, 'See you Sunday, Sis,' and then added with a grin, 'You know you'll love it!'
Sarah had grimaced the grimace of the condemned, waved him off, and then brought her attention back to the celebrations. She refused, absolutely refused, to even think about Sunday, the dreaded Mother's Day, one of the three tri-annual visits to the witch. The other two visits equally dreaded; one for her mother's birthday and a further third and final, very reluctant afternoon visit sometime over the Christmas period for the 'family celebrations'.

'Ee-Gods, was it that time already? Mother's Day is upon us again!' Sarah laughed with irony.

62

'Some mother!' Pausing, she had pulled her dread away from that particular awaiting horror and back to the celebrations at hand. *Focus, focus, Sarah! Party, party, party!* she'd thought to herself, and she'd managed to bring her attention back to the pleasure of the moment rather than the pain that Sunday would inevitably bring.

The party had gone on long after Ben and Gina had gone. Sarah couldn't quite remember how many more bottles of Champagne, well ok, Asti then, had been drunk, but the headache this morning proved it must have been a lot. Still, it had been a fabulous night! Frieda and Angie had been so excited for her, so pleased. They had promised all the help they could give and Sarah knew they would be there for her. They had been friends, the three of them, since they had all begun in infants school together. Frieda with her wild, bright red curly hair had a personality to match and had made an instant impression on the five year old Sarah. She always seemed to run everywhere, have boundless energy and a happy disposition that never seemed to be serious. She had stayed exactly the same ever since! Frieda, the wild one of the three; always in trouble, always taking risks, always having a go at anything, whether she could do it or not. Frieda's motto was that she would rather die trying than not try at all. It was a miracle she was still alive and an even bigger miracle that she still held a clean police record!

Angie on the other hand, had been the sensible one, the risk assessor, the adjudicator. With her blond pretty looks, her perfectly doll formed body, her people pleasing manner, she never wanted to get muddy, broken, battered, in trouble or take any risks whatsoever. She also was still the same. Sarah herself fitted somewhere in between the two of them in terms of her own personality. The three of them had gelled at that young, early age and had stayed gelled stronger than glue ever since. Angie was of course married, settled down and stable before she was twenty-five, ever sensible and ever practical. She had two beautiful children, a stable home and a stable life. Frieda on the other hand had been married and divorced three times, (one per decade was definitely necessary, she had laughed) with a child from each marriage. Two further engagements in between the divorces as well as countless lovers. Frieda had many adventures under her belt and a whole host of hysterically funny crazy stories at her disposal. She had entertained the three of them until the early hours of the morning. They had laughed, cried, collapsed, nearly peed themselves more than once on those stories with their alcohol filled bladders that refused to work properly after four bottles of sparkling wine, and generally had a wonderfully inebriated time. They had staggered back to Sarah's house at stupid o'clock in the morning, singing loudly and were somewhere now crashed within the safety of the house. Their heads would all be as bad as each other's today and the morning would now consist of tea and toast, paracetamol and water, recovery and the post mortem of the night-before's shenanigans.

Sarah got up gingerly out of her death-bed to go and check on her friends' states of either near

death or coming recovery. She found them both
sitting in the living room, nursing cups of tea along
with their banging heads. The curtains were still
closed, keeping the room dark to protect their fragile
eyes from the daylight outside.

'Why, oh why did we do it?' they'd both
wailed in perfect unison as Sarah entered the room,
looking as equally frail and pale as them and almost
an albino in her fluffy very white dressing gown.

'Water!' they yelled simultaneously and burst
out laughing, at what, none of them knew, but it just
seemed funny, the state of them, sitting there, all but
dying of dehydration. Sarah moved cautiously over
to the window and slowly and deliberately began to
slide the curtains open.

'Please no, spare us; let us die quietly!' they
both begged as the curtains began to let the light into
the darkened room.

'Tough! This is not the Sahara and we are not
dying of dehydration, nor are we day-walkers that
need to be sitting in the twilight zone,' she said
mercilessly, grinning as she looked at her friends.
Mind you, looking at the state of them all, herself
included, with their pale faces and red eyes, she
wasn't so sure now. Maybe they had all actually been
turned into vampires overnight! Frieda suddenly
threw herself onto the floor and began to crawl
dramatically on all fours towards the door – 'Water!'
she called hoarsely, 'Water! Help me!' she turned
round grinning, watching them watching her. 'Ah
water? Is this a miracle I see? It is a miracle, a miracle
I tell you! I see a mirage, I see an oasis – I am saved!
Oh sod, it's not an oasis, it's the kitchen tap – but it'll

65

do!' Frieda giggled, proceeding to continue crawling on all fours out the door, all three of them leaning forward from the sofa so they could watch her crawl into the kitchen, (Clarabelle was of course watching too, trying to be 'one of the girls' and join in). Still on her knees, Frieda pulled herself up dramatically by her elbows, pushing on the tap and stuck her head under it, drinking the cold, fresh water and doing a fabulous impression of a dying man finding his salvation. Sarah and Angie giggled as the water dribbled down Frieda's chin. 'I am saved!' she declared, throwing both arms in the air for effect, 'Saved!'

Clarabelle watched the girls and giggled. They really were sooo funny sometimes, though she really should be discouraging this sort of thing. She was perched on the top of the sofa between Sarah and Angie, watching with glee Frieda's antics in the kitchen. 'Bless!' she chortled.

****

They spent the morning laughing and joking about the night before. They talked about the shop and about Mr. Mac, (call me Edgar, as he would now forever be known). They screamed with laughter about the child/goblin/doctor hybrid at the hospital; they plotted and schemed about Sarah's plans and about her future, and finally, as always, they laughed and joked about the dreaded MFH, (mother from hell)! Sarah's mother was always a source of hysterical amusement to the girls. They loved to

66

regale funny stories about her appalling behaviour or actions, laughing and giggling as they slagged her mother off collectively. They joyously recalled the story of when Sarah, around twenty at the time and being between jobs, again, had run out of money and food, going to her mother's for dinner one Sunday to eat and promptly being handed a bill for thirty-seven and a half pence on her arrival. This had been broken down into five pence for carrots, nine pence for broccoli, seven pence for potatoes, fifteen pence for meat, they couldn't remember the rest. The bill had been her exact share of the dinner, her mother had explained, the charges were for the extra pound of potatoes she had to get for the extra mouth to feed, the slightly bigger joint of meat, the extra three carrots, all broken down nicely onto a neat and tidy bill by the side of her place setting. All three girls laughed at the ridiculousness of it as they recalled the memory of that incident all those years before.

'What was the half pence for?' screeched Frieda, 'electricity for boiling the kettle for your cuppa? Did she charge you for the tea-bag?' and they fell about in hysterics some more.

After a break for the loo and more tea, along with more paracetamol, the girls went onto to regale other stories of MFH, reminded by Angie's comment on the tea bag. Clarabelle watched distractedly from the sofa as she preened her feathers thinking back to that time also. *How she'd managed to get Sarah through that woman's wrath without violence occurring she really didn't know!*

67

'Like the time you went round to borrow some coffee until pay day and your mother weighed out three ounces of coffee in the weighing scales,' grinned Frieda, 'followed by exactly two ounces of sugar, pouring each carefully into the Tupperware containers for you to take home. Remember how she counted out the twenty tea bags for you one by one and put them in that little bag? OMG, she is soooo funny!'

Sarah went onto finish the story. 'Well, watch me count, Sarah!' she mimicked her mother's voice perfectly. The girls laughed. 'I don't want you to be short-changed,' Sarah mimicked again, copying Margaret's shrill harsh voice. 'Remember how she checked the labels for the price of the coffee, tea, and sugar, pulled out a calculator, worked out exactly the percentage of each that she was giving me, and totalled it up?' Sarah grinned, finishing the story. 'With a waving smile she handed me the bill and then the wicked witch of the west so generously said', (putting on cackly witches voice now), "No rush, you can pay me back when you get your giro, dear, Wednesday isn't it?" and then she put them all in a carrier bag nicely for me to take back to the bed-sit I was living in at the time.'

'You can pay me back when you get your giro!' the girls screeched in unison. 'What kind of mother charges you for bloody tea bags is what I want to know?' grinned Angie to the others. 'I can't imagine my mother doing something like that!'

'No one can imagine their mothers doing anything like that,' Frieda shrieked. 'Unreal, your mother! She's so bad you just got to love her!'

68

Clarabelle nodded in agreement. That being said, she knew the girls would be surprised to know that Margaret wasn't alone in the 'worst mother of the year' category. There were many as bad and some even worse, though in this town, she definitely won hands down! Clarabelle wondered if she should have a word upstairs and see if they should invent an award for 'worst mother of the year'! Or better still an award for 'I-could-have-so-easily-killed-my-mother-but-I-haven't Award!' *Probably a bit too long that one, but it was a smashing idea*, she decided. Perhaps they should call it something nicer, like the 'Extreme Patience Award'? *Maybe I should win one?* she wondered, *for fitting so much patience into one human award! I'd win that I'm sure!* She grinned at the thought, imagining her and Sarah picking up mutual awards for patience. Sarah had certainly needed a lot of that in her years of dealing with Margaret, she knew, and she herself had had to have heaps of it, dealing with Sarah! Clarabelle focused on the girls again. They were all smiling, loving these stories of Sarah's MFH, finding it hysterical that anyone could have such an appalling mother and Sarah laughed with them, enjoying the silly but sadly true stories as much as they did. She had long ago learned to laugh at such things, with Clarabelle's help of course.

The stories went on into the afternoon until all of their sorry bodies had recovered sufficiently for the girls to be able go home. Angie was the first, collected by the ever patient Tom, her husband of thirteen years. Frieda followed half an hour later in her own

69

car which she had driven over in the night before, prior to their night out of celebrations. She would collect her children from her mother's house, not leaving there until after she had let her ever loving pampering supportive mum, 'nurture help and heal' the remnants of her hangover for a while, of course. Sarah watched them go and was grateful for her friends; for them celebrating with her and for their support. The pain of Rob leaving had faded now, so focused had she been on her new shop that she had hardly had time to give him any thought at all. Sarah realised gratefully that she was moving onwards and upwards, not only with her life, but also her heart. *The next three months are going to be amazing,* she thought with some disbelief. *So much to do, so much to sort, a whole new life to begin.* Sarah felt an excitement in herself, an assurity, a new confidence, and knew she was more than ready for the new her.

Chapter 5

Nathaniel was sitting on the top of the forty-two inch HD LED smart screen television, watching with increasing alarm the argument that was going on in front of him. His bright orange hair was glowing with panic, standing up straight on top of his head, all the way up to its full six inches, almost doubling his height, making him look rather more like a 'Gonk' than an angel! Simon didn't have a clue that Nathaniel was there of course, or that his Angel was having a seriously bad hair day! Simon was just one of the average billions of humans who couldn't see, hear or acknowledge their Guardian Angels. That didn't mean to say they weren't there, working away in the background, just that Simon, like most people, couldn't see them.

Oh my goodness, here we go again! Nat thought. *How was he meant to rescue this one? Another 'Roger' row! It was a crisis, an absolute crisis!* 'I need Clarence and Serena, now!' he decided and immediately flew off upstairs in a flash to get the others and some much needed reinforcements.

****

Simon Brown glared at his girlfriend of two years in total disbelief.

'You have *got* to be kidding me!' he said, almost spitting through gritted teeth. 'You are doing *what?*' His hands clenched into tight fists of fury. His

71

palms began to sweat and his face drained of colour.
His normally intense blue eyes lost their intensity and
the light went out behind them as a dark anger and
frustration began to take over. Thirty-nine years old,
6'4'' tall, tanned, toned, and beautiful, Simon stood
like a Greek God; his blond hair flopping over his
now blazing eyes and for all his strength, masculinity
and testosterone, he felt totally and utterly powerless.
Simon could not believe that this was still happening
over two years into their relationship. Nothing
seemed to be changing. She still insisted on keeping
her nearly ex-husband in the family loop and nothing
he could say or do was going to change it. It certainly
hadn't over the previous two years and it didn't look
like it ever would. He shook his head again.

'No, Nadia, this is not ok! This is bloody
ridiculous! What the hell do you mean he's coming to
your birthday dinner?'

'Daaarling, you don't understand! Mummy
loves him so and she's putting on this dinner for my
birthday and she *soooo* wants him to be there.
Pleeeease understand daaarling, you know it won't
be like this forever, things will change in time, I
promise! You can come next time, darling, pleeeease?'
She looked up at him with her big beautiful brown
eyes, pleading for understanding and permission, for
him to be ok with it and he wasn't! He never had
been, not in the two years and two months they'd
been together. He had put up with it in the beginning,
when the split was so new, giving everyone time to
adjust, to get used to the fact they Nadia's seventeen-
year marriage to Roger was over, that the husband

had moved out and that, within a few months, Nadia had found Simon.

'So, *yet* again I can't come!' Simon seethed, 'Yet again I won't be joining you! Yet again I won't be meeting your mother because 'bloody Roger' will be there, yet AGAIN!' Simon's voice was raised but he just couldn't help it! She really was bloody unbelievable!

He had felt blown away by her when he had met her that night at the dance. A night out with the boys, someone's leaving do, he had seen her across the crowded floor and been mesmerised instantly. Two years his junior at that time, she at thirty-five he at thirty-seven, she had stood tall, beautiful, sexy as hell, and totally gorgeous. He had wanted her instantly and initially thought it would just be the norm for him; another casual fling. But he had found over time that Nadia had charm, wit and an amazing ability to just wrap him around her little finger like no woman ever had before. And the sex! Wow, that was just mind-blowing! Always had been from the very first time and had just got better and better as time had gone on. Nadia was incredibly beautiful with her Mediterranean looks and tall stature. At 5'11'' she had a thirty-five inch leg that seemed to go on and on; her long black thick wavy hair fell almost to her waist, framing her stunning face as it fell. She had huge deep, dark eyes that twinkled and danced with desire, large heavy breasts that she loved to press up against him, (and that he so loved to enjoy) and her long shapely legs that she loved to wrap around him. There was no part of Nadia's body that Simon did not

73

desire and desire all the time! She was a fabulous cook, a demon in the bedroom and gave him his every wish in both areas. Was it any wonder that he put up with her ex and the family situation? They were happy, passionate, their lives entwined. Only they weren't! Simon had always been kept on the fringe of Nadia's life, waiting for everyone to accept him as her boyfriend but it hadn't happened. Her two boys had met him of course, nearly men now at nineteen and seventeen. They tolerated him, of a sort. He had yet to meet her sister or her parents even after all this time. She had kept him separate from her family life from the beginning and he had assumed it would change over the first year. It hadn't nor had it changed in the second year and still nothing was changing.

Just at that moment, Nathaniel arrived back, thankfully with Clarence and Serena. The three angels surveyed the ongoing drama carefully from the top of the telly and agreed, yep, they were in trouble!

'Quick, Serena, do something!' Nathaniel implored. Serena did something, *and boy, she did it good* Nathaniel decided. Serena was pouring heat and energy into Nadia's lower regions, the injected sexual energy beginning to radiate now throughout her body. Her nipples stiffened gently, her eyes softened, her lips parted seductively. Serena smiled happily, then added in a bit of vulnerability and sadness into the mix, just for good measure, Nadia's eyes not only sparkling with sexuality now, but also with anxious unshed tears.

'Smashing, well done, girl!' both Clarence and Nathaniel chimed in unison, and all three sat back, confidently waiting for the problem to defuse.

Simon looked at Nadia's pleading face and her down-turned mouth. He saw the sadness and tears in her eyes; he saw her vulnerability and his heart melted, as it always did. She saw that moment of weakness in him immediately and seized her chance, pouncing on Simon like a lioness taking down her prey, she pressed her heavy breasts against him as she moved in for the kill.

'Daaarling, you know how much I love you, don't you?' she said in a husky, sultry voice, stroking his chest gently with her painted and perfectly manicured nail. 'You know that there's nothing to worry about, don't you, my love, my sweetheart, my baby?' She pressed her hips up against his crotch with just enough pressure to get the reaction she was hoping for. Simon felt himself react, instantly becoming aroused, his body responding immediately as it always did. His trousers tightened as he hardened, his pulse increased, his anger melted as desire took over. He pulled her into his arms, groaning and he kissed her upturned and open mouth gently, reassuringly. He was lost again. He lost every time. He just couldn't resist her! She always won him around, talked him around, seduced him around, and he was aware that he let her. *God, why was he so weak!* he asked himself silently, whilst at the same time enjoying the sensation of her tongue stroking his mouth. Despite the increasing arousal, he knew that he couldn't take much more; the family

75

dinners, the birthday meals, the constant disappointment, the many times he wasn't welcome in her home because Roger would be around visiting the kids, and he was around a lot!

Nadia's response? That Roger paid the mortgage so really it was ok for him to come and go as he pleased. It was technically his house after all she had said. They rowed about Roger often. This latest one was her thirty-seventh birthday dinner. Her mum had arranged it, inviting Roger of course and not Simon. Nadia really did act like they were still married only not living in the same house. The divorce was going through, but never seemed to come. The financial settlement agreed, but never seemed to get signed. Nadia's reasons; the children were happy, the mortgage was being paid and life was stable. She wanted and needed nothing to change. She played the children card a lot. It was easier for the children, she said, if Roger saw them in their own home, much better for them and as no one wanted the children to suffer Roger came and went as he pleased, whenever he pleased. Simon thought it was ridiculous! These were young men not tiny tots and there was no reason Roger needed to be around whatsoever!

But it was all too late to argue about it now as here he was, pulling her blouse off and her lacy bra strap down, exposing her heavy swollen breast, and stroking her right nipple again, just the way she loved it. He kissed her harder and more urgently, at the same time Nadia pulling him up the stairs into the bedroom to finish what she had started in the living room a few minutes earlier, and the moment to stand up to her was lost, and Simon knew it was lost. If he brought it up again later, he would look like a petulant, sulky little boy; jealous, possessive, or any of those other accusations that she had thrown at him when he had dared to complain or say no to Nadia, a Nadia who was used to getting her own way. Simon gave up and gave in, making love to Nadia like it was all that mattered, and in that moment, it was all that did.

Serena, Clarence, and Nathaniel high-fived each other in glee.

'Another crisis averted,' they declared happily.

'Yes, but for how long?' panicked Nat. 'I am sooo struggling with this 'keep Simon stuck' plan guys. You have *no* idea, no idea at all how hard this is getting. Has been for the last five years! Always more time, more time needed. Is she ever gonna be ready?' he wailed. Nat didn't like to admit it, but he was really fed up with Sarah now. It was her fault after all! It was *her* holding up the proceedings and keeping his boy stuck like this, and making his job *just* so much harder, almost impossible! Clarence and Serena spent the next half an hour reassuring Nathaniel that he could do it, he would succeed, that it would be ok, and slowly Nathaniel calmed, his orange 'Gonk' hair finally beginning to settle back down to its normal state of flatness down the sides of his head.

****

After the sex, the wonderful, passionate, fabulous sex, Simon lay looking at the ceiling pondering the future with Nadia as she snoozed quietly next to him. He knew that Nadia had not let go of Roger at all. In the beginning, it had suited him, he realised, another casual fling, but time was getting on now, he was getting on now. He had grown and matured in those two years and he wanted more. He wanted children of his own, a wife, and a loving home.

Nadia had married young. She and Roger had been high-school sweethearts and when she had found herself pregnant at just seventeen, they had not hesitated to get married and settle down. They had been given a council house, back then in the days where young newly married couples with babies on the way could. Some years later, they had bought it, along with most of their neighbours, making it their home and had built their life together. It had lasted seventeen years; a lifetime to Nadia and in those seventeen years another child had come, two years after the first. After that, she and Roger had begun to drift apart. She said it was because Roger was rubbish at sex, didn't have a clue apparently. Initially, Nadia had accepted it, but as time went on and her own desires went unmet and unchecked, after a series of affairs that she relished, Nadia finally asked Roger to go. He went and he went quietly. Trouble was, he never stayed 'went'! He was here just as much as he had been when he lived here. She refused to see that she was being unreasonable, seeing Simon as the one having the issue. She had asked him was he jealous? Of course he was bloody jealous! Wouldn't any man be, to see his girlfriend spend time with her ex and go for family dinners with her ex! Simon had looked at himself many times and asked himself the same question, 'Am I being unreasonable?' and each time he had found the answer to be 'no,' with a smattering of 'no, I'm bloody not!' thrown in for good measure. But each and every time that he had decided that he'd had enough, that it was time to let go and move on, they had ended up in bed and it had all been brushed under the carpet once again. Just like now.

Simon got up quietly and dressed. He looked at Nadia sleeping and let himself out of her home to return to his bachelor pad. A lonely, quiet, very male, and very empty bachelor pad. He sighed as he drove into the underground car park, for once not noticing the roar of his Jaguar's engine as it echoed off the walls. He clicked the remote locking on his key pad not noticing the soft bleep as the car locked and alarmed itself and walked the few steps to the lifts, his spirits low, his head feeling overloaded with conflict. He let himself in through the front door of his two-bedroom apartment and looked around at his home. It wasn't what he wanted anymore and he knew it.

He had loved it when he bought it seven years earlier. On the top floor of the modern apartment block that overlooked the city, this flat had been everything to him and enabled him to be part of the life that he had loved, 'the city life'. The life and the flat had suited him down to the ground then, but these days, he caught himself looking at his friends with their wives and children, their suburban family homes and had found himself desiring what they had. He had watched them get married off one by one over the years. Some had since divorced admittedly, but love wasn't guaranteed, was it?

He had been shocked initially when the thoughts had first come into his head a little over a year ago, those thoughts of settling down. He had been 'Jack the Lad' for a long time. He had sewn more wild oats than most and here he was finally watching children playing and instead of running, he had found himself smiling and wishing he too could be a father and play with his own kids. He had broached it once with Nadia the subject of children, but she had made it clear that she did not want any more. She had also made it clear that she never wanted to marry again. He had thought back then, that in time, once the divorce was through, she would change her mind. She was still young and beautiful; it wasn't too late to have another family, a family with him. But today's debacle had opened his eyes to the inevitable truth and he was seriously toying with the idea that no matter how gorgeous and sexy and funny Nadia was, and she was, maybe it was time to let go and move on.

'Simon, my boy,' he said to himself out loud, 'we have some thinking to do. It's decision time!'

Nathaniel could feel his hair beginning to rise again. Clarence and Serena had gone and he was alone with Simon in the apartments kitchen playing with Simon's toys, his 'gadgets' and 'gismo's', wondering desperately how he was going to distract him. Simon rarely pondered, and in the 'keeping Simon stuck plan' it was best to avoid any opportunity of thoughts which could possibly lead to him leaving Nadia. Nathaniel needed to act and act quickly! He concentrated fully on Simon's stomach, sending rumbles and grumbles there as best he could. It worked! *Yippee!* Simon suddenly moved from the open-plan lounge into the kitchen area beginning to prepare food. Nathaniel focused all his energy as he shouted 'telly, telly, rugby, football' at Simon and crossed his fingers, continuing with his chanting of 'telly, rugby, football' all the while that Simon cooked.

After he had fixed himself some dinner, Simon sat down, purposely leaving the ever faithful TV remote alone, despite fancying a bit of telly, deciding instead to give his life and future some proper thought.

'Argh!' yelled Nat.

Simon had toyed with the idea of leaving the city previously, to ask for a transfer to another town, any town, get away from Nadia, give him some space, but every time the thought had grown, something had always come up and got in the way. It just never seemed to happen, almost as if something were blocking it.

Nat sighed in frustration. Twenty seven times he had said 'telly,' but Simon had managed to resist his influence, yet again! He didn't feel the slightest bit guilty as he watched Simon trying to figure out how his life had been blocked from moving forward so frequently. It was the plan! The blinking 'Simon and Sarah' plan! He tried again to distract Simon, and again, he failed! *Damn, he's so stubborn!* Nat thought.

Simon was back to his pondering and Nat's orange hair was now back to 'Gonk' status!

Maybe this time he would pursue moving, have a word with head office and see what they could sort? For God's sake, in a major bank like his with hundreds of branches everywhere, there must be something somewhere! He was an experienced business accounts manager with a good record; he could go anywhere, even to another bank perhaps? Simon played more with the idea of changing employers, of moving to another bank.

Nat turned the heat up and reminded Simon suddenly of all the support the bank had given him over the years.

'Strike one!' Nat yelled, determined not to give up.

'Mm, maybe not,' Simon was now saying to himself. It seemed disloyal somehow, they'd been good to him at his bank, given him opportunities to move up and supported him enormously. It would be ok to move branch, but maybe not bank. He'd have a think and see what was on the company intranet tomorrow, see what was around, take it from there. If there was nothing, then and only then would he seriously consider moving to another bank. It was time for some action, but inside the bank he decided, for now.

'Phew!' Nat breathed, his hair thankfully now starting to wilt from its spiked state once again, but no, hang on, Simon was off again! The semi-wilted hair began to spike back up again.

Simon was now thinking about the city he had lived in for most of his life and knew he'd outgrown it. He yearned for somewhere quieter, greener, with more of a community feel. The hectic city life was no longer the fun it had been in his youth. *Time to go somewhere new, somewhere where he didn't have a reputation as a player, a stud! A fresh start? Time to start over?*

'Yes, yes, but not yet!' screeched Nat, frustration and failure burning in his now fully extended Gonk hair-state of stress!

Simon, oblivious to it all gave moving more thought. He knew that he had a stinking reputation as a ladies man and despite being with Nadia for so long, no-one would ever believe he wanted more than a shag. Before Nadia, he had been a total shit, he knew that. He had bedded most of the pretty girls in the city as well as those in the villages and towns nearby. *He had also bedded*, he thought regretfully, *a fair few of the not so pretty ones too, particularly in his earlier years. He had played the stud game and he had played it well.* He grimaced as he acknowledged his previous callousness, his lack of compassion, lack of integrity, and generally appalling behaviour; behaviour that people think they can get away with in the name of youth and fun. 'I thought I was a stud, but I was a prize prick!' groaned Simon. 'Maybe that old saying, "What goes around comes around" is true? Maybe it's my turn now to know what it feels like to be used!' *And if it was*, he thought with a new

83

understanding, *he deserved everything he was getting and more.*

Nathaniel tried another distraction. He placed a big image of Simon's family into his subconscious mind and crossed his fingers again, he added his toes and feathers for good measure.

'Strike two!' he grinned, as Simon's attention changed focus.

Simon's thoughts drifted to his family as he sat in his favourite chair overlooking the city. His parents had retired to Spain three years ago, following Dad's heart attack. It had given them all a wake-up call, had that! Once he had recovered, sixty-two year old James J Brown had reassessed his work and life balance, took his neglected, confused, and bemused wife, Linda, and legged it off to the sun. They had been back once for a brief visit, but other than the Skype conversations once a week, Simon really didn't see his parents any more. His only other family member, his sister, Jane, had long since emigrated to Australia where she lived with her flatmate in a beautiful old house over-looking Byron Bay, living the life of the spiritual seeker, surfer and 'dude.' His contact with her was sporadic. They had grown apart in the fifteen years since she'd been gone, so different now from the closeness of their earlier days. *Yes*, Simon thought, *he was well and truly alone.*

'No, no, this isn't working! Don't start with the 'lonely' thing again! That's only gonna make you want to go even more!' Nat grimaced. Determined not to give up, he tried to change Simon's focus again. It didn't work!

'Strike three, I'm out!' he said sadly, shaking his head.

Simon was regretfully acknowledging that he spent most of his time alone these days when he wasn't with Nadia. He thought back to what he used to do before her. The pub didn't have the same appeal it once did, the crowd being younger, louder, and fresher. It wasn't the same sitting at the bar on his own nursing a pint and feeling like Billy-No-Mates, nights out with the boys a rarity these days. When he called them, inviting them for a pint he was met with replies of how they'd have to see what they could do, and the inevitable, 'great to hear from you mate!', the call ending without anything being arranged or sorted.

If he did end it with Nadia, Simon knew all that he had in store for him if he stayed here in the city were the young studs' night-clubs, where he felt more like someone's granddad than a sexy bloke most of the time, or the few clubs in the city that were aimed at the over 25's. *And they say that men are predatory!* thought Simon with a wry smile. He had been into the city night scene a couple of times in the last year when he had been pissed off with Nadia, going around the clubs and bars wanting to block out the conflict in his head with loud music, fun and beer. Each time the places he'd found himself in had terrified him! He recognised the difference, the shift in himself in the last few years, going from being the 'hunter' to the 'hunted' and he didn't like it, not one

85

little bit! The pack of predatory women; single women, married women, hen nights, girl's nights, most of them dressed up to the nines, many 'mutton-dressed-as-lamb', dressing far too young for their years.

He'd tried to stay safe, hanging with the herd of other terrified men at the bar, the men who didn't want to hunt or be hunted, feeling like a lone gazelle in a David Attenborough documentary, waiting for the cougar's to pick off the weakest, drag them mercilessly onto the dance floor kicking and struggling where they would be pulled down by the predator, devoured with seduction, deep cleavage and perfume. Then there was the other predatory pack; the male pack, the wolves (or were they the hyenas?) circling the edges of the dance floor, watching, waiting, choosing their options, ready to pounce; young tasty fresh meat or the experienced and delicious Milfs! He chose to ignore them, along with the lounge lizard's lurking in the dark corners and the slimy snakes too, equally as bad, slithering their way around discretely, eyeing up their prey voyeuristically. *Animals, the bloody lot of them. Yep, it was definitely the Serengeti. Worse! Used to be a cattle market, the men the prize bulls,* he thought, *but these days it seemed it was a Safari, far more ruthless and dangerous.*

Simon stayed at the bar trying to avoid both packs, avoid being noticed. Difficult at 6'4" but he'd quickly developed a lovely stoop in his efforts to camouflage himself amongst the safety of the nervous male herd, super-glued as they were to the bar. He'd watched the female predators circling, prowling, and stalking as they neared the bar to move in for the kill.

86

Claws or sharp fangs weren't their weapon to bring down their prey, but an empty glass instead, equally effective! The nervous gazelles and bulls moved closer to each other in their vein attempt to keep the predators at bay, but somehow the cougars managed to push their way in and split the herd, moving in to their targeted prey with determination and stealth. He'd nearly passed out more than once as the pack moved in, pressing up against him at the bar, contaminating and strangulating the air he was trying to breathe with their heavy cloying perfume. He watched the cougars approach with dismay, noting most were overly made-up, shiny dance tops, cleavages heavily exposed, along with some dismal displays of unattractive flesh, some of them smacking of desperation, others a determined grit! He had been eyed up, touched up, winked at, flirted with, and pounced on! He'd had his crotch stroked, his nipples stroked, his ego stroked, his bum pinched and he'd hated every single second of it. He had left early each time, trying not to attract the attention of the pack as he slipped out the door quietly in his attempt to avoid the inevitable slow smoochy dances at the end. The finale where the women bagged their lone gazelle, their hunt complete, phone number scrawled drunkenly on a scrap of paper, clutched in their victorious hands. Simon shook his head. *Nope, definitely needed out of this city and this safari.*

'Right then, sunshine,' he said to himself with a smile, 'pad and pen, let's make a start with options.' Always a list man, (never could multi-task) Simon went to his desk and began his plans.

Nathaniel sat quietly, frozen to the spot, his hair now firmly in the 'Gonk' position. *It would take him at least a week to get it back down now*, he thought with alarm. He knew that Simon was ready to move on, but somehow he had to delay, again! He'd been delaying for five years now, pretty girl after pretty girl, keeping Simon stuck in fling after empty fling. He'd put blocks in the way for years now, bringing him to Nadia as part of the 'keep Simon stuck plan' by introducing him to her, yet another dead-end fling. Nathaniel had often turned Simon's focus to other things during that time, helped him lose track of his plans, blocking job options and generally did everything he could to mess up Simon's plans for moving forward with his life. Normally, this wasn't the practice for angels, not on a day to day level, but this was in Simon's Highest Good, (AKA, his long term future benefit), and upstairs had confirmed that it was the right thing to do, so here he was, keeping the blocks going. Nathaniel reckoned he could buy the team three months, maybe four max, and had told Clarence and the others firmly that he didn't expect to be able to stall much past June before Simon would push forward, obstacles or no obstacles. *Right, how many intranet gremlins can I get to mess up the banks internal vacancy system this time? How many pens could he dry up so that Simon couldn't write his necessary lists? How many more times could he refocus Simon's attention onto something else and away from the desire to move on?* Nathaniel wondered to himself, as he nipped off to wreak the necessary havoc required to keep Simon stuck for another few months. 'And that, Nadia, I am going to have to work with Serena so closely now to

88

tone her up or tone her down, or some-blinking-thing before Simon finally sees the light and legs it. Once that's over, he'll be gone and I won't be able to hold him back any longer. Last chance saloon, lots to do, lots to do!' he said, and he whisked himself off to cyber-space on task number one; cause havoc with the computers!

Chapter 6

Sarah arrived with Ben at Margaret's house
spot on three o'clock for the dreaded Mother's Day
visit. Her childhood home was in a nice part of
Redville, on the quiet outskirts where Margaret
wouldn't have to interact too much with life or
people, just the way she liked it. Sarah noticed the old
semi-detached house had changed little in the forty
years that Margaret had lived there. Her mother's
small, practical car sat on its drive, the lawn mowed
neatly. No flowers or boarders framed it; the front of
the house as stark and minimal as possible. Sarah felt
cold, as cold as the house. She wished Gina was there,
but as often happened her clever sister-in-law had
managed to avoid the visit with Margaret. She knew
how it would be and she got out of it as often as
possible, lucky thing! Margaret was, of course, quite
certain that no one was good enough for her beloved
son, not even the lovely Gina. Whilst she was polite,
she was frosty and Sarah knew that Ben didn't want
to put his wife through it unless he had to. It was
Mother's day for Gina too and Sarah knew that Ben
had spoilt his wife all morning with flowers and a
card, breakfast in bed, seeing to Joe, and even cooking
the Sunday roast for them all, before dropping them
off at his mother-in-law's and then going on to fetch
Sarah. It had been a lovely day so far for them and a
peaceful and relaxed day for Sarah, but the next few
hours would be difficult as they always were where
visiting Margaret was concerned.

She stared now at the dreaded front door with trepidation, anxiety building in the pit of her stomach like a volcano waiting to explode. Her throat went dry and tightened; heat and tension rose around her chest threatening to crush her ribs and begin its inevitable journey up to her throat, where it would strangle and suffocate her completely. Ben patted her clammy hands in her lap reassuringly.

'It'll be alright, Sis. It's only three hours. You can do it! Just keep thinking about the shop, think about your future. Focus on something else, something nice. Just Breathe! Breathe! Breathe!' and Sarah breathed, breathed, breathed; and … relaxed! She turned to Ben and smiled,

'Just don't leave me alone with her, not for a second, 'cos I won't be responsible for my actions,' she grimaced.

'Not even for the loo?' grinned Ben. 'I can't hold it for three hours, Sis,' and in a Frank Spenser accent, tipping his head to one side he added, 'I'm a man!' and Sarah laughed, breaking the tension.

'Don't forget your protection, child,' piped up Clarabelle, 'you'll need it in there you know!' Sarah did know! She did what Clarabelle had taught her years ago to do, she imagined a beam of beautiful, powerful white light pouring down over her, forming a cloak, a shield all around her.

'I am sealed and protected and nothing can harm me,' Sarah chanted in her mind, imagining the cloak draw strongly around her. She wrapped it closer ready for the onslaught that she knew would be waiting for her inside.

91

'Come on then, Ben,' she reluctantly agreed. 'Let's do it.' They stepped out of the car and onto the dreaded path, both sets of footsteps heavy as they approached the front door.

The clock struck three in the hall as the two siblings let themselves into Margaret's home, not wanting to be even a minute late, for Sarah knew she would be nagged, guilt tripped, and bullied for the rest of the afternoon for keeping her mother waiting. *Not that that wasn't going to happen anyway,* thought Sarah wryly to herself. Her mother was completely incapable of being nice to her; a kind word, a compliment, any praise… would be unheard of! Sarah knew the drill that was coming for the next three hours whilst they played happy families for Mother's Day. Snide digs, subtle put downs, comparisons with fabulous Ben and how wonderful he was. And then the attack would come. Why couldn't Sarah be more like him? Ben, of course, would defend, as he always did. He would calm the situation down, play peacemaker, advocate, and ally. It was exhausting for both of them really, each and every time, but it was a role they both knew and played well; they'd had plenty of practice over the years. *Ho hum*, thought Sarah to herself, *here we go*. They walked into the lion's den, the witches cavern, the spider's web, the gates of hell, and any number of other examples Sarah could think of to compare her mother's home with.

Margaret sat in the kitchen, make-up mirror in hand, applying the last of her face powder to her already heavily made-up face. Her lips pursed in annoyance as she noticed another wrinkle around her mouth. At nearly sixty years old, a lifetime of heavy smoking had taken its toll on her skin and particularly her mouth. The countless drags on her thousands of cigarettes over the years ruining her lips, which were now lined and overly wrinkled for someone of her age. She was still slim, the weight never wanting to stay around long enough to touch the sides of Margaret's cold and angry body. Weight nor people ever wanted to spend any length of time around Margaret Smith! She frowned at the new wrinkle, sending it venomous wrath.

'Old, old, old! I am getting old! And no one cares!' she lamented in self-pity.

Time had not been kind to Margaret Smith. Time and life, as she saw it, for Margaret was one of life's victims. She was not able to see or take responsibility for any actions. She was not able to see or take responsibility for any hurt and she was definitely incapable of taking any blame. The words 'I'm sorry' were not in Margaret's vocabulary. They did not register and they did not compute. Whenever anything went wrong, and it often did in Margaret's world, it was always, *always,* someone else's fault! She would play the victim, the drama queen, the 'poor helpless me' role to a tee, sucking others into the drama with relish, revelling in the attention, the 'oo's,' the 'ahh's,' and the 'oh dears' with a gusto!

'Ben! Darling, how are you my dear? You're looking wonderful as ever!' Margaret gushed. She

93

rushed over to Ben as he walked into the kitchen, the room heavy with the scent of her cloying perfume. Hugging him tightly, wearing her proud mother smile, she looked behind him and noticed Sarah standing at the doorway. The loving smile changed instantly.

'Sarah, dear, how nice to see you... for a change,' she remarked coldly. 'What *is* that you're wearing dear? I didn't realise they still made them for women nearing forty! Your hair looks nice though, for a change, although your roots need a touch up, dear. I can recommend my hairdresser if you like, they'll do a much better job than the people you use, certainly can't do much worse! And that tan!' she continued, 'Is it safe to be *that* brown? Really, dear, you're not doing any favours to your skin you know. You'll end up with cancer!' The irony did not escape Sarah, as her mother dragged on her twenty-fifth cigarette of the day, lamenting the risks of too much sunbathing and damage to the skin of her non-smoking healthy daughter. Her lovely tan from the earlier holiday now almost gone anyway, along with her boyfriend.

Sarah felt her hackles rise, her heart begin to beat a little faster, a little louder; she saw Ben's loving and sympathetic look which said, *don't let her get to you*, and she counted to ten, and then another ten, trying not to rise to it. She smiled sweetly at Margaret, ignoring the insults as best she could, saying,

'Happy Mother's Day, Mum.' With a fixed smile that didn't reach her eyes, she handed her mother the card she was holding, wondering if by some miracle she might actually be able to get through the entire three hours without a row. She was in a good mood after all, with the shop now under her name. *How good is that!* she thought to herself. She pulled her imaginary cloak in a little tighter and felt its protection from the jibes of her mother's tongue. Even so, she wondered how she was going to get through the dreaded visit without battering her mother to death! Or at the very least retaliating, which of course would do no good whatsoever, for then Margaret would have even more of a reason to despise Sarah.

On the few occasions she had tried it, tried to stand up for herself, Margaret had lamented, wailed, whined, and whinged about how nasty her daughter was to her, how horrible she was and how Ben would never, ever be so horrible to her.

Help! thought Sarah, with a panic. *I can't do this! I am going to kill her; I am going to kill her stone dead! And I am going to enjoy every single moment of pummelling her smarmy face to a pulp!* she dreamed, quietly and silently to herself, at the same time knowing she never could. She couldn't even stand up to her properly let alone kill her, but it was a nice thought, albeit for a moment.

'I am here to help you know, child, even with your mother, especially with your mother!' said Clarabelle quietly and firmly, in Sarah's left ear.

'Fine,' Sarah whispered back, 'do what you got to do! Just get me through this without a police record for assault, matricide, homicide, or battery!'

'Breathe, child, breathe!' Clarabelle whispered gently into Sarah's desperate and panicking ear.

95

Instantly a warm, calming heat began to descend into her head where Clarabelle was standing blowing in healing light. Sarah felt herself filling up with peace and for a moment, it even worked, until she heard Margaret's rising voice that is.

'She's doing *what?* Tell me you are joking please, Benjamin! You cannot be serious! Sarah, running her own shop? *Oh for God's sake!*' Margaret's voice rose in both pitch and volume as she shrilled on, increasing both with every syllable. 'She will lose it all, she will lose everything! Stupid girl! Stupid, stupid girl! I *cannot* believe what I'm hearing here!'

Sarah stepped in to her own defence.

'That's right, Mum. I bought Mackenzie's. I own it. It's mine. As of Friday, it's mine. And I will not lose it all, and by the way, I am not stupid and I would rather you didn't call me that, thank you very much!'

Margaret turned to face Sarah with fury and shock.

'How dare you back-chat me, my girl! Benjamin tell her! Tell her she is not to speak to me like that!'

Ben took his mother's shaking and increasingly hysterical hands in his, calming her down with a warm smile, a gentle touch, reassuringly. Quietly he said to her, 'Mum, you need to stop shouting. It's not good for you. Now, why don't we all sit down and talk this through over a nice cup of tea, aye?' He pulled her acquiescing body gently to the table, sitting her down on one of the four dining chairs and put the kettle on, busying himself as he looked for and found a way to deal with her.

96

Sarah sat too, on the opposite chair, seething with fury and disappointment. Why had she thought it would be any different? She had hoped of course, always hoped, that mum would support, encourage, be proud, and be nice, but it was not to be; not this time, not any time! She let her mind wander away from the table, away to her shop, her dreams, her hopes, and she switched off from the conversation around the table, as Ben explained and reassured Margaret.

He *knew* it would be ok, he said, that he was backing her, helping her, he was her business manager, would guide her, keep her safe, keep her investment safe, her house safe, and gradually, over the next half an hour, Margaret's hysteria subsided and everything calmed down.

Well, if Ben thought it was ok, well then it must be, thought Margaret, because she knew, without any doubt, that her Ben was always right! *But only because Ben is looking after her business, not because that useless daughter of mine could ever do anything properly in her life, never could, never would! But, if Ben was there to keep an eye, maybe Joan's house would be safe after all.* She didn't care about the money, but she had liked her ex-mother-in-law Joan, being the only mother figure she had ever really known. She didn't want to see Joan's lovely house being lost by her stupid, errant daughter, who, as far as Margaret was concerned, didn't deserve it in any way.

Margaret Smith allowed Ben to calm her down, taking her time and revelling in every second of the attention gained from her special, special boy

97

and she smiled. 'Such a good boy,' she said as she rubbed his hair, 'such a good boy.' She glared at Sarah, spitting through gritted teeth,

'See how you've upset me on Mother's Day! If it weren't for your brother here I'd be a nervous wreck because of you, and on Mother's Day!' she lamented, going into one of her 'woe is me' spaces of self-pity, turning again to Ben to soothe her wounded pride, lapping up every ounce of the attention.

'You upset yourself, Mother, as always, getting hysterical before you know any facts and letting yourself get into a state!' Sarah retaliated.

Her sodding mother really was unbelievable! Why she put herself through this three times a year she would never know! Hell, she realised with a shock, she had just stood up to her, not once, but twice! It was so rare for Sarah to say anything in her defence at all to her mother, that 'back-chatting' her twice within the space of a few minutes was a real break-through.

'Well, child, that's one of the things we need to look at and sort,' stated Clarabelle simply but assertively, 'but for now, just support your brother, don't batter your mother and we'll get you through the visit without any death and destruction.' Clarabelle glowed her glow. Calming warming light once again poured into Sarah, giving her the strength that she would need to get her through the next two hours and twenty-five minutes of living hell! She felt the dart holes from her mother in her invisible cloak being repaired and sealed by Clarabelle and she knew she was safe. She detached, let go, and let Ben get on with it. Bless him!

Sarah couldn't remember when it had started, this war with her mother. It went as far back as she could remember. She had been daddy's little girl and even at such a young age she could feel her mother's jealousy, resentment, and distance. She hadn't known what she had done wrong, so she had just tried harder to be good, better. She had tried to make her mother like her by doing nice things for her, but no matter how hard she tried, it never seemed to be right, or good enough, and no matter what it was, it was never what her mother wanted. Sarah guessed she must have been about thirteen when she gave up trying.

After her father had left when she was ten years old, things had become worse - much worse! Her mother turned to drink for a while in an attempt to drown out her sorrows, anaesthetise her rejection, and quash her abandonment. She indulged herself in a depth of self-pity never seen before, even for her! She blamed Sarah for everything, venting her pain on her in unlimited quantities. For the weather when it rained, for poor school results (B pluses and not A's), for the state of the world, for the strikes of the time, but mostly for her father leaving. As it was impossible for Margaret to even consider that it could be her own fault that John had gone, it fell in Margaret's mind that it therefore must be Sarah's. It couldn't possibly be hers or Ben's; she of course, was blameless and he was just a child for goodness sake! He was five years old; sweet, innocent, devoid of all blame and she, of course, had been the perfect wife!

The blame therefore belonged to Sarah and Sarah alone.

Her father had always spent a lot of time with Sarah as she had been growing up. He had helped her with her homework, run her to clubs, to friends' houses; he had been the family taxi. He had advised, counselled, supported, hugged, and loved and Margaret Smith resented every second of it! For every second that John was with Sarah, he wasn't with her and she needed and demanded every single second of her husband's time, love and affection to try to fill the limitless well, the bottomless pit of her empty and lonely heart. As Margaret's demands to her husband for forever increasing affection and attention grew, so John became more avoiding of his nagging and needy wife, less willing to please, appease, or cajole. His increasingly neurotic wife turned the pressure up and pushed more. The more she pushed, the more he pulled away and she could not see it at all. He began to avoid her, choosing to spend increasing time with his daughter instead. Margaret's resentment for Sarah grew, using her as the scapegoat for her collapsing marriage. Inevitably, John had eventually sought solace in another woman's arms, leaving Margaret after eleven years of what had mostly been to him a very unhappy marriage. He left for a much younger and much more relaxed woman, fatally meeting her when taking Sarah to a netball event. It had not lasted of course; it had just been a catalyst from which to spring John from his trapped and miserable life, but in Margaret's mind, it would not have happened if it were not for Sarah. In time John moved on and away,

100

buying a new home for himself and creating a new
life, a single life and one that he relished.

Once her father was gone, Sarah received no
love or affection from her mother at all and very little
from her absent father, whom she saw infrequently
and sporadically. The day he had left he had sat her
down, and gently holding her hand had said that he
just had to go, that he loved her very much, and that
he was sorry.

'It's not your fault, sweetheart,' he had said,
'It's just one of those things. We don't make each
other happy anymore and I can't stay. Look after your
brother for me.' He'd had tears in his eyes and Sarah
had been devastated.

'Can I come too, Daddy?' she had asked,
'Please?' He had shaken his head sadly, wiped the
tears away from her cheeks that were sliding down
her face and held her tighter still. 'Please, Daddy,
please? I'll be good, I promise!' she had pleaded.

'I wish I could, Sarah, but I can't. It's not right,
sweetheart. Now, be a brave girl for me.' And with a
kiss on her forehead and a tender ruffle of her hair,
John Smith was gone.

Throughout the next seven years, the
emotional neglect and hostility had taken its toll on
Sarah. Piece by piece Margaret had worn down
Sarah's spirit. She had grown in that time from an
awkward child into a beautiful, bright young woman,
but inside herself Sarah felt ugly, unlovable, stupid,
and unworthy, the legacy from Margaret's constant
digs and snipes. The development of Sarah from child

101

to adult went unnoticed in Margaret's insular and lonely life. Her world revolved only around the ever-present pain of her loss and her love for her son. Nothing else mattered. Sarah did not exist to Margaret except as a constant reminder of her abandonment by the man she had loved; an over-bearing, all-consuming love that had suffocated in the end and the only one who was totally unaware of this was Margaret herself.

Sarah's shiny, positive personality that had been so strong as a young child had eventually begun to dim over the years and by seventeen, she had little left at all. That was when Clarabelle had shown up, literally! An emergency meeting had been held 'upstairs' at the highest level and Clarabelle had been given permission to allow Sarah to see her, communicate with her and be openly loved and supported by her. Her mission was to fan the flames of Sarah's dwindling spirit and to counteract the coldness from her mother. It had helped to stop the rot from deepening, but it had not undone it - it had just prevented it from getting worse.

Sarah's growing popularity with the boys had helped her fragile confidence immensely as she blossomed into a beautiful young woman, but with such low self-esteem she was constantly and repeatedly drawn to boys who would use and abuse. It was a pattern that she had repeated for twenty years and each time she had got hurt, it had only served to reinforce her deeply held belief, the belief that she just wasn't good enough. Sarah did not know what it was to be loved and appreciated and Clarabelle was determined that now that Sarah was ready to finally accept help, it was time for that to change.

'It can and will be undone, this damage!' Clarabelle vowed. She determined that Sarah's light would shine as brightly as it had been intended to and she would stop at nothing to make it happen. She deserved it, she'd earned it and it was time! When Clarabelle decided something, with the might of the Universe behind her it was only a matter of time before it came about. And that time was now!

****

They sat in the car together, never closer, this brother and sister on their journey home from the afternoon from hell; his love for her was so strong, so powerful, and so protective. His guilt for being loved by Margaret when Sarah was not had eased over the years. He knew it was not his fault, but he had never ceased pitying her, sympathising with her and for her. He had been surprised to discover when he had been really quite small, that whilst Sarah seemed not to be able to do anything right in his mothers' eyes, in a bizarre twist of fate, it seemed that he could do no wrong. Maturity and wisdom had helped him to understand over the years since, that their mother had taken all of the love that she could no longer give to her husband and delivered it instead onto her son. She had also taken all of the fury, rejection, and hurt that she had felt for her husband, delivering it squarely onto Sarah's young shoulders. Ben made the decision to share the love he received from his mother with Sarah, so had allowed his mother to adorn him

103

with bucket-fulls of the stuff. He had then dumped it all over Sarah in the most loving way that he could, making sure in his own way that she got her share. He did it now, as he turned to her and reassured her that the shop was going to be a huge success, that she could do anything, be anything, that nothing was stopping her, nothing was in her way. He went on and on the entire way home about how wonderful she was, how clever, how bright, how beautiful, and that this was an amazing opportunity and one that he just knew she would seize and make happen. By the time he dropped her off at her home, Sarah was restored to fullness, the damage of their mothers' bitterness undone, again!

Ben drove away exhausted. He couldn't believe how hard his mother was on his sister. Even now, after all these years, it still shocked him. When they had left Margaret's, Sarah had seemed shrivelled somehow: smaller, quieter, defeated. He had spent the entire journey trying to undo the damage, the fragility that the visit had created, and he hoped that he had succeeded.

'You did a grand job, Laddie! Ne doubt yourself!' piped up Clarence in his soft Scottish accent, sitting as he was, squarely on Ben's right shoulder. 'She'll be alright, your sister. Don't you worry at all, not at all, lad.'

'Thanks, Clarence, as long as you say so, then I know it'll be alright,' replied Ben to his best friend of twenty years.

'Good to know that this shop is right for her, that I could help her.' Ben paused, then added, 'I do wish that you'd let me speak to my mother though, get her to back off on Sarah a bit. She's so hard on her and it's so difficult to say nothing!' pleaded Ben to Clarence, not for the first time.

'Ochhhh! My boy, I keep telling you, it has to be down to Sarah to sort her mother out. It's part of her wee lesson to find her worth and her voice. You can't do it for her, laddie, no matter how much you may want to save her; she has to want to save herself.' Clarence smiled, then added reassuringly, 'Once she's stood up to Margaret mind, feel free to step in and back her, but only once she has, aye?'

'Mmmm,' acknowledged Ben painfully, 'I suppose so,' but sounded sad as he said it. Clarence chatted away for a little bit as Ben drove, continuing to put on the soft Scottish accent as he always had done with Ben. He'd decided many years ago, when he'd first come to appear in Ben's life, that he was going to adopt the soft Scottish lilt of John Smith in an effort to comfort the confused young teenager. The accent was familiar, making it more personal. Angels don't really have an accent, Clarence knew, but if it helped, they could sound like anything the human wanted. It had helped to gain the young boy's trust quicker too, and time had been of the essence back then when Ben was closing down and withdrawing at such a crucial time in his development. *The teenage years are hard enough on this lot as it is,* Clarence thought, *without having the burden of guilt to deal with.* Clarence hadn't worried too much about manipulating the lad a bit with the accent thing, after all, it was their job to turn things around for their wards and they regularly used whatever tools they

105

needed to, to get the job done - all in their best
interests of course!

Ben drove the rest of the way home silently,
looking forward to being in the loving, easy, warm
embrace of his beautiful wife and son. They'd be
home by now, back from Gina's mums in a taxi and
he couldn't wait to see them. He thought again about
being held back by Clarence. He trusted him
implicitly, totally, and fully, always had and always
would. He knew what he was talking about, so Ben
kept his mouth shut to his mother when he wanted so
badly to wade in. He bit his tongue to stop him
interfering and he wondered how Sarah could
tolerate him for his silence, but he had followed and
heeded Clarence's advice, his guidance and his wise
words for twenty years now, since he was thirteen
years old when the guilt had first started to set in
deeply into his very bones as a young boy. He had
resented the love that his mother poured on him
when he could see that Sarah got nothing, beginning
to reject it and her, going into himself more and more
until the day that Clarence arrived in his life.

His angel was about his father's age, Ben
reckoned, mid-forties, maybe fifty? He even sounded
a bit like him too! His hair was grey and thinning, he
was a little overweight with a bit of a belly and a
crinkly crooked smile that was so kind. Ben thought
Clarence looked a bit like the angel in that film that he
liked, that old Christmas film with the angel. What
was it called? Oh yes, 'It's a Wonderful Life,' he
recalled, smiling. Clarence smiled too, grinned

actually! *Not just looked like him, laddie, I wrote it, well
dictated it!* he thought, but didn't say it out loud. Ben
would find that difficult to believe and Clarence had
always been careful to keep Ben's trust – made him so
much easier to work with! He'd never had the trouble
with Ben that Clarabelle had had with Sarah, bless
her. His picking and choosing how much to tell him,
add in the accent that was familiar and safe to Ben
had all worked a treat. Clarence grinned the grin of
the successful, the accomplished, the achiever and his
halo glowed!

Ben was thinking back to the early times again
as he drove, remembering how Clarence had
explained to the young lad how it wasn't his fault that
his mum seemed to hate Sarah and love him so. He
wasn't to blame he had said and eventually Ben let
his guilt go. He had come out of his retreating shell
within a year of Clarence's arrival and had started to
enjoy life, being a teenager and in time, a young
adult. Clarence became his best friend and he talked
to him about everything. Ben listened always to
Clarence's wise words, following the guidance that
this wise old angel offered, advice and guidance that
he knew in his heart was right. He had been listening
to Clarence ever since and had found that his life
worked for him as a result. 'Charmed life,' Sarah
often said.

If only she knew! thought Ben. *She'd never believe
me. She'd think I was nuts. Of course he could never tell
her. Tell her he had a guardian angel called Clarence? No
way! That Clarence had led him to the right job and the
right woman, that he gave him help and guidance whenever*

107

it was needed or required? She'd have him locked up! And Ben was grateful, so grateful for his charmed life! He only wished his sister could have a Clarence. Maybe her life would turn around at last and she'd find the happiness she deserved so badly.

And Clarence smiled.

Must talk to Clarabelle soon, find out where we're at, he thought to himself. And he popped off to the nearest cloud to call a meeting with his sister, establish developments and make further plans.

'Must talk to Nathaniel too; see how the blocks are coming along with Simon! All so exciting!' he chuckled to himself. 'I do love it when a plan comes together!' Clarence wondered as he 'popped off' if Nat's hair had returned to normality yet. He had a feeling that Nat would be having a lot of 'Gonk' days over the coming months, bless!

Chapter 7

The morning rose after Mother's Day and Sarah's spirits with it. She'd been through this too many times with her mother to let it affect her for days on end, the pattern old and stale, well-worn and well-used. She had developed the ability over time to shrug off the hurt and the anger fairly quickly and bring her positivity back. She'd had to, or she would have gone nuts over the years! Ben was a star of course, such a help bless him. She knew it was hard for him, being piggy in the middle as he was, but she knew he did his best for her. She also knew that he saw a side of their mother that she herself had not and could not see, making it easier for him to tolerate her, even love her. She thought he was a Saint for it, bless!

Sarah threw back the covers of her old and comfortable bed and stared out of the window, reflecting, just for a moment, on yesterday's events and with a resigned sigh, she let it go. She needed to focus on herself now. Arrangements had been made to prepare her to take over the shop and she had just two weeks to learn everything she needed to know. She pulled her attention from the morning sun and gazed determinedly at her reflection in the mirrored wardrobes opposite her double bed.

'You are ready!' she informed herself sternly and believing it for the first time ever, despite Margaret's very vocal lack of belief in her, she suddenly had a new belief in herself. Jumping out of bed with a full enthusiasm for life, Sarah walked into the shower to prepare for her training.

The following two weeks passed by in a blur of meetings, meetings, and more meetings for Sarah, followed by training, training, and more training! She learned more than she thought was possible for a person to learn in such a short space of time. She was exhausted permanently, falling into bed and into an instant sleep each and every night, but she was happier than she could ever remember being, due to Clarabelle's help of course! She had met reps with Mrs. Mac and, amazingly to Sarah, she had found that she could hold her own, building a good rapport with each and every one. She discovered that she had really good people skills and that she could mix at any level comfortably. She also discovered that she had a way of putting people at their ease immediately. She had learned how to do the banking and cash flow with Mr. Mac (call me Edgar) and learned it well. She had learned how to create spreadsheets with Ben (her wonderful and so helpful financial expert banking brother), and had found them easy to do. She had held meetings with wholesalers, suppliers, the town council, and the bank manager and with each hour of each day, her confidence and pride in herself grew stronger. She had even met with Jane from the job centre and found herself discussing her needs for a capable assistant for her new shop. Jane had come up trumps. Sarah had found herself interviewing six candidates, preparing questions in advance so that she was pulling out the best in her shortlisted people. She had chosen a young man, Tim, from the six and was confident that he would do nicely. For the first time ever, she had checked with Clarabelle before making a decision, and Clarabelle had confirmed Tim to be the right person for her shop. Sarah had been chuffed as Tim had been her first choice, but it was so nice to know that she was getting it right, for a change! Clarabelle had helped her through everything, advising, encouraging, guiding, and supporting. It was all coming together and Sarah knew it. She had been shocked at her own progress and had begun to realise that she had always been more capable than she had ever given herself credit for, slowly developing a new self-belief, personal pride, and a recognition in her strengths that had never been there before. She was feeling stronger, brighter, and better with every hour that passed. Life was good, for the first time ever!

During the two week training Clarabelle had asked her to write a list. On it she had been told to write all of her strengths, her skills, and her qualities. When she had finished, she was told to give it to Ben, then Angie, and then Frieda. Each was asked to add their own opinions and thoughts to Sarah's list and each time the list came back from one, it came back longer than when it went. Sarah knew that her friends loved her, as did Ben, but she had never realised before how wonderful they thought she was, how clever, how funny, how supportive, loyal, or trustworthy. The list just went on and on! She was beginning to believe it herself and her confidence was growing nicely, so Clarabelle had said, although she still had to correct her every now and then when

111

Sarah put herself down, criticising herself. Clarabelle would pipe up sternly, 'Self-criticism does not serve you, child!' Sarah was concerned that all this praise and pride would go to her head and that she would turn into an arrogant conceited pain in the bum, but Clarabelle consistently reassured her that a healthy amount of self-belief and self-worth was good for her.

'Recognising your own strengths is healthy, my dear,' she had insisted. All Sarah knew was that she wanted the shop not to fall down around her ears in the first week, for the regular customers to keep coming back, and for business to plod on as it had been for the best part of one hundred and twenty years.

God, she thought to herself, *imagine if it went bust in the first week that I took over and I single handed managed to destroy a business that's been standing just fine for that long! Fine before I got there; 'Sarah-The-Tornado!'*

'Now, Sarah, what have I told you about that kind of thinking! Stop it! You are not going to go bust in the first week, nor in the second. You are not going to go bust at all, everything is going to be just perfect!' and Clarabelle had bustled around her, refocusing her attention onto the forthcoming success that would be her very own business.

'Me a business woman, a shop keeper, an owner! Wowey!' Sarah pinched herself and yep, sure enough, she definitely was awake. This was very real, very happening and very marvellous! The pinch mark had even left a big white imprint on her arm just to prove how awake she was.

112

The shop was now officially hers; signed, sealed, and delivered. Mr. Mac, (call me Edgar) had reduced the price of the shop for her by thirty percent as a thank you for saving his life and despite her protestations that she wanted to give him a fair price just like anyone else, he wouldn't budge.

'How much money do ya think a person needs at my age? I won't 'ave time to spend it all before I pops me clogs!' he had laughingly said. Mr. Mackenzie had been truly astonished when he had been told the shops value by the estate agents. He couldn't believe it and was more than happy to let Sarah have it at a reduced price and a price that he felt she could manage. He didn't want it to go to the highest bidder, he wanted it to stay in the family and according to Mr. Mac, (call me Edgar,) Sarah was just that! May had agreed, just grateful to have her Edgar alive and well and all to herself for the first time in their married sixty-three years. Sarah deserved it, he had said, and he wanted to give her any help he could. A deal had been done and after training Sarah rigorously for two full weeks on every facet of the business inside and out, 'Call me Edgar' and 'His May' had packed up and shipped off, deciding to move to Australia via the scenic route on the QE2; first class no less, making an 'around the world trip' out of it at the same time. Their ship had left that morning and Sarah had waved them off from Southampton docks with tears of gratitude, sadness and with a smattering of fear mixed in for good measure. She was on her own now. No more advice, help, or support from those particular experts would be coming her way. She had to stand on her own two

113

feet and crack on and she was ready! Boy was she ready! The shop opened under her name tomorrow, April first and she prayed that she wouldn't be the April fool. She thought about how much she had learned in the last two weeks, how much she already knew, (which had astonished her!), and she just knew that she wouldn't be 'The Fool'. And anyway, she realised, she wasn't on her own! She had Ben, Clarabelle, Frieda, and Angie, as well as her own new willingness to ask for help when she needed it, as well as her growing self-belief, all of which would stand her in good stead. She would be fine, she just knew it!

****

Simon Brown lay in Nadia's bed, having just come back from a wonderful night to the theatre with her, followed by even more wonderful sex. Passionate, enticing, exciting sex! It was April first, All Fool's Day. He held her in his arms, her long legs wrapped around his, wondering what he had been thinking, to even contemplate leaving her. What a ridiculous thought! He had never had it so good! And anyway, every time he had tried to look on the company's intranet for internal vacancies or transfers, the bloody thing had crashed! And that list he had made that night when he had been so mad, he just couldn't find it anywhere; and every time he tried to make a new one, his pen ran out of ink, or the phone would ring, or something would happen.

'It just isn't meant to be,' he had told himself. 'Stop moaning with your lot and enjoy what you

114

have,' and Simon had quickly forgotten, again, all
about his frustrations, his annoyance, his dreams, his
aspirations and had gone back to enjoying the life he
had, and to enjoying Nadia!

Nathaniel smiled serenely, his orange hair
laying quietly and nicely on his head, flat as a
pancake, for a change. He was pleased as punch with
himself with what he had managed to achieve in such
a short space of time! The last two weeks had been
hard work, but Simon was back on track, that is, no
track, being stuck in his rut, which was exactly where
he needed to keep him for as long as possible.
Clarence would be pleased, not to mention Clarabelle.
Nadia had been a nightmare though! He had been
forced to have Serena, Nadia's angel, co-working
with him on a more or less full-time basis. Between
the two of them, they had managed to give her a
newer, fresher twinkle in her eye, helping her with
her on-going seduction to keep Simon where he was.
There was no problem with helping Nadia to stay
stuck, of course! She was well and truly glued to her
past like lock-tight, no-more-nails and super-glue
combined. Just toning up the sexiness, the seduction,
and the heat would be enough to keep things going
for a while on that score. Nathaniel had also
successfully managed to lose Simons list of changes
for him, as well as blocking the intranet at work every
time he tried to look at the vacancies page. He'd also
successfully managed to dry up every bit of ink in
every single pen in order to prevent him from making
more change lists! *I must go and see the others and give
them a progress report,* he thought to himself happily.

Time for a multi-angel-cy meeting with the bosses I think. They'll be delighted! he chuckled to himself as he flew off upstairs to call the meeting. Clarence, Clarabelle, himself, and Serena would all attend and maybe even the big boss Metatron would come. He didn't attend many of the multi-angel-cy meetings these days, preferring as he did to delegate most of the important stuff to one of the Archangels instead. Metatron was the boss of all the angels, whatever level they were, and he was always busy! *He was grumpy at the moment anyway,* Nathaniel thought, *still in a strop about some film or other that was a big hit 'downstairs' and it was best not to invite him anywhere until he'd calmed down.* Apparently a bunch of robots that turned themselves into cars, or was it the other way around, Nathaniel couldn't remember, had nicked his name. *What is a Transformer anyway?* Metatron was not pleased! Nearly as stroppy as Archangel Raphael had been when his name had been taken in vain by a bunch of green ninja turtles some years back, and as for Michelangelo, well, he hadn't been the same since! He pondered who'd be the best angel to invite to the meeting. *Maybe Archangel Michael?* thought Nathaniel, *He could even bring Archangel Uriel too; we could do with a bit of his help. Yes, I'll ask if they can come, that would be a massive boost and will really speed things up, take the pressure off me!* he thought with relief. Nathaniel knew the hierarchy that angels worked to and that by bringing in the extra power and help of the more senior and more powerful Archangels it would make life so much easier for both the guardian angels and the humans alike. Archangel Uriel was in charge of emotional healing and Nathaniel knew, with some displeasure, that it was Sarah's emotional baggage that was holding up the proceedings and slowing everything down. He'd have to check it with Clarabelle first of course, make sure she approved the Archangels coming, or as he liked to call them, the 'AA's', and if she said yes, then it would be all systems go.

****

Sarah fell into bed exhausted. The shops opening night could not have gone any better if she had tried. All her friends had come bringing cards and gifts. There had been 'Congratulations' Cards and 'Good Luck In Your New Venture' cards, all of which had lined the shop's counter as the champagne (proper stuff this time) had flowed. Ben and Gina had been such a marvellous help and support, bringing with them the 'good stuff', as well as bunches of flowers and cards from them, and even one from the bank. The one card that was missing and pointedly so, was one from her mother. Margaret had not acknowledged in anyway this huge turning point that was happening with such force in Sarah's life. She felt like she's been smacked in the face, despite the many cards from other loving well-wishers.

'It doesn't matter, it doesn't matter,' she chanted to herself as she climbed into bed later that night. She was determined not to let her mother's cold indifference ruin what had been such a wonderful evening.

117

'But it does, child, it does!' piped up
Clarabelle. 'And you know it does! And sooner or
later we need to address it, examine it and sort it!'

'Yes, yes. I know,' Sarah agreed, 'but not
tonight, aye? I can't deal with anything tonight,
I...am...jus'...so...tired...' and an exhausted Sarah fell
into a deep sleep with a huge smile on her face.

'Ah, bless her!' smiled Clarabelle, as she
pulled the covers over Sarah's tired and aching body.

It can wait, but not for long! thought Clarabelle,
thinking how wonderful it was that Angels didn't
need to sleep. She'd never get it all done if she had to
fit in eight hours! 'Things to do, things to do!' and
seeing Sarah sleeping peacefully, she popped off
upstairs for a chat with the others.

****

She'd heard a little earlier from Nat that a
major inter-angel-cy meeting was happening tonight
and she didn't want to be late. Apparently
Archangel's Michael and Uriel were to attend and
Clarabelle was so excited. It was to be her first one
and she wasn't quite sure what to expect, but she was
looking forward to it immensely. She'd never met any
of the Archangels before. Nathaniel had been right to
suggest it and she was only sorry she hadn't thought
of it herself. Maybe she could have got Sarah ready a
lot sooner if she had, but there was no point
admonishing herself. This was her first job, after all,
as a fully-fledged Guardian Angel and she was doing
her best. She was due another revue soon and she
would bring it up then, see what lessons could be

118

learned for the future. The ruby review had gone fine,
everyone was happy with her, happy that she had
finally managed to get some progress going with
Sarah. That had been smashing that! Being able to say
for the first time ever, 'Yes, sir, we have progress!'
Yippee! The next meeting would be the 'moving
things forward review' and she was confident that it
would be fine. Now it was time to focus on the big
meeting, find out what these AA's, as Nat called them
were all about and what help they could be to her. *Off
we go, off we go!* she thought happily.

****

'Thank you all for coming,' smiled Archangel
Michael as he looked around him at the four
Guardian Angels sitting at the large round golden
table that had appeared for them magically. They
were on Cloud 322 again. It was the best one for the
meeting as it sat right above Redfields and directly
over Sarah's house, high up in the stratosphere.
Michael had ordered the table yesterday and the
junior angels had had it delivered earlier in readiness
for this important meeting. Clarabelle was so excited
that she thought she would pass out!
Heavens, he looks so handsome! she thought as
she gazed up at him with admiration and adoration.
*So strong and macho, standing there in his full battle dress
with his shiny sword and huge wings!* She felt quite
faint! Standing at just under ten feet tall, a good three
feet taller than any of the Guardian Angels present,
Clarabelle knew that Archangel Michael was the only
angel in all the heavens that was allowed to carry a

119

sword. It was for fighting demons, darkness, and anything not of the light Clarabelle knew, and she also knew that AA Michael always won!

'What a hero! My hero!' she gushed to herself! It was an accepted fact here 'upstairs', that the light always wins over darkness. It has to! Just thinking about it logically, Clarabelle knew this to be true. When she had done her angel training some eons ago, she had questioned the power of the darkness, (AKA negativity.) She had been shown a cupboard as an example, a very dark cupboard. She hadn't understood initially what they were getting at, then the trainer, AA Samuel, had simply shone a torch into the dark cupboard. It was immediately filled with light, and Clarabelle understood, 'just like that!'

'Wherever there is darkness, simply shine the light,' AA Samuel had explained. 'Darkness cannot exist where there is light,' he had simply and truthfully stated, adding, 'Darkness is negativity, light is positivity,' just to make things crystal clear. Clarabelle knew that AA Michael's job was to banish darkness with his 'trusty sword of light' and she just *knew* that he did it *very* well indeed! And here he was, AA Michael, with his mighty sword tucked away neatly under his wings, just about to address them all.

'So you need some reinforcement then troops?' he stated simply, lovingly and oh so beautifully! Clarabelle was well and truly captivated by this mighty warrior of the light.

'May I introduce Archangel Uriel for those of you who have not met him before? Uriel, my friend, would you like to explain what help you can be to these angelic helpers, please?' Michael smiled, sitting

120

down, letting AA Uriel take over whilst he oversaw proceedings.

Uriel stood up, a similar height to Michael as all the Archangels were, his feathers magnificently flowing around him, his light so bright it lit the sky up. He prepared himself to address the group. Clarabelle knew that AA Uriel's brief was emotional healing so he was the right guy to have around that was for sure! He worked with counsellors and therapists to help them to heal others, as well as occasionally working directly with the individual themselves. He was an expert in all things emotional and she was so pleased that he was on her side. *Now, if she could only take her eyes off AA Michael for an entire second and pay attention to what Uriel was saying then she may actually learn something!*

'Sarah's issues are low self-worth and low self-esteem, all stemming from her mother's behaviour to her throughout her life,' Uriel began, 'and this has been reinforced by endless unworthy relationships. Sarah believes that it is her own fault that her mother cannot love her because she believes that she is unlovable rather than what it actually is, her mother's own pain. This belief that she is unlovable spreads into every facet of Sarah's life and worth. Sarah feels that she is not worthy of a decent, loving man because she herself is unlovable.' He paused for breath and smiled down at the group, whose attention he had totally and completely.

'We can sort this out very quickly, simply by showing her who her mother is as a person. Sarah will understand that the issue is her mother, not herself. She will release the personalisation of it and

121

see her own worth. She will have a new understanding which will then give her choice; choice she previously did not have. She will find her true self, her worth, and she will then be ready for her soul mate, Simon.' Uriel paused and smiled at the group. He knew that some did not understand and he would have to explain the actual action each needed to take to lead them gently to their own understanding.

Clarabelle was a little confused. *Aye? What?* she thought to herself. *I didn't get that at all! Should have been paying more attention instead of looking at AA Michael, oops! Must have a word with Clarence later, he can explain it to me.*

AA Uriel turned to Clarabelle smiling, he was addressing her directly,

'Clarabelle, my dear, your task is to take Sarah into trance, either through hypnosis or meditation. Take her to another time and place, a time when her mother was young and growing. Show her all aspects of her mother. Show her the marriage and her mother's fears, her abandonment, her darkness. Sarah will begin to pity rather than condemn, she will have compassion in her heart instead of hatred. As she begins to understand who and why her mother is the way she is, that hatred will melt, dissolve and Sarah's own self-love can begin to flourish. Be prepared though, that as she reaches this realisation, she will unleash much pain and sorrow held inside. She will cry and when she does, call on me and I will be there to soothe and heal. Do you understand, dear one?' Clarabelle nodded; she understood and she knew now what she had to do.

122

'Nathaniel, keep doing what you are doing. Beautiful job!' Uriel smilingly said. Nathaniel positively glowed with the praise from this powerful angelic being!

'Serena, good job, my dear. Keep up the good work.' Serena glowed happily.

He turned to Clarence directing all of his attention to the leader and mentor of this little band of guardian angels.

'Now, Clarence, have Ben ready to stand by. He should be willing to back Sarah once she has confronted her mother, which of course, she will once her release is complete.' Clarence nodded, bowed to Uriel and grinned at the others. Uriel smiled heavenly at the whole group.

'Are there any other questions?' he paused, looking around and having so eloquently explained himself to the group, sat his magnificent body back down at the table.

'Um, yes, please,' piped up Clarabelle, 'just the one. It's for 'Mighty Archangel Michael' if you please?' she gushed, wondering if she had gone a little over the top with the 'Mighty'!

'Ah, I pass the floor to the '*Mighty*' Archangel Michael,' Uriel said, grinning at Michael with a raised eyebrow. Michael stood up and Clarabelle blushed, but ploughed on with her question to him.

'Um, Archangel Michael, your job is to give strength, courage, bravery, is it not?' enquired Clarabelle. He nodded and smiled down at her. 'Well then, I was wondering, if you're not too busy, would it, could it, would it be possible for you to come and help Sarah face her mother do you think, when its

123

time?' Clarabelle gushed. 'Be there with her when she does it? She's so scared of her, you see and I'm sure your presence would be a huge help, massive help, enormous help to her, if you're not too busy, if you could make time, if it's alright sir, please?' Clarabelle knew she was gushing and rambling and sounding like a trainee angel rather than a fully qualified one, but she didn't care. These AA's were very awe inspiring, humbling and she just couldn't get her words to come out straight and sound anything other than the infatuated and blown away angel that she was!

'But of course, my dear, I shall come. She need only call and I will be there.' He smiled such a beautiful and serene smile of love and compassion that Clarabelle truly thought she would pass out with the pleasure of it!

Oh, wow, she thought, *this is big, really big!* She suddenly felt quite dizzy!

'I call this meeting adjourned,' declared AA Michael. Clarabelle sat trance like, wondering if she could call him Mike, or maybe AA, or A for short, or Mickey. *No, perhaps not,* she thought to herself, *a little disrespectful maybe, a little over-familiar?* As she was thinking those thoughts, the softest voice she had ever heard from anywhere across the cosmos whispered gently in her ear,

'You can call me whatever you please, Clarabelle, my dear' and with that, Archangel Michael was gone! Clarabelle fell back with the sheer delight of it and as she did, she promptly fell off the cloud, plummeting down through the night sky and

crashed with a large bump onto Sarah's bed in a
flurry of flying feathers!

'What the hell!' Sarah woke with a start,
jumping out of her dreams and out of her sleep.
Blowing a stray feather from her top lip she glared at
Clarabelle who was laying sprawled, face down in the
duvet, her hair upside down, bottom sticking up in
the air, tangled up in her wings with the most
ridiculous grin plastered over her face.

'Sorry, my dear, fell off my cloud!' Clarabelle
giggled.

'It's four o'clock in the bloody morning!' Sarah
shrieked. 'What cloud?' then added sleepily, 'You
ok?'

Clarabelle nodded, giggled some more,
unravelled herself from her hair and feathers, she sat
up gingerly then promptly burst out laughing,
gathered her feathers, straightened them up and then
flew back upstairs still laughing, without even a
backwards glance at a confused and bewildered
Sarah.

Very strange, she is very strange! thought Sarah,
and fell back asleep.

Chapter 8

The next week passed in a blur of activity for Sarah. Tim, the new assistant had quickly learned the ins and outs of the General Store that was Mackenzie's. He was a lanky lad, spindly looking with multi-coloured mad spiky hair, but he knew his stuff and was great with the customers. Ever willing to please, he had taken on anything and everything that Sarah had asked of him. He had worked in shops since leaving school eight years previously so he was no newcomer to it all. He simply needed to be shown the layout of this particular shop and to get to know the till and the customers. Sarah also had Mary, the Saturday girl who had worked there longer than she had. Well, she said 'girl' but Mary was well into her fifties and had been part-time at Mackenzie's for over twenty years. Rotund, motherly, smiley and bubbly, Mary was a grafter and Sarah liked her immensely. It was she and Tim who had held the fort between them for the two weeks that Sarah had been coming and going whilst doing her training.

Sarah had decided not to make any changes at the store at all for now, just intent on keeping it going as it always had been whilst she found her feet; changes could and would come in time. She knew she wanted to put her own stamp on things and the place could certainly do with a lick of paint and a fresh feel. Clarabelle had new lines she wanted to bring in too, but that could all wait for now. She was just a wee bit

reluctant to change anything straight away, fearful
that it may make it all fall down around her ears.

'It will come in time,' she said to herself, 'no
rush, no rush at all.' With a sudden realisation she
blurted out, 'Bloody hell, I sound just like Clarabelle!
I'm turning into my own nag!'

'And child,' came the instant laugh from
Clarabelle, ever present at the moment, 'just what is
wrong with that? Do I not have the most wondrous
words to be sounding like? The greatest wisdom, the
……'

She seems inordinately happy at the moment,
Sarah thought to herself. *Always been cheerful of course
but her light's been shining very brightly lately, brighter
than normal - has been all week actually, she's even been
making funnies! Most unlike her, I wonder what she's up
to?*

Clarabelle glowed. The huge smile from last
Monday's meeting with the AA's still firmly fixed on
her normally tranquil and serene face. She had been
positively glowing all week, shining and radiating
love and light all around her like a 5000 watt bulb
ever since the meeting. Clarence had told her to come
down off Cloud 999, but she couldn't! She had
remained floaty floaty all week! Clarabelle knew she
needed to get a grip and focus as she thought
sombrely then about the task ahead of her. There was
a lot of work to do this weekend and she knew that
she would need this extra energy, extra light to get
Sarah to where she needed to be by Monday. She had
persuaded Sarah to take the weekend off, that Tim
and Mary could manage the Saturday between them

and as Sarah hadn't had a day off now for nearly three weeks she really needed this time to rest and relax. Not that there will be much of either for Sarah she knew. It was very hard work on these poor humans going through emotional release work, draining on every level, but Clarabelle knew the results would be worth it for Sarah. And it would mean that she would see AA Mickey, as she had decided to call him, once again.

'Woooppppeeee!' she shouted, jumping high in the air knocking Sarah on the ear as she flung both arms up and out wide and high with pure unadulterated joy!

'Ow!' yelped Sarah. 'What was that for?'

'So sorry, my dear, so sorry,' soothed Clarabelle, 'just an accident,' and she blew some healing energy onto Sarah's reddening ear, stopping the swelling that was threatening in its tracts.

'You are sooo weird at the moment, Clarabelle! Whatever is the matter with you?' scowled Sarah. 'You're definitely up to something, spill!' she demanded. Clarabelle just grinned and glowed, then popped off again without explanation, back to Cloud 999 where she'd spent a lot of time recently – well Cloud 9 just wasn't high enough!

****

Sarah locked up at the end of the long day, the Friday night smile on her face earned from a long week, three weeks actually! The tired and weary grin on her face refused to fade as she reflected briefly on her first week as a proper businesswoman. She had

128

done well - even she was able to acknowledge it! She
climbed tiredly into her old faithful banger and
started the short drive home, ever grateful for her
wonderfully tranquil house which she would shortly
be stepping into.

'Now then, child, we have work to do this
weekend, you know that don't you?' piped up
Clarabelle, 'But I want you to rest and relax tonight,
get a good night's sleep and we will start first thing in
the morning. Make sure you eat well, we've got to
keep your energy up, up, up!' she cheered brightly.

'Mmmm, yes, ok, whatever you say,' agreed
Sarah, 'you're the boss,' and added under her breath,
'for now, but don't push your luck!'

She heard Clarabelle laugh brightly and not
for the first time this week, wondered what had got
her so ridiculously happy!

****

The morning mist the following day hung
over the valley as Sarah awakened. It was a grey,
drizzly day with a heaviness in the air and Sarah
wondered if it was an ominous sign. She felt wide
awake this morning, bright and alert and she realised
that she had slept amazingly well, falling into a deep
restful sleep as soon as her head had hit the pillow.
She wondered, not without a little nervousness what
this 'work' with Clarabelle would entail that they
were doing today. She knew it was to do with her
mother, Clarabelle had told her that much but she
really couldn't see how understanding her mother
was going to make any difference to her at all.

129

She's a prize bitch! Sarah thought, *Always has been, always will be!* But if it made Clarabelle happy and if Clarabelle thought it was important, which she apparently did, then Sarah was willing to go along with it.

Sarah showered, dressed and came down the stairs to find Clarabelle in the living room 'preparing'.

'What *are* you doing?!' Sarah asked in astonishment, seeing the room as it was. Clarabelle had clearly been at work for a while. She had closed the curtains, lit every candle in the room; incense was burning in the stand filling the room with a soft gently fragrance and soft music was already playing on her CD player.

'Just getting everything ready, child. Important to raise the vibration as high as possible to do this work,' she piped, 'it helps you know, trust me!' and she carried on with her preparations as a bemused Sarah walked on and into the kitchen shaking her head, to make herself a cup of tea.

She really is very strange sometimes, thought Sarah to herself, *but at least it gives me time to have my morning cuppa in peace*, and she sat in the kitchen window overlooking the garden, sipping her tea and waited for Clarabelle to summon her when she was ready.

'Right oh then, child, ready whenever you are,' called Clarabelle gaily from the other room some time later. Sarah got up from the kitchen chair, put her cup in the sink and walking slowly and not a little warily, she entered her living room and gasped. It was filled with a soft gentle light, not just from the candles but it seemed from Clarabelle herself. There were fresh flowers in a vase on the nearby table, the window was open just enough to feel the gentle breeze of fresh air circulating. The entire room felt warm, tranquil and incredibly relaxing! The music playing in the background was soothing, washing over her with gentle waves of peace.

'Come now, sit, sit!' beckoned Clarabelle and Sarah 'sat', 'sat' in her favourite chair and waited for the next instruction.

'Now then, my dear, I am going to take you into an altered state of consciousness, similar to meditation, similar to hypnosis and we are going to go on a little journey, alright?' she smiled warmly and reassuringly to Sarah. 'It's perfectly safe and I shall be there with you every step of the way. Are you ready?'

Sarah nodded mutely, already relaxing in the wonderful tranquillity of the room.

'Close your eyes now, dear. That's right, good girl. I want you now to imagine a lovely wave of peace washing down and through you, from your head to your toes.' Clarabelle's voice became slower, softer and more rhythmic with each word. The waves of music spread over Sarah and she could now fully imagine relaxation spreading down through her, just as Clarabelle was asking.

'Feel it spreading down all through your body, feel your muscles letting go and relax…. relax …… relax ……..' breathed Clarabelle slowly and quietly into Sarah's left ear. Sarah felt herself relax, 'with peace, with peeeeeeeeaaaaace,' soothed

131

Clarabelle on and on, and Sarah was lost, lost in the peeeeeeaaaace!

The next thing Sarah knew she was in the most beautiful garden she had ever seen! It was just magnificent! There were trees everywhere, reaching their branches tall into a clear blue sky. There were rabbits playing under one of the nearby trees, they didn't seem bothered by Sarah at all! She could hear birds singing as clear as day! There were flowers all through the garden, rich vibrant colours, their blossoms releasing a fragrance so sweet that hung in the air and she could hear the sounds of water running. As she looked across the garden, through the trees she could see a lake, fed by a waterfall cascading down the hill behind it. She suddenly felt a rustling of feathers beside her and turned. Clarabelle stood right next to her, not on her shoulder now, no longer six inches tall. She stood in her full majesty, her full height, magnificently, powerfully and quite wonderfully! She stood at about six feet tall and she looked amazing! Sarah was in awe for the second time since meeting Clarabelle all those years ago. This time though, was very different. A golden light radiated out all around Clarabelle. Sarah could see the power, the light. She could see her white feathers and long full wings in their full power and magnificence and Sarah felt humbled, honoured, special, quite gobsmacked, quite over-whelmed and quite blown-away by it all.

'Wow, Clarabelle, you're amazing!' whispered Sarah, openly emotional. She felt tears softly slide down her face as she felt the love from this magnificent and utterly beautiful angel sweep over her. Clarabelle smiled, taking her hands in her own, she pulled Sarah gently into her arms and wrapped her arms and then her wings around her, holding her in an embrace of love and warmth. 'You are much loved, child, you know,' smiled Clarabelle into Sarah's wet tear stained face. 'Never forget, you are loved and you are never ever alone.'

Clarabelle then radiated a light straight out of her heart directly into Sarah's which was pressed against her and Sarah felt an inner love, a purity that she had never before experienced or known.

'Come with me now, go into the lake. You are to be cleansed, healed, balanced, and lightened, my child,' and Clarabelle led the now very willing and very humble Sarah through the trees to the lake. It was healing water she was told and would restore her to balance. Sarah entered the water and bathed for what seemed an age and as she did, she felt herself become lighter, brighter and calmer, more at peace. Eventually she got out of the lake and returned to the bank where Clarabelle was waiting.

'Now, child, you are ready. Come with me.' Clarabelle took Sarah's hand and led her through the garden to a small temple. It was raised up from the garden with three steps onto what looked like a white marble floor. There were no walls to this temple, just pillars holding up an apex roof so that it was open to the garden. In the centre of the temple there appeared to Sarah to be what looked like a television on a stand, with a single chair in front of it. She was beyond being surprised and accepted everything before her.

'Sit down, child. Pick up the remote control and press play. You are now going to watch a movie from another time, another place. You can fast forward, rewind, pause, whatever you want to do with it,' said Clarabelle and Sarah obeyed immediately, a new respect, love and admiration for the magnificent Clarabelle, now that she could see her in her fullness. No longer the annoying little fairy-like creature that had been sitting on her shoulder bugging her for the last twenty years. Sarah now realised just how blessed she was to have this wonderful angel by her side and how blessed she was to be able to see her and communicate with her so easily. She vowed there and then that she would never, ever argue with Clarabelle again!

'Do you see, child, see how special you are?' Clarabelle asked. 'Every single person on God's earth has their own angel, but only a very few can see them, talk to them. Much loved you are, my child.'

And Sarah agreed, nodding humbly, not wanting to disagree with Clarabelle again, not now, not ever!

Clarabelle nodded at Sarah, indicating that it was movie time. She obediently pressed play on the TV remote and the screen came on instantly. She watched with fascination and then with horror as her mother's life unfolded before her and she knew that she would never be the same again!

****

Eleanor Potts lay in her bed, staring at the wall. A blank expression on her pale face, her eyes

134

filled with unshed tears. She had been lying in exactly the same position for the last four days, a position that had changed little over the previous two months. The baby girl lay in the crib nearby screaming lamented and neglected cries; cries for attention, for love, to be noticed, to be fed, to be changed and still Eleanor lay unmoved and unblinking. The postnatal depression had not changed nor had it lifted in the two months since Eleanor had given birth to her first and only child. The farmhouse bedroom that they both laid in now; cold, dirty, neglected, devoid of energy, love or care, just like the rest of the house - all being in the same state as Eleanor's mind, a total mess. No doctor had been called, no mental health professional available, not in those dark and dismal times following the post war years. Mental health was not on the radar for many years to come yet, not recognised, not understood, not acknowledged during those day of survival and rebuilding; the rebuilding of a people, a nation. Those souls that were 'touched' were generally just locked up in the asylum, usually for life, and Arthur Potts did not want that for his wife. No doctors would be called; it was far too risky. She would come out of it in time he truly believed, in his ignorance.

Sarah watched as the man came home from a long day at work at the factory. He looked familiar somehow. Arthur was a welder, fabricator, and it had been a hard day. He was dirty, tired and worried beyond belief. Worried for his wife and worried for his child, he climbed the stairs to their bedroom wearily. He lifted the wailing infant from her crib into his arms, shaking his head in disappointment,

135

discomfort and confusion at his wife's apathy.
Soothing the infant, he took her downstairs and did
what he could to feed and change his baby daughter.

'Maggie, Maggie, what are we to do, aye?' he
spoke gently to her.

The scene changed suddenly, as if the film had
skipped forward. Sarah now saw a dirty child of
about six years old, screaming hysterically as she
clung onto the man's legs, trying with her tiny half-
starved and malnourished body to prevent him from
leaving. He stood with an old battered suitcase in his
hand, the other trying to push Maggie away, unlock
her from his leg, as she screamed and screamed,
begging her father not to leave. He did not look down
at his terrified child, for he could not. He would not
have had the strength to leave had he seen her
pleading crying eyes. He had to go, he had to get
away. He was going as mad as his wife in this
hellhole and he knew he couldn't take any more. He
walked to the door with a still attached Maggie
clinging to his leg, hanging on for dear life in her vain
hope that she could prevent this from happening. She
could not. He shook her sobbing body from his leg
and walked out the door without a backward glance
and out of her life forever. It was the last time Maggie
Potts would ever see her father. She sat on the floor
and sobbed, her tears making tracks down her filthy
face, down her neck flowing over the ingrained dirt
which years of neglect had brought. Her matted long,
uncut hair lay on her filthy, louse laden head while
her clothes hung loose from her tiny, bony shoulders.
Her mother lay in the bed upstairs, still staring at the

window with the same blank gaze that had been present for the last six years. The farmhouse was falling down around her. The cupboards were devoid of food, there was no coal in the scuttle, and Maggie knew it would be another cold and hungry night. She curled up in a ball in the corner of the room and wanted to die.

The film skipped forward some more and Sarah watched with a growing horror as the doctors turned up with a van and carried Eleanor Potts off to the mental institution where she would die soon after, killing herself and successfully putting herself out of her misery. She watched with alarm as the social services of the day eventually turned up to take the half dead child into the local children's home. She watched appalled as the cold, indifferent staff scrubbed a tiny and terrified Maggie's dirt ingrained scrawny neck with a hard scrubbing brush as she screamed in pain and fear. She watched with tears as they cut off her matted lousy hair leaving cut marks on Maggie's raw and tender scalp and sent it to the incinerator, along with her clothes. She watched them take her to her dormitory and be placed with the two hundred children that lived in this hellhole and Sarah cried for her mother.

Sarah watched it skip on another five years or so and she saw a young Maggie being beaten by one of the teachers at the school. With each strike she could hear him say to her, 'Stupid girl, stupid, stupid girl!' and she saw where her mother's abusive behaviour to her had originated. She saw scenes of

137

the staff in the children's home weighing out the food
as the children watched, making sure each child got a
fair share, no more and no less than the other, and she
saw and she understood where her mother's
tightness, her lack of generosity had come from the
poverty instilled so deeply in her mother from these
awful beginnings.

She watched the film skip on another few
years and she saw the young woman, a Margaret
now, as she left the children's home that had been so
cruel and harsh to her and begin to make her way in
the world. She had no smile, no fun, no warmth in
her, her heart closed and cold, as stone cold as life
itself had been to her. She watched it skip on again,
another five years or so and she was shocked to see a
different Margaret, a smiling, happy Margaret and
then she saw why. She had a wedding ring on and by
her side stood Sarah's father John, a young man,
smiling, lovingly holding Margaret's hand. He and he
alone had succeeded in thawing out her frozen,
angry, and unloved heart. Sarah recognised with a
dawning realisation the resemblance that she had
seen earlier. Her father looked very similar to the
earlier man, Maggie's father and she understood that
Maggie had gotten her daddy back in the form of
John Smith. She understood that she would cling to
him also, in an attempt to never let him go. Too big
and too old to cling to a leg, Sarah knew that
Margaret would cling to him in the only way that she
could; emotionally, mentally, and psychologically,
until she had drained the life and the love out of the
man she adored and needed so badly.

138

Somehow, in this special place where she was being privy to this very private and inside information that was her mother's past, she was able to feel Maggie's fear, her very real and very terrifying fear, fear that her John would one day not want her anymore, that he would abandon her just like her daddy had, that he would go, he would leave, and she would be alone and afraid again, as she had been when she was little and all through her growing up years. Sarah understood everything in that second. She could see how dependant Maggie was on John, on John's love, and how her entire world and being revolved around him. She suddenly understood why her mother was so jealous of the time John spent with Sarah, how it triggered her fear, her pain, and her terror; terror that he may not want her any more, may not love her anymore, that he loved Sarah more than her. She understood how her mother's need and love for her father had ultimately driven him away. Sarah could see that her mother had sadly and inevitably created her own reality, made her own worse nightmares come true, how she had created the very thing she feared the most. She had ultimately been abandoned, not once, not twice, but three times: once by her own mother in her dark and deep mental illness, once by her father when he left her, abandoning her to a system that didn't care, a cruel and hard system in those days, and once again, the final betrayal by her husband, when she drove him away through her needy, obsessive, and unhealthy love. Maggie truly was one of life's victims and Sarah cried for her.

As her tears flowed the film skipped on again and Sarah realised with a start that she was now watching a recent scene, a scene from just a few weeks ago as Margaret prepared for her Mother's Day visit from her children. As she sat at her kitchen table getting ready she looked so sad, so very vulnerable and so incredibly lonely. Her shoulders sagged with the weight of her loneliness, her incredible, deep unhappiness a shroud all around her. Sarah heard the front door open then and watched as Margaret's back suddenly straightened. She watched her face change into the mask she always wore, a cold and hard mask. This mask prevented her children from seeing her vulnerability, protecting herself, closing herself, as she had learned to do so long ago, and Sarah understood, she finally understood it all.

Clarabelle turned the TV off silently and held Sarah in her arms as she cried. She took her back to the lake and entered it with her, holding her in the waters as she bathed away Sarah's tears of guilt, of sorrow, of remorse for her mother. When Sarah had released it all, Clarabelle returned with her to the temple and the TV and asked her to press play once again. Sarah did so. The screen was filled with image after image of her from her own childhood, images of her pleasing, helping, trying, and heaven knows she was trying so hard. Images of a child trying desperately to be loved and liked by her mother and doing everything she could possibly do came to life on the screen. They were images of a beautiful child,

140

inside and out! A child that was bright, clever, funny, helpful, caring, patient, and very confused!

'Do you see, child? You did nothing wrong.' Clarabelle spoke gently to Sarah who nodded mutely. 'You were and are a wonderful child, a wonderful person. It is not your fault that your mother could not love you. Do you see the way she only had love for her husband and that it was the only love she knew? How she was terrified to share it? Do you see how she did not know how to be a mother to you and that she had no role model, no example to follow? She could not be any other way, other than the way she was and is. *It is not your fault!*' Clarabelle continued, 'She was able to show love to Ben only because he represented a transference of her love for her husband which she gave to her son. The only love and care she could have transferred to you was her own for herself and from herself, but as she had none inside, there was nothing to give,' Clarabelle went on, determined to help Sarah understand. 'After your father left, her pain was so great, her rejection so acute, and her rage so all-consuming. She could not take that rage and blame into herself, for it would have destroyed her and your mother is nothing if not a survivor. She had to let it out somehow and she let it out to you and on you. There was nowhere else for it to go. It was wrong, she was wrong. Understanding it does not make it right, but it was what it was and it was not your fault.'

Sarah understood. She saw, she recognised, she pitied, and she cared. She cared for her mother and she cared for herself, both for the first time. She was not to blame she could see that now; she had done nothing wrong. It was not her fault; it was no-one's fault! There was no blame to apportion here, it did not exist and Sarah's blame and shame for not being good enough melted away.

Clarabelle, having completed her task of showing Sarah a new truth, led her gently out and away from the temple, back to the door of the magical garden and the next thing Sarah knew was that she was opening her eyes and she was back in her lounge. Her face was wet from the tears she had shed whilst she had been in the trance. She understood everything clearly. Now all she had to do was process it!

Archangel Uriel entered the room at exactly the same moment that Sarah came back from the garden. She was not aware of him, but she was aware of a new power, a new light, an energy, and she suddenly felt all of her pain, all of her hurt and all of her confusion within her from the years of misunderstanding, from the years of abuse, the years of neglect and it rose up within her and Sarah began to sob, long, retching, soul-shaking sobs. She sobbed and she sobbed for herself this time. For the confused child that she had been, for the pain, for the anger, the rage, for the injustice of it all and she let it all out until it was gone, until she was completely spent. A peace descended within her then, a peace that she had never before felt, known, or experienced and Sarah Smith was finally free.

Clarabelle rushed over to Archangel Uriel, thanking him profusely for all his help, his energy, his time, for being there for Sarah. She looked around, hoping to see AA Mickey, but saw disappointedly that he was nowhere to be seen.

'Ah, Archangel Michael seeking are you?' enquired Uriel, knowingly, smilingly. 'He will be there when she confronts her mother, as you requested, but he is not needed here today. Sarah has enough strength to have been able to do this alone and she did it well,' he reassured. 'She will sleep now so a goodnight I will bid.'

Archangel Uriel smiled then melted away to return upstairs and look up his old friend Yoda; his job here was done.

Chapter 9

Sarah did not recall going to bed that night, she did not recall eating; she recalled only the exhaustion, the tiredness, and the weird sense of calm. It had come through her slowly as the night wore on and she felt totally different Sunday morning when she awoke. This sunny, beautiful morning, she noticed as she awoke. She had a sudden energy today, a new energy and she suddenly wanted everything to be different, new, fresh, clean, as clean as she herself felt, as if her very soul had been washed with Daz whitener. She looked around the sunny bedroom with new eyes.

Nope, it was just perfect! she thought to herself after a moment. She got up and wandered from room to room, still in her pyjamas, assessing each and every room for what needed to change. She saw clutter where she hadn't seen it before. She saw dirt where she hadn't noticed it before. She saw beauty where she hadn't been aware of it before. Sarah seemed to have new eyes today.

'Should've gone to Specsavers!' she laughed to herself. She couldn't explain even to herself how weird this all felt, but she was happy to go with it.

She showered and dressed in old scruffy clothes and began immediately to sort out, clear out and clean out her home, working purposefully from the top of her house to the bottom. Six hours and eighteen black bags later it was done and a shattered and knackered Sarah flopped into the comfy lounge chair.

'Shit, forgot to eat!' she admonished herself and jumped straight back up again to go and find some food to feed her empty and grumbling belly. From the kitchen she looked into the utility room at the stack of bags. Some were for charity, some for the tip and others for recycling; they were all sorted, separated, and ready to go. She had to admit, the place did look better, cleaner, brighter; it also seemed to have a new vitality, somehow matching her own.

She had emptied out her wardrobes and drawers, pulling out and bagging clothes that she hadn't worn for years. She had cleared out cupboards, junk and mess from every storage area on every floor and she had been amazed just how much crap she had. The house felt better now, much better, as did she!

'Cleansing your home is as good as cleansing your mind,' piped up Clarabelle, as Sarah sat munching her sandwich.

'Mmmm, yes, I know,' replied Sarah, far more focused on the food than on Clarabelle at that moment. God she was starving, Sarah realised, relishing the food that was now making its way down to her extremely empty tummy.

'So good for the soul, a good clear out, you know, my dear? It's a fresh start for the house, for you, for everything!'

'Yes, Clarabelle, I said yes, I know,' munched Sarah with a mouth full of chicken salad on rye, her

145

newfound respect for Clarabelle briefly forgotten in
her starvation state.

'Just let me eat and I'll see what else I need to
do. It's only three o'clock and I still have bags of
energy, well, I will once I get this lot down my
throat.'

'Perhaps the bedroom may need another
look?' suggested Clarabelle, her perfectly formed
eyebrows raised expectantly.

'But I've done the bedroom, every drawer and
every cupboard! What's left to do up there?' she
replied, surprised.

'Perhaps another look, my dear?' and
Clarabelle disappeared.

Sarah allowed herself a ten minute break and
went back upstairs to the bedroom. She looked again
at the wardrobes, now neat and tidy with vastly more
space now that over fifty percent of the clothes were
gone.

'Nope, all done!' she declared out loud. She
looked again at the immaculate drawers, she looked
in the en-suite bathroom at the tidy shelves; she even
looked down the plughole.

Nope, all done! What is she talking about? she
wondered. Sarah sat on her bed and scratched her
head and in a Eureka moment, she suddenly got it. It
was the bed! It was the bloody bed itself! Jumping off
the bed she stood looking at it with fresh eyes, her
new Specsavers eyes! She took a few steps back and
sat down heavily on one of the two cushioned
window seats that sat either side of the mirrored
wardrobes and surveyed her nemesis. Her Gran had

given her that bed! It was donkey's years old, coming from her Gran's spare room, rarely used except by Sarah on her frequent visits throughout her childhood. Sarah had been so grateful for its familiarity when she had first left home at just eighteen years old, setting up her first home and independence. It had been with her ever since, through two bed-sits, three flats and eventually back to its original home, into this house, her beautiful pride and joy. She had seen the double bed as her 'old comfy', like a comfort blanket *but it actually was incredibly uncomfortable* she acknowledged now! But it wasn't the discomfort that made this bed her nemesis. It was its history; a long twenty-year history of lovers and losers, tears and pain that made this bed perfect to be on the list of things to go.

'Bloody hell!' she groaned, 'How many idiots, tosspots, jerks, and losers have been in that bed over the years? How many tears have I cried over some plank or other into that pillow?'

She thought then about Rob, the latest in the long line of disasters that had been her pattern for the last twenty years and the tears that she had shed for him just a few weeks before. Totally, completely unworthy, undeserving tears at that!

Before Rob had been Adrian. Sarah drifted into her memories now with new, fresh eyes. He had lasted eight months but as Sarah recalled, with the benefit of hindsight, he had been a casual and unworthy fling. At the time she had thought it was more of course, but in the end she had seen it for what it was and him for what he was; a loser! No job, no home, still living with mummy, an unemployed

147

photographer that dreamed big dreams and achieved absolutely nothing. Nothing but debt and a crippling dependency on everyone around him, but he had been a charmer and a wonderful lover, she recalled with a smile.

Before him, several years before had been Rod, a singer. She had spent two unworthy and unhappy years with him. 'Well, on and off,' she remembered He had moved in, he had moved out, he had moved in again. It was worse than the bloody oaky-koaky! They had never been able to stabilise their relationship, neither of them being able to get it right. There had been smatterings of happiness and joy, but they had been marred and tainted by Rod's obsessive, possessive, paranoid behaviour that had driven her demented and in the end, ruined what they had. She had worshipped the ground he walked on and during their time together Sarah didn't even know or realise that there were actually other males that existed on the planet! It had taken her the best part of four years to get over him properly. She hadn't dated for an entire year after they had split up and when she did start dating again, she realised now with a new understanding, every guy she had chosen had been 'not ready, not willing or not able' to commit, just like Sarah herself at the time; her heart still well and truly correlated to Rod long after he had gone and moved on.

There were more, probably half a dozen more in the nineteen years she'd had that bed. It had seen tears and heartache, disappointment and heartbreak, but yes, it was definitely time for a new one.

148

Clarabelle sat beside her quietly watching the dawning realisations that Sarah was experiencing and was delighted!

'Yes, yes, we are definitely making progress and excellent progress at that!' Quicker than she had hoped or expected. 'Most wonderful!' she said to herself and got on with the next task that would come very shortly.

Sarah pondered the practicalities of the bed. Now that she had seen the light, or the disaster, whichever way round you want to look at it, she didn't want to spend another night in this bed, not now, not ever!

Frieda! She would help! Sarah thought and moved towards the phone just as it began to ring on the bedside cabinet. Picking it up she heard Frieda's cheerful voice say,

'Hi, hun, I was just having my tea and you popped into my head. Everything alright?' Clarabelle smiled. Worked so well! This time, every time! All she needed to do was put a little thought in someone's head and hey, presto! She had popped over to Frieda's a few seconds ago and whispered 'Sarah, Sarah, Sarah,' into her ear, and that was all it took.

'Yes, everything's good, mate. Really good! I've been having a bit of a clear out as a matter of fact. Bloody marvellous! I don't suppose you could come over and give me a hand for an hour, could you? I need to shift my bed down the stairs and out, ready for the tip. I'm getting rid. It's not heavy, just a bit awkward, but it would be easy with the two of us.'

'Yeh, hun, no worries, I'll be with you in half,' came Frieda's willing response without any hesitation whatsoever. Sarah never asked for anything, so if she was asking, Frieda was willing. Sarah had helped her loads over the years, but had never in all the years she'd known her asked for anything for herself.

Wonder what's brought this on? she thought to herself with surprise. Frieda grabbed her handbag, mobile, and keys and flew out the door.

'Now, dear, go and get your camera and take some photos of your room as it is now,' instructed Clarabelle. 'All part of the plan, all part of the plan!' and Sarah surprisingly for her, with no argument or hesitation, did as she was told.

****

A few hours later the girls surveyed the empty bedroom. Well, it was empty apart from the two pine bedside cabinets sitting there with the large gap between them and the teak dresser which was sitting under one of the windows. Sarah and Frieda had stripped the bedding, adding it to the bags for the tip, then taken the old mattress down the three flights of stairs and out to the gate. Sarah had decided in the short space before Frieda got there to throw everything out, right down to the pillows. It was time for a fresh start and she saw no point getting a virgin bed while she still had duvets and pillows that were part of the Sodom and Gomorrah era! She would sleep in one of the two spare rooms tonight, she wasn't sure which yet, but tomorrow morning she would nip over to Redville and buy everything new.

Tim would be fine to hold the fort for a couple of hours as long as she was back by lunch for him to have his break.

A new bed, a new start, a new me! she thought with glee.

'A nice king size bed, I think,' suggested Clarabelle in her ear.

'What do I want a king size bed for?' whispered Sarah back, afraid that Frieda would hear. 'I'm only 5'4", what do I need a 6'6" bed for?'

'You just do, trust me!' whispered Clarabelle with a smile, thinking of Simon's six foot four frame, knowing perfectly well that in a few months' time if everything went to plan, he would be laying there with Sarah and love would reign! Proper love this time, none of that needy nonsense! She couldn't have his poor feet hanging off the end of the bed bless him, his toes getting cold, oh no! She clapped her hands with glee and left the girls to it.

Frieda noticed Sarah was muttering to herself again. She did that a lot, always had. Ben did it too. Come to think of it, he always had too, for as long as she'd known them both they'd been muttering to themselves in the oddest manner! Frieda thought some more – *was it always? No, actually it started in the last year of school, maybe 'A' level time.* Perhaps it was the stress of the exams? Mind you, Ben would have been much younger, around twelve or thirteen when he started muttering and he didn't have exams! Frieda always reckoned something had gone down at home that started it, but she'd never brought it up, never mentioned it. Sarah didn't seem to notice it, but

151

it wasn't just Frieda that noticed, Angie had too. They'd talked about it a few times, having caught her more than once, muttering and whispering away to herself. Angie said there was nothing to worry about, that if it was good enough for Shirley Valentine to talk to a wall it was good enough for Sarah to talk to herself. Frieda wasn't so sure; she loved her friend dearly, but she knew she was seriously weird sometimes!

When it was all done, Sarah and Frieda sat in the living room with their cups of tea in hand as Sarah explained to Frieda the events of yesterday as best she could without giving the game away about Clarabelle and the therapy session. Frieda assumed Sarah had had an epiphany, this new sudden cleaning and clearing out and on top of that Sarah was actually being very understanding about MFH, even nice! Frieda assumed that Sarah had talked to Ben, or some other explanation. All she knew and could see was that Sarah was more relaxed and happier and here she was talking about all the tosspots she'd known over the years and how it was all going to change and how she was worth more and what an idiot she had been, etc. etc.

Frieda didn't really understand what had occurred but she liked it. She'd worried about her friend for years and although they'd laughed about her disastrous men, especially 'Arthur/Martha' and 'Ring Ding Boy'! It would be wonderful to think that Sarah could finally find some happiness. She was lovely, her best friend, and she was so pleased that

152

Sarah's life seemed to be coming together. She just wondered what had brought on all this change!

Sarah was talking about the disasters now, her men, continuing on about how she'd seen the light, had new eyes, Specsavers eyes!

'Do you remember Sid, Frie?' Sarah asked. Frieda giggled. She remembered Sid! She remembered them all! Another disaster of Sarah's who hadn't liked sex and didn't want her sexually at all. Sarah had spent all of the six months she had been with him trying to work out where she was going wrong before she gave up on him as a bad job. Frieda had told her it wasn't her, it was him - he was just weird, but she hadn't listened, blaming herself as usual. They'd later found out he'd eventually gone to the doctors about it and well after Sarah had dumped him, he'd been given Viagra and counselling. Apparently he had been Sid the Stud ever since! Frieda suddenly jumped up,

'What about Arthur?' she giggled. 'Don't forget Arthur!'

'God, yes, Arthur!'

'Arthur/Martha, the transvestite!' they screeched together, laughing out loud. Of course Sarah hadn't known at the time, but the clues kept coming when her clothes kept disappearing, her nail varnish and make-up went down at an alarmingly fast rate and her shoes and belts seemed constantly to be stretched. Eventually she had caught him, of course, all dressed up when she had come home early one day after being 'let go' of whatever the latest job of the day had been and found him prancing around her bedroom in her best frock and underwear,

153

lipstick, and nails to match. She had given him a key some time before, idiot! It turned out that he'd been using it when she was at work to play Martha in privacy and peace, or so he thought. She laughed now as she went back to that time.

'How long ago was that, Frie?' she pondered. It seemed like a lifetime. She had been devastated at the time, but as the years had passed she had been able to laugh about it. She'd told Frieda and Angie all about it and the three of them had found the funny side, the hysterical side on more than one occasion. Whenever Sarah was out with the girls over the following years post Arthur, if she had found a ladder in her tights, forgotten her lippy or broke a nail, one of the girls would shout, 'Let's go find Arthur he'll have some we can borrow!' and they would all shriek and fall about hysterically. She'd even stayed with him after that fateful day when she'd discovered him; the day when his drawers fell down and his wig fell off with the shock of seeing her walk in!

Sarah had taken it upon herself she realised now, to make it her mission to understand the weird, the wacky, and the wonderful and she'd seen Arthur as all three rolled into one. She'd researched transvestites and discovered the Beaumont Society, for wives and girlfriends of TV's (as they liked to be known she had learned). She had put her best 'I understand' hat on, counselled amateurishly (as best she could), supported, and helped. She had taken him clothes shopping to the girlie shops to get proper clothes that didn't make him look like he'd been mugged, to wig shops to get something that actually

suited him; she had taught him to paint his nails
properly and apply make-up subtly.

'Do you remember how you taught him to
walk in heals like a girl without looking like he'd shit
himself!' Frieda laughed, 'And you showed him how
to use a handbag and purse? Blimey, girl, that's love!
I couldn't do it!'

Sarah remembered, grinning. She remembered
how she'd screeched at him when she caught him
shaving his arms and legs, showing him (reluctantly)
instead how to use hair removal creams that melted
the hairs instead of razor blades that strengthened
them. That had backfired when he became obsessed
with them and discovered that he could have the
even, smooth and completely hairless body that he'd
always wanted, with her help! She'd found herself
accepting the scraper that Arthur had thrust upon her
in his expectation of unconditional support; a
creamed and very hairy bum shoved in her face and a
pleading Arthur expecting her to scrape it off for him!
Really? Really!

Frieda was crying now, laughing so hard at
the memories.

'Bloody funny though, hun, bloody funny!'
She remembered that by the time Sarah had finished
with him Arthur/Martha no longer looked like the
ridiculous, sad drag queen that he had before.
He/she looked like an attractive man/girl,
eventually!

'He might have passed the chiffon-scarf test,
hun, but he still looked like a man to me though!' she
said as she wiped away a tear with the back of her
hand, taking a swig of tea. Sarah nodded, agreeing,

'Well yes, I mean, did he really think he didn't? He still had a man's arse, a man's hands and an Adams bloody apple!' Frieda nodded emphatically.

'Bloody idiot I was!' Sarah shook her head in disbelief at the things that she'd put up with. She could now spot a transvestite at twenty paces and to this day checked to see if they'd creamed or shaved! Sarah decided that she must have been totally mad, mad as a bloody hatter, to have put up with such things. Frieda couldn't agree more!

Frieda's face suddenly contorted as she remembered another one, another disaster of Sarah's.

'What about Paul,' she wailed, then fell back on the sofa in hysterics again, singing 'Pop goes the weasel' Sarah fell back too, laughing as hard as Frieda at the memories. 'Pop goes the weasel' had been Paul's nickname, due to the fact that he was always popping his cork early, bless him! That had been a great source of amusement for the girls on their giggly nights out. 'Boiled egg,' they called him. Sarah laughed now.

'Bless, it wasn't his fault he could only manage three minutes before he popped his cork!' she laughed. It hadn't been bloody funny at the time though she knew that! The nights he would get her all worked up, then 'pop' went the weasel leaving Sarah frustrated and fed up! She had tried to be patient, but it really wasn't the thing in your twenties to be having to put up with this sort of thing now, was it? She had dumped him, as kindly as she could, she just had to.

'And Jez,' Frieda was saying, 'Ring-Ting-Boy!'

Sarah burst out laughing again at the memory of the weird and wacky piercing boy!

'Studs and rings everywhere, and I mean everywhere!' she said solemnly as she and Frieda had tears in their eyes now, the laughter and giggles taking hold even more that could control themselves no more.

'His nipples were pierced, his eyebrow pierced, ears of course and even his 'thing' was pierced, with that menacing huge silver ring – Ring Ting Boy!'

'Yeh, the 'Prince Albert'!' they giggled. He had been your typical vanity man, muscles everywhere, working out on weights and benches in his own personal gym that he'd equipped in his shed, being there till all hours of the night, working up and working out, showing off his biceps and triceps and any other 'ceps' he could at any given opportunity trying to turn himself into Arnie. That had lasted a few months and in the end Sarah had to end it. Her poor bruised, bent, and battered body could take no more of the many bendy sexual positions that only a gold-medal-winning Olympic gymnast would be able to manage. Dressing up, dressing down, kinky gear, bondage, spankings; she'd endured them all, for a while! Till it all got a bit too much and the ring at the end of his thing had given her thrush!

'Bloody hell!' said Sarah, 'I don't half pick 'em!'

Tomorrow she would go and get a new bed, a virgin bed and one that would not see the backside, front side or any side for that matter of any male, Sarah decided, *not until she found someone worthy and decent,*

157

decent enough to want to stay with properly. And with her newfound gently developing self-worth, she felt her benchmark rise and it felt good!

Clarabelle smiled the smile of the 'serene and the perfect' and positively glowed!!

Chapter 10

The following morning, Sarah was in Redville waiting patiently outside the bed store for its doors to open at nine o'clock. She was oblivious to the rush hour town traffic as she stood happily on the pavement, focused on the task in hand. She didn't even notice the fabulous smells that wafted from the nearby café, smells of freshly ground coffee and chocolate muffins. Sarah pressed her nose against the window and gazed at the beds in the store, attempting to choose one from where she was standing. Clarabelle laughed.

'Patience, child!' she chirped, happy that Sarah was so excited and energised about her new start. Sarah just grinned, pressing her nose against the window even harder. It wasn't about patience! She had chosen this particular store as they guaranteed delivery the same day if it was ordered before lunchtime and she really didn't want to sleep in that single bed again! It had been like sleeping on a bale of straw, embedded with a bag of nails and was even more uncomfortable than her own double bed that she'd dumped earlier that morning.

She had been up at six o'clock today, full of beans despite the awful night's sleep and had driven to her store to pick up the works van, leaving her car there in its place. She had managed somehow to load the bed into the small van and had taken it to the tip on her way to town. The men there had smiled at her

159

attempts to lug the heavy mattress out of the van on her own and seeing a damsel in distress, a pretty damsel at that, they had rushed over from their respective parts of the dump to lend a hand. Three men had appeared, Sarah didn't know where from, but they were all so very helpful and smiling, offering their assistance. After the bed had been dumped into the huge skip by two of the men, they disappeared off with a smile, leaving the third who, leaning into Sarah leeringly said, 'Anyfing else you need helping wiv, miss?' and he'd added in a downright dirty laugh for effect. She had known exactly what he meant and it wasn't moving rubbish!

'No, thanks,' she'd firmly said, 'I'm fine, ta,' and had driven off at speed.

Three hours later, mission complete, Sarah returned to Redfields and her shop. She had bought herself a fabulous new king size bed with a cream leather frame base and a twelve inch thick memory foam mattress. Clarabelle had insisted and as she was doing as she was told these days as far as Clarabelle was concerned, she had acquiesced. She had even bought two single beds, one each for the spare rooms. Basic ones, but newer and more comfortable than the old beds that currently sat in the spare rooms now. How her friends had put up with the old ones when they stayed over she really didn't know!

'Ah that'll be the wine,' she realised. The girls only ever stayed over after they'd all had a heavy night out on the pop, as they referred to it. Their drunken bodies would have passed out instantly, not noticing the lumps and the bumps beneath them.

160

After the bed buying, she had then gone a few doors down and bought new bedding for all three beds. Clarabelle had suggested each and Sarah had ended up with the most gorgeous satin duvet set in a pale gold with embroidered sequins for her own bed, and similar style ones in a soft green and another in a pale pink for the spare rooms. She realised that there would be some decorating coming on over the coming months, matching each room to its new bedding and giving each its own style. *A home makeover!* she thought to herself happily. *How exciting!*

Another shop and another load of cash later, Sarah had two new matching bedside lamps and the softest fluffiest rug ever! Clarabelle had guided her throughout and was particularly pleased with the soft gold organza voiles she had bought, along with a curtain rod that they were to hang from. Apparently it was all for going on the wall over the bed, making a canopy. Under the guidance of Clarabelle, Sarah knew her home would be even more beautiful than it already was by the time she had finished.

****

Returning to the shop spot on one o'clock as promised, Sarah covered Tim for his lunch break before returning home for the afternoon. *No time like the present*, she'd thought to herself during the lunch cover. She had picked up a tin of cream paint and a paint pad from the shelves on the shop floor, having decided it would be far better to paint her room

161

before the bed arrived this afternoon. Ben was coming over later as the men in the shop had said they would only put it as far as the hall and Sarah knew she'd never manage the huge mattress up three flights of stairs on her own. She had text him earlier and asked for his help. *That was twice now that she'd asked for help in less than twenty-four hours,* she proudly admitted to herself. He had been more than happy to come and give her a hand after work, his text had said, and yes, he would bring his drill.

She couldn't get in the house quick enough, she was so excited at the thought of the changes she wanted to make. Arriving at her home at breakneck speed, her little car exhausted and in shock from all this activity, Sarah practically ran into the house in her haste to get on, offloading all of her bags from the earlier shopping trip into a pile in the hall. She even managed to stop long enough to make a cuppa and took it upstairs. She surveyed her bedroom, cup in hand. It was already painted white, but it was a bit stale, flat, and grubby. The old bedside lamps had gone now, the tatty rug chucked along with the rest of the junk, so all Sarah had to do was move the dresser and bedside cabinets out into the landing and she'd have a free space to work. Grabbing her old scruffy clothes out of the washing basket where she had put them last night, she pulled them on, setting to work with the paint. Two hours later it was done and looked lovely! Clarabelle was right! She paused for a moment, surveying sceptically the dresser and bedside cabinets sitting sadly on the landing. They were looking a little tatty now, a little old, but she couldn't afford new ones, not on top of what she had spent today.

'Right, my little beauties, which one of you wants to go first?' she asked, waving the paint brush in the air at them menacingly. An hour later both cabinets and dresser were made over; now cream, clean and looking good as new. It was complete!

The beds had arrived a little earlier and were clogging up the hall, the living room and the kitchen, sat there as they were in their cellophane wrappers waiting for Ben to arrive, their bases stacked against them. He arrived a little after five-thirty and after a brief coffee, helped Sarah push, pull, drag, and yank the heavy mattress up the stairs.

'God, I know they say these memory foam things are comfy, but I hope it's bloody worth it, this thing weighs a ton!' Ben exclaimed, sweat running down his brow from the effort of taking most of the weight of the heavy thing up three flights of stairs. They put the bed base together then left it in the middle of the room, away from the walls while Ben drilled holes for the net curtain rod. Sarah stood by his side, vacuum in hand catching the bits of dust the drill holes made so that it wouldn't make a mess of her nice newly painted walls. Between them they managed to push, heave, and lug the bed into place under the new hooks. Ben helped her then to pull the dresser under the window, he carried the cabinets into place either side of the bed and then he left her to get on with it, with a wave of 'Must dash, Sis. My turn to put Joe to bed,' and was gone.

163

Clarabelle and Clarence watched the proceedings from Cloud 322 with amusement, smiling as Sarah unpacked, unwrapped, and pottered in her new room. She hung the new organza voiles over the bed, the rod hanging beautifully on the new hooks that Ben had drilled for her. She placed the new lamps on the re-painted cabinets, placed the fabulous fluffy rug at the bottom of the new bed, and ironed and re-hung the curtains. She placed candles in the windows, flowers on the dresser, and put the pictures back up. The last part was to make the new bed up with all its lovely new bedding, fluff up the new feather pillows, put the new duvet set on and, finally, place the matching cushions in front of the pillows. Clarabelle flew back down from the cloud quickly, just as Sarah stood surveying her new room with pride.

'Oh my God, Clarabelle! It's better than sixty-minute makeover! It's beautiful, thank you so much!' Sarah was surprised to find that she had tears in her eyes at the beauty of it all. 'It's amazing! Fantastic! It looks like a suite at the Ritz! I feel like a princess!'

'Yes, dear, it is. And you deserve it; you deserve it all, a special room for a special girl! Now go and get the camera and take some pictures, there's a love.' Sarah obediently went to fetch the camera and spent the next half an hour taking snap after snap of her fabulous new room.

'Now, dear, go and have a nice bath and I shall see you downstairs when you are ready. I have some ideas I want to run by you for the shop. Run along now, run along.'

****

She lay in the bath some time later exhausted but unbelievably content. She just couldn't get over the transformation of her room; it had always been beautiful but now it was just magnificent! It hadn't cost her that much really. The main cost had been the bed, but taking that out, the other bits; a lick of paint, a couple of lamps, some candles and new bedding had totally transformed the room.

'Well, yes, dear, and that's what I want to talk to you about,' piped up Clarabelle, appearing once again, sitting on the taps watching Sarah as she lay in the bath, 'When you are quite ready! I've been waiting down there ages you know! You are turning into a prune, Sarah, you've been in that bath that long!' she laughed.

Sarah looked down at her wrinkled fingers and grinned.

'Yes, ok, I'm coming.' Her fingers and toes were all squashed up and funny. Love that feeling! She got out of the water and wrapping a towel around her, put her dressing gown over the top and went down the stairs.

Clarabelle sat perched in the lounge waiting. She was delighted with the progress so far on Sarah herself, now it was time to let the ripples spread into the pond that was her career, her future, and her store. She spent the next hour outlining her plans to Sarah, watched her ward's growing excitement whilst she sat as usual perched on her shoulder, planning away.

165

'So we find out who the suppliers are for the bedding and lamps that I bought today and we bring them into the shop?' confirmed Sarah warily.

'Yes, dear, but it is not *'the'* shop, it is *'your'* shop my dear!' Sarah smiled,

'Oh yes, I keep forgetting, so it is! All mine!'

'Precisely, child, precisely! And it is quite time that you started thinking of it as such. So, where was I? Oh yes, in *your* shop, you take those photographs to the local paper and ask them to make up an advert for you, full page, I think, advertising the makeover possibilities that Mackenzie's can offer. You put posters in the window, showing the before and after pictures, that's why I asked you to take them you know, planning ahead, planning ahead! The posters will show that everything you have done to makeover the room is bought and supplied by your shop. That everyone can have a room like yours, that it's easy to achieve and not too expensive.'

'But it wasn't bought from my shop!' Sarah said

'Yes, but it *will* be!' replied Clarabelle. 'Obviously you have to get that stock in place before your advertising campaign can run, but that is a matter of days my dear, just days.'

Sarah thought it through. The store already sold bedding and lamps, candles and bits, and a million other things (well, maybe not a million, but lots!), but they didn't sell those particular lines, nothing that fancy, and they had never really pushed or promoted anything. Mackenzie's had never advertised, ever. It never needed to, it just was. Always had been, always will be. The general store had been there a long time, three generations and now with Sarah taking over, four. Over the years it had diversified a little, when the big supermarkets had moved into the nearby larger town. It couldn't compete with them on price for food or anything else for that matter, but it had always prided itself on selling just about anything and everything to the local townsfolk, being convenient and offering a more personal service. Mackenzie's sold most things; it just had it all in smaller quantities and not as much choice.

There was a section for DIY, which included some basic paints; another section on household which included some cleaning products, matches, candles, a few cushions, a small selection of bedding, towels, curtains and such. Another section was dedicated to kitchenware with basic crockery, cutlery, pots and pans, and a small section of rugs and mats. Their lighting section consisted of two table lamps and some bulbs at the moment. Sarah could see the possibilities that Clarabelle was suggesting, bringing in that gorgeous bedding, increasing the lighting section to show more variety of lamps, maybe even increase the candles area. She had been blown away by the variety of candles and tea-lights at the town store she had been in earlier that day. Maybe she could make some small changes to Mackenzie's after all and if Clarabelle said to do it, she wasn't going to argue! *Yes*, she thought to herself, *let's go for it! Why not! After all, it is my shop now!*

Clarabelle glowed her glow, delighted in herself and this absolutely *smashing* progress. 'Things

167

to do, things to do!' she chortled, rushing off upstairs to meet the others, letting an excited and inspired Sarah go to bed with all her new ideas for growing the shop and the business. 'It's all coming together nicely. I do so love it when a plan comes together!' she grinned, wondering how Nat was coming on with Simon and for that matter, how his 'Gonk' hair was doing, bless him. Clarence had filled her in on the hair-up, hair-down saga and they had giggled for ages, Clarabelle picturing the scene perfectly that Clarence had described so vividly. Nat really would have to learn to deal with stress better if he was to ever get promoted and earn his Class 2 Angel status. *Aw, bless him!* She thought merrily, *bless indeed!*

Chapter 11

It was mid-May and the spring sunshine was turning into summer sun, higher, brighter, and hotter than the sun of Sarah's opening day six weeks earlier. The canopy stretched out in front of Mackenzie's window protecting the display inside from the sunlight. Several large bright red 'SALE' signs were stuck on the inside of Mackenzie's front window as they had been for the last few weeks and now, besides them, 'LAST DAY' stickers. The sale of the old stock had gone well over the past month, far better than Sarah had expected. She had still made a small profit on the sale items even though she had put the prices down and had cleared out most of the old stock, making space and room ready for the new. The bedding section was now down to its last few duvet sets, the old cushions nearly gone. The shelves were getting emptier and Sarah knew she was ready to bring in the new lines that she had found from the suppliers of the bedding that she had bought for her own house.

With Tim's help she had reorganised and reprioritised the stock and its layout; she had reduced the area for pet supplies, changed the lighting area totally and expanded the household area, all ready for the new stock that had arrived earlier that day. There were boxes of bedding sitting ready and priced in the storeroom, lush satin (effect not real of course! Sarah had to keep the costs realistic for the local

169

market) alongside boxes of crisp cotton sets in different shades and sizes all waiting to be put out on the almost empty shelves, and all the sets came with matching cushions and runners which would sit beside them. The lighting area of the shop was now stocked with a wide variety of gorgeous candles, tea lights, holders, candle stands, and the most fabulous lamps, all chosen to coordinate with the bedding sets, picked out with Clarabelle's help, of course! There were throws in soft materials, in different shades, all stacked up ready to go out. New curtain lines in similar shades and materials as the beddings were ready too. The paint section had been expanded, offering a wider range and choice to Mackenzie's customers and Sarah was ready!

The meetings with the newspaper advertising team had produced amazing results since her first discussions with them three weeks previously. Sarah was delighted with what they had done with her photographs. The before and after shots really showed what you could do with a lick of paint and a few accessories, all of which she now sold, or would be selling, by the end of the week. A full page spread was ready to go in Friday's weekly paper, running for the next four weeks, shouting from the rooftops how Mackenzie's was the place to be to makeover and transform your home, at minimal cost and with expert help. Not that Sarah considered herself to be an expert, but she could advise customers on what matched what and what colours would look nice together, what accessories would go. She knew that some people just didn't have a clue about

170

coordinating anything, so she had added that into the advertising campaign, offering her services to her customers and training Tim on 'what went with what' for when she wasn't there, well, trying to. Turned out he was one of the ones who didn't have a clue either! He just had no sense of style or colour, the mad multi-coloured spikey hair being the give-away there, and Sarah had given up in the end on Tim being an advisor, especially when he had tried to put a red duvet set with orange lamps and blue cushions!

The new banners had been produced for the front of the shop declaring to the world how wonderful the store's items could make your home, with photo's to prove it. She hadn't removed any areas of stock completely, being reluctant of upsetting or disappointing any of her local customers if they came in and found something they usually bought at the store was no longer there. She had simply reorganised and reprioritised what and how much of each item Mackenzie's now sold, making room for newer, fresher, better lines, lines, which Sarah hoped, would see Mackenzie's profits and success grow.

'But of course it will grow, dear, it's all planned, all sorted. Trust me! Trust me!' piped up Clarabelle and Sarah did trust her, she trusted her very much indeed.

****

Simon Brown sat in his favourite black leather reclining chair looking out over the city. It had been a long day at work and he was tired, a little irritable

171

and very bored. He stared at the landscape in front of him. The city was lit up like a Christmas tree as it always was at night, life going on at its usual fast and noisy pace below him. He sighed, shaking his head. *Maybe I should have gone?* He thought to himself, then dismissed the thought almost as soon as it had come. They were having a night out, the guys from the Investment Team and had invited him to join them. He'd initially thought that it may be fun, then discovered that they were planning to go to the clubs and pubs that he hated. No, he didn't fancy that at all. *Another early night then*, he thought to himself regretfully. *Great!*

Nathaniel watched sadly. 'Soon, mate, soon!' he said. 'Won't be too much longer, I promise.' Then added quietly, 'I hope, for both our sakes,' and pulled down again on his spikey 'Gonk' hair, firmly patting it into place as best he could.

****

They worked late into the evening after the shop had closed. Sarah and Tim were putting the new stock out, removing the sale signs, putting up the banners and preparing for the changes. Small changes, Sarah knew, but it was a start and it was beginning to feel like hers properly now. Profits were neither up nor down after her first six weeks and Sarah was happy, happy that she had been able to maintain a business, do it justice, and it hadn't collapsed around her ears. She was stronger, happier, and more confident and hadn't given Rob a single

172

thought in weeks she realised. Life at the moment was all about her and that was the way she wanted to keep it. Nothing else mattered, not men, not her mother, not her past; the only thing that mattered was her and building her new success.

'Ah yes, child, I thought we might have a little chat about that?' piped up Clarabelle. 'You do know that since our little session about your mother, the 'you are feeling sleeeepy' session, the peeeaaace session, that you've changed your thinking about a lot of things, don't you, dear?'

'Have I? Is this you with your counsellor hat on, Clar? Do I need to lay on a couch so you can do your Freud thing on me?' she grinned cheekily at the serious looking Clarabelle, who was now nodding quietly to herself as she sat perched on Sarah's shoulder as usual.

The Freud thing may be right, decided Clarabelle now on a mission, and immediately beamed a telepathic line into the ethers, finding the connection she was looking for. Excellent! 'How do you do Mr. Freud,' she beamed, and set to work with new inspiration, her 'counsellor hat', as Sarah insisted on calling it, now firmly in place. She piped up firmly in her most important voice, the 'listen to me' voice as she peered at Sarah intently,

'You've changed your thinking not just about your mother, my dear, it's about you, the way you see you!' she insisted. 'Do you see?'

Sarah nodded. She did see. She could see that she'd blamed herself for everything, had felt very unloved and unsuccessful, empty, a failure all round really! She realised that she'd tried to fill that

173

emptiness in herself with men and romance, but things felt different now.

'You're getting there, but you've missed a point, quite an important point, you know,' Clarabelle said gently. 'Think about your chat with Frieda that evening and what you were both saying about your past boyfriends,' she piped. 'You now see that these men were no good for you, yes?' she said hopefully. Sarah nodded, thinking that she'd been blind where men were concerned, but she could also see that she hadn't really known any better at the time. She did now though!

'So why is it, do you think, that you chose such men?' Clarabelle asked, raising an eyebrow at Sarah, waiting for her to work it out.

Sarah looked blank. Clarabelle tried again.

'Mirror mirror on the wall,' she chanted.

'Um, I chose rubbish men 'cos… I thought I was rubbish?' guessed Sarah, not quite sure if that was the right answer but having a go.

'Bingo!' squealed Clarabelle, clapping her hands in glee. Finally the penny was dropping!

'And how do you feel about those men now?' she asked.

'I was a bloody idiot!' came the instant reply.

'And also, child, because you were used to it! Your mother treated you like 'rubbish' as you put it, so you thought it was alright for men to do the same. Can you see now that you are not the disappointment that you thought you were, that you are not rubbish?' Sarah was nodding emphatically. 'That you deserve more, you deserve the best! So now you would not

choose such men, yes?' she asked. Sarah shook her
head, equally as emphatically. Clarabelle continued,

'You spent your life accepting less than you
were worth in all areas, with men, jobs, everything.
The job is sorted now, smashing!' Clarabelle beamed
at her. 'You can now see with your shop, that you
were capable of so much more than you thought you
were. It is the same with men, my dear. Once you
truly believe that that you are not 'rubbish',
everything will change. Can you see?' Sarah was
nodding and Clarabelle was chuffed. 'You must find
your own worth, Sarah. Learn to believe in yourself,
but most of all, child, you must start to love yourself!'
Sarah was nodding thoughtfully and Clarabelle
breathed a sigh of relief. 'It has to come from you,
child, from inside you. You fill up your well of love
first. Once it overflows, then you are ready, ready for
someone worthy. Can you see?' Sarah nodded
thoughtfully as Clarabelle continued.

'And what would that then make you?' she
prompted.

'Full of myself!' Sarah answered proudly.

'No!' screeched Clarabelle. Really! She'd
thought they were there, but clearly not quite! 'It will
make you whole, child, independent, strong, and
confident! It will make you a person who has worth!'

'Oh, sorry,' Sarah grinned. 'Yes, I guess it
would.'

'Well, keep working on it, dear,' Clarabelle
said with a sigh, 'we are nearly there.'

'Clar, I just want to focus on me at the mo, is
that ok? Is that right? It feels right!' she asked quietly.
'I mean, just 'cos I figured out where I've been going

175

wrong doesn't mean I'm ready to jump back in.'
Clarabelle beamed, positively beamed, nodding her
agreement! *Oh yes, this was Sarah's time to focus on her,
to grow her fledgling self-worth, and as quickly as possible!
Time was after all, of the essence! Simon was waiting, and
they didn't have forever!*

     'Me, me, me time, and it's about bloody time,'
sang Sarah to herself with delight and some relish.
Clarabelle's halo almost popped its anchor in her
glee! Sarah finally realising the importance of self-
worth! Hallelujah! She really must go and thank Mr.
Freud for his help with this little chat! Most helpful,
most helpful!

****

     The following month passed by with as much
activity and change as the previous one had. It was
the middle of June and time had literally flown by for
Sarah. She honestly didn't know it could go that fast!
Her self-worth had been growing nicely, so Clarabelle
said. She knew she was growing in confidence too,
the new self-belief was blossoming, emerging like a
butterfly from its chrysalis, growing in beauty and
strength with each and every day. She was more
aware of herself, and she no longer put herself down
the way she used to. She'd noticed that morning as
she'd cleaned her teeth, how pale her reflection in her
bathroom mirror looked. She had crooked her head
smiling at the image. It was most unlike her to be so
pale, but so far this summer she hadn't done any
sunbathing at all, she simply didn't have time. She
had always been a sun-worshipper and by now, mid-

176

June, Sarah would normally be brown as a berry! She used to feel more confident with a tan, but she realised now that it wasn't about being tanned, it was more how she felt about herself and how a bit of sun could boost her very fragile ego. It didn't seem to matter anymore. She thought back to the hours of sunbathing she put herself through every summer, baking herself in scorching heats, roasting her body as if on a spit, turning occasionally at 180 degrees to ensure an all over even golden glow.

'Mother will be pleased, no tan!' she smiled to herself. Her bitching about her mother had gone since the session with Clarabelle. She had a new quiet acceptance of it all that no longer jarred at thoughts of her mother. Sooner or later she would have to have a word with her and see if some bridges could be built, but right now, Sarah's only focus was on her, her home, her store, and to make all of it continue to grow.

****

On her days off over the last month Sarah had painted and transformed each of the two single spare bedrooms, taking before and after photographs of each transformation, each time using the new stock she had bought in for the store. Once the upstairs of her home was complete, she had then moved onto her living room. Clarabelle had taught her all about flow and light, uplifting dark corners and colour. She had brought in Christmas lights from the store with white tiny lights and had strung them above her marble fireplace; other similar ones had been woven into the

177

tall plants that now stood in the corners. Candles were everywhere, soft throws were over the sofa, and new cushions adorned each chair while a deep pile sheepskin rug lay in front of the hearth. At night as by day, the room came alive with beauty, a relaxing haven!

A new campaign of advertising was planned for the following month July, which started in two weeks' time, showing how Mackenzie's could transform your living space and sales were up. The stores bedroom stock had gone well from the last campaign in May, which was still running. More paint had been sold in the last four weeks than in the last four years, accessories such as lamps and ornaments had been flying off the shelves, and the candles had had to be re-ordered at lightning speed to meet demand. Sarah knew it would be the same for the living rooms as it had been for the bedrooms and had ordered extra supplies of Christmas lights ready, even though it was June, as well as more candles and throws. She had, on Clarabelle's advice, introduced incense and essential oils into the stock. They took very little room and made the store smell fantastic. People would remark when they came in to the shop how nice it felt, how nice it smelt and would ask what the fragrance was. Sarah or Tim would point them in the direction of the incense, sitting next to the candles and the different varieties of holders for the sticks, which were placed next to the oils and oil burners. All these new lines had been selling well.

178

Sarah had already mapped out the campaign for August; bathrooms! She was going to transform her own and add in lush, thick new towels with matching bath and pedestal mats, soft squidgy sponges (natural ones of course), and rich, thick, fancy bottles of bath oils. Fancy shower curtains would be brought in, all co-ordinating with the various towels and mats, and Sarah knew this would be a good line. She had already sourced suppliers for each of the items she wanted to introduce and made sure it was the best quality at the most reasonable and affordable price. She had discovered that she could drive a hard bargain, was a great negotiator, and a bloody good businesswoman! The campaign was prepared and ready. She was ready! The butterfly was beginning to fly!

****

Clarence and Clarabelle sat together on a cloud noticing how much softer it was this time, having been repaired, marvelling at Sarah's progress.

'She's doing so well, Clarence, I can hardly believe it myself,' Clarabelle remarked. 'It's nothing short of a miracle I tell you, a miracle!'

'Yes, I agree, it's much more than we anticipated at this stage that's true.' He scratched his head as he thought for a moment. 'Do you think we can tell Nathaniel to ease up the pressure on Simon a bit then? I know he's struggling; it's his hair, dead give-away bless, but if she's making good progress maybe we can let things move on a bit, aye? What do you think, dear?'

'Oh I'm not sure, Clar. She still has her mother to deal with; that confrontation is more than overdue and we don't know how it's going to go, how it will affect her yet, not really, do we? I mean, it could put her back, or it could bring her on,' Clarabelle worried.

'Well, it depends on how much she's grown and how strong that growth is,' Clarence stated simply. 'It will either see her crumble or it will strengthen the growth we already have in her. She will either fly higher or she will have her wings clipped and come crashing down. But yes, I agree, we'll leave things as they are until that particular task is done and dusted and then we can review. Agreed?'

'Agreed!'

Clarabelle pondered quietly to herself for a moment, deciding that she would risk going for it and arrange the show down with Margaret soon. She'd need to call in AA Mickey of course, to stand by with 'the mighty sword' to give Sarah the strength that she would need. It was essential that the team did everything they could to protect Sarah's fledgling self-worth and those delicate butterfly wings. They could then begin to move forward or backwards, depending on the outcome.

'Right oh, dear, I'll sort the meeting with Sarah and Margaret and I'll ask for Archangel Michael's attendance.' Clarabelle glowed at the thought, feeling quite faint at the prospect of seeing his mighty form again! 'And don't forget, Clarence, you have to make sure that Ben is ready to stand by with the support and back up, alright, dear?'

180

'Absolutely, just let me know when and we'll both be ready our end,' Clarence assured. They sat quietly for a moment, comfortably on their cloud, taking a break from Sarah for a moment, discussing again how they don't make clouds like they used to, this one having to be repaired so soon after it was made. Eventually, and after much pondering on the state of clouds these days, they brought their attention back to Sarah, her future, and their next step.

'So what *is* the plan once she is ready then, Clarence? How are we going to introduce them? Any thoughts?' she asked.

'Well, I was thinking her flat. He hates the city, ready to go, more than ready to go. We'll get him a transfer to Ben's bank, *and* he'll need somewhere to live. Takes time for them to sell property and buy another down there, so Sarah's little flat over the shop should do nicely as a stop-gap. Give them time to get to know each other, bond, and make a connection.'

'Oh, what a wonderful idea!' Clarabelle clapped her hands in glee. 'The flat is empty, full of boxes, hasn't been used for years, just sitting there wasting space. I can get Sarah to do a makeover on it and rent it to Simon. How perfect!'

And the brother and sister glowed from wing to wing at their little plan.

****

It was Friday afternoon and the shop was quiet. Sarah leaned on the counter at the store thinking about Sunday. Her thoughts filled with both

181

her own father as well as her mother's father. Father's Day was only two days away and Sarah had been thinking a lot about it all. She wondered whether her grandfather was still alive. *He must be in his eighties, probably dead by now!* She thought. But, if he was alive she may even be able to find him. Clarabelle would know, she could do anything and this would certainly be in her remit, finding out if her grandfather was upstairs or downstairs. *But would it be opening a can of worms, make things worse?* She wondered. She decided to discuss it with Clarabelle and take her guidance on it. She hadn't seen her for a while actually, she realised. She's been disappearing a lot lately! She'd have a word with her when she did see her, discuss it at length. There was also a growing feeling within Sarah of wanting, no needing to speak to her mother, try to build bridges, lay some foundations, and along with them, some boundaries. She definitely needed Clarabelle's help with that one! She just wasn't prepared to allow her mother to keep putting her down the way she did and Sarah knew it was time to confront the situation. *Shit, that's going to be a hard one!* She thought. But she also knew it had to be done. Her thoughts shifted to her own dad, dead now some eleven years. She would go to the pub on Sunday, she decided, to raise a glass to him. He'd always liked his beer although he wasn't a heavy drinker by any means, but he had enjoyed his Sunday afternoons in the pub with his friends. The Crown was the only pub in the small town other than the cricket club, and had been her father's favourite place to watch the football. It had a big screen, although she recognised sadly, it had more than likely just been an excuse to get away from Mum for a bit. He'd never really been a football man. *Yes*, she thought to herself, *I shall go to the pub Sunday lunchtime and raise a glass to Dad. I'll call Ben tomorrow to see if he wants to come with me. Be nice, the two of us doing that.*

With her weekend planned, and looking forward to her Friday night of peace that she had organised for later, Sarah went back to work.

Chapter 12

Simon Brown lay sprawled across the sofa with Nadia curled up against him, his arm loosely around her as they watched the end of the movie, both munching on nuts and he drinking his fourth can of beer. He liked their Friday nights together, sometimes staying in and sometimes going out. It was a great end to the week. She lay snuggled in his arms in her dressing gown, her hair still damp from the showers they'd taken together after their love making earlier. The boys were always out on a Friday night and Simon loved this private time together. It was past midnight, the movie was drawing to a close and he was tired. He'd been a bit down this week and he knew why. Father's Day was Sunday and it seemed to annoy him these days, seemed to rub salt in the wound that here he was, nearly forty, childless and wifeless. He thought for a moment of what he could be doing this coming father's day if he had little ones himself, where they would go, what they would do and he immediately felt sad, angry, and frustrated again.

Thinking of something that would lift him from his sad and intrusive thoughts he turned to Nadia,

'Darling, shall we go out for the day on Sunday?' he suggested, 'a drive somewhere maybe, go for some lunch, nice pub perhaps? I could do with

184

getting out of the city for a while. Do you fancy it, love?'

Nadia turned her head towards him, facing him warily. She knew what would come next; she had been avoiding it all week, knowing it would cause another argument. She knew that Simon was getting moodier and moodier these days, harder to please and keep happy. She also knew that he wasn't going to like what she was going to say next. Bracing herself she hesitantly said, 'I can't do Sunday, babe, how about next weekend? That sounds nice, to get out of the city and have a nice day away.'

Simon felt the hairs rise and hackle on the back of his neck. He knew too, just like she did, why she couldn't do Sunday, but he just had to ask, he had to hear her say it.

'And why's that?' His voice was already raised and he could hear it, but he couldn't help it. He paused and turned to look at her, glaring. 'Why can't you do Sunday, Nadia?' His voice was cold, angry, and knowing.

'Well the boys have arranged for Roger to come round for Father's Day, darling, you know how they are together. But we can go out for the day next Sunday, anywhere you like.' She smiled seductively into his increasingly angry eyes trying to appease him. Only it didn't work, not at all. Simon lay still, unmoved, silently, frozen like ice. He got up slowly, pushing her away from him as he raised himself from where he'd been laying, moving himself into a sitting position and away from her as he did so, automatically and without hesitation, needing to put distance between them. She watched as his mouth

closed tightly, his teeth clenched; she watched as the
veins in his neck began to pulse and she knew she
was in trouble, big trouble, she could feel it!

'And tell me, Nadia,' Simon said slowly,
almost spitting the words out, 'just why *you* need to
be there? Just why *he* has to come *here* and not take
them *out* for Father's Day like any normal bloody
father?'

'But the boys want me there, sweetheart. It's
not the same for them if I'm not there now, is it? Be
reasonable, Simon, darling, please?' she begged,
'Please try to understand, that it's best for everyone. It
will spoil it for the boys if I'm not there.' She saw
Simon's face unmoved as he stared at the floor,
unblinking, stone cold rigid. She tried again.

'Try not to be jealous, sweetheart. I do hate it
when you get so insecure, but there's no need really.
Let's not row, darling. We've had such a nice evening,
can't we just go to bed and forget it now, pleeeezzze?'

Simon looked at her upturned mouth, her
pleading face and his heart hardened in his chest,
closing down finally and fully.

'No, Nadia, we can't. Not this time.' Simon
looked at the floor. He couldn't even look at her, he
didn't want to. He'd had it with her now. Enough
was enough! He was out, gone! Only he couldn't! He
couldn't go now, he knew that, he couldn't just walk
out which is what he wanted to do and wanted to do
very badly. He was over the limit from the four beers
he'd drunk through the film as well as the bottle of
wine they'd shared earlier. He was tired and he was
undressed, sitting in the dressing gown that she'd
bought him the Christmas before, the dressing gown

that stayed here, in her house, for when he stayed over. He could get a taxi, but then he'd only have to come back for his stuff and for his car and she'd make a scene and it would be awkward. If he waited till the morning when it was safe to drive and went off quietly he'd not have to deal with her or see her again. Hopefully he could do it before she woke up. *No, I'll stay, put up with the couch, stay for one last night and go in the morning,* he decided. He'd take all his stuff, not that there was much of it here, but there were bits; a few CD's, some bathroom things, a few spare shirts in her wardrobe, and some spare underwear in the one 'man' drawer that she had given him. He turned coldly to Nadia.

'That's it, Nadia, we're finished, this is over! I am not putting up with this bullshit, this crap, this bollocks anymore! I'll sleep here on the sofa and in the morning, I am gone!' Nadia opened her mouth to protest, plead, cajole, calm him down, but Simon got there first and in an eerily quiet voice simply looked at her and said, 'Go to bed, Nadia. Get out of my sight and leave me alone. NOW!'

She went, quickly, quietly, and obediently, thinking to herself, *he'll calm down in the morning. It'll be fine, he'll come round, he always does,* and a confident Nadia went to bed alone.

Nathaniel gazed in the mirror at his 'Gonk' hair in disgust, standing fully extended as it was now, spiked up in complete panic. He couldn't fly fast enough to the cloud as he called Clarabelle in alarm with the news.

187

'Ready or not, coming!' he screamed. 'She'd better be ready, because I can't hold him back any longer!' Clarabelle went quickly upstairs, hoping to find Clarence for help with this disastrous news.

****

The next morning dawned and found Simon still sitting on the sofa, having hardly moved all night. He had dozed off for an hour or two, but that was about all that he had managed. All he wanted to do was get his stuff and get the hell out of here. He looked at his watch, 6:00. *I should be fit to drive by now,* he thought. His unshaven face and tired eyes spoke volumes. There was no doubt whatsoever in Simon Brown's mind that it was time to go. He had not had one single regret throughout all his thinking during the night. He got up quietly and began looking through the CD's for any that were his, moving from there into the kitchen, collecting up some of his 'man gadgets', followed by the bathroom, collecting as he went the spare toothbrush that he left here, along with his shaving gear. He finally walked silently into Nadia's bedroom, picking his clothes up quietly from the floor where they still lay from being pulled off in haste prior to last night's lovemaking. *No,* thought Simon, *not lovemaking, sex! It was just sex, that's all it's ever been.*

He dressed quickly trying not to wake her. Nadia began to stir, awakening just as Simon was pulling his last shirt out of the wardrobe. She watched him in dawning horror as he placed it into the carrier bag he was holding, a bag he had found in

188

the kitchen. His underwear followed it, pulled out roughly from his 'man drawer'. He turned to her, looking at her coldly,

'Goodbye, Nadia,' and she watched him walk out of her life with complete shock and disbelief.

Simon threw his bag onto his car's passenger seat almost as quickly as he threw himself into its driving seat, slamming his car door he barely noticed the screech of its tyres as he drove off at speed and away from Nadia for a final time, leaving a cloud of smoke from the wheel spin trailing behind him.

He entered his apartment fifteen minutes later, putting the bag on the kitchen counter and made himself coffee. *A small bag*, he thought to himself, *not much to show for two years of my life!* The traffic had been quiet driving home this early on a Saturday morning. *Just as well, he was bloody knackered and bloody pissed off! He couldn't have dealt with heavy city traffic with the mood he was in!* He looked at his mobile phone as it beeped for the third time in the last fifteen minutes. Another text from Nadia, a pleading, begging, shocked Nadia. *Piss off!* he thought coldly, switching it off without emotion or regret, and a tired and disappointed Simon went to bed.

****

Some hours later Simon awoke feeling better. Relief flooded his body, relief at finally finding the strength to walk away. How the hell he had put up with it for so long he didn't know. *He was going to go*

189

ages ago, March, he remembered. *Why didn't he? Why did he stay?*

Nathaniel's hair had thankfully returned to limp status and he was hugely relieved. They'd reassured him upstairs that it wasn't his fault and that he'd done a good job keeping Simon stuck for as long as he had and he wasn't to fret. As soon as he'd heard this news his 'Gonk' hair had immediately began to wilt and was now back to its normal state, lying flat once again on his head. Nat tried not to look guilty as he sat watching Simon from his perch on the bedroom mirror but couldn't help looking rather sheepish. Simon's relief was palpable and Nathaniel knew he'd held him back for far too long, longer than was good for him in his humble opinion! But those upstairs had instructed and he had followed orders. He was a foot soldier, a Class 2 Angel, not a general and hadn't dared to argue, even though he himself did think it was a bit unfair – very unfair actually! Blinking Sarah, it was her fault his Simon had had to put up with 'the bloody woman' as Simon was now calling Nadia. He himself thought that it was Sarah who was 'the bloody woman,' but again, those upstairs had said no, she wasn't, she was lovely, she just wasn't ready. He'd tried to be patient, but really? It wasn't the ticket now, was it, keeping his boy so miserable for so long! Still, he'd done his best to keep him happy focusing Simon's attention on sex and other boy stuff and it had worked, for a while! Mind you, Simon seemed to be perking up and that was all that mattered. He was chatting away to himself now wittering on about Nadia and why he'd stayed. If only he knew, bless him!

I dunno! Simon thought to himself, *maybe it wasn't the right time? It bloody is now though! No chance of me going back to that bloody woman, ever!* He looked out of the window at the city he had lived in for all of his life and decided right there and then that it was time to get from here too. He was buggered if he was going to sit here all weekend stewing. He'd go for a drive, find a nice pub, get out of the city, and stay overnight somewhere, give himself thinking time. It would give him the chance to get away from Nadia and from the city at the same time.

He showered and dressed quickly, just wanting, no needing, to go. He didn't shave; he just couldn't be bothered. He didn't even pack a razor nor did he pack any decent clothes. Normally clean shaven, well dressed, and well turned out, Simon decided he was having a weekend off from being tidy and was going to have a weekend slobbing it and that he was going to do exactly as he bloody well pleased for once. Jeans and T-shirt, fleece and trainers would do, he decided. He still looked tired and angry as he headed out the door and down to his car. He had no idea where he was going to go, but he just knew that he needed to get away for the weekend and he went. Climbing into his powerful Jaguar XKR sports car, normally his pride and joy, Simon barely noticed the roar of the powerful engine as it sprang into life nor did he notice the smell of the soft leather seats, the depth of the wood on the walnut dashboard, the feel of the leather steering wheel on his hands, or the

191

coolness of the air conditioning unit as it came on blowing softly on his face; all he noticed was a desperate need to run, to get out of the city and get the hell away from bloody Nadia!

****

Three hours and some seventy miles later, Simon Brown had calmed down and cleared his mind sufficiently to notice his surroundings. He hadn't switched his sat-nav on; he'd just pointed the car in a direction that seemed suitable and driven. He had no idea where he was right now at all. He had come off the motorway some time ago and had driven past sleepy villages, small towns, big towns, fields and countryside. With every mile that had put distance between him and Nadia he had felt better, calmer. He was getting tired and he noticed now that he was also quite hungry, bloody starving in fact, he realised. Simon looked at the small town he was driving through at that moment deciding to look for a pub, an inn, a motel, anything would do really, anything that sold food and had a bed.

Nathaniel heaved a sigh of relief. He had been keeping Simon's tummy grumbles at bay as best he could for the last hour now and had kept his mind occupied with various thoughts in his efforts to get him as close to the right location as possible. Simon had nearly stopped several times, but Nathaniel had encouraged him to push on and somehow had managed to get him to where he was now.

192

Must get Clarabelle, he thought, and winged off to find his new partner in crime.

Simon drove down quite a decent high street; he drove past a few clothes shops, an off-licence, and a general store, most closed now at six o'clock this Saturday night. He saw the pub ahead on the main road with some relief and thought it looked nice. He slowed down as he approached, looking for signs that would show him that this pub was what he wanted and indeed it was! It was open and a food menu was on display. Simon was pleased to note a B&B sign hanging over the door. 'That'll do!' he said to himself, pulling into the car park. *It seemed like a nice town,* he thought as he looked around. The pub overlooked a pond sitting in the middle of a green and seemed to be a quiet place. *It has a friendly feel to it,* he thought.
        'Yes, this will do nicely!'

He didn't know if it was a big town or a small town, but he thought it looked quite small as he looked up and down the high street, but he couldn't tell yet really. *It certainly didn't look as big as the town he had driven through just fifteen minutes before,* he suddenly thought. *Blimey, why hadn't he stopped there?* That was just before his stomach had suddenly started grumbling so loudly, he realised. There were probably more pubs, more choices in that earlier town, but Simon was too knackered and hungry to think about going back. 'Yes this will do,' he decided.
        Simon checked in, filled in the form, and leaving his credit card details, he had then gone to his room. He perused it quickly, automatically. Decent,

simple, clean, comfy. The shower was nearly tall
enough for him to get under, unlike many others. *Yep,
it'll do nicely,* he decided. Dumping his bag on the
double bed he had gone straight back down to the
pub on a mission for food and beer. An hour later, a
satisfied and more relaxed Simon was enjoying his
third beer as the waitress took his empty plate away
when he finally noticed his surroundings. It was an
old original pub, with beams, brass, and atmosphere.
It really was quite lovely and very quaint. Simon
looked around the place, people-watching for a
moment. He noticed some old chaps in the corner
playing dominoes and drinking Guinness while
another couple of guys were playing chess and
enjoying their real ale clearly as much as the game.
There were a fair few couples sitting holding hands,
chatting, and drinking by the log fire that crackled in
the large hearth, a few small mixed groups clearly out
for a Saturday night laughed raucously as they told
the jokes round the table and there were half a dozen
guys sitting by the bar. Music was playing in the
background and Simon looked for the source,
noticing a juke box on the wall and decided to go and
investigate. As he passed a large oak beam on his
quest to the music opportunity he noticed another
area of the bar through an archway behind it where a
rather magnificent pool table sat invitingly waiting
for players to rack up with a dart board nearby.

Simon focused on the juke box, spending time
carefully choosing his music selection. It was ages
since he'd been to a pub where he felt this
comfortable or where they'd had music he'd actually

heard of! He chose with relish all his favourite songs
then sat back down with his beer to enjoy his
pickings. Foot tapping and smiling happily, he didn't
notice the man approach until he heard the friendly
voice.

'Yours?' nodding to the juke box the man
smiled.

'Yes, it's one of my favourites,' Simon replied,
smiling in return.

'Yes, mine too. I'm Peter, the landlord,' he
said. 'Didn't see you when you checked in, I was in
the kitchen. Half chef, half landlord, half receptionist,
half man!' he laughed. 'You'd have met the other half,
Jen, I guess?' he asked.

Simon nodded, smiling, welcoming the
interaction. Pete asked if he was new in town and if
he knew anyone and once he'd established that
Simon was indeed 'Billy No Mates' and knew no-one,
Peter had not hesitated to invite him over to join them
at the bar where he proceeded to introduce him to
everyone. As the evening proceeded Peter continued
to introduce Simon to every man, child or beast that
came in for the rest of the night. Simon had liked
them all, particularly one chap called Tom, another
called Dick, who was a real laugh, and he was just
waiting for Harry; there had to be a Harry to
complete this rather perfect picture!

Simon made his mind up that this was a
lovely friendly town. He had become part of the pub
within the hour and almost one of the locals by the
time Peter eventually locked up. Had it really been
four am? Blimey, he didn't know any pubs in the city

195

that did lock-ins. They'd played pool, darts, drank a
yard of ale, played poker (illegally but who cared!),
and some other games he couldn't remember. The
beer had flowed, the tales and jokes had flowed, and
the night had flowed until the wee small hours.
Simon had laughed more and had more fun in that
one night here in this little pub than he'd had in such
a long time in the city! He'd pay for it in the morning,
he knew, but Simon didn't care. He liked it here and
it was exactly this kind of place that he wanted to live
he decided, as he looked out through the small
window of his room at the front of the pub to the
green and the pond opposite. *Perfect!* Thought Simon,
Just bloody perfect!

Nathaniel smiled serenely, delighted with
himself. His Gonk hair flat and beautifully styled and
all was well with the world.

Chapter 13

Sarah dressed with some thought and care on this Father's Day morning, preparing herself to go to the pub to raise a glass to her dad. She wanted to look her best and make a bit of an effort. Clarabelle had said it was important, that it would be nice for her dad, and whilst Sarah had never seen any ghosts herself, she knew from Clarabelle that loved ones who have passed over often visited those that they had left behind and even if she couldn't see him, if he was there, and she thought that he might be, he could see her, so she wanted to look good to make him proud.

She thought about her grandfather for a moment. Clarabelle had confirmed that her mother's father was indeed 'upstairs' and had been for some years. Apparently he had died of a heart attack brought on by a broken heart from guilt and loss for leaving his wife and child. He had never forgiven himself and the stress had taken its toll on his body, giving in and packing up at the premature age of fifty-two. Sarah was sad that she wouldn't be able to reunite him with her mother, but it had been a bit optimistic as well as unrealistic, she admitted to herself, to expect a happy ending out of that sad story.

Her thoughts drifted to Ben then, reflecting on their conversation yesterday morning. It was a shame

197

that he wasn't coming, but he had said he was so tired that all he wanted to do was have Father's Day at home with Gina and Joe and do absolutely nothing. He had seemed stressed when she had spoken to him on the phone, overly tired and she was a little worried about him. Apparently they still hadn't sorted out a replacement for his work colleague Charley, so he was doing the work of two and had been for over three months now and it was beginning to take its toll. He was working long hours and had a heavy workload with tight deadlines. By the sound of him, he was wiped out! The town branch of the Redville bank was meant to have two business account managers so Ben had said, but Charley had gone off on the sick with stress back in March and it was still ongoing, leaving the ever loyal and hardworking Ben holding the fort. After a bit of advice from Clarabelle on the matter, Sarah had told her brother to put his foot down and demand a replacement for Charley, even a temporary one. He had tiredly agreed, saying he would deal with it on Monday. He had a meeting scheduled with the Bank Manager and was intending to raise it then. Sarah hoped it would all sort out for him. It really wasn't fair at all on poor Ben bless him!

She put the finishing touches to her make-up and a final brush through her hair, turning to Clarabelle who hadn't left her side all morning, she asked,

'Will I do?'

'Oh, you'll do nicely, child, you'll do nicely!' beamed Clarabelle.

198

She seemed weird this morning, weirder than normal, thought Sarah. She was fussing and preening over her like some mad rabbit on speed! *Whatever was the matter with her,* Sarah wondered? *Maybe she was fussing because Dad may be there, perhaps she thought he'd have a go at her or something, for showing her what she had about her mother?*

Sarah gave up wondering what was going on with Clarabelle and set off for the pub. It was nearly twelve and she knew it would get busy in there today. It was quite a community pub and families were welcome in the daytime. Hoping to get a quiet seat at the back overlooking the beer garden, she knew if she went early enough she'd get the table she wanted. She intended to spend some time alone in peace and quietly think about her dad in some privacy.

Sarah entered the pub at twelve via the beer garden door and was disappointed to see a man, a scruffy hunched man at that, sitting where she had been intending to sit.

Probably pissed or some tramp or other, she thought in annoyance as she looked at his dishevelled appearance. Going to the bar she ordered a glass of pinot grigio and looked for another seat that would serve the privacy she wanted. She stared at the man in annoyance while she waited for them to pour the wine, thinking just for a moment that he looked familiar, but instantly dismissing it because he was such a state. She was sure she didn't know anyone that scruffy!

199

How dare he take my seat! She thought to herself. *Bloody man!* And stomped into another corner, which actually was just as quiet and would do nicely, but that wasn't the point!!

Sarah sat in her chair (in the wrong corner, bloody man!), and began to focus on her dad. She called out quietly to him, almost whispering, 'Hi Dad, how you doing? How's life upstairs? You ok? Thinking of you, love you.' She waited. She waited a little more. Nothing!

'Well, ok, Dad, but if you can hear me, here's to you, cheers!' She raised her glass in the air to the empty chair directly opposite her in her toast to him.

'God love her,' smiled Clarabelle, 'she's talking to the wrong chair, bless!' John was sitting beside Sarah in the chair to her left, as close as he could get to his daughter. He smiled as he gazed at her.

'Is he here, Clarabelle?' Sarah whispered to her shoulder.

'Yes, dear, he is here. He says to tell you that he is very proud of you, that you have come far and that you have done so well. He wants you to know that he loves his little girl very much,' came the response from her shoulder. Tears came into Sarah's eyes instantly, an emotional rush of love and loss all rolled into one, thankfulness and grateful for this gift she had been given, this gift of the love and the message from her father.

'Hi, Dad, I love you too,' she whispered tearfully.

She turned to Clarabelle then and asked hesitantly, 'Thank you, Clarabelle. Thank you so much, but is there any chance I could talk to him myself? I mean, I don't know how, or how it works, but could I, please…. is that possible?'

'Oh my, oh my! Well, I don't know, child. I haven't checked with upstairs how that would affect you. It could mess with your vibrations and cause chaos and it is rather short notice. Oh my, let me think for a minute. I could get in big trouble, let me think, let me think!' she bustled and panicked with alarm at this unexpected request. She knew she didn't have time to go upstairs and check and, hesitating for a moment or two, she made her mind up that this event called for some lateral thinking and boldness, she suddenly announced to an expectant Sarah, 'Well, alright then, dear. I just have to fine-tune you for you to be able to hear him. You can't possibly *see* him, not ready, not ready! But it may be possible for you to *hear* him, if I can just get you on the right frequency, clairaudient rather than clairvoyant, but it would do, it would do. That's hearing rather than seeing, dear, it's all I could manage at such short notice. Bear with me, bear with me, some adjustments to do my end. Be with you in a mo.'

Sarah sat quietly watching Clarabelle fuss and suddenly felt a weird whistling in her ears as if a whirlwind had just blown through. Suddenly, there was crackling in her head as if an old wireless was being tuned in. She felt a prickling sensation in her head and a sudden surge of static, then quietly, as if coming from the distance she heard her father's rich baritone Scottish voice say,

'Hello, sweetheart.'

201

Oh my God! That's him, that's really him! I can hear my dad! Bloody Nora, she thought in shock, followed immediately by wonder.

'Hi, Dad,' she shyly replied, realising instantly that she hadn't moved her lips and that the words were coming in her thoughts rather than actually being voiced.

'Can you hear me?' *Blimey, its telepathy! This is clever stuff this! Wowey, I'm telepathic!*

'Yes, sweetheart, I can hear you,' came the instant reply in her head. She would have thought it would come from her ears, but although they were still crackling like mad the voice seemed to be inside her head, inside her thoughts. It was so weird!

'Try to hear him with your thoughts, dear, rather than your ears, best way,' came Clarabelle's advice, as she stood back and let John get on with his reunion with his daughter.

'I can't stay long, sweetheart, so hard to get through the mist and veil you know from up here, takes it out of us from this end and we can only manage a few minutes here and there, but I just wanted to tell you that I am so very proud of you. You have grown into an amazing, beautiful, talented woman, Sarah.' Sarah sniffed and bowed her head to hide her tears.

'I also wanted to say that I am sorry, so very sorry, my love! I couldn't bear it, you see, couldn't bear to come around to see you and wee Ben. I stayed away when you needed me so much, stayed out the way. I let you both down so badly, so very badly. I'm so very sorry. It was having to see your mother; the ravage, the pain, the hurt on your mother's face, you

202

see, knowing that I had done that. I caused that pain that hurt. I made her like that. I was a coward Sarah. I ran away, guilty, see? I left you when you needed me and I am truly, truly sorry. Please forgive me?'

'Oh, Dad, of course I forgive you. I understand, it's ok... really it is, but thank you for what you've said. We were all scared to death of Mum and it's ok.' Sarah smiled at the empty chair opposite her with all the love she could find in her heart, trying in her smile to show her dad how much she loved him and forgave him. He sat next to her smiling back as he and Clarabelle exchanged knowing smiles at Sarah's misdirection of affection to the empty chair.

'Thank you, Sarah. Thank you so much. It's more than I deserve, much more. You always did have a big heart, a loving and forgiving heart. And talking of love, Sarah; love is coming to you, real love.' Her dad went on, 'Be ready for it when it arrives. It is near, very near. Watch for the signs, be open, be ready, it is your time.'

'What's that Dad? Love? Oh yes, I know me and love! Mess, isn't it?'

'No, Sarah, love is COMING!'

'*Careful*, yes, Dad, I know, really careful!' Sarah agreed. 'I need to be very careful, yes, but don't you worry, I won't make that mistake again Dad, I can tell you. Staying well clear of the male species, I am, and that's a fact! No more loving for me! I'm going to join a nunnery!'

'No, no!' yelled John, looking at Clarabelle for help. 'No, love is *COMING*!'

203

'Yes, yes I can hear you, love is *done with*, I know! Its ok, I know. Don't you worry about me! My heart is well and truly closed and protected, I won't get hurt again, promise.'

'Argh!' sighed John, beseeching Clarabelle to help him get through to Sarah with his message of hope.

'It's no good looking at me like that, dear,' she smiled at him and his frustration at being misheard. 'She will hear what she wants to hear and see what she wants to see. Always been the same. I know! Twenty years I've had this for!' She smiled and patted his arm. 'For now, she is closed to love and so can't hear what you are saying, but she will hear…. when she is ready and she will see…. when she is ready, of that I promise you!' They both smiled at each other, thinking of Simon then.

'Lovely man, lovely man. He'll make her so happy, so happy!' beamed Clarabelle. John nodded in agreement smiling a contented smile of happiness for his daughter and began softly to fade into mist.

'Goodbye, Sarah, my precious Sarah. I love you, my darling, always remember I love you,' he called, his voice fading further and further away.

Clarabelle called after him, 'I will not fail this mission of love. I will not fail, I assure you! No matter *how* difficult she is! On that you have my word.' She turned to Sarah then, gently saying, 'He is going now, child. He is going to see Ben and be around him too for a while, but before he goes, he wants me to tell you to remember to love yourself, care for yourself and to be happy. You deserve it. Much loved you are, child.' Clarabelle patted Sarah's shoulder reassuringly. *Well, he may not have actually said that, but a bit of poetic license wasn't beyond her remit and would help, even if John hadn't said it, she knew he would if he could, if he hadn't faded quite so fast, so it would all be fine! She'd clear it with Clarence later!*

Sarah blew her nose on a tissue that she had pulled hastily out of her bag thanking Clarabelle for being the interpreter between her and 'upstairs' and for doing whatever she had done to help her hear her fathers' voice.

'It is my pleasure, child, my absolute pleasure,' beamed the angel.

Sarah just couldn't get over it! It had been amazing to talk to her dad. She tried to take it all in. She had actually talked to her dad! Wow! She sat quietly for the next half an hour, drinking her wine and reflecting on the conversation she'd just had with her father, a conversation that Clarabelle had enabled and facilitated so beautifully. She knew how lucky she was to be able to talk to him like that. *Gee*, she thought, *people pay a fortune to go and see mediums to try to have what I just had and that was if they could get a decent one who didn't make half of it up as they went along, which Clarabelle had said, a lot of them did.* Not that there weren't some really good ones out there, just that they were few and far between and you never knew what you were getting. At least with Clarabelle she did know, she knew very well indeed!

'Clarabelle, I love you!' she declared happily, all smiling and glowing, a little angelic looking herself in that moment. 'You really are completely incredible! Thank you! Thank you, thank you!'

205

Clarabelle, of course, just beamed!

'Aw, shucks!' she smiled, 'Thanks! I am rather good, aren't I?' and popped off on the next very important job.

Chapter 14

Simon had had one of the best nights out he'd had in years and the hang-over and lack of sleep had definitely been worth it. He had walked gingerly down the stairs from his room sometime in the late morning, he wasn't sure when, entering the pub looking for Peter, who he'd found setting up for lunch. Pete regretfully informed him that he'd missed breakfast, but thankfully took pity on him and managed to rustle him up some toast, a couple of eggs and a pot of coffee, setting it up for him at the table in the front window that overlooked the green. He looked out absently at the duck pond opposite, the row of shops further up and wondered again if it was a small or large town. Simon couldn't decide.

The sun moved position as Simon finished his breakfast and was now shining brightly in through the front windows and into Simon's tired and hung-over eyes, which were objecting strongly. He decided to move from his seat at the front and was now sitting in the quiet area at the back as the clock struck twelve noon, still nursing his hangover with his third orange juice and yet another pot of coffee. He noticed his reflection in the window as he peered out over the beer garden. He looked rough as rats, awful and a total mess, but he didn't care. No one knew him here so what did it matter! Looking at the state of himself today mind, he was glad that no one knew him. He hadn't shaved in two days, his eyes were so overtired after two nights of very little sleep, and coupled with the hangover were red and blood shot, with large heavy bags underneath. His T-shirt, although clean, was terribly crumpled from where he had stuffed it in his overnight bag with such haste to get away from Nadia and the city that he had forgotten to fold it.

'Yep,' he decided, 'I definitely look like a sack of shit today!' and smiled. Simon put his head down and focused on his shoes, trying to hide his raggedy appearance a little. People were coming in now and most of them looked dressed up, neat, and tidy, everything he wasn't! It was after all Father's Day and families were out for lunch, making an effort for their nearest and dearest.

The landlord, Peter, had made an effort to make the pub looks its best today, with candles lit on every table, some in wine bottles, their wax dripping down the sides of the glass. Others were in tea holders of various shapes and sizes. Simon had to admit that it made a nice effect. Brass horseshoes, kettles, and various other bits hung from the wooden beams above, the soft lighting bouncing off them.

Maybe I should go to my room, he wondered, *Get out the way? Na, bollocks! Who cares anyway!* and Simon stayed put, giving all his attention to his shoes. Pete noticed Simon's hanging head and coming over, smiling said, 'You can get some paracetamol's at the food store over the road, mate. Past the pond, just down a bit from Mackenzie's, the general store at the end of the High Street.' Simon smiled his thanks, but decided it was best to stay put, hide quietly, and wait for the hangover to pass while he poured coffee down his throat.

As he turned back to the window, Simon noticed the girl glaring at him in its reflection. He could feel the poisonous darting looks from fifty paces!

What's her problem? he wondered. *Probably a bloody snob!* he thought to himself. *Probably thinks I'm rough as rats, common as muck, tramp or junky or some such like just because I look a little scruffy. Cheek! Bet she wouldn't be looking at me like that if I was in my work suit!*

He glanced at her then, wondering if he knew her for a moment. She looked a little familiar, but no, he didn't know anyone in this part of the country. *Maybe she just reminds me of someone,* he thought as he returned his attention to his shoes in an attempt to avoid her angry glare and where they remained firmly for the next thirty minutes, oblivious to all and everything around him.

Clarabelle looked at Nathaniel and groaned. Whilst Sarah and Simon had recognised each other on a soul level, on a human level each of the pair had dismissed that recognition as well as each other very swiftly.

'Oh my goodness, why are humans just so blind sometimes!' she exclaimed. 'Oh dear!'

Nathaniel nodded in agreement and smiled. 'Just so limited, so dense, so human!' he agreed. They'd just have to think of something else!

'Do you know what, Clar?' Sarah was saying, still in her dreamy angelic state of bliss, thinking about the conversation with her dad over the last half an hour and how blessed she was, 'You're bloody good! Bloody good! I think it's time for a little celebration, drink another toast to Dad, and even one to you. You deserve it! You're a star!'

She went to the bar to order the same again with the biggest smile on her face that she'd ever worn. Eyes dreamy and sparkly, she radiated happiness out all around her. She looked simply stunning as she shone and several people noticed the smiling girl as she walked past them to the bar. Many admiring glances were sent in her direction, glances from all directions except, of course, from Simon, who was still focused totally on his shoes and oblivious to everything but his growing embarrassment for looking so scruffy.

'Right, Clarabelle, are you ready?' shouted Nathaniel across the room to Clarabelle, who was sat on top of Sarah's head rather than on the normal left shoulder at that precise time.

'On my count of three, go for it!'

Clarabelle was ready. She'd done the family father's day reunion and now it was time for phase two, *LOVE! Yippee!*

She had met with Nathaniel last night, (and with his 'Gonk' hair), having received his urgent calls for a meeting. They had agreed between them that they might as well risk going for it and would be introducing Sarah and Simon here at the pub today.

They were to ensure that their respective wards
noticed each other, at least as a starting point, but so
far it hadn't gone that well despite Clarabelle
ensuring that Sarah looked her absolute best!

Being aware that things were not going well
so far, the angels had now decided that the situation
called for more direct active intervention. It was clear
that Simon wasn't looking at her at all, didn't know
that she was alive, exist, so busy was he with his
shoes! Clarabelle was now given the new task of
drawing Simon's attention to Sarah and to make sure
that it was in a more positive light. She absolutely had
to make sure that he noticed her and that he saw how
special she was! Clarabelle decided that she would
use all her glow, all her light, all her power, and that
she would let it shine like it had never shone before,
making sure it shone all around Sarah's head like a
beacon, a light house! He couldn't possibly fail to
notice her then! At the same time as Clarabelle was
going to do her magic, Nathaniel would make sure
that Simon looked up and saw the beauty, the
wonder of her, the fabulousness that Clarabelle
would create around Sarah.

Nathaniel sat now, perched on top of Simon's
head, looking at Clarabelle and trying to synchronise
their respective actions to within a millisecond.
'Ready, Clar? Right, on three! One, two, three!'
shouted Nathaniel, as he pulled on the back of
Simon's hair. He got the desired result as it
immediately made Simon look up from his shoes to
glare across the pub to see who or what had hit him

on the head. Standing in that moment in his direct line of vision was Sarah at the bar, at exactly the moment that Clarabelle, perched on top of Sarah's head, puffed her halo and her power up on every level and radiated out a brilliant and stunning golden light all around Sarah's head. She even made sure there were some golden sparks in there too for good measure!

Oh my God! a more than startled Simon thought, forgetting all about his head being hit. He saw the bright light of the glow around the beautiful girl in front of him at the bar. He saw the sparks, he saw the power of the light all around her head, and he was gobsmacked! He also saw the candle on the bar-counter just behind her. In his befuddled and confused brain, a brain that does not compute halo's to the average person on the average day, Simon put two and two together, came up with five, and in his overtired and hung-over brain, decided quite reasonably as any sane person not accustomed to angelic glows would, that the poor girl's hair was on fire!

No one is doing anything! Simon thought with even more alarm. She herself, 'Fire Girl', hadn't even noticed that she was on fire! *'Shit!'* Finally spurred into action, Simon jumped up from his seat and raced across the room towards her. Grabbing the first glass that he ran past in his panic and haste to be the hero, he promptly poured a full pint of freezing cold beer all over Sarah's head!

'What the f....!' Sarah screamed. 'What the *hell* do you think you're doing?' She stood in shock, dripping wet with brown sticky real ale sliding down her cheeks. Her hair was saturated, her dress ruined, and on top of that, the entire pub was looking at her in shocked amusement.

'Oh my God!' Sarah shouted. 'This isn't happening to me! What the hell is your problem?!'

'Your hair was on fire!' Simon proudly said. 'I was helping, helping to save you, to put you out.'

'The only one here who should be put out, *pall*, is you!' Sarah blurted in horror and disgust. 'Put out or put down, I really don't care! You're a bloody animal! A mad man! What do you mean 'my hair is on fire'? There's nothing wrong with my bloody hair! Well, there wasn't, till you!' Sarah glanced at herself in the mirror behind the bar and reddened seeing the state of her and got even madder.

Simon hesitated. Could he have been wrong? Was that possible? How? He now looked at her soaked hair, searching for evidence of burned, singed locks and seeing none, he began to pale. Simon looked at her furious face and was panicking now. Confusion poured through him. He cringed as he defended himself as best he could, trying to make sense of it.

'I'm so sorry; oh my God, I'm so sorry! I saw a light, a light around your head, it looked like you were on fire. I'm so sorry! There was a candle and I thought you'd caught fire, your hair. I-I, oh shit! It must have been the reflection of the sun or something, coming in through the window, I don't know. I don't understand. I'm so sorry.'

Simon knew he was sounding like a mad man rambling and could understand why she was so angry with him, but he really truly had thought that

213

she had been on fire! His face reddened and deep shame and embarrassment came over him.

'Oh my God, what an idiot! What was I thinking!! I'm so sorry, let me pay for your dry cleaning, anything, let me make amends, please?' Simon grabbed a beer towel off the bar and was now desperately patting Sarah's face and arms in his panic of getting it so wrong. She snatched the towel from his shaking hands and glared at him, saying each word slowly, one syllable at a time, at this idiot man in front of her,

'Just, get, the, hell, away, from, me, you *NUTTER!*'

Simon didn't have to be told twice! He legged it from the bar and up to his room at the speed of light, throwing himself into the chair in his room he put his head in his hands and wailed,

'What the hell was I *thinking!* Shit, fuck, bollocks!' He could have died with embarrassment. Every instinct in him was on fight or flight mode and Simon decided the latter was definitely preferable! He grabbed his bag and practically ran out of his room to his car, needing to get away from his shame as fast as possible. He'd have to sort the bill out over the phone; no way was he going back in there now! They had his credit card details so it wasn't like he was doing a runner, well kind of, but not from the bill, from her, from his mistake, from the lady he'd just soaked, the very pretty, very angry lady! *But it was an accident, well, but, oh!* He knew what he meant!

Sarah stormed out of the pub and marched down the road towards her home with as much dignity as she could muster in her dripping wet, sticky state.

What an absolute plank! she thought as she stomped every footstep home in squelching wet shoes, soaked legs, and dripping hair.

'Oops!' said Clarabelle.

'I thought that went rather well,' declared Nathaniel optimistically!

'What part of that went well?' retorted Clarabelle, standing as she did, herself soaked from halo to foot; her normally beautiful blond, wavy hair now plastered to her head, flattened down with the weight of an entire pint of brown sticky liquid having been poured over her delicate form. Her feathers, normally so white and fluffy, lay flat and lifeless, stained brown from the real ale, drowned and saturated! They were drying now but as they were fully encased with beer, each feather was sticking together as it dried forming a gooey mess! Clarabelle looked anything but angelic!

'But it's a start,' they said in unison and laughed.

'I'm going to have to go upstairs and clean up, cleanse in the angelic temples to restore my feathers!' Clarabelle declared with alarm. 'I can't fly like this, Nat. My feathers don't work!' she noted with growing horror as she tried unsuccessfully to flap her wings and found that they wouldn't move, stuck solid with dried beer as they now were!

'No worries, Clar. I'll give you a lift, hang onto mine!' Nathaniel offered, spreading out a wing to a bedraggled and flightless Clarabelle.

215

'Hop on!' he said cheerily and she grabbed his wing to make her way back home to sort out her sorry feathers. Clarabelle knew she'd have to declare today's goings on to both Sarah and Clarence and have a chat with her brother about the disaster that had been Sarah and Simon's first meet. *Whatever will he think?* She wondered! *Oops!*

****

Simon returned to his flat some hours later, the humiliation of the events earlier still making his ears burn with the shame. That being said, he had a great time on the Saturday night and it had made him more sure than he ever was that he definitely wanted out of the city. These small towns had such a community feel and everyone was so friendly, apart from the fire girl of course, but he could hardly blame her! After making himself a coffee, Simon telephoned Peter at the Crown, apologising profusely. He settled the bill with a huge tip and after ringing his dad and wishing him a happy Father's Day he then set about updating his CV. Tomorrow he would apply for a transfer and if his bank didn't have anything, he would look elsewhere. Nothing was going to stop him now. He pulled his mobile phone out of his bag. It had been turned off since Saturday morning to give him some peace, some privacy. Simon turned his mobile back on to find twenty-eight texts as well as seventeen voice messages, all from Nadia. He deleted each without reading or listening to any of them. His home phone answer machine was laden with her pleading voice too. Those messages got the same

216

treatment as the ones on his mobile, being deleted quickly, firmly, decisively.

'Simon, my boy,' he said to himself, 'there's no going back!'

The following morning found Simon in work early searching the company's intranet for vacancies, transfers, secondments, anything! This time it seemed to work and it worked well. There were a few possibilities he could see, but nothing that grabbed him. He'd have a look properly when he finished work, before he left for the day, he decided. The bank was just opening up at the moment, customers lining the doors. There was no time to look properly now, but he vowed he would not go home until he had applied for something, somewhere!

Chapter 15

Ben sat in the manager's office of Redville's main bank at nine o'clock. A medium sized branch of the National banking chain, they had been in a meeting for some thirty minutes so far and Ben was stating his case to his boss, a case that justified and proved that they simply had to get someone in to cover Charley. He had come prepared with facts, figures, spreadsheets, and account details. Mr Godwin looked at all the information and after some discussion agreed that yes, they couldn't go on as they were any longer. He would contact head office immediately and get the ball rolling. The post would be on the company's intranet by the close of play today and they would do everything they could to expedite things, he promised.

'It will probably be a secondment or similar for now,' he said, thinking to himself that they couldn't just go filling Charley's job while he was off sick. They'd get hauled over the coals in a tribunal if they tried that, but he would get human resources onto it, find out the state of play with Charley's health, and get someone in temporarily to cover the role for now. No one had expected Charley's sickness to go on this long and he knew it was time for some action. Ben was so relieved he felt his shoulders drop from his ears immediately. They had seemed to be permanently locked there since Charley had been gone, making his shoulders and back ache with the pressure. He could feel it ease, just with the

218

knowledge that things would change soon. He left the meeting and walked back to his desk feeling lighter and brighter than he had for some time.

A few hours later, a surprised Mr. Godwin asked Ben if he could please come into his office for a moment. Human resources had emailed him, he said, before he had even had a chance to email them. The email explained that just that very morning they had received a letter from Charley's doctor saying he was unfit to return to work at the bank permanently. A meeting had then hastily taken place with senior managers to discuss said letter, and on the advice of HR, it had been agreed and decided that it was in Charley's best interests to retire him on medical grounds, with a nice pay packet to see him through. Charley was happy, HR was happy and Mr. Godwin was happy! On hearing this news, Ben was bloody ecstatic! Charley's job would now be able to be advertised properly. Mr. Godwin went on to explain to a very happy Ben, that whilst this would take time (unless a miracle happened and someone at the same level within the company doing the same job wanted a transfer, which was highly unlikely), it would be sorted very soon, within a month or two. In the meantime, pending the miracle transfer request that they didn't expect to happen, they would ask for someone as a secondment, or even an agency temp to fill the void. It was all going on the company's intranet within the hour and he would let Ben know as soon as he knew anything.

219

A delighted Ben went back to work with a huge smile on his face. He had liked Charley, but he also knew that it was the right thing. The poor bloke really hadn't been up to the job and the stress of trying to cope above his level had caused the breakdown.

'All as it's meant to be,' piped up Clarence, sitting on Ben's shoulder. 'Don't you worry about him, he'll be fine. He'll be guided to the right job for him when he's ready, a job that will help him grow rather than debilitate him! The poor boy was on the floor he was so stressed! Needed some R&R he did, that's for sure,' Clarence went on. 'And don't you worry about his replacement; we have just the right man for the job. All in hand, all in hand.' Ben smiled a relieved smile, believing and trusting in Clarence that it would all sort out. He switched his focus to the next task of the day and got on with his work.

****

Simon could not believe his eyes! It was five o'clock, the bank was closed, and he was trawling the company intranet again, this time with more focus. A job had just come onto the intranet this very afternoon, the exact same role as his! He would be able to simply transfer, unless there were others at the same level that wanted it, in which case, it would have to be interview and competition, but that was extremely unlikely. Most people wanted to advance *into* the city, not out of it. Nor did they want to go down in salary. The role was slightly less money than he was on now, but it was out of the city so that was

220

to be expected. He wouldn't have the same outgoings once he'd moved out, so he figured that it would work out about the same in terms of balancing his personal finances. *And anyway,* he thought to himself, *money isn't everything!*

The job was in a place he'd never heard of but it turned out to be a town a few hours away. He had 'Googled' it immediately after he had seen the vacancy to find out where it was. It wasn't far according to the directional map; three hours it said, but that was far enough! He then looked up the town on a satellite map and saw that it was quite large. It was surrounded by countryside, small towns, and villages and was exactly what he wanted. It wasn't in a city and it wasn't near Nadia, so that made it just bloody perfect!

Simon didn't notice when he had looked at the Google maps to research the location of this new post, the proximity of the job to the small town he had left just twenty-four hours ago. That fact had escaped his attention, with a little help from Nathaniel, who was ensuring Simon's focus was on the job not on 'A' roads or directions. Nathaniel knew that in his drive to the pub on Saturday, Simon had been so wrapped up in his anger at Nadia that he hadn't noticed where he was driving. Simon had been equally oblivious to his surroundings on his Sunday drive home, filled with thoughts of the humiliation of the incident with Sarah. Not knowing what town he was in nor how to get home from the pub, he had used his sat-nav to guide him, like breadcrumbs back to base. He had

driven home following the instructions of the
seductive female automated voice, paying absolutely
no attention whatsoever to any road signs or
locations, his mind being fully occupied, playing over
and over again how he could have got it so wrong
with the fire girl!

Nathaniel made sure of course that Simon
didn't notice that the vacancy was in a town that was
within fifteen minutes of the humiliation of The
Crown incident. Simon, mind now fully focused on
the vacancy, really didn't care where it was, he had
already decided it was perfect and he applied
immediately, leaving the bank just minutes later
having placed his application for transfer into HR. He
went home happy for the first time in ages!

****

Sarah sat in her kitchen at the end of the long
day at the store thinking back to yesterday's
humiliation. *What an absolute plank,* she thought in
disgust as she pictured the scruffy man pouring a pint
of beer all over her head.
'Ah well now, child, I'm sorry to say that may
have been my fault,' admitted Clarabelle guiltily from
her left shoulder. She was on a mission to change
Sarah's opinion of Simon before it became too
ingrained and she hated him forever. It was
confession time and Clarabelle piped up earnestly,
'You see, child, I got a little over-excited in the pub
and my light glowed a little brighter than normal. I
believe that it was shining so brightly around your

head that it is very possible that the young man saw it and in doing so, he mistook my halo glowing for your hair on fire. There was a candle on the bar behind you and from where he was sitting, he may have seen the flame, seen the glow around you….' She trailed off, it sounded weak, but it was the truth and Clarabelle firmly believed that the truth will always serve you, no matter how far-fetched it may sound. She ploughed on, 'and you know how much hair spray and the like people use these days don't you! Makes people's heads very flammable. I truly believe he was trying to be a hero! I am sure that he thought your hair was alight and just reacted, trying to help, to save you.'

'Humph, yeah right! And how did he manage to see you?!' Sarah asked sceptically.

'Well, that might have been my fault too,' Clarabelle admitted. 'You see, when people are very tired, or stressed, or under the influence, they can sometimes see us, or feel us, or sense us; sometimes fully, sometimes just for a split second. My halo was very bright, positively glowing! I think he saw it, just for a second and seeing the candle behind you and with your hair so long and lovely, he must have put two and two together and made five.'

'Oh my God, you're right!' Sarah screeched, suddenly realising the mistake.

'Bloody hell, Clarabelle! That was all your fault? You caused that? Me being soaked, the humiliation, the nightmare? The poor man practically ran out of that pub! I was so awful to him, horrible! Oh shit!'

'Now, dear, it's not your fault. I was a little wet myself you know, soaked in fact, but we angels don't get mad, it's not in our make-up you see, but it's understandable that you did, so don't admonish yourself now, child. I am sorry for the mix up, truly I am.'

Sarah thought about the man for a bit longer. She had been horrible to him and if he had truly believed that she was on fire, he really had been trying to be a hero, bless him! But a scruffy hero and Sarah decided not to give him another second's thought.

****

The shop was busy the following day and Sarah and Tim were flat out. Clarabelle had been trying to talk to her all morning, kept butting in, trying to get Sarah's attention, but she just didn't have time for a chat right now, she was far too busy.

'Later!' she whispered for the tenth time to her shoulder, 'Not now!'

Three seconds later Sarah suddenly had an urge to pee, a strong urge. She ignored it, pushed it away, but it persisted, her bladder telling her 'now, or you're going to wet yourself!' She practically ran from the shop floor to the loo, annoyed at the interruption. Sitting on the toilet some minutes later, nothing was happening, her bladder was empty it seemed! Clarabelle suddenly appeared from nowhere, piping up,

'I thought we could do something with the flat upstairs, Sarah, what do you think?'

224

'Jesus H Christ! Is nothing bloody sacred?' Sarah squealed. 'I'm having a bloody pee for God's sake! Well, trying to! Bit of privacy wouldn't go amiss here!'

'Sorry, dear, but I really want to talk to you about the flat. It's most important! I really think we need to do something with that flat upstairs!' Clarabelle insisted.

'Oh for God's sake, fine! We'll sort it.' Sarah glared at her then. 'Did you do this? Make me think I needed the loo when I didn't, just to get my attention?' she accused. Clarabelle nodded solemnly.

'Bloody hell, Clarabelle, you're getting out of hand! I'll talk to you later, now please let me get back to work!' and Sarah stomped back to the shop floor in frustration and annoyance.

Some hours later, a calmer Sarah sat with Clarabelle in the empty flat above Mackenzie's, planning together how to decorate it and get it ready to let. Sarah had to admit the income would be good to have and it was just wasted space, but she also knew that it would be difficult to let as the entrance door to the flat came right into the back of the shop by the counter. It would have to be someone extremely trustworthy, someone with impeccable credentials as they would have to have a set of shop keys as well as the flat keys. Then there would be their visitors to consider too. They would all have access to the shop and its stock in the evenings and on Sundays, she realised, that was way too risky!

'Don't you worry about a thing, dear, I will make sure it's the right person. Someone honest, someone you can trust,' assured Clarabelle with glee. 'Just you leave that to me, I will send the right person, I promise! The shop will be in safe hands and you will not only have the income, but added security for the store with someone living over-head.' This was a good point, Sarah recognised, although the town was hardly known for its crime levels! The local paper's stories usually ran about noisy neighbours, or dogs fouling the pavements, or bins being knocked over! Her town was hardly 'The Bronx. It was a good idea to let the flat and Sarah agreed to start the makeover on the weekend.

'Perfect,' smiled Clarabelle, and popped off upstairs to have a word with the others.

****

It was Wednesday morning in the bank and an excited Mr. Godwin was beckoning Ben to come into his office.

'You are not going to believe this Ben, my boy! I can hardly believe it myself! We've had an application in for Charley's job, for *a transfer!* What a *coincidence!*' he raved.

'Coincidence my eye!' humphed Clarence, sitting on Ben's shoulder as usual.

Mr. Godwin was going on, all excited, 'It just came now in the internal email. What a surprise, what a surprise!' He was beaming from ear to ear. 'Look! Have a look at this!' He thrust the application he'd printed off at Ben, motioning him to sit down and read it. Ben looked at the application with surprise and delight.

226

'Transfer Request - Simon J Brown,' he read, 'aged thirty-nine, BA Hons. first class in business and marketing; went into banking aged twenty-one as a graduate, has worked in customer service, customer accounts, business accounts, and investment banking, was currently a senior business accounts manager in a major city branch. Wants to transfer, relocate for personal reasons.'

Ben was bemused. *Why would someone with his credentials and qualifications want to come here? Maybe he has family here?* Ben wondered. *Either way it didn't matter. They had an applicant and a more than suitable one at that!*

'He looks great! A bit over-qualified, Mr. Godwin, but if he's going to be happy here I'll be more than happy to have him!' Ben nodded. Turning to Clarence on his shoulder as subtly as he could, he whispered, 'Any good?'

Clarence whispered back, 'Oh yes!' He was grinning like a Cheshire cat.

Ben grinned back happily.

Mr. Godwin was excitedly saying, 'Well, I think we should get him in and have a chat! If all's well, we can agree a start date for the transfer in a few weeks' time. I'll have a word with his manager. It should be a month, but it's a large city branch that he's with, so it's possible his manager will negotiate on start dates. They certainly have a lot more staff than us and we are desperate. I'll certainly push all I can to make it happen as soon as possible. Now, bringing him in, how is Monday for you? I'll ask him to come down around two o'clock I think. He can have the afternoon with us, spend a bit of time so that

227

we can all see if it's going to fit, going to work. He can have a chat with me for an hour and then spend a few hours with you, all right, Ben?' Ben nodded, delighted at the prospect.

'Leave it with me and I'll come back to you later on in the day to confirm it all.'

Sitting back at his own desk a few minutes later Ben smiled happily. 'Amazing news!' he grinned, 'Just amazing!'

'It is indeed,' came the reply from Clarence on his shoulder. 'Told you I'd sort it didn't I, laddie?'

'You did, mate, you did yes. Ta very much!'

Ben felt his shoulder being patted reassuringly by a satisfied Clarence.

Clarence thought back over the last weeks' work. It had taken a huge amount of time and effort to coordinate the Charley, Sarah, Simon trilogy, but he had been able to work it. Once Nathaniel had called him with the news of Simon and Nadia's break up on Friday night, he had immediately called Charley's angel to release the blocks on him quitting. It had been hard work keeping those in place! They had been holding Charley back since March, three months now, to make sure it would all tie in with when Sarah was ready, as much as they possibly could. They had been going for six, but that had always been optimistic!

Clarence knew that Charley had decided the day he walked out the door at the bank back in March that he was never going back, but the angels had worked their magic and managed to persuade him to go on long term sick rather than quitting, to buy them time. Charley was no longer sick with stress and had been feeling guilty about it for a while now, guilty at milking the bank's sick policy of full pay when he'd been out playing football for the last six weeks and having a jolly time! Once he'd left the bank, his stress levels had actually sorted themselves out fairly quickly. Clarence had to admit it that it had been a bit of relief when Nathaniel had called with the news Friday night. All blocks were lifted on Charley immediately and the following morning, as Simon had been sleeping and then later packing to leave the city for the weekend, Charley had had a sudden urge (with a bit of help via Clarence) to go to the docs and get signed off permanently from the role, freeing him up from his guilt and freeing the job up for Simon. That had taken some work, more than most! Trying to get the receptionists at the doctor to co-operate and give Charley an emergency appointment for the Saturday morning had been the toughest task out of them all! Those reception staff were like gladiators in their protection of their doctors and the elusive Saturday morning appointments! Clarence had even had to call in reinforcements to break down their gladiator spirit! It had taken three angels and two Archangels to sort that one, but they had got there in the end - Charley had his appointment! The angel team had then worked their magic on the doctor and not only was the letter written there and then that day, stating Charley was not fit to return to work in the bank permanently, it had also been faxed rather than posted by the newly co-operating reception/gladiator staff! It had been sent straight

229

over to the banks HR department, all tying in with
Ben's chat with Mr. Godwin over being short staffed
for the Monday morning.

Really! Clarence thought. *These humans just
have no idea how much organisation and co-ordination go
into these things at all! Arranging circumstances so that
they all coincide, synchronise, match and balance were
extremely complicated, some more than most!* This
particular plan had involved Charley, Charley's
doctor, the reception staff, HR, the bank, Ben, Simon,
and Nadia, not to mention Roger, the children, and
many others on the fringes, all of whose actions had a
direct effect on the plans being mapped out by
'upstairs'. And then there had been each of those
human's respective angels to coordinate and
cooperate with as well; it had been a nightmare! The
inter-angel-cy meetings that had gone on in the last
few days had been intense! Clarence was still
bemused, nay amazed, that the humans 'downstairs'
never realised just what went on up here to make
these things happen, how everything was linked and
planned! He was always surprised how those
downstairs put all the angelic hard work down to
coincidence or *accidents!*

Clarence was just grateful that he'd had the
time to do it all. Having Ben as a ward was so easy
because he always followed his guidance. That
cooperation of Ben's gave Clarence free time, time
away from his job as his Guardian Angel and able to
take the lead to coordinate circumstances around Ben.
Everything and everyone was linked and Clarence
knew that all these particular links impacted on Ben

directly or indirectly, whether he was aware of it or not! He took some comfort in the knowledge that at least Ben was aware of the work that went on upstairs to some degree. *At least he isn't one of the millions who declare another 'wow, what a coincidence!' moment and at least says thank you!* Clarence thought. He knew that Ben didn't believe in coincidences. In any serendipity moment Ben recognised that there were forces at work and powerful forces at that! It was nice that Ben acknowledged it and was grateful for the help. Angels do so love gratitude!

'Always nice to have a thank you!' Clarence declared loudly, having a little rant for a moment. 'A thank you never goes amiss, not that we get many mind, but that's the way the cookie crumbles in this work! Little acknowledgment or praise! A thankless task indeed!' But Clarence didn't mind really, not in the least, loving his job with every atom of his being, from his halo to the tips of his feathers. Thinking about the progress so far, he was happy. *Yes, a good days work,* he thought and went off upstairs to tell Clarabelle the news.

****

Simon received the call just after lunch.

'Yes, he would be delighted to come for the afternoon on Monday. Yes, two o'clock would be fine. Yes, he will look forward to meeting Mr. Godwin too and to spending time with the Business Accounts Manager, Ben Smith, who would be his colleague if all was agreed.'

231

Simon was delighted. It was all coming together. His boss had agreed to release him for the day and was already in discussions with Mr. Godwin regarding possible start dates for the transfer. It was simply a matter of dotting the 'I's' and crossing the 'T's' now.

'Bloody marvellous!' Simon sighed with a smile. 'Another couple of weeks and I'll be gone! Can't wait!' He didn't care what the bank was like; it felt right and he was going if they'd have him, and he thought they probably would.

'Simon, my boy, time to make plans!' he said to himself out loud.

Chapter 16

Sarah was looking forward to Sunday. Ben was coming over to the shop for the day to help her paint the flat. He'd thought it was a great idea and knew the extra income and the added security would be great for Sarah, and he was more than happy to help. *His tiredness of last week's Father's Day seemed to have passed now,* Sarah thought. He had been much more cheerful and upbeat on the phone when she'd spoken to him earlier. Some changes were happening at work for him he had said and she was pleased for him.

She had already picked out the paint for the flat, having decided to decorate it with a simple neutral magnolia. It hadn't been let for years and needed a fair bit of work, but she had got on the case the day after Clarabelle had persuaded her to let it and she had already arranged for a carpenter to come and fit a new kitchen worktop tomorrow. The cupboards under the top were fine and a new work surface was all that was needed apart from the white goods, cooker, fridge-freezer, and washer-dryer. Sarah had already bought all three from the electrical store down the road; just basic ones, but they were new and clean. It was amazing how helpful people were now that she was a shop owner! She was surprised how easily discounts had been arranged and agreed. The shower was knackered so a new one was arranged and a local electrician was fitting it later that day. The tiles in the shower cubicle were fine, just a bit grubby.

On Clarabelle's advice, she had decided to let it out unfurnished, going along with the suggestion that most people had their own things and if they didn't, she would supply what they needed, within reason. White goods though, most people had built in these days, so Sarah had made the decision to buy those. Other than that, it just needed a lick of paint and a good clean, so that was the plan for the weekend. She would be able to advertise it in next week's paper and hopefully, the right person would apply. The flat consisted of two rooms; a large lounge and dining area with an open plan kitchen at one end and off that, a decent size double bedroom with an en-suite shower room. It would be perfect for a single person or a couple, and Sarah was looking forward to getting it done. In time, if the shop kept developing the way it had been over the last three months, she may give some thought to stop letting the flat and allow the shop to expand upstairs. Sarah couldn't believe that she'd had the shop nearly three months now; it had gone so quickly! *Expansion's for the future* she thought, but for now, it made sense to let it. Clarabelle was right. *Actually,* she thought slowly with a growing realisation, *she's always right! Every suggestion she's made has come off, every idea's turned out to be a good one! Bugger me she's converted me! How did she manage that?* Sarah smiled a happy smile, a contented smile, a smile that said, 'Yes, asking for help and accepting it is a bloody good idea!'

234

****

As the week went on the end of June turned into July. Mary, the Saturday girl was holding the fort in the shop while Sarah and Tim emptied the remaining boxes and junk from the flat upstairs. Sarah was pleased with it all. The electrician had been and a great new power shower had been installed in the en-suite bathroom, the carpenter had done a lovely job on the new worktop in the kitchen, and the flat was almost ready. Sarah let Tim get back to the shop after he'd helped her with the boxes and she set about cleaning it thoroughly. She washed the windows and paintwork, scrubbed the bathroom, steam cleaned the tiles and the carpets, and finally cleaned the kitchen. The new appliances were in place and connected. New locks had been fitted on the entrance door to the flat and she was ready to start the glossing on the woodwork. The tins of magnolia emulsion paint for the walls sat waiting with the brushes and rollers, new curtain tracks sat next to them waiting to be fitted by Ben after the decoration tomorrow, and new curtains were in their packets waiting to be hung. Sarah set about painting the window frames, doors, and skirting with the one coat white gloss and was exhausted but happy as she left for the day some hours later, feeling strangely excited and apprehensive, though she had no idea why!

Clarabelle sat serenely on her shoulder with a knowing smile. *Yes, all going nicely!* she thought to herself and popped off upstairs to check plans with Clarence and Nathaniel.

235

****

Sarah and Ben sat covered in paint munching fish and chips out of newspaper surveying their handiwork from the day. The flat was ready. The paint had gone on easily and with the two of them it had only taken a few hours. They were having their lunch sitting waiting for it to fully dry so that Ben could put the tracks up for Sarah to hang the curtains, their last task. The vacuum cleaner from the shop stood waiting for the inevitable mess that the drilling would cause and they were both pleased with the results.

'Be fair, Sis, it looks good. When you gonna advertise it?' Ben asked, with a mouthful of chips.

'The weekly paper comes out Friday so I'll talk to them tomorrow or Tuesday about an advert. I think Wednesday is the deadline, though I thought I may put a postcard in the shop window too, see what comes from that.' She paused, wishing for the third time that she'd remembered to bring the ketchup. Mackenzie's didn't sell any food and the local corner shop was closed so they'd had to manage. Wrapping the leftovers of their chips up, they tested the walls and yep, they were dry enough to crack on. After another hour later it was done. Going down the stairs to the shop together, Ben carrying the vacuum, Sarah hugged her brother, thanking him for his help and began to lock up.

236

'Oh by the way,' she asked, 'what's made you so happy this week? Did you sort it at work with your boss, then?'

Ben grinned, 'Better than that! Charley's resigned so we were able to advertise it properly and some bloke from another branch wants it. Means if he's ok, he can just transfer and we'll have a new Charley quick-sharp! I tell you, Sis, it's like a weight's been taken off my shoulders! Bloody great news, just great! I'm meeting him tomorrow as a matter of fact, this new bloke. He's coming down from the city for half a day to make sure he's happy, we're happy and if everyone is, then its game on!'

'Oh that's great Ben, I'm so pleased for you!' And Sarah was! Delighted in fact! If Ben was happy then she was happy. She gave him another hug and wished him luck for tomorrow. She was going home to her bath for a soak, followed by her sofa and a film for the evening and she couldn't wait! Thinking about the day as she put her seat belt on, then the week, then the last three months Sarah declared out loud suddenly, 'Bloody amazing the way it's all coming together so quick!' She felt so proud of herself and of her life that was moving forward so well. She was doing great, she knew that. She was stronger, more focused and definitely much happier! She realised that she felt like a different person these days, all since she'd let Clarabelle help, so different from just a few months before. *Blimey!* she suddenly thought, *if Rob tried to come back now, or anyone like Rob tried to come into my life I'd tell him where to go without a seconds hesitation!* She was happy on her own. For the first time in her life, she was really happy. She didn't miss having a boyfriend at all! It just wasn't on her radar! That was different! *She* was different!

'And you are, child,' piped up Clarabelle from her shoulder, 'you are!'

Chapter 17

It was Monday afternoon in the bank and Ben saw the tall man in a sharp suit and briefcase go into Mr. Godwin's office and the 'in a meeting' sign go across the door.

Bloody marvellous! He thought to himself. *Super smashing great!* He grinned, hoping that he wouldn't have to add later, *let's have a look at what you could-a-won!* Clarence had said it would be fine though and that he didn't have anything to worry about so that was great. He was looking forward to meeting this Simon chap and getting to know him; it had been quite lonely working on his own these past three months and he'd missed the banter that he and Charley had shared in their joint office. *Be good to have someone again,* Ben thought happily. He looked up from his accounts as Mr. Godwin came in with Simon some time later noting that Mr. Godwin was beaming, so the meeting had clearly gone well. He smiled at Simon, standing up he put his outstretched hand to him to shake his hand enthusiastically, welcoming him to his office. Ben decided immediately that he liked Simon. He had a warm open friendly face and he noticed that Simon's smile reached his eyes too, always a good sign. So many people smiled, but it never reached their eyes, this Simon's smile did! Ben looked up at him to get eye contact. He was ridiculously tall, dwarfing Ben's six foot frame and stood rather like a giant in the small office, a smiling giant! *God, he must be about 6'5" or*

239

even 6'6", Ben thought, although he didn't ask, it seemed rude to, especially as an opening line to a newcomer.

'Hi, Simon, good to meet you,' he said instead, 'How are you finding it so far? Bit different from the big city bank you're in now, aye?'

Simon smiled easily. 'It's a breath of fresh air, mate! Just perfect!' Simon replied and Ben could see that he meant it.

'I'll leave you to it then, gentlemen,' Mr. Godwin said, smiling happily at the occurrence that was this seemingly perfect applicant and the miraculous luck of this transfer request. 'I'll see you back in my office, Simon, around four thirty pm? We can discuss your thoughts then and firm everything up then, alright?'

'Yes, Mr. Godwin, I'll look forward to it,' Simon replied and set about getting to know Ben, the office, the clients, the work, the workload, and the expectations of the manager, Mr. Godwin, for the rest of the afternoon. They discussed the other staff in the bank one by one; the strengths and weaknesses of each, the branch and the town, and by the end of the afternoon he had learned what he needed to know. Simon didn't have a doubt in his head and neither did Ben.

'So do you have family here then, Simon? Is that why you want to move?' Ben enquired, trying not to pry, but still surprised that Simon would want to move from the city to this much smaller place.

'Nope, don't know a soul, mate!' Simon smilingly replied.

'Oh?' Ben was even more surprised. 'So what made you want to come here? Hope you don't mind me asking?'

'I've just had enough of the city, Ben. Fancy a change of scene, quieter pace, bit of green, you know?'

Ben did know. He didn't know how anyone could live in the city with its concrete jungle and lack of space, light or green. *Each to their own though, aye!* He thought to himself.

'Things have just ended with the girl I've been seeing too, so it felt like the right time to make the break,' Simon said, finding himself opening up to Ben, thinking how easy he was to talk to and that he just had an easiness about him. Simon decided that he liked him very much. *Maybe we'll even be mates?* He thought to himself. While he was thinking that thought Ben was now saying,

'I'll have to show you around, Simon, take you out and about, help you get your bearings and introduce you to the locals. They're a nice bunch; I think you'll like them. There's quite a lot going on for a town, depending what you're into.'

'That sounds great, Ben. Thanks, I'd like that.'

'What about living arrangements then, Simon? Where you gonna live, mate? You presumably won't be commuting from the city!' Ben laughingly said.

'God, no! I'll start looking for a flat as soon as I get home tonight. Start trawling the internet for places to rent round here. Something will come up, I'm sure. If it doesn't, I'll just have to go into a B&B for now till it does!'

241

'Oh?' Ben said, with an idea forming in his head. 'What kind of place are you looking for?' He looked at Clarence then who was smiling and nodding emphatically.

'Aye, laddie, do the boy a favour, he'd be perfect for the flat and it'd be helping him ooot no end,' Clarence beamed.

'Oh, anything really, it's only for now. I've got my own pad in the city and once that's sold I'll buy something down here. That'll take a few months I guess, so it doesn't really matter what I have here, it'll only be a stopgap. Why, do you know of anything?'

'I do indeed!' Ben grinned, 'My sister's literally just finished doing up a flat she owns, got it ready to rent out. She's going to be advertising it this week. I can have a word if you want me to? Give her a ring?'

'Oh mate, that would be great, cheers. I don't suppose there's any chance I could see it today, is there? I know it's short notice, but it'd be doing me a massive favour. Saves me having to come back out from the city again if we could do it today, while I'm here,' Simon asked, wondering if he was pushing his luck with Ben, knowing him for only a few hours and asking favours so soon. But Ben was nodding, smiling as he replied, 'I'm sure we could, probably be fine to go and have a look at it today before you go back to the city to see if it's what you want.'

'Perfect!' Simon was chuffed! 'What kind of flat is it? Where is it? Any parking?'

Ben filled him in on the details explaining it was a one bedroom flat over a shop in a smaller town about fifteen minutes away. Because it was over a

242

shop, it would be quiet in the evenings and Sunday's since the shop was closed, and as he'd be at work during the day the noise and the activity from the shop in the day wouldn't be an issue. There was parking around the back. It was unfurnished, but had white goods, carpets, and curtains and was ready now.

'It would be perfect for you to have it actually 'cos the one issue with it is that the entrance to the flat is actually within the shop itself, at the back, so it's really important that she gets someone in that she can trust. Couldn't get better credentials than you now, could she!'

'Sounds ideal!' Simon said excitedly.

'And I guess you won't be having many visitors either, being from the city? She'll like that too. Shall I ring her then?'

Simon nodded enthusiastically.

Ten minutes later, it was all arranged. Ben would be taking Simon round after work to meet Sarah and have a look at the flat. She'd agreed with Ben that this new bank colleague sounded perfect as a tenant! He was fully checked and legit of course. The bank would have done all the checks they needed and wouldn't be employing him if he had been dodgy and no visitors had been perfect too. Everyone was happy!

Five o'clock came quickly and the meeting with Mr. Godwin had been just as they all thought, just to confirm the transfer. They agreed a start date in two weeks' time that Simon's boss had approved in

243

an earlier phone call with Mr. Godwin. The necessary paperwork would be sent tomorrow to HR who would be arranging that side of it and Mr. Godwin looked forward to seeing Simon again in a fortnight. With a shake of hands, Ben and Simon left the bank to head off together to Sarah's flat.

Ben had suggested that they both jump into his car and go together to see the flat, that way he was sure that they would arrive at the same time and then he could do the introductions properly. It also ensured that Simon wouldn't get lost on the way as it was always difficult to follow another car and keep together, especially getting out of the town in rush hour traffic. The plan was that after they had seen the flat he would return Simon back to his own car in the town car park. Ben lived in Redville so had to return there anyway, so it wasn't putting him out, he had assured a grateful Simon. They walked together to the town car park where both cars were parked and Ben watched with awe as Simon walked to a flash and fab Jaguar XKR, clicked the remote which popped the boot automatically, and dumped his briefcase into it.

'No way! Is that yours? You lucky bastard! Nice wheels, man!' Ben envied, turning increasingly green with every second. 'I'd love a two-seater sports, trade it in for my people carrier any day!'

Simon smiled. His car often had this effect on family men, men who'd love the rush of the drive that the jag gave, not to mention the low chassis style of the sports model, family men who'd given up their sporty boy's toys and engine torque for baby seats and buggies. Ben reluctantly pulled his attention away from Simon's wheels and headed with him

towards his own car, wondering briefly and
hopefully if they couldn't go in Simon's car instead.
He knew that he'd have to direct the non-local Simon
all the way to the flat and also knew that Simon had a
long drive back to the city later. Tempting as it was to
ask, Ben kept his mouth shut and opened his own car
door regretfully.

Ben, as usual, took the short cuts to the small
town eight miles away that Sarah lived in, going
through all the quieter back roads to avoid the traffic.
It took them fifteen minutes to get out of the town
and in another fifteen minutes, they pulled up at the
rear of the store. They'd chatted all the way, getting to
know each other more with each passing mile.
    'Much quicker this way, mate, although it
does mean you won't get to see the high street or
much of the town this way 'cos this road comes in the
back, not that it's that big anyway! It's quite a small
town compared to where we are at the bank,' Ben
went on, 'but if you want the flat, we could go and
have a wander round for half an hour after, if you
like? There's a decent pub just up the road from the
flat. Give you a chance to get your bearings.'
    'Sounds great, Ben. Yeh, thanks, be good to
have a drink and a break before I start the drive back,
as long as you have time? Did you say you were
married? Won't your wife be wanting you back?'
Simon asked.
    'Oh, Gina's fine, I had a word earlier. Told her
I was bringing you out here to see Sarah's flat. She'll
be cool with it, mate, no worries!'

245

Simon couldn't believe how well it was coming together. It was all so perfect! This flat he was going to see sounded great and he preferred to be out of the larger town if he was honest. He wanted a quieter place with more of a community feel and a small town would give him that. *Much easier to make friends and fit into a small place,* he thought. *A bit like that town I was in last weekend. They were really nice, friendly, apart from 'Fire Girl,' of course! Yes, something like that town would be great!* He decided.

He followed Ben to the rear door of the store and as they waited for someone to answer the bell, Simon looked up at the windows of the flat above. It seemed a decent size. The door suddenly opened and a lanky lad with mad multi-coloured hair stood there smiling at Ben,

'Hiya, mate, come on in. She's just in the office doing the cashing up. She won't be a minute. We just closed up for the day. You know how she likes to get the till out quick and sort it.'

'I do indeed, Tim,' Ben smiled. 'I taught her that! Safety, you know!'

The two men followed Tim into the store and waited by the counter for Sarah to arrive.

'Sarah, they're here!' Tim yelled into the abyss of the back office. 'Right oh, I'm off. Catch ya laters!' and Tim disappeared back out the door they'd just come in.

A few minutes later, Sarah appeared. She walked up to Ben, hugged him and then turned to see Simon standing behind him. It took a full ten seconds for the penny to slowly slide into place as she looked at him, wondering where she'd seen him before. He looked

246

completely different, almost a different person! It
was only the increasingly reddening face of Simon
that finally gave it away, coupled with his slowly
reversing body towards the exit that the penny finally
dropped into place.

'Oh my God!' she squealed. 'It's YOU!'

Simon could not believe his eyes! It was 'Fire
Girl', standing there in front of him with a look of
shock horror on her equally reddening face.

'You two know each other!' Ben exclaimed.
'How the f....!'

Simon, having backed almost to the door by
now and knowing there was no escape, continued to
redden to an almost equal level of Fire Girl. Both their
mouths were open, their jaws having dropped at
exactly the same moment and both now stood looking
at each other in an embarrassed and shocked silence.

'I, um, I ruined your sister's day last Sunday,'
Simon admitted, finally breaking the silence. He
looked down at his shoes suddenly as he always did
when he was lost for words.
Sarah could have died! Oh my God, this was not
happening! This was the man she had been so rude
to, so awful too, because of bloody Clarabelle!

'Just tell him you're sorry,' piped up
Clarabelle, 'he'll understand, trust me.'

Sarah didn't think twice, she just blurted out
'I'm so sorry!' at exactly the same time that Simon
said exactly the same.

'No, I'm sorry'
'No, I'm sorry!'
'No, I'm the one who should be sorry!'
'No, me!'

247

'Alright, alright!' Ben yelled, jumping in to sort the mutual 'sorries'! 'We've established that you're both sorry. Good! Now what exactly are you both sorry for and how the hell do you two know each other?'

Both Simon and Sarah jumped in with their explanations at the same time, both talking over each other and Ben couldn't understand either of them.

'RIGHT! STOP!' he yelled. He glared at them both like a scolding parent to naughty children. 'Right, Simon, you first.' He looked at Simon accusingly, waiting for the explanation of these increasingly strange events.

Simon began, 'Well, I went away for the weekend last weekend, ended up in this town, don't know how, didn't know it was here, this town, in the pub down the road, The Crown, yeah?' Ben nodded, amazed that Simon knew The Crown.

'Go on,' Ben nodded, waiting to hear the rest of this bizarre story.

'Your sister was in there and I thought her hair was on fire. So…' Simon looked at his shoes and then back to Ben, 'so… I poured a pint of beer over her head to put her out!'

'Oh my God! You did WHAT?!' Ben looked at Simon's guilty face and promptly burst into uncontrollable hysterics!

'A pint of beer all over my sis? You poured a pint of beer over my sis? And you're still alive!? Oh wow! I wish I'd been there to see that!' Ben doubled up with more hysterics, holding his stomach now he was laughing so hard.

248

'It wasn't that funny, Ben!' Sarah admonished.
Ben was still roaring with belly aching laughter.

'It was really embarrassing! And I was really
mad! And I was horrible to him. Really horrible! I
thought he was a total nutter! Well, you would,
wouldn't you? Someone pouring a pint over you out
of the blue when you're just standing there minding
your own business!'

'You would, indeed!' Ben replied, between
gulps of laughter.

'So what actually happened?'

Sarah looked at the floor. She couldn't
possibly tell Ben the truth, or Simon of course; that
she knew it was Clarabelle's fault and not Simon's.

'It was an easy mistake to make,' she said. Ben
stopped laughing mid roar, both men looking at her
in surprise, raising their eyebrows sceptically at her.
'Well, it was!' she defended, 'he was only trying to
help and I was very ungrateful! And I was very rude!'
Simon was gobsmacked! 'And I'm very sorry that I
was so horrible to you.' She turned to look Simon in
the eye now, so that he would feel the depths and the
honest truth of her apology. She was mortified.
Bloody Clarabelle! God, his eyes were very blue, she
noticed suddenly, and he had a really smart suit on!
He looked so different, a nice different! And he was *so*
tall!! Really quite gorgeous as a matter of fact, with
his fair hair flopping over his eyes like that! *Probably a
player, twit, or tosspot though, and I don't have time for
men or dating, even if I wanted to - which I don't! And he's
going to be my tenant so that puts that out of the question
anyway!*

249

'So, shall we go and see this flat then?' Sarah asked the two bewildered men and started walking towards the door of the flat with purpose. Simon was in shock! She had forgiven him, just like that! It didn't make sense at all!

Clarabelle, Clarence, and Nat all grinned, perched on the shop counter watching the mens' confusion.

Wonder why she's changed her mind? Simon wondered silently to himself. Ben was thinking along similar lines. He couldn't imagine why Sarah was being so forgiving or so apologetic! Simon was the one who had poured a pint over her head not the other way around! *Why was she apologising?* He wondered. Ah well, he never would figure out the mind of a woman, not even his sister, but as long as these two were cool, it didn't matter. *Bloody funny though*, Ben thought with a grin. *Bloody funny!*

Simon followed Sarah up the stairs to the flat and couldn't help but notice her bum as she wiggled up each stair in tight jeans. *Nice!* He thought with admiration. She had gorgeous eyes too he'd noticed. *Pretty girl, very pretty girl!*

Now, Simon, my boy, he said to himself in his head, *she's going to be your landlady so no funny business!* and he pulled his attention reluctantly away from her bum to the flat that they were now walking into. It was a nice flat, he decided; clean, tidy, newly decorated, and had all the space that he needed. He had a huge bed and a long sofa back in the city,

250

bought when he had moved in to his apartment seven years before; they would fit here just great! Both had been expensive purchases and he didn't want to leave them behind. He especially loved his bed! Simon surveyed the space again and declared to the siblings that it was great and that it would do nicely, and yes, thank you, he'd like to take it.

All three then moved up the road to the pub to hash out the details over a pie and a pint. The landlord Peter greeted Simon like a long lost friend and dismissed his apology with a wave.

'It's already forgotten, don't worry,' he'd smiled as he served him the round of drinks and ordered the pies from the kitchen. His eyebrows raised with surprise when he'd seen who Simon was with though!

'Are you going to drink this one, mate, or shall I just pour it over her head for you?' he grinned, nodding towards Sarah. Simon laughed awkwardly and thought back to that afternoon and the disastrous pint throwing affair. He'd telephoned Peter at the Crown when he'd got in that night and had, at the time, thought that he would never see him again. And here he was, back in the Crown with Peter serving him and chatting away and joking with him like he'd known him forever. Pete was relieved to see that they'd settled their differences, whatever they were, wondering what had caused it in the first place, but he was also wise enough to know when to keep his nose out. He watched the three with interest, knowing he'd find out soon enough. This was a small town after all!

251

Simon brought the pies and drinks back to the table and informed Sarah between munches that he would be bringing his own furniture and no, he didn't need her to provide anything other than a wardrobe if possible, as the ones he had in his apartment were built in. They discussed the security of the shop as Sarah explained that he'd need to use the back entrance and always make sure he had double locked the main door of the shop for safety. She had no doubt that Simon would be responsible and her shop would be in safe hands, as would the flat. They agreed a move in day of the Saturday before he started at the bank, just under two weeks' time. He would drive down with a van in the day, he said, and probably stay in the pub again for that night. He'd be there by the time the store closed and move in that evening if it was ok with her. Sarah had nodded happily. Ben offered to give him a hand if he needed it, but Simon assured him that he had a mate or two who would help and he'd need one to drive the van down and back anyway as he'd be driving his own car.

A few smiles later and a happy Simon handed over a cheque for the deposit to his new landlady and the deal was done! Finishing up their pints the two men prepared to leave. Simon had a long drive ahead, he said, and Gina was waiting for Ben to serve up dinner so they needed to be making a move. Thanking her again for the flat and the forgiveness, which he still couldn't figure out, Simon left his new landlady finishing her drink, waved to Peter, and walked out of The Crown with Ben.

Sarah sat in shock, finally able to process the events in the store now that Simon had gone.

'Un-bloody-believable!' she announced to the empty chair next to her where Simon had been sat a few minutes before. 'Just bloody unbelievable!'

'Precisely, child!' piped up Clarabelle with a huge delighted grin on her face.

'Precisely!'

Chapter 18

It had been a difficult week for Sarah. Every Tom, Dick, and Harry seemed to be taking the piss lately and she'd spent most of the week in confrontations of one sort or another. Two of the suppliers had sent her the wrong stock and tried to get away with it, then another had left off the discount previously agreed and then tried to backtrack on it. She'd had problems with the phone people and even the window cleaner had taken advantage. Well tried to, she admitted to herself, but she had stood up to them all, not backed down from any of the issues and she knew she had handled each situation with dignity and assertiveness. She had won every battle, each time growing in confidence as she had stood up to be counted. Sarah decided she was now a force to be reckoned with!

'Humph, take the mick out of me would they? I don't *think* so!' she had declared more than once that week. She really didn't know what was going on with all this shit! It was like the world had suddenly gone mad, everyone wanting an argument! *Must be the heat,* she thought. It was stifling hot at the moment, the country being in a heat wave that had lasted at least three days now! That was more than the average Brit could cope with!

'Bloody people thinking they can rip *me* off! I don't *think* so!' she said again, ranting away to herself. She had stood up to the suppliers and sent the stuff

254

back that had wrongly been delivered and made sure it had been at their cost! She had dealt with the phone people in the best way she knew how, by treating them like naughty school children, *it's the only thing that works with telecom people!* They'd been out the same day to fix the phone after she'd sorted *them* out! She'd told the window cleaner to wash the windows again and no, she wasn't going to pay him until they were smudge free!

No one's gonna take the piss out of me, mate! she'd said to herself. *No more Miss Nice Girl here!*

Sarah knew she'd always been a bit of a push over, but she was becoming increasingly assertive with her new growing business and her new growing confidence.

'Precisely!' piped up Clarabelle, 'Precisely!'

'Am I turning into a prize bitch though, Clar?' Sarah asked, a little concerned at this new attitude that had been building gradually over the last few months.

'Not at all, dear, not at all!' Clarabelle smilingly said. 'Self-assertion is a good thing, it's all about boundaries, as long as you handle the situation with respect, of course. Being firm with someone and standing your ground does not harm you or others, dear. You're learning to respect yourself more that's all. Don't you worry about a thing. It's all just perfect!'

'Yay! All I've got to do now is stand up to my mother and I'll have conquered the world!' Sarah jokingly replied.

'When you're ready, dear, when you're ready,' Clarabelle chirped.

'I think I might be actually!' she stated matter-of-factly, surprising herself with the admission. 'I've had enough practice recently that's for sure! Maybe it's time for a little chat! Mmmm,' she hesitated with some thought. 'I'll have to have a think about that one. Do I really want to go back into the witch's cavern and go *voluntarily!* Bloody hell, I must be going potty!' But the words rang with some truth in Sarah's ears and she knew it was time to face that situation. She hadn't spoken to her mother since Mother's Day, back in the middle of March. It was now July for God's sake! She'd avoided her like the plague, put her out of her life and her mind while she'd been building a new one of both!

Ben, of course, rang her mother every week, every Sunday without fail, doing the dutiful son thing. Sarah never had and probably never would. She knew she'd never have what Ben had with her mother, but if she could back down a bit on the bitching maybe her mother could too. Maybe it was possible that they could build some bridges, at least be able to have a sort of relationship where she rang her once a month if not once a week like Ben. It would be a start.

'Yes, it's time. I'm going to ring her and arrange to go and see her tomorrow night.'

That would be Saturday and if it all went to pot, which it probably would, at least Sarah could go and drown her sorrows after and not worry about the hangover Sunday.

'I thought you didn't drink except to celebrate, my dear?' enquired Clarabelle quietly in Sarah's ear.

256

'Well, it would be a celebration wouldn't it?!'
Sarah retorted. 'If mother throws me out when I tell
her to stop giving me shit and it ends our so called
relationship then what the hell have I lost? Not
exactly bosom buddies are we? More like David and
Goliath!' she laughed.
Thinking a bit more sombrely, she realised that at
least she would have put some boundaries down with
her mother, boundaries that were sorely needed and
if her mother didn't accept them, well then, that was
her loss. She wasn't going to put up with the abuse
any more. *Yes, abuse,* she thought to herself, *let's call it
by its rightful name! She doesn't bitch at me or tease me.
Her behaviour to me is nothing short of abuse and I'm
simply not having it anymore! I know why she does it, but
that doesn't make it right and it certainly doesn't make it
acceptable.*
Sarah marched purposefully into her office at the
back of the shop and dialled her mother's number.

'No time like the present!' she said to herself,
mobile in hand where she'd had to look it up from
before dialling it on the office phone. Ben probably
knew it off by heart, but she certainly didn't! It would
have been easier to have simply dialled it from her
mobile, but the signal was never good at the back of
the shop and she didn't want any crackles. She
wouldn't be sure if it was her mother's cackle or the
phone! 'Hubble bubble, toil and trouble,' she
mouthed silently, imagining her mother sitting
stirring a cauldron with her broomstick. 'Eye of toad
and thingy of newt,' said Sarah, not quite
remembering the line from Shakespeare's Macbeth, or
was it another play? She couldn't recall.

257

'Now, Sarah, that was unkind!' she admonished herself, but she couldn't help grinning at the thought, picturing her mother in a witches hat and cape, black cat on lap, fag in hand, of course, cackling away to herself from her latest evil deed!

Margaret answered the phone with a wary, 'Hello? Who is this please?' so unused to receiving calls was she that she was in some shock at the thought of someone actually calling her!

'Hello, Mum, it's Sarah. How are you?'

'Sarah? Sarah? I don't know a Sarah; you must have the wrong number.'

Margaret was just about to put down the phone when Sarah shouted, 'Your daughter, Sarah, your *daughter*'

Bloody hell! Sarah thought, *I'm so far off her radar that she's actually forgotten I exist!*

'Oh *that* Sarah!' She paused, 'What do you want?' Margaret asked coldly.

'I thought I'd pop in and see you tomorrow night, Mum, have a bit of a chat, if that's alright with you?' Sarah couldn't believe the words that were coming out of her mouth! She was being nice to her mum!

'Why?' Margaret replied, even more warily now. 'What do you want?' The cold tone in Margaret's voice was clear and obvious, but Sarah managed not to react to it, just.

'I don't want anything, Mum, just a chat. I'll be round about seven o'clock, ok?'

'I suppose so, if you must,' and with that, Margaret hung up.

Sarah looked at the phone in her hand, which she noticed regretfully was shaking a bit. She was trembling, but she knew she'd done well. She'd managed to do it! She'd managed to volunteer to go to her mother's house for the first time in nineteen years! Every visit since she'd left home she'd had to be dragged to, almost kicking and screaming and only ever because of some family event, never 'just for a chat'! Ok, so the hand was a bit shaky! Ok, so she'd got a bit rattled, but all in all, at least she hadn't wanted to kill her, not even once in their whole three minute conversation! That was progress! She looked at Clarabelle who was positively glowing!

'What's going on with you?' she enquired, 'You're all glowy!'

'Just pleased for you, dear, just pleased!' But Clarabelle wasn't pleased. She was absolutely totally completely one hundred percent delighted!

'Yipppeeeeeee!' she screeched, throwing her arms in the air and doing a dance on Sarah's shoulder.

'What on *earth* are you doing?!' Sarah asked in shock. 'A bit of an overreaction here, don't you think? I mean, I know you're pleased and all, happy for me that I'm gonna sort my mother out at last, but calm down, aye, Clarabelle! You're gonna punch holes in my shoulder at this rate the way you're bouncing up and down on it like a demented rabbit!'

'Sorry, dear, sorry. Must dash off for a bit, see you later.' Clarabelle was gone!

What is the matter with her? Sarah wondered as she walked back to the shop floor. Tim was calling her about a customer who wanted some advice

259

matching a lamp with a throw. She would think about tomorrow's meeting with the witch later. 'No, not witch! *Mother!*' she corrected herself as she walked behind the counter. They'd never build any bridges with that attitude!

****

Clarabelle had flown upstairs in a huge rush so excited was she at the prospect of calling in her 'Mighty AA Micky'!

'*Yours*, aye?' smiled Clarence, suddenly by her side.

'Since when did Archangel Michael become *yours* exactly?! And since when was he called 'Micky'!'

'Oh, um, oh, I,' Clarabelle was embarrassed, being caught out so by her brother. Now she knew he'd tease her mercilessly. Angel brothers were no different to human brothers; they just had to tease, it was in the genes, the atoms, and in the feathers!

Clarence was laughing at her now.

'So, my little sister! We have a little crush, do we? How funny!' and Clarence pushed her playfully. She pushed him back and before they knew it they were wrestling around and promptly fell off the cloud they had been on!

'Ok, ok, enough teasing, I surrender!' Clarence giggled, flying back up to the cloud and retaking his seat. 'Let's be serious now.' His face became stern and Clarabelle sighed with relief.

'She's ready then, your Sarah? Ready for the last battle, the battle with MFH?!'

260

'Clarence!' Clarabelle admonished with horror, 'You can't call her that!'

Clarence grinned. 'Yes, I know we're not meant to, but you have to admit, Clar, it is funny! MFH! Some of those down there are really quite comical, you know.'

Clarabelle glared at him.

'Ok, ok. I'll behave! You've done well by the way, Clar, arranging all those problems for Sarah this week, helping her grow a backbone at last. I was particularly impressed with the phone problem handling, very good, very good indeed. Right then, I'll go and put the call in for Archangel Michael to attend. When do you want him? Tomorrow evening? Seven-ish?'

'No, no!' she screeched in horror. 'Far too late! Sarah will be a nervous wreck by then! We'll need him *much* earlier than that! At least all day I would have thought!'

'Mmmm, and that's nothing to do with you wanting to spend the whole day with him then?' Clarence grinned knowingly at his sister.

'Not at all!' she replied in horror. '*As if* I'd think of doing such a thing! Wasting his time like that! Of *course* I wouldn't do that! It's absolutely *essential* that he be there all day! Essential!'

Seeing that Clarabelle truly believed that, but also knowing it was not 'essential' at all, Clarence went off to put the call in to the Higher Realms for assistance.

'All day, my eye! I don't *think* so! I think we'll go for lunchtime, even early evening,' he decided. 'That'll be plenty. I'm not having my sister wasting

261

senior management's time, however much she's managed to convince herself otherwise, I know the truth! And besides, Sarah's much tougher these days, just look at the way she's handled all those confrontations that Clarabelle organised! I'm not sure she even needs AA Michaels help at all! Probably better to ask for AA Gabriel instead! He's in charge of communication and this meeting with her mother is after all, all about her speaking her truth!' Clarence had to admit that Gabriel wasn't quite the warrior that Michael was, but his sister would just have to fly with it!

****

The following morning saw Clarabelle preening her feathers, fluffing up her light and cleaning her halo till it shone. She was incredibly excited and was having trouble focusing on Sarah's needs at all today!

'Now focus, Clarabelle!' she said to herself, 'this is a big day for Sarah, huge!'

The day dragged on and on for both Sarah and for Clarabelle! Sarah was already beginning to stress about what she would say to her mother later and Clarabelle had spent the entire day looking over her shoulder, above her, below her and all around her, keeping a look out for her mighty AA Micky, but there was sadly no sign of him! Sarah locked up at the end of the day with a sigh.

'Here we go then, Clar. Time to go home and plan the defence or assault at The Battle of Britain, Gallipolis, Waterloo, Hastings, or whatever!'

The pair of them sat in the car in silence the entire five minute drive home, neither of them saying anything! Sarah was a little surprised that Clarabelle wasn't coming out with her usual pearls of wisdom but she was glad of the peace. It gave her time to think until they pulled up at the house.

Sarah walked into her house with heavy steps, dreading the ordeal that would come later, but knowing with a determination that it was necessary. Making herself a cup of tea and a sandwich, only then to discover that she couldn't eat or drink a thing, Sarah sat in her chair in the living room and pondered what to say to her mother, how to build these bridges.

How much should I tell her? Nothing I guess, she thought to herself. *She'll only be mad that I've found out about her secret past and fair enough too I suppose.* She was beginning to feel a little lost, a little scared, bloody terrified actually, when all of a sudden she felt hot, really hot! A tremendous heat had suddenly come into the room. She looked at the fire to see if it had somehow switched itself on. Nope! Was the window open, she wondered, letting in the heat wave from outside? Nope! It wasn't that hot out there now anyway, the day had cooled considerably since the high temperatures they'd had earlier in the week. Sarah wondered what the heat was, pondering for a moment if she was too young at thirty seven to have a hot flush!

263

'Oh my, oh my!' exclaimed Clarabelle from her shoulder. 'Oh my!'

'What?' Sarah shook her head at Clarabelle. 'What are you 'oh my-ing' about now?'

Clarabelle gazed adoringly in front of her. In the centre of the room stood Archangels Michael and Gabriel, radiating out light and power around them like the core of a nuclear reactor! The sudden heat in the room was coming from them, their very presence creating an energy that pulsated all around them. Clarabelle knew that Sarah couldn't see them. They never appeared to humans, well, hardly ever; their power being so strong that they knew it would scare the average person to death! But they were here! At last!

'You called, my dear?' AA Mickey said to her in a beautifully soft voice. Clarabelle almost passed out with delight.

'Yes, thank you,' she stammered, 'thank you for being here. She needs some help, my Sarah. She needs some strength, some confidence, it's been fading all day, all day!'

Michael smiled at Clarabelle and then she swore she saw him *wink* at her! No, she must be dreaming! He was going towards Sarah, standing over her he pointed his sword directly into her stomach and began to shine the light that now poured out of its tip. Gabriel was also standing over her, pouring power and light from his hands into her heart and her throat.

The anxiety was a solid, twisted ball in Sarah's stomach, a grenade of torturous power, a volcano full of competing emotions, each and every one of them

264

vying for position wrestling with each other in their desire to escape and explode inside her. Anxiety, dread, fear, each and every one of them now suddenly melted away like the morning mist on a sunny day under the power of Michael's sword of light, creating an intense heat in her belly. Her neck felt like it was on fire, burning away the lump that had been gathering in her throat and Sarah began to cough uncontrollably. Gabriel was working hard on Sarah's throat helping her communicate effectively, assertively, making her ready to say what she wanted and needed to say and then they were gone! Just like that!

As they disappeared Clarabelle felt just gutted! Two minutes? She'd been so looking forward to spending the whole day! Her disappointment was crushing and devastating, but even more than that! For the first time in her entire existence, Clarabelle wanted to cry!

Clarence! Clarabelle thought. *I bet he only asked them to pop in for a minute instead of the whole day like I asked!* Immediately her devastation was replaced by frustration, annoyance, and even a little anger, all new feelings for Clarabelle who really didn't know how to manage any of them at all!

'Clarence! The little demon! I'll de-feather him! I'll pluck them out one by one! I'll smash his halo! I'll rip his wings off! I'll, I'll, Oh! Brothers!' But now she had to focus on Sarah, who was looking all hot and flushed.

'I must have dozed off for a minute,' Sarah was saying, 'I swear I saw a bright light in the middle of the room and then I felt all this heat in my tummy and chest and my throat feels weird too!'

'Oh it's probably because you haven't eaten, child. You need to keep your strength up, you know. Hard task ahead you have, you'll need your strength.

'Yeh, you're right, I'm starving actually!' Sarah realised, forgetting all about the funny heat and with a bit of help from Clarabelle who had discreetly redirected her attention to her belly and made it suddenly rumble. She began munching hungrily on the sandwiches she'd made herself when she'd first come in. They were still sitting there, beginning to curl at the edges, half-baked from the intense heat of a few minutes earlier. Her cuppa was still warm and she drank it quickly. She was feeling heaps better, much stronger, focused, and ready. She had absolutely no idea why!

'Right! Let's get on with it! Come on, Clar.' And a newly confident and stronger Sarah marched purposefully out of the house to the car.

****

She sat in her little car outside Margaret's house thirty minutes later and stared at the door. She focused for a minute on the session she'd had with Clarabelle about her mother's past and allowed compassion to surface.

'Right oh, let's go!'

Sarah walked into the house and through to the kitchen where Margaret was sitting. She didn't get up.

266

'Hello, Sarah. And to what do I owe this honour?' she sarcastically remarked. Sarah ignored both the sarcasm and the attitude.

'Hello, Mum, how are you?'

'Like you care! I'm fine, thank you, apart from my back and my knees, of course, and my sinuses not to mention my bowels and my migraines, and my chest is all congested, but I'll live!' She paused and looked at Sarah warily.

'What do you want, Sarah? You never come and see me, you never ring, so why are you here? I'm not stupid, you know!' Margaret stared at her daughter coldly, accusingly.

'I've been doing a lot of thinking, Mum. I know we've never got on, never been close,'

'That's the understatement of the century!' Margaret sniped.

'Thing is, Mum, I think it's just that we don't understand each other, don't know each other, not at all. I'd like to try and build some bridges, get to know you a bit, make a bit more effort, come round a bit more, ring more often. Try to be a better daughter. What do you think?' Sarah asked hopefully.

'I don't see any point in that whatsoever!' Margaret's look was of horror. 'Why would I want *you* to visit *me*? You don't care! You're a total waste of space, Sarah! I have nothing to say to you!' Margaret's eyes were cold and hard as she dismissed her daughter.

'Well, there's the thing, Mum,' Sarah looked her mother in the eyes, keeping her voice level and calm as she said, 'I'm not. I'm not a waste of space, but you think I am and I haven't helped by not challenging you on your opinion of me or on the way you treat me. I've let you treat me like dirt all my life, Mum, and it's not ok.'

Margaret looked shocked and then angry. Sarah continued before she had time to deny it.

'I think you've always blamed me for Dad going, for him letting you down, and it's not my fault Mum, it's not. I was a child and any problems you two had were not my fault. You need to stop blaming me and let it go Mum.' Margaret physically jumped at the mention of her husband. Sarah saw the look of raw pain flit briefly across Margaret's face before it closed down once again into the cold unemotional mask she normally wore. Sarah saw the heat rise in Margaret's face and a red mist of rage develop within her eyes as they began to flash.

Here we go, she thought to herself, but hanging onto her calmness, her courage, and her strength, Sarah decided to ignore the anger building within Margaret's eyes and ploughed on with her speech.

'Let's start again, aye, Mum? Let the past go? Build some bridges? Get to know each other? Make friends a bit, aye?'

Margaret jumped up from her seat and took a step over to Sarah. Standing over her menacingly she bent down, right into her face she spat the words, 'How *dare* you speak to me like that! How *dare* you accuse me of such things! Get out of my house! Get out now!' Her voice had risen with hysteria and volume with each word, nearly screaming by the end.

Sarah stood up slowly from the chair, matching her mother's height. She stood close and looked her mother square in the eyes. Calmly, quietly, and with authority she said, 'Do not raise your voice to me, Mother. Do not scream in my face. Do not abuse me. You will not speak to me like this anymore, do you understand me? Do you understand me, *Mother*?!'

Margaret recoiled with shock, sitting suddenly with a bump, staring up at her daughter in stunned surprise and disbelief!

Sarah watched her mother's confusion and shock, shock that her daughter was counter-attacking and defending. She saw her mother's anger and for once, she was not afraid nor was she angry in return. She realised, now that she understood her it somehow meant that she could detach, take a step back. It no longer hurt. It just was the way it was. She also realised that it was very unlikely to change, despite her best efforts. She picked up her bag from the back of the chair and turned to her mother.

'I'm going now, Mum. Have a think about what I've said. I'd like to be friends with you, but only if you want that too and only if you can treat me with some care and respect. If not, Mother dear, sad to say, but we are finished. I'd rather that not happen, but that's up to you, your choice. Bye.' And Sarah walked out of Margaret's kitchen and out of her childhood home, knowing that it may well be the last time she ever did.

Chapter 19

She drove home quickly, automatically, her mind almost blank. Walking in her front door she went straight to her kitchen and poured herself a huge glass of wine. She downed it in one.

'You did so well, child! I am sooo proud of you, dear! How do you feel?' enquired Clarabelle gently.

'Do you know what, Clar? I feel bloody marvellous! I did it! I actually told her!' and with that Sarah promptly burst into tears! 'I dunno why I'm crying but,' she gulped, 'I just need to!'

'It'll be the tension coming out, dear and the build-up, all being released. You just let it go.' Clarabelle patted her shoulder reassuringly.

'Part of me feels free, but the other part feels sad. Some part of me feels liberated and the other squashed. I dunno, Clar; it just feels weird. I do feel proud of myself, glad that I did it. I just have to accept that I may never see her again and that a huge part of my life is over. It's just weird.'

Sarah poured another glass of wine and took it into the living room. She lit all the candles, put on some nice music, and curled up with her glass of wine. She felt a need to treat herself, be kind to herself, relax, and let go. She also felt the need to get very drunk! She laughed then.

'Bloody hell! I did it! I'm free!' and she set about indulging herself and celebrating her newfound freedom with gusto!

****

The call came about nine o'clock. Ben was in bed in the middle of making love to Gina, just about to orgasm when the phone shrilled on the bedside cabinet.

'Leave it,' Gina whispered, writhing underneath him, close to her own climax and enjoying this moment when Joe was asleep and neither of them were too tired for sex, a rarity these days!

Ben carried on for a moment, but was really losing his stride with the shrilling of the phone going on and on near his ear.

'I'd better get it, babe, it might be important.' Ben reluctantly reached over for the phone, not moving off Gina while he did so. His mother's voice immediately shrilled in his ear,

'Benjamin, Benjamin!' she wailed hysterically, 'I need you! I've tried to deal with this abuse, this nightmare on my own, but I can't, I just can't, I need you, I need you now!'

Ben felt his erection immediately disappear and both he and Gina groaned with disappointment and frustration at the same time. He climbed off his wife and sat up, trying to make sense of what his hysterically sobbing mother was saying, or trying to!

'Calm down, mum, I can't understand you. Start again.'

271

'She said I blamed her for her father going. She said horrible, horrible things to me. She said… she said…' Margaret hiccupped, 'she said that she wouldn't let me shout at her again; I wasn't shouting, I wasn't! She was nasty. She scared me and she was horrible. Why oh why would she be so nasty to me? What have I done? What have I ever done to that girl? I don't deserve this, to be abused by my own daughter, bullied so. Horrible child, horrible, horrible child!'

Sarah didn't have an abusive bone in her body, of that, Ben was absolutely sure. *Ah,* he thought, *she's finally stood up to her! About bloody time! Brilliant!*

'Well, Mum,' Ben knew this was his chance, a chance that he had been waiting for nearly twenty years to take, the chance to defend his sister. 'She's right! You do blame her for Dad going! I love you, Mum, but you do treat her horribly, you always have! I don't know how she's put up with it for so long! And if she's finally stood up to you Mum, it's because she needed to and I back her a hundred percent. Whatever she said to you, I agree with. Sorry, Mum, but that's the way it is.' Ben heard her gasp with shock. 'Got to go now, Mum, I'm busy. I'll ring you tomorrow, bye.' And Ben hung up on his mother for the first time in his life. Gina looked at him in surprise.

'What's happened, babe?' she asked with concern. Ben relayed the conversation to his wife, saying then that he thought he should go over and see how Sarah was. 'She may be traumatised, upset; she shouldn't be on her own. Do you mind, babe?'

272

'Did you just hang up on your mother?' Gina looked gobsmacked! Then she looked delighted. She grinned at him, pulling him to her she whispered, 'My hero! Come back to bed for a mo and let me show you how much my hero turns me on! This won't take long, trust me!' and pulled him in one hard yank right on top of her. Ben felt his erection return and play resumed from the brief interval that had been his mother's distracting call. *Sarah can hang on for five,* he thought briefly, enjoying both his wife and his honesty to his mother, almost as much as each other. A while later, and not a very long while later, a satisfied Gina and Ben lay panting, waiting for their breathing to return to normal from what had just been quite an intense release for them both.

'I'd better get over there, hun. You sure you're ok with it?' Ben asked, stroking his wife's arm as he held her.

'You go, darling. I've taken what I need from my hero, thank you,' she grinned. 'Sarah will need you, go do your brother-hero thing for your sis now,' she reassured, then added, 'Do you want me to wait up?'

'No thanks, honey, you go to sleep. I don't know how late it will be; it could be an all-nighter. Is that ok with you?'

'Of course! You just go and do what you need to do.'

Ben dressed quickly and left for Sarah's to go and rescue her, help, and support her, the way he had wanted to for years.

****

Sarah was on her second bottle of wine sitting merrily drinking and singing Roger Daltrey's 'I'm Free' from the musical Tommy when Ben walked in.

'Hiya, Bro!' she yelled, in between bars of song, 'I'm Free! I'm Freeeeeeeeee and I'm waiting for you… to follow meeeeeeeeeeeeee, I'm freeeeeeee, I'm freeeeeeeeee!' Sarah sang at the top of her voice, swinging her glass around with each line of the song, in rhythm with the music playing full blast on the CD. Ben was gobsmacked! He thought she'd be in a right state! Well, not that she wasn't, she was as pissed as a fart, but she was happy and that was all that mattered.

'What you singing, Sis?' he shouted, trying to get her attention above the din.

'Who!'

'Who?'

'Yeh, Who!' Sarah yelled.

'Ah, Who!' Ben laughed. 'I like 'Pin Ball Wizard' best, but I guess that wouldn't go so well with the moment.'

'Not unless she's the silver ball getting battered by the pingy things, no!' Sarah yelled, 'I'm freeeeeeeee, I am freeeeeee!' as she returned to her song, carrying on with her favourite line of the night, a line that had already been sung a million times due to the repeat button having been pressed for that particular track, a track which clearly meant so much to Sarah at that moment in time. Ben laughed and left her to it as he went to the fridge to get himself a beer.

I'll stay and join her, look after her. She may be happy now, but she might go down like a sack of spuds

274

later and I'd better be here if she does! he thought to
himself.

'Hello, Clarence!' said Clarabelle as she glared
menacingly at her interfering brother who was sitting
on Ben's right shoulder trying his best to look
innocent. 'Two minutes? Just two!'
'Now, Clarabelle, don't start! It was best! And
leave my feathers alone!' he laughed. 'De-feather me
indeed! And you an angel, a fully qualified one at
that, allowing yourself to get angry! They won't like
that, you know, in the higher realms!' he grinned.
'But I won't say a word, you can trust me!'
'Humph!' said Clarabelle, turning her back
silently on Clarence, sending him to Coventry, she
absolutely refused to ever speak to him again! She
turned her full attention to a singing Sarah.

Ben let Sarah sing and dance while he sat with
his beer keeping an eye on things. Eventually, she got
tired of the loud music and the singing and put
something quieter on so that they could sit and talk.
They chatted about the store, about her business, and
about his work. Ben didn't bring up their mother or
her call, waiting for Sarah to talk about it when she
was ready. The beer flowed and the wine poured as
the evening drew on, Ben catching up with Sarah on
the inebriated levels after a while. Eventually, Sarah
opened up and started telling Ben all about her
mother and the visit earlier that evening, how she had
rung her, arranged to go over, confront her, stand up
to her, and to do it nicely! How she had tried to build
bridges and set boundaries and that she'd done her

best. Ben knew exactly what had occurred and knew that it would take time for their mother to even begin to process this confrontation with Sarah.

'Give it time, Sis. She may come round, she may ease up, you never know. Don't expect miracles to happen overnight though, this is our mother we're talking about not Mother Theresa!'

'Well, I've done all I can and I've done what I needed to do, so bollocks to the rest!' a pissed Sarah replied. *A pissed but strong, assertive, confident Sarah*, Ben thought, noticing this new attitude with interest. He was intrigued!

'So what's brought all this on then, hun?' Ben asked, 'I mean, it's a bit of a shock after all these years, you standing up to her like this! What's brought it all on, aye?'

Sarah eyed her brother carefully. She knew she was pissed. She weighed up how much to tell him. *Oh bollocks!* She thought, *he was pissed too, he'd forget anyway by the morning* and so in her drunken state she blurted out,

'Clarabelle, it's all down to Clarabelle!' she slurred. She smiled at Ben, 'Started listening to her, I did, decided it was time, may as well give it a go, everything was so fucked up, didn't have anything to lose. She sorted the shop you know? She sorted me out too and she showed me stuff about Mum, stuff that made me see her differently, anyway, its 'cos of Clarabelle.'

'Who's Clarabelle?' *What the hell was she wittering on about*, Ben wondered!

Oh, here we go, Sarah thought, and giggled. 'Clarabelle's my angel. My guardian angel! Been with

276

me forever, well since I was about seventeen, I think. Anyway, never listened to her before, do now though! She's bloody good is Clarabelle. Wish I'd listened to her years before, I wouldn't have made such a mess of everything!'

Ben was in shock! His jaw dropped, his face paled, his eyes bulged!

'She's like my own personal advice line, my psychologist, counsellor, and guru all rolled into one, and oh yeah, she's like a fortune teller 'cos she knows the future, and she's my friend too, oh and she's about six inches high normally, but sometimes she's six *foot* high, and oh yeah, she lives on my shoulder most of the time. That one!' said Sarah, pointing to her left shoulder, grinning at Ben and then took another mouthful of wine.

'Oh... my... good... God!' he yelled, 'I can't believe it! Bloody hell!'

'Well, I know it sounds far-fetched and I don't expect you to believe me, but I'm not potty, really I'm not!' Sarah defended. She looked at Ben who was now grinning stupidly from ear to ear. She didn't expect him to believe her, but it was nice to let it out at last, even if she did have to make out tomorrow that she'd been joking. Ben was looking at her in total shock. She'd thought he would laugh, think she was joking, but he was looking happy! Shocked happy, but happy!

'Don't look at me like that, Ben, I'm *not* mad! I know you think I am, but I'm not, truly!'

'I don't think you're mad, Sis. I think its bloody brilliant!'

'You don't? Think I'm mad?'

277

'Nope!'

'Why not! It sounds mad! Ah, you think I'm joking!'

'Nope!'

'Why don't you think I'm joking then?'

'Cos,' Ben took a deep breath, 'cos I got one too!'

'One what?'

'One angel!' Ben grinned.

Sarah both screeched and jumped at the same time, her wine sloshing onto her lap, but she didn't even feel it in her shock. She stared at Ben in wonder. *How could she have not known, not noticed? It all made sense; his charmed life, his perfect judgement, his constant muttering (did she do that, she wondered?) OMG! He would have been talking to his angel when he muttered, just like I did when I was talking to Clarabelle.*

'Yep! He's called Clarence, mine is! 'Clarence-The-Angel'. Been with me since I was about thirteen. Been listening to him all my life, always have, always will. He's always right! He's always there! Here! He's here now as a matter of fact!'

'*No way!*' Sarah shouted with delight. 'Clarence?! That's my Clarabelle's brother!' She turned to her shoulder excitedly,

'Clarabelle, is *his* Clarence, *your* Clarence? Your brother?!'

'Unfortunately, it is so, child, yes.' Clarabelle replied, still fuming with her brother for spoiling her plans that she'd had to spend the day with her hero AA Micky.

'It was in your best interest!' Clarence defended and grinned.

278

He thought it was wonderful that these two finally knew about each other's angels. Smashing in fact! Clarabelle would get over her disappointment about her hero, eventually!

'That'll be why your life's always been so bloody perfect then?' Sarah suddenly realised, 'Always so charmed!'

'Yep! Wanted to tell you, Sis, but how could I? I didn't know you had one too! I thought you'd think I was nuts!'

'So did I, think you'd think I was nuts!'

'Well!' Sarah and Ben said together in shocked amazement.

'Who'd have thought it?'

Sarah told her brother everything then. She shared all that she had found out about Margaret in that session and how she had seen Clarabelle in her full height, her full glory, how blown away she had been, how sorry she had felt for her mother and for herself, and how all of it had changed her. Ben talked about Clarence, how he'd held Ben back from defending Sarah to their mother, said he had to wait, how he'd found Gina for him, his job, his house, and how he had followed his guidance, always. They regaled stories and talked through the night till the wee small hours, stories about each other's angels and all the help they'd had over the years from them, or not, in Sarah's case, until recently. She even told him about Simon and the pint over her head all being down to Clarabelle because of her halo glowing and they both laughed, Ben finally understanding why

279

she'd forgiven Simon so easily and at the same time, feeling sorry for the poor bloke who'd soon be moving into Sarah's flat. The pair finally fell asleep on the sofa where they had been sitting together, passed out in a drunken haze and contented happiness. Always close this brother and sister, now never closer.

Chapter 20

The following week passed by in a blur of activity for Sarah. The new advertising campaign was out and business was booming! Loads of people wanted to makeover their living rooms; lamps and throws were flying off the shelves, she'd run out of candles again, and the Christmas lights were going well too, considering that it was only July! People had liked her ideas, well strictly speaking they were Clarabelle's ideas and it was all going nicely. It was Saturday and Simon was moving in after work later that day. She'd already seen a van parked out the back of the store, along with a flash car, presumably his, although there was no sign of him.

Probably in the pub with his mate, Sarah thought. She brought her mind back to last weekend and the strange events of Saturday night.

She and Ben had had tremendous hangovers on Sunday morning, but they had talked it all through again, sober this time and all was good. It was lovely to know that Ben had an angel too! Clarabelle wouldn't discuss it for some reason. Whenever she'd asked about Ben's angel Clarabelle had just 'humphed!' and changed the subject. She seemed particularly grumpy with him about something, though Sarah couldn't imagine what! She didn't know angels got grumpy!

Ben had said when he'd left that Sunday that he was going to go and see their mother to try to calm her down and talk some sense into her. He'd assured Sarah that he would be backing her and hopefully Margaret might see what Sarah was saying, with Ben's help.

Well, if anyone's going to convince her that she's been a bitch to me for years it's Ben! He was the only one she ever listened to, but Ben had reported back later Sunday night saying that Margaret had turned on him too, for the first time ever, when he had defended Sarah and her actions. She had refused to discuss it and told him to go home. He was in the doghouse apparently and was happy to stay there!

'She's just sulking, Sis. She'll come round in time,' he'd cheerfully said, and that was that!

The bell went on the back door bringing Sarah's attention back to the present with a jolt. *That'll be Simon, I expect*, she thought to herself and sure enough it was. He stood smiling, looking particularly sexy in his T-shirt and jeans! Sarah dismissed that treacherous thought immediately, focusing instead on his flash car and his Greek God image. *Definitely a player*, she decided, summing Simon up in precisely one-point-two seconds flat!

Fire Girl looks pretty today! thought Simon to himself, looking her up and down discretely.

'Hi,' she said, smiling back. 'Come on in, I've got the keys all ready for you and if you can just sign the agreement I can leave you to it. You had a chance to look over the one I emailed you?' Simon nodded, following her and her decidedly scrummy arse into the shop.

'Smashing, just here then, on the dotted line, great, thanks.' Sarah was being incredibly business-like and professional, friendly, but not overly so she decided. *Don't want to give him the wrong impression, just because he's gorgeous!* she thought, wondering why she was focusing so much on his gorgeousness! His mate came in then, having opened the van up ready to unload.

'Hi, I'm Dave. Pleased to meet you.' He reached out his hand to her and Sarah shook it.

'Hi, Dave, nice to meet you too. Right then, gentlemen, I'll leave you to it. You have my number if you need anything. Don't forget about locking the back door, will you? See you later, boys, bye bye.'

Simon let himself into his new flat and looked around the empty space, empty that is apart from the card and the bottle of wine that was propped on the kitchen counter. He opened the card with surprise, finding it was a 'Welcome to Your New Home' card from Sarah, wishing him luck and happiness and leaving the bottle of wine for him to toast his new home.

'What a nice thing to do!' he said, showing Dave.

'She seems a nice girl, mate, a lot better than that Nadia and that's for sure! I can see what you saw in her Si, great tits an all, but be fair, I know she was probably a fabulous shag an' all, but definitely not a keeper! Heard from her have you?'

Simon groaned, 'All the time! The bloody woman just won't leave me alone! She rings, she texts, she pleads, she begs. I just tell her to fuck off, nicely of course, but it's getting harder to be nice. She's practically stalking me now! I'm glad I got rid of her, mate, I can tell you! So glad she's out of my life, bloody woman!'

As the two men carried on about Nadia neither noticed Sarah standing at the door, arms folded, judging the conversation she had just overheard. She'd got to the bottom of the staircase before she'd realised she'd forgotten to tell him about the meter readings so had run back up them again, getting to the door of the flat just as this exchange had begun.

I knew it! She thought to herself, *Another pig who thinks he can go around just dumping girls and breaking their hearts! I bet the poor girls bereft! Clearly she was just a shag to him, probably a one night stand or three! Men like him did things like that, but it must have been more to her, she wouldn't be so upset otherwise now would she! What a pig! He obviously got bored with her after he'd had what he wanted and dumped her! Tosspot!* Sarah wondered then how many girls, women and various ex's would be showing up over the coming months that Simon would be toying with without a care and wondered then if she'd made a huge mistake letting him have her flat.

Clarabelle groaned! *No, no, this wasn't right at all! Blimey, another hurdle to jump!* She noticed that Nat's hair was, as predicted, standing up in its 'Gonk' like position once again, sticking up and sticking out like a lighthouse, an orange lighthouse, on top of his head.

284

'Argh!' groaned Nat, 'I thought we were done with this!' *He'd have to get himself a hat,* he decided, *till this stress was over, if it was ever going to be over!*

Simon turned as he heard a polite tap on the door and saw Fire Girl in the doorway. She seemed deep in thought and not looking happy about something.

'Oh hi, thanks for the card, Sarah that was really nice of you. Would you like to join us for a glass, once I've found the glasses?' he laughed, grinning at her.

Sarah looked at him coldly. 'No, thanks, I must get back. I just came up to tell you that I've read the meter, but if you want to do it too that would be best. Right, I'll let you get on.' She stomped back down the stairs and out to her car.

Bloody men, they're all the same! She thought to herself as she slammed the car door and drove off angrily.

Clarabelle and Nat sighed. 'Oh dear!' they both chimed. 'Oh dear, indeed!'

Over the next month, Sarah saw Simon practically every evening, bumping in to him each night as he was coming back to his home and as she was going home to hers, their watches almost synchronised to coincide each night! He left the bank each day at five pm, getting back to the flat at five-thirty, just as she was either cashing up or locking up. He consistently tried to be friendly and chatty, but she was cool and distant. Each night he would make

the effort to chat as he came in, she constantly
excusing herself saying she was busy or just leaving.
She was polite, but frosty, determined not to be one of
his victims, keeping her distance in every way that
she could. She'd worked too hard on herself and her
heart to lose it to another player or tosspot, which she
had decided he most definitely was, so she kept him
at arm's length, both emotionally and physically. She
did notice that she never saw any of the expected
women visitors come and go, no visitors at all in fact,
but Sarah's mind was made up that Simon was
'dangerous' despite the lack of any evidence of 'toss-
potted-ness' or 'player-of-women-extraordinaire' and
kept her distance.

Clarabelle sighed, knowing that Simon was
neither tosspot nor player; not that she knew really
what they were, but she knew enough to know that
neither was good! Somehow she had to convince
Sarah that she and her heart would be safe with
Simon. She just wondered how she was going to do it!
Nat scratched his head, itching as it was under his
new baseball cap. He didn't have a clue either!

Clarence, she thought with a sigh. *She was going
to have to speak to Clarence; there was no avoiding it.
She'd sent him to Coventry for long enough now and
besides which, she needed some help!*

****

'So what am I going to do Clarence?' she
asked her brother some time later, back on their

286

favourite cloud. 'A month he's been living there now and she can't stand him! How am I going to get them together?'

'Simple, my dear, just push them together! Use the flat, use the shop, use Ben, use anything that they have linked and don't forget you need to make sure that she sees him in a better light. If she knew about Nadia and what Simon put up with she'd change her mind about him, same if she knew all he really wants is to settle down. I'll have a word with Nathaniel, get him to work with you. May have to bring in Serena too, Nadia's angel, see what we can co-ordinate between us. Leave it with me, my dear.' He smiled at her as he sheepishly added, 'And, Clar, I'm glad you're talking to me again. Sorry my dear! I didn't mean to upset you.'

Clarabelle hugged her brother and went back downstairs to conjure up a plan.

****

The next day Clarabelle sat on Sarah's left shoulder and put her plan into action. Nathaniel was standing by his end, Serena too, and it was game on!

'Action!' she imagined her invisible director saying as she launched herself into 'The Plan'!

'So what I thought, Sarah, as the shop's doing so well, is that you could think about expanding the opening hours. How about opening up on a Sunday? Give it a go for a few weeks, a month trial maybe? If it turns out not to be worth it, go back to the six days, but I think it will be worth it. See if Tim or Mary would work it? I think Mary might, she's often bored

287

and lost on a Sunday and I know she could do with the money.' Clarabelle beamed at Sarah.

'Do you know what, Clar, that's a bloody good idea! Yes, I'll have a word with them both and see if they'll do it. Don't know why I didn't think of that before!'

'And you'll have to have a word with Simon as well, of course, dear. It affects his tenancy having the shop open on a Sunday. You'll need to discuss it with him, make sure he doesn't mind. I'm sure if you opened at ten o'clock he'd be alright, he's always up by then.'

'Mmmm, good point, I would, wouldn't I? Need to get him to agree, I mean. If I had a shop suddenly opening under me on my one day of peace I know I wouldn't be too happy! I'd better talk to him first then, yes. If he's alright with it then I'll talk to Tim and Mary.' Sarah gave it more thought as the day wore on and decided that she'd have a word with Simon tonight when he came home from work. If she was going to do this Sunday thing then she would need to get her advert altered and the deadline for any changes in that week's paper was in two days' time.

'Excellent, my dear! Give him a chance to get in and have a cuppa first though, aye? No one likes to be pounced on the minute they get in the door. Leave it half an hour and then have a word, aye? I think that would be best.'

'Mmmm, ok, if you say so.' Sarah agreed.

Simon came home as normal at five-thirty that day feeling hot, sweaty, and sticky. The air conditioning on his car had played up all the way home and he needed a shower badly. Normally he just chilled when he got in with a beer or a cuppa, but today he'd need to get out of his suit straight away and shower and change.

Bloody nuisance! he thought. *Wonder what's the matter with it? It was fine yesterday!*

Nathaniel smiled happily, pleased with his handiwork of placing gremlins in Simons air con! It was all going to plan perfectly! Now all he needed to do was synchronise with Clarabelle to get Sarah to knock the flat door at the perfect moment.

'Stand by, Clarabelle!' Nathaniel yelled down the stairs.

'We're ready this end, just let me know when!' came her reply from the distance.

Simon was just getting out of the shower when he heard the knocking on the door of the flat. Grabbing a towel and putting it around his waist he walked to the door, opening it to see 'Fire Girl' standing there.

'Hiya!' he smilingly said, 'How are you, Sarah? What can I do for you?'

He clocked Sarah's jaw drop and he also clocked her eyes moving from his chest down to his toes and back up again. He grinned.

'Yeh, sorry, just got out the shower. Bloody air cons gone in the car! It was a nightmare drive home in this heat! Come on in, I'll just grab some clothes.'

Sarah was motionless for a split second before following Simon into the living room. She watched

289

him disappear into the bedroom and finally let out the breath that she'd been holding.

Oh my God! she thought to herself, *He truly is a God! A Greek God! Like Apollo, or Zeus... Or Orion - he was a Greek Giant God! Stunning, just stunningly beautiful, for a man!* And he was, there was no mistaking his masculinity or his beauty! His tall six foot four inches frame was perfectly proportioned, she'd been able to see that from his stance, and the fact that he only had a towel around his waist had been most helpful in determining that fact! There wasn't an ounce of fat on him anywhere. He was tanned, toned, and muscly, in all the right places. His wet body had been shimmering with the water still on it and she'd had one hell of a job to stop herself reaching out and wiping one particular water droplet that had been trickling down his chest.

Jesus, girl! Get a grip, the man's a player and a tosspot and your bloody tenant, she said to herself as she waited for him to come back out of his bedroom.

Sarah was aware, very much so in that moment, that she hadn't had sex since the end of February and it was now the middle of August! Positively barren for half a year, for God's sake! She wondered then whether it had closed up down there the way that pierced ears do if you don't wear earrings for long enough. Was that possible? Does it close up if it's not been used for long enough?! She hoped not! She was also aware that she hadn't been held, kissed, touched, cuddled, or had any form of contact with the male species for a whole six months.

'Oh Godddddddd!' she groaned. The desire rose in her as she again pictured the image she had

290

seen of him seconds before, standing at the door almost naked and she knew that she fancied him, *God, she fancied him so bad! Shit!*

Simon came out of the bedroom to find Sarah sat in his chair holding her head and groaning.

'You ok?' he asked

'Yes, yes, I'm fine, just fine!' Sarah jumped up, trying to regain some composure, trying her best to push down the desire that was now consuming her! *Fire Girl looks a bit flushed,* Simon thought.

'You sure you're ok? Do you want a beer, cuppa, glass of wine?' he asked.

'Yes, yes, that would be nice, thank you. Glass of wine please, large one!' *Probably not wise*, she thought to herself, *but bollocks!* She needed something to calm down the raging heat that was growing between her legs!

Simon smiled and fetched her a large glass of wine as requested, handing it to Sarah just as his mobile rang. He answered it without checking the number and groaned with regret as soon as he heard the voice. Shit, it was Nadia, again!

Serena sat on Nadia's shoulder watching her ward in action. Nathaniel had called earlier and asked her to get Nadia to call Simon at exactly six o'clock. She didn't know what was going on, but had gone along with the request. She listened to Nadia, watched her put on her seductive voice and despaired at her ward!

'Simon daaarling, pleeeezzz can't we talk about this? Daaaarling, I miss you sooooo much!'

Sarah watched Simon's face drop as he took the call; she heard the tone in his voice and she heard his frustration as he said,

'No, Nadia, we cannot talk! There is nothing to talk about, not now, not ever, now please stop ringing me. It's getting ridiculous, it's practically stalking and if you keep calling like this I will seriously have to consider changing my number. Goodbye!' He pressed the end call button and then turned the phone off immediately.

'Sorry about that,' he said, 'I don't know what to do with her, how to get rid of her! I've tried everything, but she just won't give up. It's bloody scary! Like something out of Fatal Attraction! Bunny boiler!'

Sarah looked at him in surprise. He didn't seem the type to be bothered by a woman chasing him or to get annoyed or scared by it. She would have thought that he'd have revelled in the attention, but he clearly was not.

'Sorry, I shouldn't be telling you all this anyway, I'll sort it out. It's my problem.'

Sarah was intrigued now, wanting to know more.

'Well, maybe I could help?' she suggested, 'Give you a woman's perspective? I don't mind, really. I'm a good listener.'

'Really?' Simon hesitated, wondering if this was a good idea or not. He didn't know her that well to be asking advice so he shook his head.

'Cheers, but I've talked to the lads about it, they tell me to ignore the calls or change my number. I don't really want to, shouldn't have to, just because

292

of an ex who won't take no for an answer! Should I?'
he hesitated then.

'Well, why don't you tell me about it and I'll
let you know?' Sarah replied, dying to know now
what was going on.

Serena watched Nadia's face as the phone
went dead in her hand. She saw the anger on her face
at the rejection, then watched with amusement as
Nadia picked the phone straight back up again
ringing Roger for support, again.

Job done, she thought, having carried out her
instructions for Nathaniel to the letter. Now all she
had to do was sort Nadia out.

Nathaniel was delighted and Clarabelle was
beaming! They both heaved a huge sigh of relief as
Simon caved in and started filling Sarah in, fairly
quickly really, explaining how he'd met Nadia and
how it had just been a fling for them both for months,
suited them equally at the time, but as time had gone
on that he'd wanted to make it serious, move in, talk
about long-term and futures, and stuff. He explained
about how Nadia hadn't let go of Roger and how she
wanted to keep it all casual with Simon and how in
the end, he'd given up and ended it, realising that it
was going nowhere. Sarah was gobsmacked! She
didn't have him pegged as that kind of bloke at all,
not the settling down type! She suddenly realised
how badly she'd got him wrong, how she'd
misjudged him. He didn't seem like a player or a
tosspot. He seemed a genuinely nice guy!

'So when did all this end?' she asked.

'The weekend of Father's Day, middle of June. The weekend I came down here. I'd finally had enough, finished it and then buggered off for the weekend. Ended up here, with you, 'Fire Girl'!'

Sarah laughed, ''Fire Girl'?'

'Yep, sorry. I'll always think of you as 'Fire Girl'!' Simon laughed. 'Anyway, it was after that weekend that I decided to make a completely clean break and move away, apply for other jobs and ended up back here again, in the bank with your brother. Weird, really, isn't it?'

'Yes, it is,' Sarah admitted, thinking that it was just a bit too weird. Something was going on! She didn't know what, but something definitely was, she could feel it in her bones! It had been a long time now since she'd believed in coincidences, knowing that everything happens for a reason. She brought her attention back to the problem of Simon's stalker.

'Well, I think you're right! She sounds like a selfish spoilt madam who likes her own way, Simon. It sounds as if she's not used to rejection either, she doesn't know how to let go. She hasn't let go of her husband and now she's not letting go of you. I'd change my number if I were you. Just get a new one and give it to your friends and start again.'

'You think?'

'Yep, I think! I mean be fair, how long were you with her, two years? And in all that time she didn't let go of her husband at all? She'll probably be the same with you and you don't want her still hassling you in two years like him now, do you?'

'God, no!'

'Well, then?'

'Yes, thanks, you're right. I'll do it tomorrow. Cheers.' Simon looked relieved. 'Can I top you up?' he asked, as he walked to the kitchen to get the bottle of wine from the fridge and a beer for himself.

'Oh go on then, I'll force another one down,' grinned Sarah. 'Seriously, though, I think you should just change your number, accept that she can't let go and that it could be ages before she does, if ever! She probably won't let go till she's found someone new.'

'Yes, it's good advice. Looking at it now, seeing it like that, it makes sense. I just haven't known what to do about it, I've never had this kind of thing before!'

Sarah smiled, 'I'm happy to have been able to help. Anytime, really, anytime!' And she meant it! He was nothing like she'd thought! He wasn't a tosspot and he wasn't a player. He was a really nice bloke and a totally gorgeous bloke at that! And he was single and he wanted to settle down not run away like every other guy she'd met over the last ten years! Bloody hell, Sarah suddenly realised, not only that but he's actually suitable! Good job, secure, own property, well dressed, well spoken, intelligent, educated, the list just went on and on! Sarah felt her guard come down, her desire go up, and she decided there and then that she was going to be open to whatever unfolded. She didn't know if he fancied her, but if he did, and if he wanted to chase her, she may just let him catch her!

****

295

She left the flat a little after eleven o'clock that night, having had a really nice evening with Simon, who'd insisted on walking her home like the gentleman he was. As she lay in her bed later reflecting on the evening, she realised he was great company. They'd talked easily about everything and anything. There didn't seem to be any caginess, any barriers. They'd found themselves being really open to each other, talking freely about themselves and their dreams as well as their desires, aspirations, and goals. Sarah had told him about the shop, the Mackenzie's, and her friends. He talked more about Nadia, his life in the city, his career, and his desire to move out and reprioritise his life. The more she'd got to know him, the more she'd liked him. He was funny, easy to be with, and he seemed to really care about people; he took responsibility for his life, the way he lived it, and how it affected others around him. They'd even talked about spiritual matters, one of Sarah's favourite subjects! Simon had agreed with her that there were things that you couldn't see and couldn't prove, but it didn't mean they didn't exist. He also agreed with her that many things happened for a reason, although you may not see it or understand what that reason is or could be at the time. They talked more about him coming to her town and how it had all happened, both coming to the conclusion that weird stuff like coincidences usually worked out for the best. Sarah decided that Simon had integrity and depth, as well as being charming and gorgeous!

'Mmmm, how interesting!' she said to herself, now surveying him as possible boyfriend material and liking the thought of getting to know him better very much!

They'd finally got round to talking about why she'd knocked at his door in the first place, but only as he walked her home, having forgotten all about it. He'd said it was no problem on the Sunday opening thing at all and made her promise to pop in for a drink or a cuppa more often. As she closed her front door slowly, watching Simon walk down her path she felt a little dazed, a little shell shocked and a little excited. He was amazing!

'Yep,' she decided, as she lay in her bed dreaming now about a besotted Simon chasing her and her playing hard to get of course, but not too hard! 'Yep, he can definitely catch me!' she grinned, picturing herself on his arm and them as a couple, letting her imagination run riot, including of course, what he'd be like in bed! Well after seeing *that* body you couldn't imagine it not to be fab! And then another thought came into her head, a thought that said, *What if I'm wrong again? What if he is a tosspot after all?* She immediately came out of her imaginary world, a world where she and Simon were fabulously happily shagging their brains out, and bumped back into the real world, a world where hurt and disappointment reign. She hesitated, took a step back from the daydream and began to process carefully everything she knew about him in a very realistic sense. After examining everything that she knew about him in the minutest detail, Sarah still thought he was nice, very nice!

297

Nope! She thought, *Can't find a thing wrong with him, not one single thing! But...we've been here before my girl, so let's check with Clarabelle first before we get carried away, aye?!*

Simon was processing too as he walked slowly back to his flat. He thought 'Fire Girl' was just amazing! She had a really good business head on her pretty shoulders, was go-getting, dynamic, hardworking, dedicated, and loyal (her staff clearly adored her.) On top of that she was very attractive, funny, honest, open, intelligent, interesting, strong, and very much his type, if he had a type! And if he didn't, he'd make one and she'd fit! He'd never felt so at ease so quickly with anyone! She was also sexy as hell and he fancied her rotten! The only problem was, would it be a good idea to pursue her? He hadn't long come out of the Nadia disaster for one, two it was a new town, and three it was a new job. He needed time to let the dust settle on all three before he started thinking about dating again. And then there were the risks! She was his landlady *and* she was his new work colleague's sister! If he dated her and it went pear-shaped he'd lose his home and probably have to leave his job!

'Bloody risky, mate!' he said to himself. It was just a matter of deciding whether he thought she was worth taking that risk for.

'Dunno, sunshine, better get to know her a bit better first, aye? Then decide!' he said to himself. *Yes,* he thought, *just get to know her first and be friends.* And then he thought about her smile, her eyes, her figure;

she was slim and trim and bloody gorgeous and she had a fabulous arse!

Hmmm, maybe friends is pushing it, but I'll have a go!

Clarabelle and Nathaniel did high-fives to each other and grinned.

'That went well!' they both said in unison, and this time, it was true!

'It's all coming together nicely!'

'Well done on the air con, Nat! That was sneaky!' Clarabelle said.

'Worked though, aye?!' he replied. 'And well done you on the Sunday opening plan, Clar! Brill timing too on getting her up there just as he came out of the shower, perfect!' Nathaniel said.

'Serena did a good job too, getting Nadia to ring at just the right minute,' they both agreed. Sarah finally knew the Nadia story and as predicted, it had done the trick! Her opinion of Simon had changed dramatically, the door was open and now all they had to do was get the pair to walk through it! Their halo's glowed with happiness at a job well done and then they both popped off upstairs to report in to Clarence with the good news.

Chapter 21

The next month passed by with the speed of light. August had turned to September and the summer sun was fading. Sarah was busy in the shop with the new campaign, Sunday openings were going really well and business was booming! The bathroom makeovers were being advertised and the stock was beginning to shift from August's advertising campaign. Tim and Mary had agreed to work every other Sunday on a trial basis and a new assistant had been brought in to support them. They'd been open Sundays for nearly a month now and after some discussion earlier that day, it was agreed by all to continue with it permanently.

She'd had her 38th birthday with the girls in the pub the week before and Ben and Gina had come, bringing Simon along too. Simon had blown Frieda and Angie away! They'd thought he was sexy, gorgeous, and just scrummy in every way, being particularly impressed with the gift he'd bought her, a small silver angel necklace. Simon had asked Ben what she would like, what her tastes were and Ben had said that Sarah loved angels so he'd gone off and found this pretty little necklace that now hung around her neck. Sarah had been delighted!

'Hey, Sarah, if you don't want him, mate, I'll be more than happy to take him off your hands!' Frieda had laughed to Sarah in the girl's toilets. 'He's huge! Gorgeous! Hey, do you reckon he's in those proportions everywhere?!' she'd said grinning. They'd laughed, Sarah admitting she'd wondered the same! Simon's hands were like shovels, his feet a size thirteen, and his whole body matching his large frame.

'Mmmm, be nice to think so,' she giggled, 'but we're just friends, Frie, just friends!'

'Yeh right! Not for long, girlie! I've seen the way you two look at each other! Bloody fireworks there, mate!' and they'd gone back into the birthday celebrations still giggling. Sarah was glad that Simon had met her friends and they liked him; it seemed everyone did. He was 'Mr. Popularity'!

****

Simon had been on a mission since moving to Redfields to settle in, settle down, and build a life here. He'd joined the rotary club in Redville with Ben, the cricket club in Redfields and was now a regular in the Crown. He'd developed a friendship with Tom, the chap he'd met the weekend he'd first come down that he'd liked and got drunk with, and was pleased to find out that he was Angie's husband, a friend of Sarah's. It seemed everyone here knew everyone else. Tom knew Ben, Angie knew Gina, everyone knew Sarah! He'd been teased mercilessly by all and sundry about pouring a pint over her head that day and despite it being three months since the fateful day, still had comments of 'Do you want to drink this one or pour it over someone?'

Yes, Simon decided, *he'd definitely done the right thing moving here.* He was happy and settled.

301

He'd spent increasing time with Sarah since he'd told her about Nadia. She had been so helpful, understanding, and really, just great! They were getting on like a house on fire and he was finding it increasingly difficult not to make a pass at her, especially when he'd had a few. She was just lovely! He'd spent ages choosing that angel necklace for her birthday and was aware that it was more than was normal for 'just a friend'. He'd been really nervous giving it to her last week, desperate for her to like it. She'd loved it and he was chuffed to bits! He'd thrown himself into the many events over the summer, partly to give him a distraction from his increasing desire for her, but partly to help build a life and friendships with the locals. He'd changed his number and there'd been no more calls from Nadia and life was just nigh on bloody perfect.

'Yep, Simon, my boy, you done good!' he grinned to himself.

****

Sarah was pondering on Simon too. They had spent more and more time together over the last few weeks since that night when she'd decided he was definitely a nice guy as opposed to a tosspot! Their friendship had been building and they'd spent quite a few evenings together, some at the pub, others at the flat. He'd not been to hers yet, but that would come in time. They'd had a few take-away's together, even a couple of meals in the pub after work, but all just as friends. They were easy together, they got on well, and just seemed to fit. Mutual admiration had been developing and they were getting closer with every week that had passed. Whispers had been growing in the town, Chinese whispers and gossip of the budding romance between them, the locals seeing Sarah and Simon together so often now. Sarah knew they probably had them down for being in a full blown torrid romance by now, rather than the 'just friends' that they actually were, but she didn't care at all, not a jot!

Nothing was hard work between them, other than suppressing the mutual desire for each other that was building all the time and which they both felt; they never argued and although they did disagree at times, it was healthy and respectful disagreements, not that there were many of them, but you can't agree all the time! Sarah had asked Clarabelle about Simon, but all she would say was that he was a nice man and that Sarah should make her own mind up. Even without Clarabelle's confirmation that he was safe, Sarah was becoming more and more sure of Simon. She was also becoming surer that she wanted to be more than 'just friends'. She didn't obsess about him, didn't spend every waking minute thinking about him like she had with the previous men that she'd fancied, but she did look forward to seeing him each night when he came back from work and she enjoyed the evenings they'd had together where he'd asked her up for a drink or they'd gone to the pub. He hadn't made a move in all those times over the last month, but she thought, and hoped, that he might fancy her too.

She knew she had changed a lot in the last six months. The days seemed to be long gone now when her world revolved around a man. Her world was so full now, so fulfilling; her store was her focus, her home her sanctuary, she needed nothing, feeling independent and whole for the first time in her life. Her life was busy, yes, full, yes, but she knew she had room to fit a relationship into it, if it was what she wanted. And she did, she did want it! She wanted him! It was just a matter of whether he wanted her too!

****

'Ben, I wanted to have a word, mate?' Simon said that afternoon at work.

'Oh, yeah? What about?' Ben enquired. 'What's up, Si?'

'Well, I was thinking of asking your sister out on a date and wondered what you thought? If it was ok with you?' Simon felt like he was an eighteen year old in Victorian times asking someone's dad for permission to court their daughter, rather than a grown man nearing forty, but it felt right to ask Ben somehow! He knew Sarah's dad was dead and that she had no real relationship with her mother, so Ben was Sarah's only family really and it seemed fair that he would probably play the protective brother role.

'Yeh! Go for it! That's great! I'm happy for you, I know she likes you, she's told me. So, yes, you kids go have fun!' Ben grinned, playing the father role that Simon had given him with relish.

Ben couldn't be happier. He'd been really pleased with the way Sarah and Simon had been getting on recently. He knew they spent a fair bit of time together after work. Simon had been here two months now nearly and Ben liked him, trusted him and thought he was a great bloke. Everyone at work liked and respected him too, no one had a bad word to say about him and he knew that Simon was someone finally worthy of his big sister.

'Thanks,' a relieved Simon said. 'Any idea where a really nice restaurant is round here? I'd like to make it special for her, especially for the first date. I mean I know we've been out a couple of times to the pub, had a few meals there too but that's been as friends, not as a date and not somewhere classy. I want to do it right.'

'Oooo posh, aye! She'll like that, mate! Not used to being courted is our Sarah, not properly at any rate! Yes, now let me think. There's Gino's,'

'No, not Gino's' Clarence suddenly piped up from Ben's right shoulder. 'Remember Rob! Bad memories there, bad memories!'

Ben hesitated, thinking back, *oh God yes, Rob! Thank God for Clarence!*

'No, no, I wouldn't! Not Gino's! Um, let me think.'

'Florentino's!' Clarence's voice urgently and insistently piped up in his ear. 'Florentino's! That's where he should take her!'

Ben picked up the ball that Clarence had thrown him.

'Well, there's Florentino's, that's nice; pricey, but nice. I take Gina there sometimes on special

305

occasions, anniversaries and the like, she loves it.
That's probably the best one round here. Do you want
the number?'

'Great, cheers, mate!' and Simon was set.

'Phew!' said Clarence to himself, 'That was a
close call!'

****

Sarah was pricing new stock on the shop floor,
totally focused on her work when her mother walked
in to Mackenzie's that afternoon. She couldn't believe
her eyes! She gawped at Margaret in open disbelief!

'Um, hi, Mum. What are you doing here?' a
more than surprised Sarah asked.

'I'm here to see you. Do you have a moment?'
a nervous Margaret asked.

Bloody hell! Was this for real? Was her mother
actually here? Taken the time to drive over to see her!
And was that really her mother *asking* if she had a
moment rather than assuming that she did!? Bloody
hell, this was a turn up! Sarah rose slowly from the
boxes, putting the pricing gun down on top of them;
she turned to her mother, 'Um, yes, Mum! Yes, I have
a moment. Come through to the back office, I'll make
us some tea.'

'No need for tea, Sarah. I shall not be staying
long.'

Margaret followed Sarah through the shop,
looking around her as she did. Sarah pulled out a
chair for her mother in her small office and sat in the
smaller guest chair opposite wondering what she was

doing here. She didn't have to wait long for the answer.

'I've been doing some thinking since your visit, Sarah,' her mother said, pausing for dramatic effect, 'I've discussed your accusations with your brother, of course. I have decided, after much thought, that I *may* have been a little harsh with you over the years. It is *possible*,' she paused again, 'that I *may* have been a little unfair.'

Sarah could see that her mother was really struggling with this admission, really finding it difficult to admit any wrong doing on her part, but she was, she actually was! Admitting responsibility, *bugger me!*

'So I have decided, after much thought, that I am in agreement with starting afresh. I shall try to be a little kinder from now on.' She smiled then at Sarah, a small and weak smile, but it was a smile and not the usual glare! She continued her speech to a silent and shell-shocked Sarah.

'Ben tells me how well you have been doing with this little shop of yours. It was a surprise to me I must admit, but it seems that you *may* have some of your brother's know-how after all. It is *possible* that you are not the disappointment that I thought you were. I am pleased for you.'

Sarah managed to find her voice and respond to this monumental back down that her mother had offered,

'Thank you!'

'Yes, well, I shall leave you to it now. Perhaps I may see you for tea one afternoon, when you have some free time? I should like that.'

307

'Um, yes, me too.'

Margaret picked up her handbag and walked out of the small office and through Sarah's store firmly and purposefully, while Sarah sat in stunned and shocked bemusement for the next two hours!

'Well, bugger me! Bugger me!'

****

Sarah was still sitting in the office trying to get her head around her mother's visit when Simon came back from work. She heard him call her name from the counter and somehow managed to shake herself out of her stupor to go and say hi to him.

'Hi, Fire Girl! How you doing today, babe?' he asked

Babe? Did he just call her babe? She must have got that wrong! No, apparently she hadn't because he was now asking her if she'd like to go to Florentino's with him for dinner Friday night on a date, a proper date, if she'd like to!

Double bugger me! Sarah thought, *It's all happening today!*

She nodded her head in agreement, grinning from ear to ear she had said yes, she would like that very much. Simon's blue eyes had twinkled as she had nodded her smiling agreement and he'd almost skipped out the shop to his flat door with a, 'Great, eight o'clock, ok?' and disappeared as Sarah sat in shock, grinning stupidly from ear to ear.

Clarabelle beamed, positively beamed. Simon was ready. She *knew* her Sarah was ready. Even MFH was coming round!

'Finally!' she squealed, 'Yippee!'

Chapter 22

Sarah prepared carefully for her night out
with Simon, their first proper date!

'Oh my God, just let it be perfect please!' she
breathed. She'd bought a new dress for this special
date with Simon, (another one!) green this time; she
was avoiding blue like the plague, not wanting to
jeopardise anything. She certainly didn't want to
wear the same blue dress she'd worn out with Rob
that awful night so long ago. The 'EA's' were ready,
although the 'essential accessories' hadn't seen the
light of day since her date with Rob either; she simply
had not either had the time or the inclination to be
dating anyone! The WWB knickers had been put on
and then taken off again, sexy knickers replacing
them instead, not that she intended anything to
happen that would warrant underwear being on view
of course, but she just felt sexier and more confident
in pretty knickers! And besides which there were
definitely less wibbly wobbly bits now than there had
been before and even if it wasn't the perfect body of a
twenty year old, it was good enough!

Must have lost some weight since having the shop,
she thought to herself, although she was also aware
that most of this attitude was down to her increased
confidence and self-worth rather than a huge change
in her body, which had actually changed very little.

Simon was collecting her at eight o'clock and it was now seven forty-five. Her make-up and hair was already done, along with her nails. She pulled the dress over her head and stepped into the 'God-awful lethal high-heeled shoes', adding her earrings, a squirt of her favourite perfume, then finally putting the angel necklace around her neck that he'd bought her for her birthday. With a 'da da!' to herself, she was ready! Sarah surveyed herself in the mirror with a smile, proclaiming to her reflection,

'Yep! You'll do, girl, you'll do!'

'You'll more than do, child!' piped up Clarabelle. 'You look radiant, just positively radiant! Beautiful! Stunning!'

'Yes, not too shabby, am I!' Sarah was pleased with her reflection. She went downstairs and waited for Simon nervously. Spot on eight o'clock he rang her doorbell, handing her an orchid plant as she opened the door to him. Sarah looked at the plant in wonder. No one had ever bought her anything like that before! Flowers, yes, but never something like this! Wow! It was a plant, a real plant with roots and everything! She hoped the plant's longevity was an indicator of things to come with Simon, hopefully lasting longer than the week the average bunch of flowers did.

Simon was looking at her in the same way that she was gazing at the orchid.

God, she's beautiful! he thought, as he looked her up and down. She was wearing a dress of gentle green that clung to her curves softly. Her slim legs were shown off to their best in the high heels and her smile, well, it just lit up the place! Simon couldn't take

311

his eyes off her! He'd never seen her properly 'done up' before and my God, if he thought she was lovely before, he *knew* she was lovely now!

'You look beautiful, Sarah!' he said to her admiringly. 'Just gorgeous! May I?' and he bent down, kissing her softly on her cheek. Sarah blushed, a little embarrassed at this new attentive, almost gawping Simon.

She looked at him now, managing to pull her attention away from the beautiful white petals of the orchid plant that was in her hand. He looked magnificent!

Bloody hell, he looks like James Bond in that black suit, really utterly gorgeous and so sexy! she thought to herself. He was wearing a black suit with a white dress shirt underneath, the collar was open just enough. His black shoes shone with fresh polish and she almost stopped breathing with the rush of emotion that she suddenly felt as she gazed at him then.

Greek God with bells on! she thought to herself, *Wow, and this was my date for the night! Bloody Nora, the girl's come far!* She was amazed by the way he was looking at her, as if he felt exactly the same about her, which to Sarah was even more amazing!

'Are you ready, babe?' he asked tenderly. She put the plant down on the nearby hall table, nodding her head. She was speechless at the perfection of it all! He took her hand and led her out to the car, opening the door for her, and waiting till she was seated before he closed it.

312

'Jesus! I've died and gone to heaven!' Sarah exclaimed to herself while he walked around the car to the driver's side and let himself in. She watched in wonder as he took her hand, holding it in the car all the way to the restaurant, letting the automatic gear box do the work so that he could keep his left hand firmly in hers. He was nervous, she could feel it!

That means this is really important to him! That I'm really important to him! Blimey! and she smiled serenely to herself at the thought of the beautiful and gorgeous Greek God being nervous of *her!*

The evening was wonderful from start to finish. Florentino's was amazing! Soft music played gently in the background, the lighting was discrete, casting warm shadows around the room, and the whole place had a beauty, elegance, and style that was simply perfection. Simon ordered the best wine, holding her hand between courses, stroking her fingers gently as he did so. They talked about their day and week, but she really couldn't remember what they'd talked about, she couldn't take it in! All she could remember later was the way he'd been gazing into her eyes throughout the whole evening and on several occasions, he had held her hand across the table, lifting it to his lips, kissing it softly every now and then.

Yep, definitely died and gone to heaven! Sarah decided. She was loving every second, every nanosecond of it! She'd never had anyone so attentive, so affectionate, not ever! She was lapping it up like a sponge, revelling in it! He was spoiling her like she'd never been spoilt and adoring her like she'd never been adored! When they'd finished the meal, the coffee, and the after dinner drinks, he paid the bill, leaving a generous tip, thanking the wonderful staff profusely, and escorted a stunned and besotted Sarah back to the car in the moonlight, his hand in hers every step of the way. She felt protected, cared for, pampered, and bewildered, never having known this kind of care before.

Standing in the car park by the side of the car, he took her gently in his arms, pulled her closely into him and bent down, kissing her fully and properly for the first time. Sarah felt his lips on hers and then her legs go weak, her stomach flip and her heart jump out of her chest to fall into her stomach to join in with the flipping! Her throat went dry, her palms became clammy, her head span and she thought that she would pass out with the sheer delight of this one kiss, this one embrace. But oh my God, *what* a kiss! *What* an embrace! She was trembling from head to foot by the time he let her go and she wasn't at all sure if she wasn't going to fall over, especially balanced as she was precariously, on those God-awful lethal five inch heels! She grabbed the car door handle to steady herself as he put his hand over hers, pulling the door open for her.

'Milady?' he said, beckoning her to get into the car with a smile that made her heart melt even more.

The drive back to her place was surreal. They just sat smiling, her at him and him at her, when he could, when he was able to safely take his eyes off the road, which she noticed he did a lot! Just as well, the roads were quiet! They smiled at each other, fingers wrapped around each other's hand in a contented silence. He walked her to her front door and she opened it, taking his hand she led him inside to her hall, where she turned to him this time, wrapping her arms around his neck as she leaned up to kiss him again. The kiss went on and on and on! She felt his passion as they kissed; she felt herself melt with desire for him and as she pulled back from the embrace, her arms still around his neck, she whispered to him, 'Thank you for a wonderful evening. It was magical!'

Simon smiled, his eyes dancing with desire he shook his head, as if to clear it. A little dazed, he stepped back from her, took her hand and said simply, 'Same time next week, Milady?' and moved towards her front door. Opening it, he turned back to face her, took her hand and kissed the back of it like a chivalrous gent from the last century, then disappeared back up her path, saying as he went, 'Must go, darling, while I still can!'

Sarah closed the door gently behind him, still trembling from their embrace, she walked up the three flights of stairs slowly and fell onto her bed with a bump.

'Oh my God, Clarabelle!' she shrieked to her smiling sidekick. 'Oh my good God!'

'Precisely, child, precisely!' came the grinning reply.

****

315

The week passed by in a blur for Sarah. The following day he had called her and asked if he could take her to lunch. After a lovely meal in a quiet country pub that overlooked a river, they had walked along the meandering river bank hand in hand, gazing at each other, stopping for little kisses every other step it seemed, managing somehow not to fall into the water despite spending more time looking at each other than the path they were on. Returning her home from their walk, he had come in with her, complimenting her on her home as he followed her from the lounge to the kitchen, saying how perfect it was and asking if he could light the log fire that was laid in the hearth of the living room. Sarah had grinned, throwing him the matches, even though it was a warm September's afternoon, letting him enjoy his delight in the coals and logs whilst she'd made them both a large pot of coffee. Returning to the living room, she'd switched the tiny lights on that were subtly hidden around the room, lighting the dark corners with their soft glow. As the logs began to crackle, she'd lit the candles and together they'd curled up in front of the fire for the rest of the afternoon and talked long into the evening.
There had been more kisses, each becoming more intense, their passion and desire for each other building. Simon had excused himself several times during the evening, going to the kitchen for more coffee, mainly to allow their mutual desires to be pulled into check with a little distance. Eventually he had left, leaving her flushed from their embraces, her heart pounding and her legs wobbling.

316

This pattern continued through the week, Simon spending more time at Sarah's house, staying ever later each evening, both finding it increasingly difficult to tear themselves away from each other. A week after the first date he took her to the theatre, giving her another magical evening. As he returned her home that night and held her in his arms on her sofa, glass of wine in hand, she turned to him and said simply, perfectly and so sweetly,

'Would you like to stay, Si?'

He had nodded mutely and then he smiled the biggest smile she had ever seen anyone smile. She led him up the three flights of stairs to her bedroom with nervous anticipation. She wanted him, this wonderful man whom she adored, and she didn't just want sex with him, she wanted everything, she wanted it all!

Simon pulled her again into his arms in the bedroom and slowly kissed her face, her eyes, and her neck with slow simple kisses. He lifted her hand to his lips and kissed each finger, trailing kisses then from her fingers up along her arms to her shoulders and on to her neck. He turned her around then, away from him, unzipping her dress, turning her back towards him as he slowly pulled the straps of the dress down, beginning now to undress her. He took off her bra and bent to gently kiss each breast; he pulled down her knickers slowly, kissing her tummy and her thighs. She undressed him at the same time, unbuttoning his shirt, stroking his chest with her trembling hands, before she undid his trousers and let them fall. He kicked them off and let her go briefly for a moment to remove his socks and briefs, and then Simon Brown did what no man had ever done before

317

to Sarah Smith; he picked her up in his arms and carried her to the bed, just like something out of the films! Laying her down gently on her bed he made love to her then, like she'd never been made love to before!

It had been incredible! Sarah lay on her side now, wrapped in Simon's arms as he was stroking her hair with one hand and holding her close with the other, placing little kisses on her forehead and her nose, smiling at her with a tenderness that she had never seen before. Sarah thought she might cry! To be cared for like this, desired like this, held like this! She'd never had any of it before and it was all very new to her. She'd been seduced of course; lust and wanting were things Sarah knew well, but she did not know tenderness or care, nor did she know real passion. This was simply, breathtakingly wonderful and Sarah prayed it would never stop!

Clarabelle and Nathaniel stood some time later, gazing at the sleeping couple, wrapped around each other in their warmth, love and togetherness.

'Good job,' they both said in unison, smiling broadly, then they left Sarah and Simon to enjoy each other in private.

Chapter 23

Sarah had prayed it wouldn't stop and it didn't! Over the next two months it carried on and with each passing week it grew deeper and stronger between them. It was a Tuesday evening just twelve days after their first date when he had said it, the words that she'd been waiting for, longing for, although she really hadn't expected it so soon! They had been curled up together in her living room with a glass of wine and half watching a film, half chatting when he suddenly interrupted her and said gently, quietly,

'Sarah? I'm in love with you. I've fallen in love with you.'

She had looked at him then to see if she had heard right, *did he just tell her that he loved her? Oh my God, he did!* Her heart jumped out of her chest with the pure joy of hearing those words from him. She wrapped her arms around his neck saying tearfully, emotionally,

'Oh, Simon, I love you too! I'm in love with you too!'

'I know it's soon, early days, very quick, but I just do! I love you!' he said and they had kissed, a deep and passionate kiss that only lovers falling even deeper in love can kiss.

'Aw bless!' Clarabelle and Nathaniel chimed in perfect unison.

319

'Our work here is done, I do believe!'
Nathaniel said to Clarabelle, 'Let's go play on a cloud.
I'm badly in need of a harp lesson, got very rusty over
the last few years trying to manage this lot! I just
haven't had the time to practice like I should be!'

'I know the feeling! My bell ringing is getting
a bit rusty too, not to mention the choir practice!'

And they flew upstairs to get back to normal.

****

Sarah felt incredibly secure with Simon on
every level. He had added her to Facebook after her
birthday bash as a friend, but after the declaration of
love that night he had changed his status from 'being
single' to 'being in a relationship with Sarah Smith!'
and there was her photo just to prove it! He was
declaring to the world that he was with her and she
felt honoured and touched that he would be that open
to his friends and family about her. It made her feel
incredibly safe and loved. Then there was the evening
he'd asked her up to the flat to meet his mum and
dad, via Skype of course. He'd pulled her onto his lap
in front of his computer and announced to the smiling
couple on the screen, 'Mum, Dad, this is Sarah. Isn't
she just beautiful?'

Aw bless! she'd thought, *he's showing me off to
his mum and dad!*

They'd chatted for a while and then Sarah had
left them to it for their weekly catch up, but she'd felt
really touched that he wanted his parents to see her
and meet her like that. It showed how important she
was to him and if felt wonderful!

320

****

Clarabelle and Nathaniel were on a mission, again! Now that their wards were finally together they had thought they could relax, but no, it seemed there was more to do. They had been told by 'upstairs' that a whirlwind romance was needed for the pair and the angels had been instructed to do everything within their power to expedite things and move the happy couple along.

'We don't have the two years that it usually takes, Nat,' she'd said to her friend one afternoon. 'We need to get them to get on with it!' she insisted. 'It's not like they need to be sure they're right together is it, they know that bit; well, they should do and they are five years late as it is!' she had fretted. Nat had nodded absentminded.

'How long?' he asked.

'Oh dear, I'm not sure. Shall we go for six months?' she considered, wondering if that would be more like a tornado than a whirlwind!

'We need a plan, a proper plan!' she determined. After much deliberation, they finally came up with a plan together, a plan that they *hoped* would work!

'No time like the present. Come on, Nat!' she instructed, and the pair flew off on their mission.

Sometime later the pair were returning from a successful morning at the radio station. It was the same station that Sarah and Simon listened to and both Clarabelle and Nathaniel had dripped their

321

influence into the producer's ear repeatedly all
morning. The play list was sorted. Over the coming
months their wards were to be bombarded with songs
which would hopefully help the process along, the
angels making sure the radio was on whenever
possible.

'Love is all around us!' sang Clarabelle, 'It's
everywhere we go!'

'She's the one!' sang Nat. 'If there's somebody
calling me on, she's the one!'

'Everything I do, I do it for youuuuuuuu!'
sang Clarabelle

'Sheeeeee may be the beauty or the beast, the
famine or the feeeeeast' warbled Nat.

****

Simon was courting Sarah with a
determination, a charm and a passion. They spent as
much time together as possible, falling in love more
and more each and every day. Simon was often
singing these days, repeatedly singing 'She's the One'
as he drove, walked, made coffee, or whatever else he
was doing. If he wasn't singing that, he was warbling
'Sheeeee may be the face I can't forget, she may be the
reason I'm alive, sheeeee may be the beauty or the
beeeeeast, the famine or the feeeeeast!' Sarah didn't
know Simon even liked Robbie Williams or Charles
Aznavour and he'd assured her that he didn't much,
but just couldn't get the damned songs out of his
head for some reason! He did particularly like singing
one song by Thin Lizzy, often singing to her and
grinning, 'When you came in my life, you changed

322

my world, my Sarah.' Sarah too seemed to be
constantly singing or humming Bryan Adams'
'Everything I do, I do it for you'. Simon caught her
singing that song quite often, and others with it,
especially Wet Wet Wet, which she sang often. He
enjoyed listening to her singing to herself as she
cooked or as she washed the dishes with him.

'I feel it in my fingers, I feel it in my toes,'
she'd sing away to herself. He thought it was really
sweet!

****

The courtship continued. He took her to the
city for the weekend, booking them into a five star
hotel and spoiling her rotten! He had wanted her to
meet his friends and they'd spent the afternoon with
Dave and Jane at their home and had a great time
getting to know each other. Sarah liked his friends
and was chuffed to bits to hear Dave whisper to
Simon as they were leaving,

'She's great, mate! You got a right cracker
there! She's a keeper!'

They'd returned to the hotel, making love of
course in the enormous bed the room sported, then
enjoying the fabulous marble bathroom with its
luxurious Jacuzzi bath together afterwards. He had
then taken her to the theatre to watch a high
production musical with named and known stars.
Sarah had never been to a proper show before and
was enthralled. He booked dinner for after the show
in one of the restaurants near the theatre, a little

French place with fantastic food. It had been late September and they were having an Indian summer; the evening was warm so they had sat outside at the tables on the pavements under the restaurant's canopy, each table with little candles on them and it was all so incredibly romantic! Afterwards he had called over one of those little rickshaw taxis and had the man cycle them around the sites as they sat arm in arm in the back watching the world go by.

Other times, he had taken her to concerts, big ones outside and smaller theatre ones. They'd gone to comedy clubs and to the cinema; there had been more dinners, he had brought her flowers, he always told her she looked gorgeous, noticing when she had made an effort; he noticed everything! If she had any worries, he picked it up straight away and was there to support and help. As late summer turned, the autumn leaves began to fall, and Simon fast became Sarah's best friend, lover, and confidant in every way. She completely adored him and still found it amazing that everything she felt for him was reciprocated.

To Simon, Sarah was everything he had ever wanted in a woman and he loved spoiling her. He'd say to her that she deserved it and she was worth it and if he wanted to spoil her she'd just better let him get on with it 'cos it made him happy! Sarah didn't argue!

Simon had joined all manner of things since moving to the town. He was now part of the five-aside football team, the rotary club, cricket club, and the golf club. He took her to meet everyone that he knew over the next two months, showing her off to his new friends, his arm always around her in a protective 'mine', but easy way. They were always holding hands or had an arm around a shoulder or waist; it was just normal, natural for them to be so tactile with each other. Frieda and Angie thought it was lovely the way they were together. Tom would tease him, pushing him playfully, threatening to throw up, they were just so sickeningly good together, but he was chuffed for his new mate. They all were! They were just so right; they fitted, just like 'peas and carrots' as Forrest Gump would say! Life had never been better for Sarah and she was ecstatic on every level.

Simon too was happy. He was loving the community life that the small town was giving him; he'd made new friends, was out and about after work a lot, and seeing Sarah too, whenever he could. His life in the city was closed and now his flat was nearly sold, moving him more towards the full closure he wanted and was more than ready for. He'd accepted an offer on the apartment just after he and Sarah had got together and the sale was expected to complete in a week or two. He would be going up to the city to sign all the paperwork and fetch the last of his things from there and then begin to look for a property here. He'd never been happier! He knew he must be happy as he was constantly singing these days, something he rarely did before meeting Sarah.

'Simon, my boy,' he said to himself, 'life is good, bloody good!

Nat grinned happily.

325

****

Simon was in his apartment packing up boxes, singing away as usual to the radio playing on his smart phone when his doorbell rang. He had come up to the city last night on his own, Sarah being tied to the shop this late in November, the Christmas rush on and not being able to get away. He'd seen his friends for a few hours, staying over at Dave's and was now in his apartment putting the last of the things into the boxes he'd brought with him ready to transport. The doorbell rang again more insistently. He answered the door and was horrified to see a smiling Nadia standing there.

'Hello, Simon, daaaarling, you don't mind if I come in do you?' and she swept passed him into his apartment in a rush of perfume and fur with determination.

'Nadia, what are you doing here? What do you want?' a frustrated Simon asked, as if he didn't know! 'How did you know I was here?'

'Oh, I bumped into one of your friends and I just *had* to come and say hi, see how you are, it's been months, daaaarling!'

'I'm busy, Nadia!' Simon was still standing by the door, holding it open, but Nadia had settled herself down on a box and was clearly not going to move! Simon closed the door and walked over to her warily. She smiled sweetly at him, stretching a long slim leg out of her coat, allowing it to fall open just enough at the leg to emphasise the slim calves and the extremely high heeled shoes that she wore. She leaned forward, subtly pulling the neckline of the fur

326

coat open just enough for him to see a glimpse of her perfumed cleavage.

'The thing is, daaarling, I just wanted to say that you were absolutely right! I was a total bitch to you and I understand, daarling, I truly do, but it's all changed now. Roger doesn't come around anymore, he's moved on and so have I. I'm ready now, daarling, ready to be with you properly. We can be together now, just like you wanted. I've missed you, baby.' Nadia stood up slowly and pressed herself against Simon seductively, lifting her face to his and pouting her lips ready for his kiss. She pushed her hips into his crotch and traced her finger down his chest just like she used to. Simon was horrified! He felt like he was in a time warp! He pushed her firmly away from him, stepping back to give himself space.

'Forget it, Nadia, it isn't going to happen, not now, not ever!'

'But, darling! What we had was so good! You can't possibly want to throw that away! I forgive you for leaving me, really I do. Let me show you how much I've missed you. Remember all our nights, baby, and the way you love to touch me?' Nadia smiled her most seductive smile and opened her ankle length fur coat slowly, showing Simon exactly what he'd been missing. She was standing completely naked under the fur coat that she was now holding wide open!

'Nadia!' Simon yelled in horror! Horror and anger! Anger at his arousal that was beginning to be evident in his trousers, despite his mind telling it not too! She saw it instantly and pounced the way she always had, seeing his weakness she stepped into him again, pressing her naked, hot body against his.

'I want you, daaarling' she breathed huskily, 'let's make love here, on the floor now, daaaarling. You know you want to!'

At that exact moment an image of Sarah's smiling face came into Simon's mind. A smiling, honest, trustworthy Sarah! His beautiful Sarah! A Sarah whom he loved and loved deeply! Simon pushed Nadia roughly away from him.

'Get the fuck off me, Nadia! Get your coat closed and get the hell out of my flat!' he shouted at her. 'Just give it up, will you!'

Nadia sat down with a bump in shock and disappointment. She couldn't believe that he was rejecting her like this! She promptly burst into tears, sobbing into her hands that were now clutched to her face. Simon calmed immediately on seeing her tears, but he had no doubt whatsoever that he still wanted her out, he still wanted her to go and would do even if she cried enough tears to fill his bloody bath!

'Just go, Nadia,' he said, more kindly now. 'It's over, just accept it, aye?'

'But what am I going to do?' she wailed, and then it all came out, the real reason that she was there.

'What am I going to do? Roger's gone, Simon, he's got someone new! He's moved on and she's younger, his new woman, only twenty-eight! And he wants to sell the house! I'm just so lonely, so lost! Simon, I need you, help me, baby? Please take me back, darling.'

'Ah, now it all makes sense, Nadia! You're looking for a mug to pick up the pieces! You just can't stand being on your own can you? Can't take it! Have to have someone there! Some sad sap willing to pay the mortgage so that you don't have to move! Bloody hell, woman, you're unbelievable!' Simon shook his head. 'You really are a prize bitch, aren't you? It's all about you! Your needs, your wants, and you don't give a flying fuck who you use or who you trample on to get what you need!' Simon looked at her in disgust. 'Just get out, Nadia. You make me sick!'

Simon walked over to her, pulled her up by her arms and frog-marched her to the door, pushing her through it without remorse or hesitation, he closed it firmly behind her.

'Goodbye, Nadia,' he said to the closed door and went back to his packing.

'Phew, that was close!' Nathaniel said to himself with a flutter of wings. His hat was trying desperately to stay on, despite the risen, fluffed up Gonk hair that had sprouted at Nadia's sudden appearance! *Why had no one upstairs thought to check what was going on with Nadia or with Roger for that matter? Heavens above, that had come out of the blue! No one had seen that one coming! He'd have to have a word with Clarence, find out what's occurred!*

'I managed to save the day though, bringing Sarah's face into Simon's mind like that,' he said with relief, 'snapping him out of his trance, a trance that Nadia and lots of women like her seem to have on the majority of men down here! Makes them think with their downstairs bits instead of their head, bless 'em!' Nathaniel decided that he did not understand at all the ways of the human world. 'I need more training!'

329

he decided, 'must ask Clarence about that!' He
remembered Clarence going on about some book or
other the humans used in these times; something
about Mars and Venus, though he couldn't quite
figure out how the planets had anything to do with
men being ruled by their nether-regions instead of
their brain. It didn't make sense to him at all! How
could a man as decent as Simon react like that when
he loved Sarah? He wouldn't have done anything
about it of course, not in him, just not in him, but his
thingy had other ideas and it had tried to take over!
Poor, Si, just 'cos some boobs were on show and some
sexy, vampy woman was thrusting them at him!
Nope, didn't make sense at all! He knew Simon had
been telling his erection to go away, (he could hear
his thoughts,) but it had just refused! Had a life and
mind of its own, so it did! Nathaniel tried harder to
work it all out in an attempt to avoid having to run to
Clarence for advice. 'Maybe Nadia was one of those
Milf women, or was it Wilf,' he couldn't remember,
but he knew it was something about being older and
being very sexy and desirable and knowing what
they were doing. Apparently there were lots of male-
trances and nether-region-rulings where they were
concerned. Nadia definitely knew what *she* was doing
that was for sure! But she'd failed, ha! She couldn't
trick his boy, no sirrree! The penny dropped suddenly
as Nat worked out what had happened. The nether-
region-boing thing had taken over, just for a moment,
blinding and blocking Simon's mind, but as soon as
he'd given him the image of Sarah the trance had
been broken, like a spell.

'Hey, presto! Ta da!' he announced proudly. He knew how to break a spell now! Wicked! He didn't need Clarence at all! Nat pulled out an imaginary wand then, practicing his 'breaking spells' technique and dancing around Simon's apartment as he wrapped and packed, oblivious to it all. Nat noticed Simon was quiet but wasn't at all concerned. The crisis was over, Simon was fine and Nat had learned something new so all was well.

Simon wasn't fine, Simon was wracked with guilt! Deep in thought for the rest of the afternoon, he continued packing. He was disappointed in himself at his reaction to her seduction. How could he even think about getting a hard-on when he had his Sarah? He just couldn't understand it. He felt disloyal, dirty almost, just thinking about it. *By his age he really should be in control of his dick not the other way around!* Simon humphed and banged as he packed. *Bloody Nadia!* Her appearance and behaviour brought home to him just how glad he was that he was out of it, out of her life and out of the city. He was incredibly happy with Sarah and with his new town, his new job and with his new life! He'd never do anything to risk it! He'd never had it so good! It worked, it all worked and he knew now more than ever that the new life he had created for himself was the life he wanted to keep, make permanent, solidify it. He rang Sarah then, needing to hear her voice.

'Hello, Fire Girl! How's my gorgeous woman today?'

'Hi, babe, I'm great, thanks, missing you. Can't wait to see you later.'

331

'Nor me. Sarah, I love you, fire girl! Very much!'

'Love you too, babe. Got to go, sweetheart, shop's full, sorry. Hugs and snogs, darling, byeee!'

Simon smiled at the phone in his hand and knew how lucky he was to have her. She was everything he'd ever wanted and he wanted her for keeps, he'd never been more sure of anything. They were right together, she was right for him. He was ready. He didn't care that he'd only been seeing her seriously for two months, he'd known her for five and he knew enough to know she was it! She's the one, he just *knew* it!

'Simon, my boy, it's time to put your money where your mouth is!' he said to himself, grabbing his coat and his wallet as he headed out of the door on a mission to the high street.

'Diamond, I think, nice one. Yes! God knows what size she is but it'll be fine!'

Nathaniel was in a panic at this development. He hadn't seen that one coming either, so busy was he with his magic spell breaking and 'hey-presto-ing'! The hat, already struggling to contain the orange spiked force beneath it which had been standing to Gonk-like-attention since Nadia's arrival earlier, now with the additional stress of the ring size issue, the hair just erupted and with a 'boing', the hat gave up the battle and shot off like it had been fired from a cannon! Nat rushed over to the ineffective cap, picking it up, he dusted it off and flew off upstairs. *How had this happened? How had they not seen that coming? This was early, earlier than expected, but it was*

332

wonderful, just wonderful! The songs had worked then! Wicked! Simon wanting to propose so soon, just wonderful, but ready to propose and no ring size ready? Really! They really were all getting very slack up here, missing things right left and centre!

Clarabelle, I need Clarabelle! he thought to himself. *She'll know what size ring Sarah is.* And he darted off to find Clarabelle quick before Simon bought the wrong one!

Chapter 24

The ring had been burning a hole in Simon's pocket for four weeks now, ever since he'd got back from the city. He was dying to get on with it, but he wanted to make it special and perfect and what would be more perfect than proposing to her on Christmas Day! Two days to go! No one knew except for Ben. He smiled as he remembered his visit to Ben.

He'd gone to Ben's house the day he had got back from the city with the ring, even before he'd gone to see Sarah and solemnly asked Ben for her hand in marriage. Ben had muttered to himself, (he always did that!) then patted Simon on the back and with a serious face had asked him if he thought he was worthy of his sister, and if so, could he provide for her and keep her safe? Seeing Simon's face as he contemplated these questions with his full attention was just classic and Ben could hold in his mirth no more, bursting out laughing and saying of course he could marry his sister, he'd be delighted to have him as his brother-in-law, he was just winding him up! They'd hugged, patting each other's backs, then Simon had gone to Sarah's to be with his girl. He'd left Ben with,

'Say nothing, nothing at all! It's a surprise!'

And here he was, finally! Sarah was out tonight, taking her staff out for their Christmas meal to the Crown and Simon knew that he wouldn't be

disturbed. She'd popped in earlier, arms laden with
the presents that she'd bought for each of them, just
stopping long enough at his flat for a kiss on her way
to the pub. She often popped in here and there and he
needed to know he wouldn't be interrupted so had
waited for this staff party night when he knew the
coast would be clear. Simon looked at his watch.
She'd been gone long enough now. He took out the
engagement ring, examining the diamond closely,
wondering quite how a tiny rock could cost three
months wages and hoped she would like it, hoped it
would fit. He put it back in the box and wrapped it
carefully. Then, pulling the cracker apart, opening it
carefully, trying not to spoil it, he placed the box
inside and re-sealed it. Not quite as tidy as it was but
it'll do! He grinned to himself,

'Yep, bloody perfect! She'll never guess!'

****

It was Christmas Eve and they'd closed the
shop up early. Sarah was incredibly excited! She
loved Christmas and this one was going to be so
special, so perfect, now that she had her shop, Simon
and her new life. They were having a big family
Christmas this year. Ben and Gina were coming for
Christmas lunch and bringing Joe, even her mother
was coming.

God, I hope she behaves, Sarah thought to
herself, but she was glad that her mother was coming
even if she didn't behave. Margaret had been making
an effort since her visit to the store that day and
bridges had been built, small bridges admittedly, but

335

they were making progress. Her mum still couldn't resist the odd dig, but she was trying and that was good enough for Sarah.

Simon's parents were over from Spain and were staying in The Crown, enjoying the old pub and the honeymoon suite with its four-poster bed that Simon had paid for. They were joining them for Christmas lunch too. Sarah had offered for them to stay in her home with her and Simon, but he had thought that it was better if they stayed in the hotel, seeing as she only had single beds in the spare rooms anyway.

'And besides, darling, I want you all to myself at night! I don't want my mum and dad hearing us celebrating our first Christmas together! Not the noise we make!' and they'd both laughed, nodding in agreement. Their lovemaking was not known for being quiet, Sarah screaming the house down most of the time as she did!

Angie, Tom, and their children as well as Frieda with hers would be joining them in the afternoon, so there was going to be a houseful! She couldn't wait!

****

Simon was nervous. It was Christmas Day. He didn't think he would be, but he was! His special cracker was hidden in his overnight bag in Sarah's bedroom, kept separate in case it got mixed up with the rest and ended up on someone else's plate. He wanted it to be perfect, his proposal, especially with all the family there. He couldn't wait!

The table looked just beautiful! It sat in the centre of the small dining room and more or less filled it. It was laid ready with eight place settings, holly sprigs adorned the crisp white tablecloth, candles burned in the silver candelabra, and the golden wine goblets were sat next to each setting, all apart from Joe's of course; there was a plastic beaker for him! Champagne was on ice with several spares ready in the fridge. The smell of roast turkey wafted through the house, tantalising and teasing everyone with its promise. Sarah was dishing up with Simon's help while their parents were in the living room, sitting near the enormous Christmas tree chatting in front of the roaring log fire, getting to know each other and downing wine like it was going out of fashion. Christmas lights adorned every room, twinkling away catching the light off the tinsel that was placed strategically around the ground floor. Wine in hand, Sarah had had a few herself, particularly noticeable when she missed the sink while she was draining the peas and managed to get it all over the floor.

'Oops!' she laughed, smiling at Simon as she took another swig of wine from the large glass.

'God, I love you, Fire Girl!' and he grabbed her, peas, colander and all, and swung her round the kitchen trailing wine and water on the floor as he did.

'Get off, get off! Things to do here! Hello? We have the world in there waiting to be fed! Get off me!' but she was laughing as she said it. Simon did as he was told, put her down reluctantly and began to carry in the food to the dining room, calling the family to the feast as he did. When they were all sat at the table 'ooing' and 'aahing' about how wonderful it all looked and how clever Sarah was for putting on such a magnificent spread, he excused himself for a moment and rushed upstairs, leaving Sarah to top up everyone's wine.

'Crackers!' he yelled as he returned to his seat, 'Got to have crackers! Can't have Christmas dinner without silly hats on!'

'Nor without silly jokes!' Ben added, pulling his cracker with Gina and grabbing the hat that fell out onto the table.

'This one's for you, darling,' Simon said, handing Sarah one end of *'The Cracker'*. It was quite a lot bigger than everyone else's cracker, but she barely noticed as she smiled into his eyes. She pulled it hard and with a bang a small box fell out and onto her lap. She looked at it in surprise. Everyone else's cracker seemed to have plastic rings, toys and silly things, but hers had a little box wrapped in gold Christmas paper and even had a little bow on it. She looked at Simon in confusion.

'Open it, open it!' he smiled nervously. As she unwrapped the box, fully focusing on it, she did not notice Simon get up from his chair, bending down on one knee besides her. Sarah, oblivious to Simon's new position, so focused on the little box as she was, opened it curiously to see the most exquisite diamond solitaire ring, sitting proudly in its velvet casing. It sparkled and shimmered, catching the light from the candles. It was absolutely beautiful! She looked at Simon questioningly, noticing then his position on the floor besides her. He took her hand in his. She

338

thought for a moment that he had dropped something on the floor and was reaching down to pick it up, when she noticed the expression on his face as he looked up at her nervously. She suddenly took it all in and her mind finally comprehended what was happening.

'Oh my God!' she exclaimed, as tears filled her eyes.

'Sarah,' he began. The table suddenly fell silent as the whole family noticed his position at the same time.

'Oh my!' Gina gasped

'Aw!' said Ben, grinning happily.

'Oh my goodness!' said Margaret, Linda, and James in unison.

'Yay!' Clarabelle, Clarence, and Nathaniel yelled simultaneously.

'Sarah, my darling, my wonderful, gorgeous 'Fire Girl'. You are everything I have ever wanted, dreamed of and much more.' The tears now spilled embarrassingly out of Sarah's eyes and down her cheeks. Simon continued,

'I love you with all my heart, my darling, and if you will do me the honour of becoming my wife, I will do everything in my power to make you as happy as you have made me. Will you marry me darling?'

You could have heard a pin drop in the room as everyone held their breath. Gina had a tear in her eye, as did Simon's mother Linda. Even Margaret looked happy! Sarah could not have smiled a bigger smile if she had tried, as she looked at this amazing

339

man who she had fallen so deeply in love with and who she adored with every ounce of her being.

'Yes! Yes, I'll marry you! Of course I'll marry you! Yes, please!'

The whole table burst into rapturous applause and with whoops of 'congratulations' they all jumped up to hug and pat Sarah and Simon. He took the open box then; still clutched in her shaking hands, taking out the ring he placed it on her trembling finger. It fitted perfectly!

Clarabelle and Nathaniel were beaming, glowing with pure joy!

'But of course it fits perfectly!' they both shouted in unison. 'Of course it does!'

As the champagne popped and everyone rushed around excitedly, Margaret was eyeing the ring that Sarah was now showing. She was impressed with its carat and value, which she judged correctly to be of considerable worth. Clearly this nice man adored her Sarah! She also noted with some concern the steam coming from the magnificent spread on the table, steam which was reducing with every passing moment. The lovely dinner was slowly going cold, ruining the feast that Sarah had so clearly worked very hard on, and Margaret did so like her food piping hot! *Most inconvenient*, she thought to herself, *really, could this proposal not have waited until after lunch!* But she managed to keep her mouth shut for once and let Sarah enjoy her moment, her special incredible moment and the really rather special ring! *Maybe the microwave?* Margaret thought to herself, deciding for once to try to be flexible and go with the flow. Sarah after all, did look inordinately happy at the moment. *Perhaps it wouldn't be the end of the world if my dinner is not quite piping hot, this once!* she decided, and smiled, feeling for some strange reason, really rather happy!

****

The celebrations went on all day for the happy couple. All of the Champagne was drunk plus a few of the normal bottles of wine along with the spirits. Everyone was rather merry, in more ways than one! Angie, Tom, and their kids had all turned up at the same time as Frieda turned up with hers. There were squeals of delight as they found out the news, both wanting to look at the ring and find out the details of the proposal.

'No way! In a cracker! One knee and everything!' squealed Angie.

'Oh my God, girl! You've got a star there! He's bloody perfect! I want one!' laughed Frieda, hugging her friend. She was so pleased for her, so happy for her, they all were. It was wonderful news!

'So when's the day? When you gonna marry him?' Frieda asked. 'I want to be bridesmaid!'

'And me!' joined in Angie.

Simon walked into the kitchen at that exact moment,

'Whenever she wants to marry me!' he smiled. 'I thought June, maybe? Our anniversary? When we met that day, the day I poured beer all over your head!' he grinned. They all laughed. 'But if you want

341

to do it sooner, darling, that's fine with me. I'd marry you tomorrow!'

I've truly died and gone to heaven! thought a truly, happy, contended Sarah.

****

Sarah walked down the aisle of the small chapel slowly, revelling in each step that she took, savouring every moment of this monumental day in her life. The church organ filled the room with its rich tones, its music echoing off the old stone walls and ceilings as she matched her footsteps to its slow beat. She looked around her at the smiling faces of the friends and loved ones that were now turned towards her, watching her every step as she approached the alter, almost floating down the aisle. She saw Simon's mum and dad proudly watching her, standing with all his friends, old and new. Gina, her beautiful supportive sister-in-law stood smiling in the second row, holding a suited 'mini-Ben' in the form of little Joe, nearly three now and dressed so sweetly in a miniature kilt, jacket, tiny shirt and tie, and even the sporran bless him! Tom was standing with his and Angie's children who were behaving beautifully, Frieda's mum stood with her grandchildren. The place was packed! Half the town was there including Pete from the Crown, the rotary, football, and cricket club chaps and most of Sarah's regular customers. Margaret smiled a big smile as Sarah walked nearer, dressed in the soft pink mother-of-the-bride outfit with matching hat that Sarah had helped her to pick out on their first ever shopping trip as mother and daughter some weeks before. Sarah smiled back at Margaret with warmth, genuinely meaning it.

Flowers adorned the church, each row of seats having its own floral display, filling her senses as she passed. The fragrance of roses, mixed it seemed, with half the flowers in the florists shop, (Clarabelle having added in far more than Sarah ordered when she wasn't looking) filling the chapel up to the high vaulted ceiling with their many scents. Sarah wore a beautiful ivory lace wedding dress with a long train, veil over her face, a beautiful bouquet in her left hand and holding tightly onto Ben's arm with her right. It was a glorious day in the middle of June, the sun shining perfectly, as ordered from above by Clarence and Clarabelle of course, who now walked behind them in their full glory and in their full height. Angie and Frieda followed them; both proudly holding their posies of yellow daisies. A host of angels sat in the rafters of the church singing along with the organ, joining the happy couple on their special day.

Simon stood in front of the alter in this lovely little church, the church where Sarah had been christened so long ago as her father before her, repeatedly tapping his pocket to make sure the ring hadn't mysteriously gone missing since he'd last checked two seconds ago!

'It's still there, mate!' both Dave and Nathaniel said together. Dave was the official best man, but Nathaniel knew he was really, or should be, all the work he'd done to get these two here! He'd even managed to get his hair to behave which was now

lying flat, as it should be, as he stood next to Simon
looking him in the eye. Nat, like all the other angels
here today, due to being in the energy of a church and
of so much love, also stood in his full height and size.
At just under seven feet tall he looked smashing, very
smart, even if he did say so himself! He was so
pleased, he really hadn't wanted to wear the baseball
cap at a wedding as it just didn't go with the new
outfit he'd ordered for today, conjured up of course
with his new wand! Clarabelle had told him off about
it, said this was not Hogwarts and that he was not
Harry Potter and that he didn't need the wand. She'd
also corrected him insisting that they weren't spells,
they were *miracles*, but Nat liked his wand and the
'abracadabra' so she'd given up and let him get on
with it.

Ben handed Sarah's hand to Simon and
stepped back, just like he'd been shown in the
rehearsals last week.

'Phew, that's my job done!' he said to himself,
relieved he hadn't fallen, farted, fucked up, or messed
up his sister's special day.

'Good job, laddie!' said Clarence in his ear.

'Thanks, mate.' He smiled.

'Yes, well done, my son,' whispered John
Smith in Ben's ear, 'grand job, lad, I'm so proud of
you', but knew he could not hear him.

John, unknown to either Ben or Sarah, had
walked with them as they had proceeded down the
aisle together. He was delighted that he had been able
to be here today to walk his daughter down the aisle,
just as any proud father should. Ben felt a shiver go

344

down his spine as his father patted his shoulder proudly, feeling the hairs standing up at the back of his neck, he looked around him for a moment. Seeing only smiling happy faces he shrugged off the shiver and took the few steps back from the alter to the front row, taking his place by his mother. John smiled at Clarabelle then, waving, he called gently to her,

'Couldn't miss my little girl's special day now, could I, my friend?'

'Indeed not,' came the choked reply from an emotional Clarabelle. 'As if!'

Simon stared at his Sarah standing next to him now in front of the church alter. She looked radiant, beautiful, amazing, and he felt the tears prick at the back of his own eyes as he gazed at her with pure adoration and love.

'You look beautiful, Sarah!' he whispered to her, dragging his eyes away from her and turning slowly to face the vicar.

'She does, aye, lad, that's for sure,' agreed John, gazing at his beautiful daughter as he stood close to her, holding her arm. 'Sarah, my lovely girl,' he whispered in her ear, 'I could not be more proud. I'm only sorry I could not be here for you fully, on your special day, my darling, to walk you down the aisle properly.' John shook his head as a tear slid down his cheek silently. He took a deep breath, trying to take control of his emotions, the overpowering and overwhelming love he felt for his daughter in that moment pouring out of his very being. He hugged her, whispering, 'Ben did us both proud though, aye, lass? You couldn't get a better stand in, aye?'

345

Sarah put her hand on her arm absently, feeling a warmth, a softness there.

'Dad?' she whispered, 'are you here, Dad?'

She turned to Clarabelle who was standing behind her holding a tissue to her face. Wiping away a tear she nodded to Sarah.

'Yes, child, of course he is here,' she whispered softly, 'he wouldn't have missed this for the world. He couldn't be here in person, of course, though goodness knows how much he'd love to have been, he did the next best thing he could. Not the same, I know, and so does he, but he's here in the only way he can be. Your grandmother Joan is also here, sat next to Ben there.' Clarabelle smiled, nodding to Ben and Margaret. Sarah looked surprised, then delighted!

'All your loved ones are here for you, Sarah, on your special day, whether they be from upstairs or downstairs, they are all here.' Sarah smiled a happy and contented smile, feeling so incredibly blessed to have so much love around her.

John, moving slowly away from Sarah, now stood next to Ben. He needed his son to know, to listen, to hear. He turned to Clarence then, nodding.

'Please?' he asked, 'Please tell him after the wedding what I say now.' Clarence nodded, smiling gently to John who was earnestly speaking, with love, with gratitude, with pride, into Ben's ear;

'Thank you, Ben. Thank you so much for being there for her, protecting her, minding her, when I could not. You could not have done more as her wee brother, son. You have done your job and you have also done mine. Thank you for doing both and for

346

doing them so well.' John paused, nodding over to Simon, standing in front of them with Sarah now, both focusing on the vicar.

'I think it's time to hand that job over to Simon now, aye, lad? Your job is done, and a grand job it was laddie, a grand job indeed! Simon will take it from here, we both know that. You can let go now, son, relax, take a break, you've earned it!' John beamed a beautiful and peaceful beam at both children, then moved over to join Joan standing the other side of Margaret.

'Hi, Mum,' he smilingly said, taking her hand he placed it in his arm and stood back to enjoy his daughter's wedding.

'Dearly beloved,' the vicar began, 'We are gathered here today, before this congregation, and before God, to join together this man and this woman in holy matrimony...'

Clarabelle burst into tears, Nat and Clarence followed and the host of angels at the top of the church struck up a choir! There was even a harp and some bells thrown in for good measure!

'Good job,' Clarabelle sniffed to her brother and Nat.

'You too,' came the sniffed replies.

Epilogue

Clarabelle was excited! Beyond excited actually! She was just about to go into a major inter-angel-cy meeting and she knew who'd be there!

'Yippee!' she yelled, throwing her arms and wings in the air at the same time and nearly falling off the cloud again!

'Now, Clar, calm down. Serious is this! Awards an all!' a stern Clarence said, looking at his sister with disapproval.

'Sorry, yes, serious. Ok, I'm calm, I'm ready!'

'Come on, time to go.'

The huge doors swung open as they approached the grand hall of the Angelic Temple. Side by side they walked through the open doors, descending down the wide sweeping steps into the magnificence of the hall that opened up below them. An enormously huge amphitheatre, pillars, and posts stood tall around the sides of the temple, adorned with thousands of candles and golden bells. The pillars, carved exquisitely dominated the perimeter of the temple as far as the eye could see, holding up the high domed ceiling which was lit up like a Christmas tree with millions of twinkling stars. White mist swirled around the hundreds of gathered angels who were standing on the many tiered rows applauding enthusiastically as they walked in. On the circular stage in the centre of the room below them, at the very bottom of the many steps stood Metatron, his

348

regal wings open to their full and powerful thirty feet span. He stood majestically, commanding everyone's attention. Clarabelle and Clarence took their places at the front in the seats that had been reserved for them and stood, waiting for the ceremony to commence.

'Be seated,' Metatron boomed, his voice reverberating around the room, bouncing off the ceilings and cylindrical walls. Everyone sat.

'Second Level Angel, Class 2, Clarence, please step forward.' Clarence did so; walking up to Metatron he knelt before him in awe. He bowed his head as a golden feather was placed on his shoulder.

'For services to Benjamin Smith, please accept this golden feather of honour with our love and thanks,' he boomed. 'You have earned the right and light to now be promoted up to a First Level Angel, Class 2. Well done, Clarence, good job.' Clarence beamed and returned to his place.

'Third Level Angel, Class 2, Clarabelle, please step forward.' Clarabelle followed suit, nervously bending down before Metatron and bowing her head as a golden feather of light was placed on her shoulder.

'For services to Sarah Smith, please accept this golden feather of honour with our love and thanks,' he boomed again. 'You have now earned the right and light to be promoted up to a Second Level Angel, Class 1. Well done, Clarabelle, good job.'

The ceremony went on, with awards being given to Nathaniel for services to Simon of course, earning him an extra Level and a whole class! Well it had been incredibly hard work keeping Simon stuck

349

for five whole years! Nat didn't know how he'd managed to do it, but he was chuffed to bits to have been awarded two promotions. He was sooo happy, he didn't think he'd *ever* need his cap again! There was even one for Margaret's angel Ishra for her work with softening Margaret's heart, a little bit, although it was acknowledged that there was still much work to do with that one!

'It is essential,' Metatron had boomed away in the ceremony, 'that all angels work together as a team. Nothing is independent in these realms. Nothing stands alone. We are a team, a team that loves, cares and protects all of the humans down on planet Earth. Never forget our purpose - to bring joy, guidance, and help, but above all, to bring love! We are Angels,' he boomed. 'We are ONE!' Metatron finished his speech and lifted his wings wide for dramatic effect, flooding the entire hall as he did so with their bright light and incredible power. The crowd erupted in rapturous applause.

Clarabelle clapping joyously, suddenly noticed Fred and Frank standing in the next row and thought how lucky she was to be part of this team, this special team of Guardian Angels. She felt blessed and honoured to be Sarah's Guardian Angel.

It must be sooo boring to work in transport, she thought. *I couldn't be a Grim Reaper! Just up and down collecting souls, all day, every day!* She grimaced at the idea of it, squishing her pretty face up at the very thought. Clarabelle *loved* being a guardian angel, simply *loved it* and never wanted to be anything else! So exciting her job, different every day and *so* worthwhile! Smashing!

350

'By the way, Clar, do you think she knows she's pregnant yet?' Clarence whispered, 'Your Sarah?'

'No,' she giggled, 'but she'll find out soon enough! They'll know when they come back from their honeymoon. They'll be delighted! I've already arranged everything for the shop. I'm going to get her to promote Tim to manager, even with that hair! He can move into the flat above the shop and Sarah can let go a bit then, be able to focus on her baby. I've already had a word with Tim's angel to clear it.'

'Oh well done, Clarabelle, good work!' Clarence beamed.

'Pregnant? Pregnant? Was anyone going to tell me!' fretted Nat, thrown by this gem of information, his orange 'Gonk' hair on full alert at the news! 'Where's me cap!' he grimaced and flopped down heavily onto the seat below him. Clarence grinned,

'Shush now, he's talking again.'

Metatron was booming out to the packed hall again.

'Seraphina, my dear, please come down.' A small and dainty angel walked down the steps into the big hall and stood before Metatron respectfully.

'Second Level Angel, Class 3, Seraphina, you are hereby charged with being the Guardian Angel of Angelica Brown, Simon and Sarah Brown's new baby daughter. Please ensure everything is ready for her arrival next March. Love and support her, guide and help her through her life and beyond.' He placed a feather on Seraphina's shoulder to enthusiastic applause from the hall.

It would be Seraphina's first ward and she was thrilled.

351

'How exciting!' she beamed to herself, 'how exciting!'

Clarabelle clapped her hands in glee!

Smashing! she thought, *I'll need to get to know Seraphina really well if we're going to be working together.*

'You will indeed, my dear Clarabelle, you will indeed!' agreed the Mighty Archangel Michael, standing right behind her in full battle dress.

Oh my! Oh my! thought Clarabelle and immediately went into a tizzy.

'And I thought *we* might get to know each other a little better too!' smiled AA Mickey, as he stroked one of her feathers lovingly, gently, his powerful energy and dazzling smile directed straight into Clarabelle's shocked and besotted eyes.

'Oh my!' said Clarabelle and promptly fainted, falling right into his arms!

'Oh dear!' said Clarence with a shake of his head!

'Oh dear, indeed!' sighed Nat, pulling his cap out of his pocket. 'May as well just sew it on permanently and be done with it! Argh!'

The End

Coming Soon

Angel In My Heart
Julie Poole

Following on from 'Angel On My Shoulder', Sarah is finally having a good day! At 38¾, life is now going fantastically! She's just married her soul-mate Simon, her store is doing great and she's even getting on with her mother. (Miracles really do happen!), and to top it all, she's pregnant! Her 'Guardian Angel' Clarabelle is of course, 'smashingly' happy, but is she risking it all with her crush on Arch Angel Michael? How will Simon cope with finding out that his new wife has a Guardian Angel that she can see and talk to? Will Nathaniel ever sort out his Gonk hair, and what will Metatron do when he finds out about Clarabelle's crush? Or will she be banished from the Angelic Realms forever?

In this sequel, Angel In My Heart, it is Sarah's turn to help her angelic best friend Clarabelle and prevent a disaster. Can she do it? Enter 'Fred the Fantastic' to save the day. Fred is, of course, Sarah and Simon's new dog; a Golden Retriever, who being a genius can speak three languages (dog, angel and human). Whether he can help 'Mum' and 'Aunty Clarabelle' sort the mess out that they've got themselves into though, is quite another matter!

Order your copy now!

353